To Barbara,
Happy Birthday 1991.

Didn't we have a
lovely day!

Ray xxx

MY BELOVED SON

OTHER BOOKS BY
CATHERINE COOKSON

NOVELS   Kate Hannigan   The Gambling Man
          The Fifteen Streets   Miss Martha Mary Crawford
          Colour Blind   The Tide of Life
          Maggie Rowan   The Slow Awakening
          Rooney   The Iron Façade
          The Menagerie   The Girl
          Slinky Jane   The Cinder Path
          Fanny McBride   The Man Who Cried
          Fenwick Houses   Tilly Trotter
          The Garment   Tilly Trotter Wed
          The Blind Miller   Tilly Trotter Widowed
          Hannah Massey   The Whip
          The Long Corridor   Hamilton
          The Unbaited Trap   The Black Velvet Gown
          Katie Mulholland   Goodbye Hamilton
          The Round Tower   A Dinner of Herbs
          The Nice Bloke   Harold
          The Glass Virgin   The Moth
          The Invitation   Bill Bailey
          The Dwelling Place   The Parson's Daughter
          Feathers in the Fire   Bill Bailey's Lot
          Pure as the Lily   The Cultured Handmaiden
          The Mallen Streak   Bill Bailey's Daughter
          The Mallen Girl   The Harrogate Secret
          The Mallen Litter   The Black Candle
          The Invisible Cord   The Wingless Bird
                                      The Gillyvors

THE MARY ANN STORIES
          A Grand Man   Life and Mary Ann
          The Lord and Mary Ann   Marriage and Mary Ann
          The Devil and Mary Ann   Mary Ann's Angels
          Love and Mary Ann   Mary Ann and Bill

FOR CHILDREN
          Matty Doolin   Mrs Flannagan's Trumpet
          Joe and the Gladiator   Go Tell It To Mrs Golightly
          The Nipper   Lanky Jones
          Blue Baccy   Nancy Nutall and the Mongrel
          Our John Willie

AUTOBIOGRAPHY
          Our Kate   Catherine Cookson Country
          Let Me Make Myself Plain

WRITING AS CATHERINE MARCHANT
          House of Men   Heritage of Folly
          The Fen Tiger

CATHERINE COOKSON

My Beloved Son

BANTAM PRESS

LONDON · NEW YORK · TORONTO · SYDNEY · AUCKLAND

TRANSWORLD PUBLISHERS LTD
61–63 Uxbridge Road, London W5 5SA

TRANSWORLD PUBLISHERS (AUSTRALIA) PTY LTD
15–23 Helles Avenue, Moorebank, NSW 2170

TRANSWORLD PUBLISHERS (NZ) LTD
Cnr Moselle and Waipareira Aves,
Henderson, Auckland

Published 1991 by Bantam Press
a division of Transworld Publishers Ltd
Copyright © Catherine Cookson 1991

British Library Cataloguing in Publication Data
Cookson, Catherine, 1906–
My beloved son.
I. Title
823.914

ISBN 0-593-01434-0

Photoset in 12 on 13pt Linotron Sabon by
Chippendale Type Limited
Otley, West Yorkshire.
Printed in Great Britain by
Mackays of Chatham plc, Chatham, Kent

*To Bill McBrien who, in 1950, tactfully
sorted out a tax demand for £2.10s.0d on
the first novel of an irate and raw
beginner, and has continued along the same
lines over the past forty years.*

Thank you, Bill.

PART ONE
1926
9

PART TWO
1937
77

PART THREE
Maggie
151

PART FOUR
The Residue
303

PART ONE

1926

1

The tall woman lifted the small boy from the railway carriage and into the flurry of drifting snow being blown from the top of the train; then, as she stood looking first one way and then the other along the small platform, two men came hurrying through a far door and made their way towards her. They were muffled to the eyes. It was the man in the check cap with the ear-flaps who spoke, saying, 'My dear Ellen, we're just in time!' He had taken her hand but, without pausing in his greeting, he had looked down on the little boy, saying, 'Here we are then!' then turned back to the woman and still without pausing said, 'Where's your luggage? In the van? See to it, Dick.'

For the first time the woman spoke, saying quietly, 'I've only two travelling cases with me' – she motioned back into the carriage – 'the rest were sent on three days ago.'

'Three days? Never arrived. Well, let's get going. Oh, I am pleased to see you, Ellen. But the weather! I don't know how you're going to put up with our weather after the south. If it isn't the weather it's wars, if it isn't wars it's strikes. What are we coming to?' He laughed loudly now as, with one hand on her arm and the other holding that of the child, he guided them towards the exit, then through the booking hall, and outside to the car, which had a small trailer attached to the back.

The snow appeared to be falling in a thin, vertical spray and as he helped them into the car he said, 'Be a bit of a rough ride, but we'll get through; at least I hope so.' He laughed again; then shouted to the man who was now strapping the luggage on the trailer: 'Get a move on, Dick, if you don't want to walk.' Again he laughed, and the small boy, looking at him as he was on the point of closing the door, laughed too, a high squeaking laugh that brought two responses: the man cried, 'That's it, boy. That's it. It's a good sign you can laugh,' and from his mother a whispered remonstration: 'Don't giggle, Joseph.'

The child stared up at his mother for a moment; then screwing himself along the seat he began to rub at the window with his gloved hand, until his mother spoke again: 'The snow's on the outside,' she said.

'I know.'

She now smiled at him and shook her head as if in amused despair.

The man called Dick had taken his place in the front of the car, which now started with a jerk that brought them all forward in their seats, and again the child laughed, but this time Ellen Jebeau did not check him, only put her hand out quickly to arrest his fall. Then, pulling him close to her side, she put her arm around his shoulder and slowly allowed her body to relax against the back of the seat, while her eyes remained on the man in front of her, her brother-in-law, Sir Arthur James Jebeau, whom she had met only twice during the five years she had been married to his younger brother; and she pondered now, as she had done then, on the difference in their personalities. This man was garrulous, full-blooded, alive, a doer, while her late husband had been in all ways his opposite, a dreamer of dreams that never came true. His last dream had killed him, and in a foreign

12

country, attempting again to make money overnight in an enterprise that took most men a lifetime to accomplish: the making of wine.

She wondered how they had come together in life, because her own character was as far removed from her husband's as was his brother's. She never dreamed dreams; she had desires, strong desires that were based on practicality, not on flimsy imaginings. In a way she was not sorry Joe had died, for sooner or later there would have been a parting. She knew in her heart that if she had had any money of her own that parting would surely have happened. Yet that wasn't the whole truth; the custody of the child would have been the deciding factor as to whether she went or stayed. But this decision had mercifully been taken from her. She said mercifully, but she certainly hadn't thought that way when she found that he had left her a legacy of debt and a smothering mortgage on the old, cold, grim farmhouse to which he had taken her with such pride, as if presenting her with a royal palace.

A month ago the man sitting in front of her had come over to France and seen to the burial of his brother, leaving her sufficient funds to clear up his affairs: also he had spontaneously offered her a home until such time as she would want to make plans of her own.

Beneath her mantle of mourning the offer had brought not only relief but a certain form of joy. Her brother-in-law had been a widower for five years and he had so loved his wife that he didn't seem ready to replace her. His home, she recalled, was beautiful, and lying awake at nights in that dreary, bare farmhouse, she had pondered with not a little envy why one brother should live in such style while the other, mainly through his own fault, should live in a way that was no better than a peasant's.

And what was bringing more comfort to her now was the thought that there wasn't even a housekeeper as such running the place; the wife and daughters of the groom, who was now seated next to his master, managed the place, so there was no person in charge to contend with, no mistress for her to feel subservient to.

Her head sank into her shoulders, and she let out a long slow breath as she saw the future stretching out from the narrow confines of winters, as it were, through springs into high summers. But being of the character she was, she knew that springs would bring storms, as would the summers also. But one thing at a time, she told herself, one thing at a time: she was beginning a new life, not only for herself but for her son. Instinctively she pulled him closer to her until he whimpered, 'Mother, you're hurting my arm.'

It had taken them an hour and a half to reach the house. She had seen none of the landscape through which they had come; she could only recall it from the past journeys and think that she had missed nothing, because the barren hills and scree slopes would have presented no picture of grandeur to her.

She did glance at the façade of the house and her eyes lifted to the blackened strip of stone of the old chimney and noted the smoke billowing out of its tall pot.

Then she was in the hall and there all around them was bustle: there was the fat face above the equally fat hulk of Jessie Smith smiling a welcome that did not touch her eyes; her daughter Mary, a nineteen-year-old, unlike her mother, thin and wiry, her head moving slowly up and down in welcome and, also unlike her mother, smiling with her eyes. They helped her and the child off with their outdoor things, while opposite them stood two boys, silent and embarrassed-looking as their father talked to them non-stop: 'It's getting worse; we won't be able to move tomorrow. Did you get the animals out? If this keeps up and they don't exercise, their bellies will burst. Well, don't stand there like stooks, speak to your aunt. Martin and you, Harry, you remember your aunt, don't you?'

The twelve-year-old Martin now stepped forward and, holding out his hand, said politely, 'How do you do, Aunt Ellen?' Then ten-year-old Harry, following his brother's lead, as always, held out his hand saying, 'How do you do, Aunt Ellen?' Then, simultaneously, they both turned to the small boy, and when he lifted his face and grinned at them and said, 'Hello,' they grinned widely back at him and almost simultaneously they answered, 'Hello.'

'That's a nice fire.' The child point to the log fire blazing high in the wire basket, and Martin said, 'Well, you won't remember, but when you were one year old you nearly fell into there.'

'Did I?'

'Yes, and on your birthday too. It's on Christmas Eve, your birthday, isn't it?'

'Yes, and I'll be five.'

'Crikey! what an age.' Martin assumed a mock solemn face now and they all laughed.

'Come on over and get warm.' As Harry held out his hand to Joseph, Ellen said, 'I think he had better come upstairs and get changed; his feet are bound to be damp.'

'But I want to go with . . . well, them.' The child pointed and the boys laughed, and Ellen, holding out her hand, said, 'Come on; be a good boy.'

Joseph now looked first towards his cousins and their father, then towards his mother, who was waiting with her hand extended towards him, and with a sigh that might have come from a much older child he turned from the boys. He did not, however, place his hand in his mother's but walked before her towards the stairs. And he did not raise his eyes to the fine gallery, nor wonder at his wonderful surroundings. The pattern was set: it was personalities not things that were to attract him; but as yet he had no cognizance of what this was to mean to him.

*　　*　　*

15

Joseph was to remember his fifth birthday always; even during that time when he was to remember nothing else, the atmosphere of that house, particularly the hall, was to remain with him. Early in the morning of Christmas Eve, Martin and Harry had put him on the back of one of the horses and led him around the yard, which had been cleared of most of its snow. They had taken him up into the hay-loft and tumbled him in the hay; then later in the day he had gone with them, helping to carry presents to the Smith family. They had walked in single file through the narrow path between the drifts of snow, down to where the three cottages stood, and there he had met the family en masse for the first time.

Mr Smith he already knew, and his wife, a big fat woman who made lovely puddings; and, of course, by now he knew Mary, her daughter, who helped with the cooking and waited on the table, and Helen, the housemaid, the one who looked like her mother – she was sixteen, so she had told him. Then there was Charlie. He, too, worked in the house: he blackened the boots and washed the bottles and glasses in the little room he had all to himself, and he was one of twins. Florrie was his twin and she worked in the kitchen washing up the dishes. And there was Mick, who seemed to do all kinds of things, from helping the gardeners to assisting with the horse shoeing. But there were two of the Smiths he met for the first time this Christmas Eve, and one was called Janet. She was thirteen and still at school. But the one who interested him the more was the youngest, Carrie.

He first saw Carrie sitting on a cracket by the open fire. She seemed dwarfed by the family about her but for him she shone out, as Mick was to say later, like a star that had dropped on a midden. It wasn't that she was pretty. Janet was the pretty one, whereas Carrie seemed to have no outstanding feature, except perhaps her eyes. These were round, the colour indefinable as yet because the firelight, with each flicker of its flames, was changing

16

their hue from brown to black; her mouth still retained the rosebud shape of the child but the corners of her lips seemed to droop as a mouth might do when a mind was sad.

Joseph stood staring shyly at the little girl on the cracket, while the voices seemed to pass around his head in circles as they cried, 'Merry Christmas!'

'Merry Christmas!'

'Merry Christmas!'

'Oh ta. Ta, thanks.'

'Eeh! The master is kind.'

'He won't be kind much longer, our Mary, if you don't get over there and see to that dinner.'

'Oh Ma! I haven't been here a minute and Mrs Paxstone is giving an eye to things.'

'Then you thank God for burnt offerings. Now get yourself away, our Mary, until I can come.'

'Oh, thank you, Master Harry.'

'Oh, thank you, Master Martin.'

Joseph rose above the wave of voices as Martin pushed something into his hand, saying, 'Here, Joe; you give that to Carrie.' Martin pointed to the little girl on the cracket, and Joseph, without a moment's hesitation, went towards her and thrust the box into her hand.

'Say ta to Master Joseph.'

The room was silent now, waiting. For answer, Carrie, with one deft stroke of her small hand, ripped the Christmas paper from the box amid exclamations of 'Oh! My! Look what the imp's done.'

'Oh, you naughty girl!'

'Well, would you believe that!'

'It's for your stocking, you little tinker.'

'Let her open it now.' It was Mick Smith speaking. The ten-year-old boy seemed to have the voice of an adult, and as if he were an adult the others made no protest and the mother said, 'Go on then, Carrie, open it.'

By this time the child had already lifted the lid of the cardboard box and her hands were pulling away the tissue to reveal a doll that was dressed like a baby in long clothes, and as she held it up, Charlie Smith cried, 'Coo! That's funny; he's giving her a bairn.'

The stable knowledge behind the laughing remark did not go unnoticed by his father, and when the boy almost landed on his back in the corner of the room, saved only by Mick's arm, his father said, 'That should learn you. Keep your big mouth shut except when you're shovellin' in your grub.'

There was an uneasy murmur in the kitchen now and Martin, adopting almost the manner of his father, said heartily, 'Well, well; we must be off. I . . . I haven't any of my parcels wrapped yet. As for Harry here' – he nudged his brother – 'I don't think he's done his shopping.'

'Then he's had it then, hasn't he?' The pert remark came from Janet and caused a little ripple of laughter. Joseph laughed too, but he wasn't certain what he was laughing at. He only knew that he would like to stay and play with the little girl, but Martin had him by the hand again and so, following the example of his cousin, he was calling, 'Merry Christmas. Merry Christmas.' Then, just as they were about to leave the cottage through the door being held open by Dick Smith, he turned and looked back into the small room which seemed crammed with people and said, 'It's my birthday today, I'm five.' At this there was a genuine roar of laughter and the voices came to him crying, 'Happy birthday, Master Joseph. Happy birthday.'

Martin, pulling him along the path, said laughingly, 'You're daft you know, Joe; they knew it was your birthday; you've been telling everybody since you've got up. And didn't Dick give you the present of the little wooden horse?'

'Yes, yes, I know, but . . . but it's a long time since this mornin' and they could have forgotten.'

The two brothers let out great peals of laughter, and when they reached the yard Harry took Joseph's other hand and the brothers skipped him across it, lifting him at intervals off his feet as he ran; and when presently they entered the house they vied with each other in pulling off his wellington boots, his coat and his muffler and cap, then almost threw him on to the rug before the fire; and there they tumbled and tickled him until the uproar brought his mother down the stairs.

But on this occasion Ellen Jebeau did not say, as was her wont, 'Stop it, Joseph! Behave yourself. Be a good boy now,' she quietly took a chair to the side of the fire, and when the boys stopped their tumbling they all lay in a heap and stared at her.

She was no longer wearing black but was dressed in a midnight blue velvet gown, her fair hair was piled on top of her head and she looked like something that only needed a frame to make a beautiful picture.

Martin screwed up his eyes as he stared at her: she reminded him of something, someone; he wasn't sure what until there flashed through his mind the memory of his mother coming down the staircase wearing a gown just like the one his aunt was dressed in now.

Ellen was aware of the boy's eyes on her and she guessed what was passing through his mind. Yesterday, his father had said to her, 'Don't look so sad, Ellen; the dead are dead. I've had to face up to that this last year and you'll have to do the same. I know how you must be missing Joe, for he was the most lovable creature on God's earth. Impractical, yes, but that's no sin; in fact, I think his impracticality was an asset. He had a trust in him that gave him that strange quality of innocence. I mourned Vera. For four years I wouldn't let her go. I kept the dressing-room almost as a shrine; in fact all her clothes are still there. I often thought about giving them to Jessie for her tribe, but somehow I couldn't bear the thought of them wearing her things. But it's different with you. In a way, you know, you're not unlike her; you're about the same height and the same colouring and so, if you don't object, please make use of her things. I am sure she'd be pleased to know that they were being worn. She loved clothes, she had taste.'

She had managed to mutter, 'Yes; yes, I remember how smart she was, and beautiful.' And then she had added, 'I could never be like her; I know my limitations both in looks and character.'

And to this he had said, 'Go on with you, Ellen, you're too modest. But it will please me if you do as I ask.'

And with barely concealed excitement she had done as he asked, and now she had a large wardrobe and a cupboard packed with clothes, most of them beautiful, all of them expensive. She recalled that she hadn't envied her sister-in-law without cause.

The boys were still lying gasping when their father entered the hall, where he stopped for a second and gazed at Ellen; then making his way towards the fire, he shouted at the boys, 'Up with you! Out of that, and see if you can act like young gentlemen for once in your life. Up with you!' he shouted again, hauling his sons by their collars and shaking them whilst laughing down on them. Then pushing them towards the staircase, he said, 'Go and get changed; you smell of the stables. Take this young scamp with you and see to him; see that his ears are washed and take a pick to his nails.'

Again the boys had Joseph by the hands, hauling him up two stairs at a time while they yelled together, 'One, two, three, alairy ally-oop!!'

Arthur now walked slowly towards the small French gilt table that stood against the wall, its fragility in sharp contrast with the strength of the stone, and took a cigarette from a silver box. But as he was about to light it, he turned abruptly towards Ellen, saying, 'Manners! Manners! How do I expect my sons to behave like gentlemen with such a pattern for a father. I'm sorry, my dear.' He handed the box towards her. 'This comes of not having a woman in the house, and Vera didn't indulge.'

'Nor do I. Thank you.'

'Oh, well, in a way I'm pleased, because it's a dirty habit really. Women do try to make it elegant by using long holders, but the nicotine all goes down the same way and it can't do any good, you know. I cough like the devil at times.' He demonstrated here by thumping his chest. Then, his attitude changing abruptly, his face unsmiling, and his voice serious, he said, 'You look beautiful, Ellen.'

'Thank you, Arthur, but I'm afraid, as clothes maketh the man, they go further with the woman. It's the dress, the beautiful gown. I hesitated to wear it in case it upset you.'

'No, no' – he shook his head – 'it doesn't upset me. Mind, it might have done a couple of years back but, as the old tag goes, time is a great healer. Well now' – again his attitude changed and he was once more the boisterous, boyish host – 'what about a drink? You do like a drink, if I remember, don't you?' He turned his head to the side and slanted his eyes towards her; and she laughed a light, gay laugh as she said, 'Well, I should have died of thirst long before this if I didn't, for Joe wisely wouldn't let us drink the water.'

'Good. Good.'

He marched now to a cabinet that stood to the side of the staircase and after opening the double doors he called over his shoulder: 'Sherry, port, or something harder?'

'Port with a dash of brandy, please.'

'Well! Well! Well!' He turned from the cabinet. 'I've never heard of that one before.'

'Joe invented it as a pick-me-up . . . for special occasions only.'

'And this is a special occasion; yes, yes, I must try this one myself.'

A moment or so later, having handed her the glass, he raised his own to her, saying, 'Here's to the future, and may you be happy here, Ellen.'

As they clinked their glasses she answered, 'I am sure I shall, Arthur. And I must say again, my heart is full of gratitude for your kindness to us. What we would have done without you, I don't know, and if ever I can repay you in any way I'll be only too willing.'

'Nonsense! Nonsense!' He turned from her now and took a seat on the other side of the fireplace before saying, 'I'm only too pleased to have you here; one misses a woman around the house. Oh, I'm not saying that Jessie and her brood haven't looked after me and the boys very well, but it's not the same . . . You know what I mean?'

She inclined her head slowly towards him and answered, 'Yes, I know what you mean.'

'But mind, you might find it pretty dull here after a time; not very much happens. As you know, it's like an island; we're at the back of beyond and in winter we can be cut off for weeks. For the most part we're self-supporting, but the nerves get frayed when you can't get out and about.'

'That won't worry me; I'm used to being on my own, used to loneliness. Joe was out a lot. Of course he had to be to see to things. I . . . I can assure you that lack of outside company will be the least of my troubles.'

'Oh, now I'm not trying to suggest that we live bereft of company altogether. There's the Doltons and the Hallidays. The Doltons have three youngsters and the Hallidays have two. You'll like Joan Dolton. She's sparkish, is Joan. Anyway, you'll meet them all on New Year's Eve, if not before. We've always had a do here on New Year's Eve. I dropped it for two years after Vera died; but then, as Tom said – Tom Halliday you know – they missed it, and so this year, because I have two extra in my family, it will be a better turn-out than usual.'

22

She made no reply to this but sat looking at him, and he went on talking in his nervous, jerky way. 'It's been a good year. We won the Ashes, didn't we?' He jerked his head towards her and repeated, 'Yes, we won the Ashes. And Cobham flew to Australia and back, and Betty Nuttall knocked the stuffing out of Mrs Mallory . . . Do you like sport?'

'I like swimming. That's about the only thing I can do in the sporting line, except I can shoot a bit. Joe taught me that.'

'Oh, I'm glad you can shoot; there's some good shooting round about. But it's funny, I'm not a very good shot. I swear the birds pass the wink when I'm out.'

They laughed together now; then presently he said, 'You still play the piano?'

'Yes, a little.'

He stared at her now through narrowed lids and his tongue swept round his upper lip and he took another sip from his glass; and his manner further suggested that he was embarrassed and searching for a further topic of conversation; then seemingly finding it, he blurted out, 'Politics . . . do you go for politics?'

'Oh no, not politics. That's the last thing I'd meddle with.'

'Quite rightly, too. Women should keep out of politics. You'll have heard about the strike when you were over there, though?'

'Oh yes, the General Strike.'

'Awful time; the country was at a standstill. That didn't last long, but the poor beggars, the miners, they were out for months. It was terrible around this quarter, pitiable. Dirty deal, dirty deal they had. I had a few of them over here doing odd jobs: willing to work just for potatoes. Dreadful, dreadful state to bring men to.' He rose abruptly from his chair. 'Things are badly divided in this world. Oh . . . oh I admit it' – he pointed to her now, his arm outstretched

as if he were contradicting some statement she had made
– 'I'm talking from the position, in a smaller way, of the
lord in his castle, and the poor man at the gate. I was the
third down the line; but you know I never wanted the title
. . . never dreamed of it, for Cousins John and Thomas were
both hale and hearty, you would have taken a bet on them
reaching senility. But John was whipped off with influenza
just before he was to be married and Thomas goes and breaks
his neck on a mountain. It came as a great shock to me, I can
tell you, I mean, being saddled with a title, me a baronet,
because . . . well' – he turned around now and faced the
fire, thrust his foot out and pressed a log further into the
heart of the basket – 'I don't feel I fit in with the titled type.
Solicitor was all I aimed at . . . and living on the farm. We
had a farm, you know.'

'Why not? Why don't you consider yourself fit to carry
the title?' The question was sharp and he turned his head
towards her, saying now, 'Well, apart from everything else,
it carries responsibilities. I'm an easy-going chap, free and
easy would be a better description, and I like mucking in
with all types. I suppose it's because, in my work, I meet all
types. My father was the same and Grandfather too; although
Great-grandfather was a judge. But he was a jolly judge, I
understand. You know, this place' – he now waved his hand
over his head – 'in its beginnings consisted of nothing but
this very hall we're sitting in. And then only the top part
was habitable for human beings: where you're sitting now
would be the cow byres; the pig-sties were over there near
the staircase. There's a sketch of it in one of the albums in the
library. I must show it to you. The next stage was when they
turfed the animals out and built this chimney. That must have
been all of a hundred years ago. Then my great-grandfather
had a windfall, practically a storm' – he put his head back
and laughed loudly now – 'half a million dollars left to him
by an American relative. But, of course, when you change

24

dollars into sovereigns it doesn't sound nearly as much. And then the lawyers washed their hands in it on the way down. I was about to say, as lawyers are apt to do, but that would be hitting my profession, wouldn't it?' His laugh now turned into a bellow. Then he went on: 'But nevertheless it was a fortune, and at one fell swoop. He built the east and west wings, altered the front. Oh, he practically rebuilt the place.'

'And a beautiful job he made of it.'

'I couldn't agree with you more, Ellen, I couldn't agree with you more. Ah!' He held up his hand. 'Our peace is at an end, look what's coming.'

They both turned towards the staircase now to see the two boys, again with Joseph between them, coming down the stairs.

At the bottom, Joseph tugged himself away from his cousins and, running towards his mother, he cried, 'They did wash my ears out and they were clean! I told them they were clean but they said they had to be red and shining, else they wouldn't pass mustard with the lord and master.'

As the laughter ran through the hall, Arthur's voice rose above it, crying, 'I'll pass muster with you two before you're much older.'

As the boys hung their heads and giggled Mary Smith came from the direction of the dining room and, standing on the outskirts of the group, said, 'Dinner's ready, Mr Arthur.'

'Thanks, Mary. And we're ready for it.'

As he was holding out his arm to Ellen, Joseph looked up at him and asked, 'Why does she call you Mr Arthur? Martin said you were a sir, nearly a lord . . . are you?'

'I am not a lord, but I am called "sir".'

'Oh' – there was a note of regret in the child's tone now – 'I wish you were a lord, like God, in Our Father which art in heaven.'

As the boys hung on to each other in paroxysms of laughter, Joseph, realising that he had caused the amusement, took it further as he demanded, in childish glee now, 'Will I be a "sir" when I grown up?'

The question seemed to silence the group, and as Ellen Jebeau shook her son's arm Arthur said quietly, even solemnly, 'I hope not, Joe, I hope not; the implications are too great.'

Years later, when these words, long forgotten, came back to his mind Joe was to remember the sound of his uncle's voice, and the look on his face as he said them, on his first Christmas in the house called Screehaugh.

2

1932

'Are you looking forward to Oxford?'

Martin screwed up his face as he glanced at Harry and said, 'Yes and no. Yes, because, well, there'll be some life up there, things going on, yet at the same time I'll miss coming home at weekends. I love this old shanty, you know' – he looked towards his bedroom window – 'but at the same time I know I'd have to get away from it at times, and if it ever does become mine' – he turned quickly to Harry – 'God forbid that won't happen until I'm in my dotage, but what I mean is, when it does, I think I'd still have to escape now and again. You know the feeling?'

'No, 'cos I never want to escape.'

'No, you wouldn't, you old stick-in-the-mud.' Martin pushed his brother backwards, and Harry fell with a laugh on to the side of the bed. But then, his face becoming serious, he asked quietly, 'How would you take towards Father marrying again?'

Martin narrowed his eyes at him. 'You've heard something fresh?' he asked.

'No, nothing really, just keeping my eyes open.'

'What have you seen?'

'Oh, just that Aunt Ellen is . . . well, losing control, I think, because every time Vanessa Southall goes riding with Father, she acts up mad. In fact, just before you came home last Saturday she knocked the hell out of Joe.'

'She hit him?' Martin's face screwed up in disbelief. 'She hit Joe?'

'Yes, she did, and not just hit him, either. I would say bashed him, for she knocked him flying up against the wall; then seemingly full of contrition, she gathered him into her arms and cried over him.'

'Where did this happen?'

Harry jerked his head upwards. 'I was upstairs rummaging about among the old train sets as I thought I might find an axle. I did, but it was too small for what I wanted, and I was just about to come down when I heard them on the stairs. I thought they'd be coming into the old nursery looking for something, books or something, because she's always reading to him and keeping him at it. She's aiming to make him into a walking encyclopedia and naturally he's kicking against it, but they went across the landing and into the schoolroom, and as I opened the door I saw her take her hand and swipe the lad across the room. I felt like going and swiping *her*, but then she got down on her knees and started to howl over him. It . . . well, it was embarrassing the way she was whimpering and saying over and over again, "I'm only thinking of you, Joe, only you. It's all for you, Joe, it's all for you." Well, whatever was all for Joe, I thought she had a funny way of showing it. Somehow she made the hair stand up on my neck and I did a quiet disappearing trick. You know I've always liked her, but after that scene last week it showed me another side of her. Perhaps it's the side you've seen all along, because you've never cottoned to her, have you?'

'No, I never have.'

'Was it from the time you found out about her and father?'

28

'No, I don't think so, although one can't be sure, looking back to when you were twelve. Yet she didn't seem to be in the house five minutes before she had him into her bed. Never forget the night I found out. It made me sick; I couldn't look her in the face for ages afterwards. It affected my school work. It was old Baldy Wrighton who relieved my mind. He got it out of me what I was worrying about. I can see him now, sitting behind his desk stroking his bald pate with his fingers spread wide as if he was running them through his hair, and showing all his bad teeth as he grinned and said, "Well, your worries should be all over, Jebeau; she'll never be your stepmother because a man can't legally marry his brother's wife."

'I can feel my jaw dropping now as I stared at him in relief and said, "How's that?" Then he had me laughing as he used to do with the lot of us at the end of a lesson. "It's the law," he said. "And as for the act of copulation, dogs, cats, bulls and rams do it without being reminded, so you can't expect an unintelligent beast such as a man to restrain the urge. Now can you, Jebeau?" '

As Martin chuckled Harry said, 'I'm afraid of old Wrighton, he's much too clever for me. Everybody says he's the cleverest bloke in the school and that he turned down a lectureship in the University just to stay there.'

'Yes, that's true; but this time next year I bet, like everybody else in his form, you'll sing his praises. At the same time, though, you'll be making up couplets about his rotten teeth and the drop at the end of his nose . . . But to get back to Father: there's going to be a hell of a rumpus if he does take up with Vanessa Southall. What do you say?'

Harry remained silent; then getting up from the bed, he walked to the window and, sitting on the wide sill, he said, 'There'll be more than the hell of a rumpus, there'll be one mighty upheaval, because you can't see Aunt Ellen knuckling down to any other woman in the house; she already considers

29

herself mistress of it. She acts like one. To make matters worse, her rival is so much younger, not yet thirty and very attractive into the bargain.'

Martin went and stood by Harry's side and, looking out of the window, he said, 'Somehow I can't see Father playing the dirty on her. I'm not fond of her but I wouldn't like to see her humiliated. Perhaps you with your serious old head' – he now rumpled his brother's hair – 'are seeing things that aren't there.'

'You haven't come home with me every weekend this term, so you've missed quite a bit. A lot can happen in a couple of months.'

'I've only missed four weekends.'

'Well, on two of those particular weekends there were high jinks, albeit refined, in the drawing-room on one occasion, and another up in my lady's chamber.'

Again there was silence between them, and then Martin, pointing, said, 'There's Joe and Carrie coming back.'

Harry looked to where two small figures were racing down the hillside and into the belt of trees at the bottom, and as they disappeared from view he said, 'The only thing Aunt Ellen's got to hang on to is that Father wouldn't do anything to alienate himself from Joe. He's too fond of him, and I can't imagine the house without Joe.'

'No, no; I can't either; he has a strange fascination, has Joe; he exudes love and somehow you want to give it back, yet one senses a need in him at times; I feel he's lonely . . . lonely inside.'

Harry stared at his brother. He was like their father, a boisterous extrovert on the one hand and a secret, thoughtful even poetic, creature on the other.

Martin said now, 'I bet Aunt Ellen doesn't know he's running wild with Carrie; she's not partial to that friendship.'

'Carrie . . . yes, that's what it was about.' Harry was now digging Martin in the arm with his finger. 'The belting he got last week, that's what she was saying as she went into the room; "I'll carry you!" I thought she said; but I didn't connect it with little Carrie. Good lord! Yes, that was it. Poor Joe, he's going to find the going hard.'

'Yes, and not only with Aunt Ellen' – Martin was now nodding slowly – 'but from Mother Jessie too, for if she gets her way, she'll have 'em into bed before they know what's hit them.'

'Jessie?'

'Yes, our fat motherly Jessie. For your further education I'd better tell you that our dear retainer is a cow of the first order.'

'Our Jessie? Go on!'

'Yes, our Jessie.'

'What makes you say that?'

'Because she would sell off her daughters one at a time. Oh, she's got her head screwed on firmly, has our Jessie.'

'I don't follow you.' Harry's tone was flat and he added, 'I like Jessie.'

'Well, brother, all I can advise you is not to cast an eye towards Janet or Carrie. As for Florrie, she's already got her settled in her own mind. In a way, I can understand the old bitch's reasoning; she wants a better life for her girls than she's had, so she aims to marry one of them off into our family by fair means or foul, mostly foul.'

'*You're joking!*'

'Oh no, I'm not joking, Harry.' Martin's voice was deeply serious now. 'She has thrown Florrie at me since I was fourteen. And Florrie was only too willing. She's always been too willing to oblige, and she knows how to oblige an' all. Of course, I've only been made use of, I suppose, at holiday times, but . . .'

'You mean?' Harry's head was thrust forward now, his voice a mere whisper, and he repeated, 'You mean . . . well' – he swallowed and pulled his chin in – 'you mean?'

Martin, now imitating his brother's voice and attitude, thrust his head towards him and whispered, 'Yes, that's what I mean, brother. And don't look so shocked.'

'I'm . . . I . . . I'm not shocked, merely astounded, I mean . . . well, surprised and sort of disappointed. What I mean is, about Jessie; I thought she was nice, motherly.'

'Oh, she's motherly all right, so motherly she even pushed Mary into father's path just before Aunt Ellen came. Although, mind, I don't think Mary would have stood it; she's too much like her father . . . as Carrie is. Our Jessie'll have a job to get Carrie to tread her prepared path, but Florrie and Janet take after their mother.'

Harry's expression caused Martin to exclaim on a laugh, 'Don't be so shocked, lad. Come on, let's go for a ride and sweat some of the passion out of us, eh?' He dug Harry in the shoulder. 'We'll run over to the Doltons'.'

At the mention of the neighbour's name Harry rose from the window seat, grinning now as he said, 'Sweat some of the passion out of us! Well, if we're riding to the Doltons' you're riding in the wrong direction, aren't you?'

'Subtle reasoning. Subtle reasoning. On with you!'

Martin now grabbed Harry's arm, and as they used to do years ago when they were small boys, they ran from the room and down the stairs. And as they ran across the yard Harry shouted, 'I'm going to get a motorcycle.'

'You'll not bring a motor-cycle into this yard as long as there's a horse in it.'

'We'll see. We'll see.'

As they entered the stable Dick Smith was coming out and they stopped almost simultaneously, for the man they looked upon as a friend, who had first taught them to ride, who, whatever the weather, had never failed to meet them at the station when they returned from school, passed them without a word, a look on his face like thunder.

As they exchanged glances Harry muttered, 'What's up with him?'

'Don't ask me. But it must be something pretty bad. I've never seen Dick look like that in my life: something's wrong somewhere. Ah well, come on; I suppose the day won't be over before we'll find out.'

3

'Eat your dinner.'

'I don't want my bloody dinner.'

'Well, you'll eat it afore it eats you. There!' Jessie Smith lifted the plate heaped high with potatoes, cabbage and stewed meat from the table and, going to the oven, she thrust it in, saying as she banged the door, 'You can take it out of there, 'cos I won't. Standin' here cookin' all mornin.' She heaved up her bulbous breasts with her forearm, pushed her greying hair back from her brow; then taking up the corner of her apron, she passed it over her face before turning and looking at her husband, who was standing near the corner of the table glaring at her, and she said, 'You're a fool, Dick Smith, that's what you are. You've always been a fool. You were born one, you'll die one. What have you got for your years of slaving for them, eh?'

'What have I got; I've got food to bring up a family and a clear conscience to go to bed with, that's up to now. Now I feel I'll never hold me head up again.'

Ignoring her husband's last remark, Jessie Smith picked up his first words, saying, 'Food to feed your family with and a hovel for them to live in, 'cos look at it!' She swung her fat body around. 'Compare it with what they've got across

34

there.' She jerked her head towards the door. 'Have they ever suggested building us a decent place? And your wage a pound a week!'

'Don't be so bloody ignorant, woman; I don't only earn a pound a week; there's most of our food can be added on to it, and the heating. And what's more, they've employed every one of us. You should go down on your knees at the present moment and thank God for that, with the roads packed with men begging their bread. Many a miner would give his eye teeth and those of his whole family to be in our shoes the day.'

'Ah, Dick Smith, you make me sick, you do. I've listened to that parable for years. Begod! If we were Catholics like the Paxstones, you'd have us bloody well saying a Mass for them. Why don't you go and crawl up the front steps and thank them for allowing us to exist at all? You know, sometimes I believe you're grateful to them for being born because it happened in this very pig-sty. Anyway, we've been through all this afore, so let's get down to the present. Are you going to go and face him, or am I?'

Dick Smith drew in a long shuddering breath, then patted the stubble on his chin and his head moved slowly back and forward for a moment before he asked, 'And what do you propose I say to him? "Your son, master, has taken our Florrie down and she's going to have a bairn. When can you arrange for the wedding?" ' His teeth now ground against each other and his eyes narrowed as he squinted at her, adding, 'You're the bloody fool, Jessie; in fact, I think you're a bit of a maniac even to imagine he'd make his son toe the line and marry her. She's two years older than him to start with, not that that needs to be a stumbling block if she was of his class . . . '

'Oh, class! Here we go again.'

'Shut your mouth, woman, and let me finish. And I'm gonna say this: I haven't been entirely blind to what's been going on, at least in our Florrie's and our Janet's case; they've both made the hay hotter, I know that, so how are you gonna prove its Master Martin who's responsible for the swelling in her belly?'

'Because she said so and they were at it at Easter and for many a long day afore that.'

'Oh, I bet you saw to it that they were at it, oh aye. You're a long schemer, Jessie. Just afore Mrs Ellen came on the scene you had a plan in your mind. Oh, oh!' He now tossed his head from side to side. 'Get into your napper at last, woman, I'm not the bloody fool you take me for. I don't say much but I keep me eyes open, an' me ears an' all. But from now on things are gonna be different: if anybody's gonna have any say in this matter it's gonna be me. And I'm tellin' you now, there's nobody going up to the house. Aw! Hold your hand, woman! Hold your hand.' He lifted his own hand. 'Don't say it! Don't say she's not goin' to stand this alone.'

'Not say it! By God! but I will. An' I'll see you again in hell's flames afore you keep me tongue tied about this. He's put her in this condition, and one way or t'other something's got to be done about it, an' I'm going to see to it, an' right now.'

As she made for the door he sprang in front of her and from his medium height he seemed to tower over her for a moment as he said, 'I've never hit you, I've never raised me hand to you, and I'm not gonna demean meself by doin' it now, but I say this, if you go up to the house and cause trouble over this, then life as it has been atween us is finished. And you know me well enough by now to know that I don't talk idly. Do this and I'll never touch you again, Jessie. And I'll speak to you when I must, that's how strongly I'm feelin' in this matter.'

36

He now moved aside and he stood watching indecision play on her face; then when he saw her push up her breasts with her forearm he knew what she intended to do, and when her hand came out and she grabbed open the door he made no movement to stop her.

Arthur stared at the woman whom he had seen almost every day for the past twenty-six years, from the very day she had married Dick, but only in this moment did he admit to himself his real personal opinion of her; he had always smothered the feeling of dislike that would arise at intervals by reminding himself that she was a damned good servant and that she had trained her family along similar lines. But now as he looked at the fat bulk of her, the sly devious creature he had always suspected lay behind that too-ready smile was very much in evidence.

'You tell me,' he said, 'that Florrie is pregnant and that Martin is the culprit. You've also inferred that Florrie is very . . . smitten, that was the word you used, wasn't it? smitten by Martin, and she's heartbroken in case her condition causes a break between Martin and her, if he doesn't stand by her. Well now, Jessie, let's get things straight.' His voice was ominously quiet. 'It's got to be proved that my son has brought this thing about. If I know Florrie, and I think I do, she's quite a gay spark. I may as well tell you I have often thought that it's a good job there's very little hay to be gathered in, otherwise the household duties would have been more neglected than they were on these occasions. How do you answer that, Jessie?'

Jessie Smith's face became tight. She sucked in her cheeks, causing her lips to purse, then she rotated them as if she was sucking on a sweet before she said, 'He's got to stand by her.'

Arthur had been seated in the leather chair behind his desk, but now he sprang to his feet with such force as to dislodge the heavy desk an inch or so; then banging his fist down upon it, he said, 'Like hell he will! And let me tell you, Jessie, and I never thought to say this to you, especially as you are Dick's wife and I have a regard for him, but should you make anything big out of this, you and your family will find yourselves out of jobs. And mind, I mean that. I will also tell you, while we're on that, you and your daughter between you have spoiled the good condition of friendship; and I'm not thinking at this moment so much of you, Jessie, but of your man. Now, get yourself away back to your work, and when my son comes home from wherever he's gone I'll talk with him, and if he says he's responsible, but begod I don't believe it for a moment that he is, but should he say he is, you can draft your daughter off to one of her many relatives and I'll pay her expenses up to a certain point, and when the child comes we'll discuss the matter further. But if my son denies that this child could be his then I'd still advise you to get your daughter away . . . and out of my sight!'

As they stared at each other for a moment it seemed that she was about to spit a virulent mouthful of abuse at him, but thinking better of it she brought her teeth down on to her lower lip and, flinging her heavy body about, made for the door. But there, his voice stopped her as he asked grimly now, 'How far is she gone?'

'On three months.' She hadn't looked around; but then, turning her head slightly, she said slowly, 'And she can pinpoint the day and the time when it happened.'

The door had been closed for a full minute before he sat down heavily in the chair again. God! for a thing like this to happen. Blast the young fool! why couldn't he have gone in for his training further afield. But that Florrie, she was like a bitch on heat. And Janet was almost as bad. Helen hadn't been much better, but she must have eased herself when she married Paxstone. The only decent ones among them were Mary and the little one, Carrie. But then, she was a bit young yet, that one, to know which way she would go.

He leant his elbow upon the desk and held his brow in the palm of his hand, and aloud he said, 'Lordie! Lordie!' As if he hadn't enough on his mind at the present moment with Ellen and this other business. He had left the office in Newcastle early yesterday telling himself he couldn't let it go on any longer, that he must bring it out into the open; she would understand, she was sensible, but when he arrived home and looked at her he knew that she wouldn't understand and that where he was concerned she wasn't sensible.

He pulled himself up abruptly as a tap came on the door and, as if she were walking out of his thoughts, Ellen entered the room. After closing the door behind her she asked, 'What did Jessie want? Something wrong, I mean about the house?'

'Oh.' He closed his eyes tightly for a moment, then said slowly, 'I only wish it were.'

She was facing him across the desk now as she said, 'What is it? Something serious?'

'Serious enough. To be brief, Florrie's pregnant and she's naming Martin.'

'*No. No . . . No.* She's daring to blame Martin?'

'Oh, Ellen!' Again he closed his eyes. 'Don't look so shocked; Martin's a young man and Florrie's a very presentable young woman.'

'I'm well aware that Martin is a young man and that Florrie may be a presentable young woman, but she's a loose piece, nevertheless. They're all a much of a muchness over there. I've seen . . .'

He held up his hand and silenced her, and as he gazed at her he thought with some cynicism how strange it was for the frying pan to call the kettle black: it was all right for her to serve his wants and in such a way that some would call brazen, for even when he didn't want to be served she was there, but it wasn't right for Florrie to do the same thing.

'What are you going to do about it?'

'I don't know yet until I speak to Martin. It's got to be proved.'

'Yes, it's got to be proved. And that particular young miss will find it very hard to prove, I'm sure.' Turning to the side, she sat down now and, looking at him again, she said, 'You wanted to see me?'

He did not answer, but stared at her. Seeing her like this, who would think she was capable of such passion that at times he likened it to lava, for it was burning him up. In the six years she had been in this house she hadn't seemed to change, at least not in appearance; she had filled out slightly, but she was still thin and had that aloof, cool air about her that was so deceiving. It had certainly deceived him.

During the first weeks of her sojourn here he had become so fascinated by her that the only thought in his mind was to woo her to his bed; and then when he had broached the subject tentatively he had found he could dispense with the wooing and start the honeymoon straightaway.

Through time he had learned that besides hiding an unusual passion, her cool exterior also hid a fierce temper that could be likened to rage. He had first experienced the onslaught of this when she knew he couldn't marry her. She hadn't been aware that it was unlawful for a man to marry his brother's wife. At the time he made this clear to her he would have been willing to end the physical association, but she had other ideas.

Now he had fallen in love again, really fallen in love, and wanted to marry. He'd had the feeling for some time now that he'd like youngsters around the house once more. It was a house made for young people and the boys were growing up; there was only Joe and he was no longer a child. That was another odd thing about her: her attitude towards her son. She smothered him, or aimed to do so.

He'd have to fight her for his freedom one day, would Joe.

'What are you thinking about?'

'Well, Ellen, to tell you the truth I was thinking about us.'

'Well, I can say you're not alone, I'm always thinking about us.' Her face did not soften as she said the words that should have inferred tenderness.

'Oh.' He got to his feet now and walked the length of the long, narrow room and back again before he said, 'This is going to be very difficult, Ellen, because . . . well, I know how you feel, and I appreciate all you've done for me, in all ways' – he nodded his head deeply at her now – 'in all ways. You know that.'

He waited for her to make some comment but she sat, her back straight, her eyes fixed tight on him; and so he went on, stumbling now: 'I feel a swine about this, Ellen. I do, I do; but you see I'm not getting any younger and . . . well, I'd better come out with it.' He now went and sat down in the chair and looking down at his joined hands on top of the desk, he said, 'The top and bottom of it is, Ellen, I'm thinking of marrying again . . . You know her . . . Vanessa Southall.' His head drooped further towards his chest as he ended, 'I know I'm almost twice her age, but . . . but she's willing and . . .'

He started back in the chair as she flung herself across the desk and gripped the sleeve of his coat below the elbow and, her face now just inches from his, she hissed at him, 'You'll not! You can't. What's more, you won't! I won't have it, do you hear? You've used me all these years, you've made me feel this is my home, and now you throw me aside for a bit of a girl. You'll not do it. I'll see you dead first. Do you hear me?'

With a jerk of his arm he freed himself from her grasp as he ground out, 'Don't you threaten me, Ellen. That's the last thing you should do, threaten. As for using you, I think the

boot's been on the other foot more times than not ... Oh
God!' He put his hand over his eyes for a moment, and his
voice dropping, he went on, 'Don't make me say such things,
woman. Yet it's true, and you know it is. As for the work
you've done running the house, well, you know I've tried to
repay you: you've got a good allowance, and ... and you
won't lose it, I'll double it when you have to leave.' He
turned his head aside and, like that, continued to talk to her,
'You won't be without a home. There's a property going just
outside Hexham, a nice little house with a garden, and it'll
be nearer Joe's school. I'll do everything in my power ... '
  'Shut up!'
  He rose to his feet, his eyes wide, and looked at her. Her
face was livid. In all respects she now bore no resemblance
to the woman who had just a few minutes earlier entered the
room: her shoulders were hunched, almost touching her jaw
line, her body was bent forward as if she were on the point
of springing, and like this she repeated, 'Shut up!'
  'Ellen.' Her name was a plea, but before he could go on her
hands had come out and were gripping the lapels of his coat;
and in this way she brought her body tight against his and,
her mouth wide, she caught his chin between her teeth, and
as he gave a low cry against the pain, he brought his forearm
up between them and thrust her away with such force that
she stumbled backwards, tripped over a foot-stool and fell
into a huddle against the corner of the break-front bookcase
that lined one wall of the room. And it was as she lay huddled
on the floor and Arthur stood gripping his bleeding chin that
the door opened and Joe entered the room ...
  Joe never knocked on doors, at least not on the door of
the office, where he was used to walking in and having a
chat with his uncle; nor on the drawing-room door; nor
the dining-room door, nor any of the kitchen doors; the
only doors he was told he must knock on were bedroom
doors. He stared now at the two figures before him and

42

as he saw his uncle go and help his mother to her feet, he thought with amazement that they must have been fighting, but what he said, as he stepped towards them, was 'Did you slip, Mother?'

She did not answer, her head was deeply bowed, but in a strange voice his uncle said, 'Yes . . . yes, your mother slipped. Take her to her room, there's a good fellow'; and obediently Joe put his arm on his mother's elbow, and she allowed him to lead her from the room and up the stairs and into her bedroom. But once in the room, she did a strange thing: she dropped onto her knees on the floor and, pulling him into her embrace, held him so tightly that he wanted to cry out against it.

He had no desire to return the embrace, perhaps because he wasn't used to embraces, not embraces such as this, anyway. And then she puzzled him still further for, letting him go as quickly as she had caught him to her, she flung herself on the bed, and he watched her hammering the eiderdown with her clenched fists as she kept saying, 'He shan't do it! He shan't do it!'

Strangely, he noted that she wasn't crying. People usually cried when they were vexed, but then his mother wasn't like other people.

4

Mick Smith said, 'They're not rising,' and Joe replied, 'No, they're not, are they? It's the weather perhaps?'

'Aye, it's the weather. They're keeping under the banks, and we'd be more sensible like if we went and sat under a tree. You're sweatin' like a bullock.'

The sixteen-year-old boy grinned widely at Joe and Joe, returning the grin, said, 'Aye, you're right.' He knew he shouldn't have said aye, but somehow he thought it was kinder to use the same words as Mick did when in conversation with him.

A few minutes later they were seated with their backs to the bole of the gnarled willow and the silence of the sultry afternoon hung over them. It was Mick's rough voice that broke the silence, saying, 'Your last day then, school the morrow?'

'Yes, aye.'

'Glad to be going back?'

Joe didn't answer for a moment; then bending sidewards, he tugged at a stem of stiff grass and when he had broken it he put it in his mouth and, closing his teeth on it, he drew the sap on to his tongue before he answered the question with a statement: 'It's been a funny holiday, not like the others.'

'No; you've said it, 'tain't been like the others. No . . . no, you're right there.'

Joe began to examine the limp piece of grass that he was now holding between his finger and thumb as he said, 'Why has your father forbidden Carrie to play with me?'

'Oh well.' Mick now bent forward between his stretched legs and, snapping off the head of a clover he pulled at one of its myriad petals and, putting it into his mouth, nipped it between his front teeth, then muttered slowly, 'Aye, well, you know there's been trouble, don't you?'

'Yes, but I didn't know what it was all about. I only know that Uncle was very angry with Martin, and he went away to stay with a friend and when I asked Harry why, he snapped my head off. It wasn't like Harry. But then, he's been at sixes and sevens all the holiday. I like Harry' – his voice became thoughtful – 'but I didn't know that I didn't like him as much as I like Martin. I love Martin.'

'Aye now, aye now, Master Joe.' Mick hitched himself straighter against the bole of the tree and there was a little note of laughter in his voice. 'You don't say you love a chap.'

'No?'

'No. It doesn't do to say you love a chap. You love your mam and dad and . . . well, you love a lass, but you don't say you love a boy, a man . . . a young man like Master Martin.'

'Why not? If you feel you like someone very much. Why not?'

'Cos . . . well just 'tain't done, Master Joe. Oh, you're not old enough yet to understand these things, but just for future use, don't say you love any lad. Well, you know what I mean, like.'

'No, I don't really.'

'Oh my!' Mick turned his head away now, a half-smile on his face as he muttered, 'You're always the one for

45

the straightforward question and answer. It'll get you into trouble one of these days.'

He had hardly finished speaking when his head jerked round towards the young boy as Joe said 'Then I may say I love Carrie and no one would mind?'

'Eeh, God above! don't you start, Joe . . . I mean Master Joe. Eeh! now, you can say you like people but don't go about saying you love 'em. And as for our Carrie, well now, you don't want to cause any more trouble, do you?'

'Why should that cause you trouble? I've always loved Carrie. I've never said so, but I always have.'

Mick screwed his eyes up tightly and, like that, he said, 'You're not eleven till Christmas, are you?'

'No; you know I'm not.'

'Aye, I do. Well, at this minute I wish I could put three or four years on you.'

'Why?'

'Oh, Master Joe.' Mick was now on his knees bending towards Joe. 'You've got to learn that you can't go round saying you love people. I know how you feel, I love people. Aye, I do' – he nodded – 'but I can't go openin' me mouth about it. An' you are in a worse position than me because you are of the house. An' now you say you love our Carrie. Well . . . well now, I must say this to you, all the trouble that's been lately, it's concerned with just that, somebody sayin' they loved somebody. You follow me?'

There was a pause before Joe shook his head and said, 'No.'

'Oh, God above!' Mick pursed his thin mouth, ran his fingers through his thick sandy hair, then said, 'Well, laddie, I think it's a bit early to open your eyes but for your own sake it's got to be done. You know that besides Master Martin going away, our Florrie went away an' all; you know that too, don't you?'

'Aye yes, Mick.'

'Well, she went away because ... well—' The beads of sweat were standing out on Mick's brow and he wiped them off with his fingers before he continued, 'She said she loved Master Martin and that's why she had to go away.'

Joe now swung around on to his knees, the look on his face one of sheer astonishment as he said, 'You mean, just because she said she loved ... ?'

'No, no, I don't mean *just* because she said that. You know, Joe, you being brought up alongside Master Martin and Master Harry and being among the horses and animals every holiday, you've kept your eyes closed, haven't you?'

Joe made no answer, he just continued to stare at Mick; and Mick, heaving in a big deep breath now, said, 'Our Florrie's gonna have a bairn and she says it was given to her by Master Martin.' His voice faded away on the name, and he now sat back on his hunkers and returned Joe's stare; and like this they remained for some time before Joe, turning slowly around, lay face down on the grass and began once again to pull at the tough stems. It was a full minute before he turned his head and looked at Mick and asked calmly, 'Aren't they going to be married then?'

'No, 'tain't possible.'

'I see.'

Rising to his feet now, Joe stood looking towards the river as he asked, 'Am I backward for my age, Mick?'

'No, no, Joe: I'd say you've a head on your shoulders, but at the same time ... well, you're a bit airy-fairy.'

'Airy-fairy?'

'Oh, I'm not very good at explaining things but, you know, you get lost at times, Joe, when you start writing your bits of poetry.'

'Does that make me airy-fairy?'

'Aye, in a way, 'cos you don't see things that are happenin' under your nose.'

'I'll have to stop being airy-fairy then, won't I?'

'No. Now, no; don't you do no such thing; you're all right as you are. I heard Master saying he wouldn't be surprised if you make something of yourself one day with your bits and pieces, 'cos you've got a head for it, and I agree with him. It'll be fine if one day I can say to somebody, "Oh, Mr. Joseph Jebeau? Oh aye, I know him. I'll say I do, 'cos I was practically brought up alongside of him. We walked together, fished together, and one early mornin' around dawn he slipped out and we saw the dawn from the top of the moor." That was a mornin' I'll always remember; I'll take it with me down the years, that mornin'.'

The muscles of Joe's face twitched slightly as he stared up at his tall gangling friend and more than anything at this moment he wanted to say, 'I have the same feeling for you as I have for Martin and Carrie'; instead he said, 'You could write poetry yourself, Mick.'

'Me write poetry! You're kiddin', aren't you?'

'No, no, I'm not. Sometimes it's the way you say things, it sounds like poetry to me.'

'That'll be the day when I write me first line of poetry. Mind you' – he nodded at Joe – 'it isn't because I can't write; I write a very good hand and I can put a letter together better than most, oh aye' – he jerked his head in praise of himself – 'but poetry, no. No, Joe; me mind doesn't run along those lines, in fact I can never get me mind higher than me head, and me feet are so firmly planted on the ground that I couldn't fly even if God gave me wings this minute.'

'There you are, that's what I mean, Mick' – Joe laughed outright – 'you could write poetry.'

'Ah well, I'll let you have your joke, but now let's pick up the lines and get back to the yard. I've got work to do in the stables an' I'd better be there when Master Harry comes back, because Neptune will be running grease, if I know anything the day. For a young man who says he doesn't care for horse ridin', Master Harry certainly takes it out of a beast when he gets on its back. The quicker he gets that motor-cycle of his the better, that's what I say. And then there's your mother; she should be back about five. And another thing, we'd better make our way around the back, because if Bill Swann and Danny spot me, they're not above tellin' the boss I was skivin'. Why do gardeners always think it's only them who does any work, eh?'

'Do they? I mean, do they think they're the only ones who do any work?'

'Oh aye, oh aye. Well now, have we got everything? Come on, let's get going.' . . .

Five minutes later they were nearing the house when Joe drew them to a stop by saying, 'Will you do something for me, Mick?'

Mick turned and, looking down on Joe, said, 'Aye, anything I can, short of kicking you in the backside.'

He laughed while waiting for Joe to speak again, but when Joe said, 'Will you let me see Carrie just once to say goodbye, because . . . because I have a present for her.' The grin slipped from Mick's face, his eyes narrowed and he said, 'Well now, that's asking something, but—' He jerked his head up out of his collarless shirt and remained silent for a moment, before ending, 'Well, it's your last day, an' from where I stand I can see no harm in it, but you'll be careful, now, won't you?'

'Oh yes, Mick, I'll be careful.'

'It'll all depend if she's outside the house. If she's indoors I can't do anything about it; if she's outside I'll send her round to the back. Meanwhile, you keep out of the way. Stand in the doorway to the back stairs; and don't keep her long, mind, for if you're found, you'll get me into a hell of a row. Me dad would skin me! I wouldn't do it at all if he was about the place. Go on, put your stuff away, then look slippy.'

They parted, Mick making his way now directly to the yard while Joe skirted the shrubbery and the rose garden, then ran over the stretch of lawn towards the back of the house. He paused for a moment near the staircase door. If he were to go and put his tackle away it might mean missing a few moments extra with Carrie, so, slipping the bag from his shoulder, he threw it into the corner of the passageway from which the back stairs led, and leaned his rod up against the wall; he then rubbed his hands down the length of his short trousers and stroked the dark lick of hair from his brow before, standing within the shadow of the doorway, he moved his head slightly forward until he could take in the length of the house to where the kitchen quarters jutted out.

It was only minutes later when he saw Carrie coming around the end wall. She was running with her head down, and she didn't lift it until she came to the doorway where, moving quickly into its shelter, she stood panting for a moment before raising her head and looking at him.

As he gazed back into her round eyes he found, as usual, it was difficult to formulate words. When he was with her he just wanted to keep looking at her. Presently he did speak, but his voice was low and weighted as if with sorrow as he said, 'I go back to school tomorrow.'

'I know.'

'I'll miss seeing you.'

'I know.' She nodded. 'So will I.'

She never seemed to waste words, she always came straight to the point. That's what he liked about her. Other people, young and old, seemed to beat about the bush; and girls of his own age he found always acted coy, but not Carrie.

'I have a present for you,' he said. 'I . . . I did it from memory. I . . . I don't think it's very good.'

'What is it?'

'It's your picture.'

'Me picture!' Her mouth widened into a smile. 'You've drawn me?'

He nodded at her, answering her smile now. Then, his voice eager, he said, 'I'll go and get it, I won't be a minute.'

He had reached the third step when he stopped and looked down on her. His mind was telling him that there was no-one in the house, not of any importance. His uncle was at work in Newcastle. His mother was in Newcastle, too; and she would likely return with his uncle. She used to do that a lot at one time, go to Newcastle and have dinner with his uncle, but not so lately. Still she had gone today. And Harry wasn't in, either.

Holding out his hand, he said, briskly now, 'Come on. Come on up to my room.'

When she hesitated he said, 'There's no-one in; and I've written some poetry; it's about you an' all. Come on.'

Her eyes wide, her lips apart, she gave him her hand; then they were running up the stairs together. But at the door leading on to the landing he brought them to a halt before gently pushing it open and peeping round it. As he paused, Carrie whispered, 'Our Helen's down in the kitchen with Mary.'

'Oh, they won't mind.' He grinned at her now, pushed the door wide, then still holding her hand he hurried her along the gallery, down the wide corridor to the end and so into his room. There, releasing her hand, he went hurriedly to a chest of drawers and, pulling open the bottom drawer, he took out a piece of cardboard edged with passe-partout. Returning to where she was standing near the closed door, he thrust it into her hand saying, 'There!'

Carrie looked down at the drawing and she recognised herself immediately, and such was her pleasure that her face became alight: her eyes shone, her rosy coloured cheeks formed apples at each side of her nose, her lips stretched themselves into a wide smile, showing her teeth and the gap in the left side of her upper set.

Gazing at him, she said, 'It's me!'

'You think it looks like you?'

'Aye. Oh aye! Yes; it's lovely. Thank you, Joe.'

51

His expression now as tentative as his words, he said, 'Do you think your mother will let you keep it?'

For answer she said, 'I won't let anybody see it. I've got a hidey place, it's down by the burn. If I get any extra pennies I keep them down there.'

'You do?'

'Yes.' She nodded at him.

As they looked at each other a silence fell on them. It was like a pressure on them. He knew he was sweating, and he could see that she was too. Her chin was wet and there was a damp patch near her oxter. 'I've got a bottle of pop in the drawer,' he said. 'It's American cream soda. It'll be warm. Would you like a drink?'

'Yes, please.'

He went again to the chest of drawers and now rummaged under some underwear in the top drawer. Bringing out the bottle, he took it to the wash-hand stand where he opened it and poured half the contents into a tooth-mug. As he handed it to her he said, 'It's still fizzy, so that might cool you.'

Before she drank it she looked towards the wash-hand stand, saying, 'Have you got any left?'

'Oh yes; but I've only got the one mug. Anyway, I can drink out of the bottle.' He now went and picked up the bottle, and having taken a drink from it, he sat down on the side of his bed. It was an automatic action and he seemed to realise this for, getting up quickly, he said, 'Come and sit down; you can sit on that chair.' He pointed to the chair to the left of him. But Carrie didn't take the chair; she sat down on the side of the bed near the foot, hooking one arm over the lower wooden rail as she continued to sip slowly from the mug.

'Would you like to hear the piece I wrote about you?'

She gulped on the soda, wrinkled her nose, then nodded.

He rose from the bed and walked towards a desk that was set under the window, pulled open a drawer, took out a notebook and from it a loose sheet; then returning to the bed, he sat near her, but not too near, saying, 'It's very short;' then swallowing deeply, he began to read:

> 'The morning brings the chorus of the birds;
> And the lark soars to the sun at noon,
> And evening the thrush and blackbird vie,
> And night brings the moon,
> The stars, and the owl's cry;
> But the song in my heart beats them all,
> For it sings: Carrie, Carrie, Carrie.'

His face was scarlet as he finished and he kept his head down for a moment, and when there was no comment forthcoming from her he said, 'You think it silly?'

'Oh no!' The words were firm, her voice loud, and again she said, 'Oh no! No! I think it's lovely.'

He was gazing at her; they were gazing at each other, and what she said now almost brought the tears to his eyes. 'Our Mick says you're clever with words an' . . . an' he says you're goin' places. He . . . he likes you, our Mick does.'

There was a catch in his voice as he said, 'And I like him very much too.'

'I . . . I love our Mick, I . . . I love him better than anybody else in the family; he's good, is our Mick, I do love him . . . An' there's something else.'

He waited.

'I love you, Joe, I do. I know I shouldn't – me da would lather me if he was to know I said such a thing – but you're goin' to school the morrow and . . . and I likely won't see you again ever, ever.'

He seemed stunned by her declaration of love, but her last remark brought him jerking along the bed towards her, asking, 'What do you mean?'

'Me dad's talkin' about sendin' me to Cousin Alice's. He's been fightin' with me ma over it; if he gets his way I'll have to go. I don't want to, but I'll have to go, so I might never see you again, 'cos she lives miles away in a place called Howdon. It's miles and miles away.'

'Oh, Carrie!' He reached out and took the mug from her hand and, stooping, put it on the floor; then he was holding both her hands in his tightly against his damp shirt front. And now there were actual tears in his eyes as he said, 'I couldn't bear it if I was never to see you again, Carrie, because I love you too. Oh I do. Yes, I do.'

Her head was moving in small jerks now and her voice was a whisper as she said, 'I'll never forget you, and if I go I'll take your picture with me.'

'And I'll never forget you, Carrie, never, never, never. And when I'm old enough to leave school I'll come and find you and . . . '

For a seeming age they gazed at each other; then their hands still joined together they swayed, their bodies in unison. Slowly they fell sidewards onto the bed. The action seemed to freeze them for a moment, until a little self-conscious giggle rippled through Carrie and she bit on her lip; and this brought a grin and a chuckle from Joe too, and their brows came together as they laughed softly.

And there the compromising situation would have ended for Carrie, wriggling her legs, which were hanging over the edge of the bed and still mostly covered by her ankle-length frock, was about to raise herself on her elbow, when the door opened and a gasp that sounded like a roar swept over them and caused them to huddle together for a moment in sheer terror.

Then the figure was above them, glaring down at them, the face so distorted that Joe couldn't recognise it as his mother's and when Carrie was wrenched from his hold he went to cry out, but the sound seemed to be knocked down his throat with his mother screaming, 'You dirty little hussy! You filthy little scheming little hussy, you!' When her hand came with resounding cracks on both sides of Carrie's face, Joe sprang from the bed and, clutching his mother's arm, he yelled at her, 'Stop it! Stop it! Don't!'

'Out of my way! I'll deal with you later.' The thrust of her arm sent him flying against the wash-hand stand, and then her two hands gripped the terrified girl's shoulders and Carrie, crying, struggling and screaming, was thrust out through the open door, across the landing and gallery and down the main staircase with such force that they both nearly tumbled the last steps into the hall.

Mary and Helen Paxstone had come running from the direction of the kitchen, only to be brought to a wide-eyed and open-mouthed stop by the sight of the mistress, as they now thought of Ellen, shaking their Carrie like a terrier shakes a rat, and their Carrie sobbing as they'd never heard her sob and holding out her hands in appeal to them.

It was Mary who now rushed forward demanding, 'What's this! What you done to her, ma'am? What's she done, anyway? Leave go of her!'

It was Ellen Jebeau's turn now to find herself thrust so roughly aside that she almost fell back on to the stairs; and now Mary Smith, holding her young sister to her, dared to look at her mistress and say, 'You gone mad?'

Ellen stood gasping while beads of sweat dripped from the ends of her chin, and she had to draw in a deep breath before she could speak. 'Yes, I have gone mad, for I have just seen that dirty little creature aiming to seduce my son.'

'You're out of your mind, ma'am.' Helen Paxstone's voice was quiet and her eyes narrowed as she squinted at the enraged woman.

'Out of my mind, am I? I can't believe my own eyes? She had him on the bed, her arms about him.'

'It could have been t'other way about, he could have had her on the bed, his arms about her; an' it was on his bed.' It was Mary speaking now. 'And they're but children.'

'Children! None of your family are children where sex is concerned; you're all sex mad.'

'Well, 'twould appear we're in good company, wouldn't it, ma'am?'

Ellen now rounded on the housemaid and her voice almost a thin scream, she cried, 'Don't you dare talk in that fashion to me!'

'Well, don't you dare talk in that fashion to us, ma'am. You be careful what you're sayin' about our family. I have a good name, so has Mary here, and there's no one can point a smirking finger at us. And it isn't everybody that's in that position the day, ma'am, is it, ma'am?'

'Get into the kitchen! I'll report you to your master when he comes in.'

'Well, there'll be more than one doin' that, ma'am, let me tell you. It isn't finished this, not by the looks of Carrie's face; there's a weal rising right down by her eye.' She nodded down to Carrie where the child was clinging to her waist. 'An' that didn't get there by a tap. Oh yes, there'll be more than you seein' the master afore the night's out. Come! The air stinks around here.' Helen now grabbed hold of her elder sister's arm and with her other hand on Carrie's shoulder she propelled them towards the kitchen; but before she passed through the door she turned her head back and looked at Ellen Jebeau, who was standing rigidly stiff, the nails of her joined hands pressing into her flesh, and she called to her, 'We was here afore you came and we'll be here when you're gone.'

For a moment Ellen thought she was going to choke. Unclasping her hands, she began to stroke her neck, and after a moment she turned and rushed up the stairs.

Once again she was in the bedroom and staring at her son.

Joe seemed to have been waiting for her, for he was standing with his back to his desk, and when she stopped

56

a yard or so from him and stood glaring at him, he said, 'We weren't doing anything bad. And it was me to blame. I brought her upstairs to give her a present, a going-away present.' He put out his hand and picked up the passe-partout picture from the desk and, turning it towards her, he said, 'I had done a drawing of her.'

Her action was so quick that she had the picture out of his hands and was tearing it in two before he could draw a second breath.

As he watched her tear it again, then again, the tears came to his eyes. He blinked them away and his lips pressed tightly over each other for a moment before he said, brokenly, 'It doesn't matter, I can draw another one; and I will, because I love her.'

The blow sent him flying. He felt himself toppling backwards; his head hit something sharp; then as if he had dropped off to sleep he went into nothingness . . .

When he came to he was lying on the bed and her face was hanging over him and she kept dabbing his brow with a wet flannel. His mind was still muzzy and her voice seemed to be coming from a distance as she kept saying, 'Oh, I'm sorry, I'm sorry, Joe. I'm sorry. Oh, if you could only understand. You're all I've got now, all I've got, and I don't want your life ruined by sluts. You can do anything you choose if only you put your mind to it; you're like me inside, I know, I know. Come, wake up, wake up, Joe. I'm sorry, I'm sorry. I love you. Don't you understand, I love you?'

As her voice dragged him back into full consciousness he thought, it had been a strange day, everybody he had spoken to or listened to had talked of love. It had started early this morning when he overheard Bernard Paxstone talking to Rob Burnip. Bernard was saying that the master was in love with Miss Southall and it wouldn't surprise him a bit if they got hitched. In some sort of a way he had connected this news with his mother and it gave him the reason why she had been acting odd lately. He recalled that she hadn't seemed happy for some time and especially so from the morning he inadvertently went into his uncle's office and found her on the floor and his uncle with his chin bleeding. He had sensed a great unhappiness in her then.

Nobody seemed happy, nobody; yet it was all connected with love and love should make you happy. He knew now he would never see Carrie again, for they would surely send her far away to that place in Howdon. The loss within himself linked up in a strange way with the loss his mother was experiencing, so he could forgive her for hitting him; but he wasn't so sure if he could forgive her for hitting Carrie.

Carrie had walked by her father's side through the grounds to where the garden ended and the grassland and the hills began. There was one hill still within the grounds and when they reached the top he made for an outcrop of rock where three sheep were grazing. They had evidently jumped the wall at some point. Another time Dick Smith would have shooed them down by the side of the wall until he found the gap or perhaps a section where the top had crumbled, and then shooed them over it. But today he took no notice of the sheep, which ran away at their approach. Standing with his back to the rock, he looked around him. There in the distance, to the right of him, ran the thread of the river; away to the left, spreading onwards and onwards, were hills and more hills showing great swards of reddy-brown heather merging into purple in the far distance. He kept his gaze fixed straight ahead as he spoke to his daughter, saying, 'You've never told me a lie in your life, have you, Carrie?'

'No, Da.' Her voice was a whisper.

'And you're not going to start now, are you?'

'No, Da.'

'Well then, tell me exactly what happened back there s'afternoon. Exactly mind, bit by bit.'

'Well!' Her voice still small and each word seeming to hold a trembling note, she began, 'It was like this, Da. Our Mick came and said Master Joe had to go to school the morrow and would I like to go and say good-bye to him, and I said, "Aye, I would". So I went and . . . and . . . '

'Aye. Go on.'

She she went on, giving him a minute picture of everything that had happened as she remembered it, and when she stopped speaking he looked down at her and asked quietly, 'But did he touch you?'

She blinked her eyes, stared up at him and seemed to consider for a moment, and his voice urged her by repeating, 'Did he touch you? I said.'

'Yes, Da. Well . . . '

'Well what?'

'Well, he caught my hands like this.'

She demonstrated. 'And when we fell over on the bed he . . . put his brow against mine, like this.' She poked her head forward and looked towards the ground, and when she lifted her eyes to him he was looking away from her again and what he said was, 'Aw, hinny. Hinny.'

'I've told you the truth, Da.'

'And I believe you, lass.' He was nodding down at her now. 'And what you told me only goes to prove what I learned a long time ago, that women are like vampires. You know what a vampire is?'

'No, Da.'

'Well, it's something that sticks to you and sucks your blood, lass. And women are like that . . . and young lasses are like that. A lad or a man has no chance against them, once the urge gets them.' He bent his head now towards her, bringing his face close to hers, and he said, 'You'll soon be a young lass, Carrie. You mightn't know what I'm gettin' at now but, later on, just remember what your da's saying at this minute, and he says to you this: no matter what your feelings, try to keep them to yourself until the right time comes. And you'll know when the right time comes, and it doesn't always come through going to church or chapel and having a ring put on your finger. 'Tis better that way for respectability like, but it doesn't always bring happiness. Can you follow what I'm saying?'

She stared at him for a moment in silence before she said, 'I think I can, Da. You're telling me I've got to be a good girl.'

'Aye, that's it, you've got it, that's what I'm tellin' you. Now, I've got to tell you something else. I'm sendin' you to Howdon. You'll be better there in all ways. As you know, your Aunt Alice and her husband Stan haven't any bairns. You remember them, don't you, when they came and visited us?'

She gulped and nodded.

'Well, they've always fancied you, and it was our Alice who put it to me last year that she'd like to give you a chance in life. Your uncle's got a good job; he's a gaffer in a glass works and he comes from a very respectable family. They brought him up well. He plays the piano lovely. An' they've got a big house, well, not like the big house here' – he jerked his head back – 'but a biggish house in a street, a terrace, it is. Besides a big kitchen, they've got a dining-room and sitting-room and lavatory to themselves. What do you think of that?'

Whatever she thought of it she made no comment; she couldn't speak.

'Don't cry, lass,' he said, 'don't cry. It'll finish me if you cry.' He gulped in his throat, ran his forefinger under his nose, then muttered, 'We've come up here a lot, you and me, over the years, and this will be the last time we'll look towards the hills together until you come on your holidays, or visitin' like, and so I'm gonna tell you something now, me bairn, an' it's this: of all me brood I've loved you the best.'

60

'Oh, Da! Da!' She had her arms around his waist now, and his hands were cupping her fair hair and his eyes were moist as he turned and looked towards the hills and only his tightly pressed lips stopped the words coming out: And you're one she won't send whoring.

5

'Ellen, you've got to face up to it. I mean to marry Vanessa.'

Ellen was sitting at the side of the fireplace in the drawing-room. Her knees pressed tightly together, she was sitting more like a man would, her hands covering the knee caps, her body bent slightly forward, her eyes directed towards the blazing logs. She didn't speak, and Arthur went on, 'I'm doing the very best possible for you and the boy, you must admit that. The house is nice, charming. I wouldn't mind living in it myself. I wouldn't have the responsibility of this one then.' He swept his hand backwards while keeping his eyes on her. 'I know it's going to be a wrench for you, I understand that, because you've grown to love this place and you've managed things so well over the past years; no one could have done it better, but there won't be room for two women in it. You know that yourself. Your suggestion that you stay on here as a kind of housekeeper wouldn't work. You know it wouldn't. Anyway' – he jerked his chin upwards – 'I couldn't stand that kind of situation, not after what has happened between us.'

For the first time she turned her head towards him and her voice was quiet as she said, 'You admit then that there has been something between us?'

'Oh, don't be ridiculous, Ellen.' His voice was almost a bawl. Realising this, he looked down the room towards the door; then taking a step nearer to her, he said, 'Don't make me angry.'

'Don't make you angry!' There was a note of bitter laughter in her voice. 'You have nothing to be angry about; you've had the best of both worlds, you're going on having the best of both worlds. No' – she cast her eyes towards the fire again – 'that isn't correct. You won't allow yourself a mistress and a wife, the prig in you wouldn't countenance that, would it?' Again she was looking at him, and he remarked somewhat grimly, 'No, it wouldn't.' Then almost beseechingly he bent down towards her and said, 'Look, Ellen, don't let us spend your last few days in the house warring. Vanessa will be here at any minute; don't, I beg you, make it awkward for her. She's been very good; she understands the situation.'

She was on her feet now confronting him, her face ablaze, 'You mean to say you've told her?'

'Yes; yes, I did. At my age she wasn't expecting to find me a monk.'

'How long has she known?'

'Oh, I think she must have guessed pretty much from the first, but I came clean only a few days ago.'

'You unthinking, callous, garrulous, stupid individual!'

'*Ellen!*' The name was drawn out. 'You go too far, and if you have hysterics this time, I warn you, you won't be the only one who'll use their hands, for I'll slap you down. Now just think on that.'

As they glared at each other, it was evident to him that she was making a great effort to control a spasm of her ungovernable temper. It amazed him that anyone so composed on the surface could lose control to such an extent as to appear almost insane. Sometimes he was made to wonder if there wasn't a streak of insanity in her.

He turned from her now and walked towards the door

saying angrily, 'I won't expect to see you at lunch.'

It was a dismissal, and she felt in this moment that he was placing her on a level with the Smiths. Her suppressed rage rose up, her face became almost purple, and she swung around as if looking for a way to escape. Yet it was because she didn't want to escape, never to escape from him, that she was feeling like this. It wasn't to be borne. She told herself this repeatedly: it wasn't to be borne. The thought of that young girl and him made her feel physically sick, she wanted to retch. She hurried up the length of the room and stood as if meaning to leave by the French windows, but she stooped in front of them and placed her flat palms on the frost-grimed glass. In this moment she had the desire to crash through it, to break something, see the fragments flying through the air, broken, finished in the way she saw her life from now on. She tried to remember that she still had Joe to live for; but she had also seen a fulfilling of a different part of her life, the ambitious part. She wanted for him, even craved for him, the things, the position, that she had missed. At one time she had imagined herself becoming fulfilled in that way through him. However, her love for her son was only part of the whole of her; the love she had for Arthur came under the heading of passion, a burning body demanding passion, a consuming flame that refuelled itself each day and which she felt would never die out.

Lifting her head from the window pane, she stared through the glass on to the terrace and down over it to the gardens to where, in the distance, lay the dim outlines of the hills. Everything was covered with frost. It had held since yesterday. As she continued to gaze out of the window her mind kept saying: 'What am I to do? What am I to do?' Then slowly the germ of an answer came to her. It came in the shape of a car which had emerged from the belt of trees, continued round the drive, and was now passing along the front of the house.

Miss Vanessa Southall had arrived in her sporty MG. She

was so young, so tough, she hadn't even bothered to put the hood up; that she had arrived in a car at all and on a frosty day like this, when the roads would be unsafe, showed what kind of person she was, resilient, fearless in a way. Other people in this part of the world put their cars away for the winter, but not Miss Vanessa Southall.

She turned from the window and went down the room towards the door, repeating the name to herself as she went: 'Miss Vanessa Southall. Miss Vanessa Southall.'

Joe looked at his two cousins standing before him. They were in Martin's room and although it was a large room furnished with a rosewood bedroom suite, to his mind at that moment it was the two young men that seemed to fill it, especially Martin.

With the pain in Joe's chest growing deeper and deeper, Martin seemed to swell before his eyes; then the hand came on his shoulder and Martin's voice, jovial now and very like his father's said, 'Come on, nipper. Cheer up. You won't be all that far away. And . . . and you'll be coming back on Christmas Day.'

'I won't.'

'What makes you say that?' It was Harry asking the question, and Joe answered, 'Just, I know I won't; once we're gone we'll be gone.'

'Nonsense! Nonsense!' Martin's voice was loud and he turned away as he spoke and rubbed his hands together as if they were cold, which they were, as the bedroom had no heat whatever.

'I'm . . . I'm not a little kid any longer, Martin.'

'What!' Martin turned abruptly and faced him; then he looked down on him for a moment before he said, 'I'm sorry, Joe, you're quite right; you're not a little kid any longer. We should have realised that, both of us.' He glanced at his brother. 'You've never been a little kid, really. Anyway, we know where we stand now, don't we? And as you've just said, I doubt if you'll be here for Christmas, and that being the case we've brought your presents.' He nodded towards the table. 'Those are to take with you.'

Joe moved his head to the side and gave a short sharp cough, then said, 'I've . . . I've got something for you both. I . . . I gave them to Mary to put on the tree.'

There followed a long pause: they stood in awkward silence, Martin and Harry looking down on the dark bent head that was hiding the pale, drawn face of the boy. Presently Harry spoke, saying, 'Time soon passes; it won't be long before you'll be able to go your own way . . . What I mean is—' he hesitated, glanced at Martin, then finished, 'to decide things for himself, won't he, Martin?'

'Yes. Yes.'

Joe's next words, however, seemed both to belie his previous manly statement and to deny the truth of Martin's words. 'I'm nearly eleven,' he said, 'and sixteen, seventeen or eighteen appears to me like next Christmas; it'll never come.'

Martin bit on his lip before saying, in a voice that was almost a gabble, 'I know how you feel. I was like that myself; in fact, I still am. At times I feel I can't wait until I'm twenty-one, when I'll come into my grandmother's money, and the things I want to do with it is nobody's business. Not that father keeps me short, but it isn't like having cash of your own, and I can't see me earning any for some time.' He grinned now at Joe and, realising that he had succeeded in taking his attention away from himself, he went on, 'I want to breed horses. I'm going to breed horses. As you know I'm quite daft about horses, like he is' – he nudged his brother now – 'about motor-bikes. You, too, will go daft about something that'll take your mind off everything else. What do you think you'll go daft about, Joe?'

Joe replied quietly, 'Writing, or painting.'

'Oh.' The word was said simultaneously by Martin and

Harry and they turned and looked at each other, Harry saying, 'Well, he's good at both, isn't he?'

'Yes. Yes.'

'And what about cricket and football?' Martin had his head on one side and a grin on his face as he asked the question, and Joe replied, 'No; they don't really appeal to me.'

'You're a funny fellow,' Martin now put out his hand and ruffled Joe's hair, then he added, 'It's a wonder you don't take an interest in cars. Now that would be exciting. I'm surprised they don't attract you 'cos your mother can drive as good as a man. She can change a tyre, too, and that always surprises me, for she doesn't look mechanical. Now does she?'

'No.' As Joe stared back at his cousins he was asking himself when they were going to stop being kind, because if they didn't stop soon he knew he would cry. They were talking about things that didn't matter, to them or to him. He wished he could get out of the room. He wished he was leaving today instead of tomorrow morning. He wished his heart would stop aching for Carrie. He wished he could die, yes, he wished he could die because, from now on, he would have to live with his mother. There would be no-one else but himself and her; she would have no-one to love but him because, he reasoned, she couldn't love his uncle now he was going to be married, and he didn't know how he was going to bear her love.

He couldn't really explain the effect her love had on him. It was like when he had a nightmare and got tangled up in the bedclothes and couldn't breathe. And yet he knew he loved her and wanted to comfort her because she was very unhappy. She'd be sitting alone now. He ought to go to her. His uncle and Miss Southall had gone walking through the estate. They had gone out after lunch. His mother hadn't gone into lunch and she had told him not to either. He hadn't minded because he wasn't hungry.

It was four o'clock now and it was getting dark; he must

go and find her. His legs suddenly moved. His head down, he made a rush for the door, mumbling, 'I'll see you in the morning.' He ran the length of the corridor to his mother's room. After tapping on the door and hearing no answer, he pushed it gently open, then peered into the room. It was empty. He walked slowly now to his room and there, standing at the window, he looked down on to the back of the stables and the little barn that was used as a garage on this side of the yard. He could just make out the main yard. There was no movement there. They had been short-handed in the yard all week: Mr Smith was off with a bad cold and today it was Bernard Paxstone's half-day. Rob Burnip had been working on his own, but from the light in one of the windows above the harness room at yon side of the yard, he guessed that Rob would be working up there. He liked Rob. He was another one he'd miss and it wasn't because he always had a bag of black bullets in his pocket and was never mean with them.

He was about to turn from the window when his attention was caught by a figure emerging from the back door of the garage. He recognised it instantly as that of his mother. He wasn't surprised to know that she had been to the garage – perhaps she had been taking one last look at uncle's car, knowing that she wouldn't be driving it any more. He noticed that she was walking with her head and shoulders bent forward as if she were thrusting against the wind; but there had been no wind for two days, not since the frost had settled. He watched her stop now and straighten up, nip the hood of her coat under her chin, then lean with her back against the wall, as a person often did when out of breath. He pressed his face to the window pane and narrowed his eyes the better to see through the gloom. She was walking again, not as he would have expected, towards the back staircase, but was going down the grassy bank that led into the gardens. She was likely going to walk round them for the last time. He stood back from the window and shook his head. It was so cold out and soon it would be quite dark: should he go after her and walk with her to keep her company?

'No.' He said the word aloud and blinked rapidly at the sound of it. Then going to the wardrobe, he took down his greatcoat and a scarf, and having put them on he drew a chair up to the window and sat staring out into the coming night.

She would likely return by the back staircase, and any minute now Mary would be lighting the lamp that was above the back door, because this also opened on to the passage which gave on to the kitchen, and so he would see his mother's return, and when she was once more in her room he would go in and talk to her . . . well – his head jerked – he would say something, and he must think now what to say to bring her comfort.

The light had been lit for some time and he was still sitting watching when he heard his name being called, and before he could reach the door Harry thrust it open, exclaiming loudly, 'Why are you sitting there in the dark? We've been looking for you. Where's your mother?'

'I . . . I don't know.'

'Well, Father's just off with Miss Southall. They've changed their plans; they're going to a play in Newcastle and he's spending the night with her people.'

'Oh.'

Harry stood looking down on the boy; then with a sigh as if at the end of a long run, he said quietly, 'I suppose Aunt Ellen is keeping out of the way, but I think Father would have liked to explain to her the change in plan and to say goodbye for the present, because he won't be here in the morning, will he?'

'No.' Joe walked past Harry now and into the corridor. For some unknown reason he had a great urge to find his mother. He could see himself leading her by the hand into the hall and presenting her to his uncle. Perhaps, he thought, he was remembering the song that his uncle would sing derisively when he'd drunk a lot of wine. It was apparently one that his own father used to sing when he was in some war or other: 'A little child shall lead them, lead them gently on their way'. For a moment he thought of himself as the little child leading his mother to his uncle, but deep within himself he knew that this was just wishful thinking, for his uncle didn't want his mother, at least not the way his mother wanted him.

He was running now down the corridor shouting over his shoulder, 'I'll find her. I'll find her.'

As he ran across the gallery he could see heads bobbing down below in the hall: Martin, Mary Smith, his uncle. He couldn't see Miss Southall, but amid the hubbub he recognised her laugh; he had heard it before and liked it. It was a young, gay laugh, a laugh like he used to laugh himself when he chased Carrie on the hills and caught her, or when Mick said something funny in the dry way he had, without laughing or even smiling himself.

He was down at the bottom of the back stairs now, dragging open the door. The night wasn't as black as he had expected; there were a lot of stars out but the cold air rushing up his nostrils made him want to sneeze.

He told himself that it was no use running into the shrubbery; she wouldn't have been sitting there – unless she had kept walking she would be frozen with the cold.

Through the gap in the hedge and and now in seemingly pitch blackness, he couldn't see his hand before him, so he called softly, 'Mother! Mother! Are you there?'

He groped his way along by the hedge to where it opened into the rose garden. Here it was less dark, and again he called, 'Mother! Mother!' He was across the rose garden now and slithering down the slope towards the tennis court. He looked upwards. The heavens were dotted with stars. The sceptical side of his mind came to him for the

70

moment and said, 'They can't be millions of miles away, it's an impossibility. God would never have made stars and placed them so far away.' He was learning about light-years at school, but that didn't explain things.

'Mother! Mother! Are you there, Mother?'

He drew in a breath, then let it out as he ran forward to meet the figure coming slowly towards him by the wire-netting of the tennis court. He seemed to fling himself at her and his voice was a gabble now as he said, 'I . . . I've been looking all over for you. They're going. They want to say good-bye. Come on. Come on.' He took her hand and went to pull her, but she remained stiff as she asked, 'Who's going?'

'Uncle and Miss Southall. Harry says they've changed their plans; they're going to a play . . . Uncle, he won't be here in the morning to say good-bye; he was looking for you.'

'*What!*' She was leaning over him now, her hands like claws digging into his shoulders. 'What did you say?'

'Well' – he wriggled under her grasp – 'well, I've told you, they're going to a play.'

When she let loose of him he hunched his shoulders as he watched her hand go out and the fingers being thrust through the wire netting as though for support. The next minute she was running from him and he after her. It had seemed a great distance from the back door to the tennis court, but now they appeared to have covered it in seconds.

She did not make for the back stairs, but went towards the kitchen, where she banged open the door, and was through the room without stopping, almost knocking Mary on to her back as she entered by the far door.

'Oh! ma'am . . . missis, what's the matter?'

'Where are they?' She was now standing in the hall. Martin was about to enter the drawing-room and Harry was halfway up the stairs and her voice was a yell as she cried again, 'Where are they?'

Both Harry and Martin turned quickly and hurried towards her, and it was Martin who said gently, 'Father's been looking for you, Aunt Ellen, for quite some time. What is it?' He had hold of her by the arm and she gasped at him, 'How long? How far?'

He narrowed his eyes at her as he said, 'Oh, three or four minutes ago, about that.' He looked at Harry who nodded, saying, 'Yes, about that. We saw them off and came in . . . Good Lord! Catch hold of her.'

As she swayed away from him towards Harry, Martin thrust his arm around her shoulder; then her dead weight brought him bending over towards the floor.

'She's fainted. Let's get her into the drawing-room. Mary!' He jerked his head to where Mary was hovering. 'Get some water.'

His mouth and eyes open, Joe followed them as they hurriedly carried his mother into the drawing-room and laid her on the couch. She looked already dead: her body was limp, her face ashen. He watched Mary come running into the room with a jug of water, a glass in her hand, and it was Harry who said almost harshly to her, 'She won't be able to drink; it's a wet cloth we wanted.'

'Here!' Martin pulled a folded white handkerchief from the breast-pocket of his coat, and Mary, thrusting it into the jug, squeezed out the water and handed it back to him.

Joe watched Martin dabbing his mother's face, but she still looked dead.

'Smelling salts.'

'There's some on her dressing-table.'

Martin glanced up at Mary; then looking towards Joe, he said, 'Run and get them.'

Joe ran, taking the stairs two at a time, and he almost dived into his mother's bedroom and was half across it when he had to return to the door and switch the light on. He knew what kind of bottle he was looking for, but it wasn't on the dressing-table; it was on her bedside table. He grabbed it up and was running again. One hand on the bannister, he jumped the last three steps into the hall and when he entered the room there were only his cousins and his mother there; Mary had gone. Martin was saying, 'This is the result of her feeling for him. Father should never have done it; it wasn't fair.'

Harry answered in a whisper, 'But you said yourself it was the best thing.'

'Yes, I did, for him to marry again, but not someone as young as Vanessa. It must have been an insult to her.' He was nodding down to the white face as Joe handed him the bottle.

Joe watched the smelling salts bring his mother back to life, but it was almost fifteen minutes later before she spoke and as he listened, he was made to realise that his mother was a very clever woman; in fact, that she was two distinct people, although the realisation was just a misty thought in the back of his mind, so misty that it was to fade later that evening, together with the memory of the incident that followed, and was not to be resurrected until he was a young man, for what his mother said was, in a quiet, even, ordinary voice as she put her hand on that of Martin's, 'I . . . I thought to say goodbye to him pri . . . privately. You understand?'

And Martin inclined his head towards her as he answered softly, 'Yes, Aunt, I understand, I understand perfectly.'

The boys had suggested to Joe that his mother go to bed and rest, but she seemed reluctant to walk upstairs. He thought that, this being her last night in the house, perhaps she wanted to make the most of it because, after rising from the couch, she sat in the big chair quite close to the fire and kept holding her hands out to the warmth.

Mary brought her a light meal on a tray but she couldn't eat it; all she wanted was a warm drink, she said. When it came to eight o'clock and Harry showed concern for her still sitting there, she assured him that she was all right and insisted that he and Martin play their usual game of billiards.

However, at nine o'clock, when they returned after their game, she at last rose from the seat, saying with a weak smile she now thought she'd be able to sleep and that they were not to worry, she could make the stairs by herself, that she wasn't yet quite an old woman. Martin turned his head to the side and was about to make some gallant retort when the bell rang and startled them all, for the bell never rang after dark; if they were expecting friends the door was nearly always open; even in the winter there'd be someone waiting to welcome the visitor; as for the staff, they, of course, used the back way.

Mary had already gone home.

Martin and Harry exchanged glances and Joe looked at his mother. She had her hand to her throat and her head was making almost imperceivable movements backwards and forwards.

'Who can this be?' Martin was striding up the drawing-room, Harry following him; Ellen didn't move, neither did Joe.

A few minutes later Martin and Harry re-entered the room, a uniformed man with them and another in plain clothes.

Joe watched Martin stagger to a seat like someone drunk, and from there gaze at his mother.

Joe turned towards Harry, who was crying. He now looked at the man in plain clothes. He was talking quietly like the doctor talked when you were ill and as he listened, Joe knew he was going to die himself, not only because of what the man was saying about them having to cut the car to bits to get both his uncle and Miss Southall out, and also the two dead men out of the lorry, but for something else that was so big, so enormous that it wasn't to be borne, because in some strange way he was part of it.

74

The only things that Joe was to remember of this night, until the door of his mind was thrust open again, was his mother having a sort of seizure, the result of which was to keep her in bed for two months, and of Mary's gabbling through her tears that one man's meat was another man's poison. Years later, he was to know that that hadn't really been applicable to the situation but that it was the only way Mary could explain the advantageous change in his mother's position, for at the eleventh hour she had been saved from leaving the house.

PART TWO

1937

1

Joe and Harry stood on the platform side by side. There was now no difference in their height although Harry was twenty-one and Joe sixteen. Even in physique they were very much alike, both being thick in the shoulders and almost of the same colouring, except that Joe's hair showed a black sheen whereas Harry's was a dark brown, thick matt. It was only when you looked at their faces that you saw the difference in both age and expression: Harry's face was round, his eyes merry, while Joe's features inclined to length and his grey eyes, which at times seemed colourless, had in their depths a touch of melancholy that had deepened with the years.

Joe started when Harry's elbow caught him in the ribs as he said, 'I wonder if my illustrious brother will be as insufferable as he was during the Christmas holidays?'

'Martin's never insufferable.'

'Of course he is. All those fellows who get to Oxford become insufferable . . . It used to be "I'm doing my law moderations" ' – he pursed his lips and wagged his head – 'but these last couple of years it's been, "I'm reading for my finals". Gosh! how sick-making.'

'You're only envious, and you know you were the most

concerned when he had to lose almost a year to that fever. Anyway, you know you love him.'

Harry had been about to make a jovial retort, as was his nature, but he stopped and, screwing up his face, he said, 'Joe, the things you come out with. You don't say you love people.'

'Why not, when you do?'

'Well, just because . . . '

'That's what Mick once said to me.'

'Mick?'

'Yes, years ago he told me you don't say you love people. Yet when you don't love many people I think you should tell those whom you do.'

'Oh, lad.' Harry stepped back from Joe now, but poked his head forward as, under his breath, he asked, 'You don't come out with things like that at school, do you?'

'No.'

'It's a damn good job you don't, laddie, or I could see you being hauled up before the old man.'

Harry now looked at his watch, saying, 'It's nearly fifteen minutes late; I bet it's got diverted to London.' He grinned. 'Must be marvellous up there today.' He looked upwards now at the bunting stretched across the girders of the platform, then said, 'With a little imagination you know I could dismiss the Coronation and take it that this show of affection was all for my being twenty-one today. I'm twenty-one today, I'm twenty-one today.' He began to whistle now, accompanying it with a little shuffle of his feet which brought a wide grin from Joe; then becoming serious for a moment, he said, 'You know, I do appreciate Martin getting leave to come home for my twenty-first. He could easily have gone into London and enjoyed the jollifications. But there'll be some jollification around the old homestead tonight and nobody likes tripping the light fantastic better than wor Martin.' He had dropped into a thick Geordie twang and, after laughing, he looked up and down the platform now, saying, 'We must be the only ones expecting a passenger.'

'They'll all be glued to their wireless sets, I suppose.'

'Yes, that's it.'

'They say he's going to speak tonight, the King. Amazing, isn't it? Amazing.' He moved his head slowly from side to side.

'Oh, here it comes at last.' Harry again looked at his watch. 'Almost twenty minutes late. I'm going to report this.'

The train puffed to a stop; only five passengers alighted, and the only male among them a tall young man, his hair so fair that from a distance it appeared almost white, waved to them before turning back to the carriage and lifting out a case.

Now they were all together, clapping each other on the arm, shaking hands, laughing; then Martin, gripping his brother by the shoulders, said, 'Happy days ahead, laddie.'

'Thanks, Martin. Thanks.' Harry's answer was low, even serious sounding.

They turned and made their way along the platform, through the small waiting-room and so into the road to where the horse and trap waited.

It was Martin who took the reins and as he cried, 'Gee-up! you there, you flibbertigibbet!' the horse, as if recognising the voice, tossed its head and went off at a spanking pace down the road, and as they laughed, Harry said, 'Would you believe it! He never goes like that for me.'

'Well, he knows you prefer stinking machines. By the way, how do you like it?'

'Like what?'

Martin tugged on the reins for a moment, then turned and looked at his brother, saying, 'It hasn't arrived?'

'If I knew what had to arrive I would tell you.'

'Good God! I'll murder them; they promised.'

'Promised what?'

81

'Your birthday present, thickhead.'

'Oh, don't tell me it's a horse.'

'It's your kind of horse.'

Harry's eyes and mouth stretched: then he was leaning over Joe and gripping Martin's shoulder, saying, 'You haven't . . . it isn't?'

'I have and it is, and I'm mad, because I hate your damned machines.'

'Aw! Martin. What is it?'

'It's what you're always on about.'

'An AJS!' Harry turned quickly to Joe and cried excitedly, 'Did you ever know such a brother as mine, spending his money on something he hates!'

Joe smiled but didn't answer, and Harry, again in a thoughtful tone, said, 'What would you like when you're twenty-one, Joe?'

But before he could answer, Martin, turning his head to the side, called over his shoulder, 'Why need you ask! A set of encyclopedias, of course. How's the writing going, Joe?'

'Not so good.'

'What! And you aiming to come up and read English Lit.'

'That's the point,' Joe called back now, 'I have to do so much reading I've hardly any time for writing, at least not the kind I want to do.'

'Poetry?' There was a scornful note in Martin's voice and Joe answered, 'Well, no, not just poetry; in fact, not poetry at all.'

'No? Don't tell me you've gone in for politics. There's been enough trouble without you starting. Or are you aiming to take Kipling's place?' Quickly switching the conversation, he addressed the next remark to Harry, saying, 'I wonder how the Duke is feeling today; I wonder if he still thinks the exchange was worth it.'

'I'm sure he does. He loved her; he must have.'

82

The brothers turned and looked at Joe and presently Martin said on a laugh, 'That's what he's going to be, Harry, a romantic novelist. You can tell, can't you? In fact, it's a pity he isn't in the game now. Look at the material he could have had this past year. Besides the Duke's romance, there was Princess Juliana marrying a German prince; and then there's our bleached beauty, Miss Jean Harlow. By! there'll never again be a year like this for you to get your teeth into.'

'Shut up!'

Martin and Harry laughed together and Harry thumped Joe in the shoulder, saying, 'Take no notice, lad; you'll get there. I only wish I had half your grey matter.'

For the rest of the journey Joe listened to the brothers talking about their futures, particularly that of Martin after he came down in June.

As for Harry, his aim was engineering and he was now in his third year at the College of Science in Newcastle.

It was as they approached the gates that Joe pointed away to the left and towards the hills where a man was walking and he cried excitedly, 'There's Mick!'

'Mick? Mick Smith?' Martin screwed up his eyes and looked towards the hills, saying, 'How can you tell from here?'

'Oh, I know his walk.'

'Is he back home for good?'

'No' – Joe shook his head – 'he's taking a holiday; he's twenty-one an' all, you know; well, he was last month.'

'Is he still working in the factory?'

'Yes, he was promoted, he's head of his department now.'

'Well, that's not surprising, he was always a wizard with wireless.'

'Yes, he was. He is.'

Joe continued to look over his shoulder to where the figure in the distance had become a mere speck.

83

When they came in sight of the house it was to see Ellen Jebeau standing on the terrace, and when Martin drew the horse to a standstill at the foot of the steps she was there to meet them. Holding out her hand, her smile wide, she said, 'It's good to see you home again, Martin,' and his answer was to take her hand and kiss her on the cheek and say, 'It's good to be home, Aunt. How are you?'

'Very well. Very well . . . and what do you think about the new man?' She extended a hand towards Harry, and Martin said derisively, 'New man! He'll never be a man, he's still in the nursery playing with toy bikes.'

Again the two brothers were pushing at each other and as they all mounted the steps Ellen stepped back and walked by the side of her son, something she was in the habit of doing whenever they were in company, and which Joe had been aware of from the time she had recovered after his uncle's death. He hadn't known whether to put it down to the fact that she imagined he was being left outside the cameraderie of the brothers or that in some strange way she was laying claim on him. Her action always embarrassed him, but as it was unobtrusive he doubted if anyone else noticed it.

In the hall, turning to Martin, she said, 'Come and see the table before you go upstairs,' and hurried forward to the dining-room, where Martin exclaimed in genuine appreciation of the table, beautifully decorated with flowers, glass, and silver and set for sixteen people.

'It's wonderful, Aunt! Beautiful. Better than I had on *my* twenty-first.' He turned a comically aggressive face towards Harry, saying, 'Mine was never like this.'

''Twas; it was even better. You had two tables, the second one to accommodate your lady friends; I don't have so many.'

'Well, that's your fault, isn't it? You've got to acquire charm and have a presence.' He walked around the table now in an exaggerated pose, and Harry, laughing, said, 'If

84

it wasn't for spoiling Aunt Ellen's work I would throw that centrepiece at you.'

'Anyway, who's coming?' Martin was addressing Ellen, and she, looking at Harry, said, 'Well, it was up to Harry, and he wanted the Doltons . . . '

'Oh yes! We must have the Doltons' – Martin nodded and winked at Harry – 'especially Rachel . . . What about Betty? Isn't she married yet?'

'No; she's not married yet; I think she's waiting for you.' Harry pulled a face at his brother now as Ellen put in quickly, 'The Hallidays too and their cousins, two young ladies who are staying with them.' She turned towards Harry now, saying, 'The Crosbie sisters?'

When Harry nodded Martin said, 'How old are they?'

'Nell is nineteen and Marion eighteen,' Harry said and, poking his head forward with emphasis, he added, 'And neither of them is a beauty.'

'Oh!' Martin craned his head up out of his collar. 'Well, that cuts them out of my book, unless, of course, they're entertaining, witty, rich, and—' Here he turned and began to march from the room, saying, 'have the sense to appreciate my worth.'

They all laughed. Even Ellen laughed and, looking at Harry, she said, 'He doesn't change.'

'No, he doesn't.' Harry now stood looking along the table as he added thoughtfully, 'It would be awful if he did, wouldn't it?'

Ellen paused for just a fraction of a second before she answered, 'Yes; yes, I suppose it would.'

Joe looked at his mother and there came into his mind a thought that wasn't new: his mother didn't like Martin; she liked Harry but not Martin; and Martin didn't like her.

It was two o'clock in the afternoon. The sky was high, the air so clear that he imagined he could see to the ends of the earth. He was sitting with Mick at the top of a hill and he was wishing with a deep desire that he could remain in time, this present time, forever. Somehow he always had this feeling when he was with Mick. Mick made him feel rested: his brain didn't churn and ask questions when he was with Mick. Mostly he listened; not that Mick talked a lot, but when he did everything he said seemed to have meaning. Now, as the thought came into his mind he spoke it aloud, and had he spoken like this to anyone else it would have been taken as an insult, for what he said was, 'It's a pity you haven't had education, Mick.'

And Mick, looking straight ahead, was silent for a moment, then said, 'Yes, I've often thought that, Joe, but not so much of late. Years ago when I used to see the young masters going off to their boarding schools . . . you too, I used to envy you all. But not any more, because you see this is how I look at it now: those kind of schools grind you into a certain way of thinking and . . . and somehow, unless you become very careful, you're stuck that way for the rest of your life. You've been set in a certain class and no matter how your opinions change and you want to throw that class off, if ever a man does, it won't let him, it's there in his voice, in his manner; even if a gentleman was to take to the road he'd still be a gentleman; I mean, according to the kind of education he's received, so to my mind that has become a kind of cage. Do you follow me?'

They looked at each other, then returning their gaze to the far distance there was a silence between them before Mick went on again, 'As I see it now, real education is what you get from life: not what life gives you, but what you give to it. I read a lot, Joe, and it appears to me that every man, even every thinking man has always had a different view of the same subject; the more I read of men and their lives and their ideas the more I realise there's no black and white in the world; there's good points to be found even in the

86

blackest, and there's some very dark streaks in the so-called saints. As for heaven and hell, well, Joe, as I see it we make them both ourselves.'

'You don't believe in God then, Mick?'

'Yes and no, Joe. I don't believe in the God the parson used to present to us three times on a Sunday.'

He laughed now. 'Eeh! his idea did put the fear of God into me. You know, Joe' – he leant towards him now, a wide grin spreading over his face – 'I used to wet me pants every Sunday morning. It's true.'

As Joe bowed his head and laughed, Mick went on, 'And every Sunday night for years and years it happened, because every Sunday night I'd go down to hell. You know where it was, Joe?' Now he was laughing at himself and he could hardly get the words out. 'You know old Farmer Bolton's place before it was burned down, you know, where the pig-sties were and the stink? Well' – he choked now with laughter – 'I would go in among those pigs and they would all start scratching a hole and there I would be standing on a clapboard looking down and nearly sick with the smell. And when it was so deep I couldn't see the bottom, Old Bolton's prize sow, you know the one who had borne so many litters, there was no space atween her belly and the ground. Well, I used to wait for her, trembling like a leaf; then she would come behind me and bump me, and down I would go, down, down, down, into hell and wake up screaming and our Charlie shaking the life out of me . . .'

Now both of them were choking with their laughter as Mick ended, 'It got so bad that they used to wait for it every Sunday night and try to smother me with a pillow. It's a wonder I survived.'

'Oh, Mick! Mick!' Joe was rocking himself now, the tears running down his face. Then he set Mick off into another spasm of laughter when he asked, 'Do you think I could get a job alongside you in the factory?'

Some time later, Joe, looking at his wrist watch, said on a note of deep regret, 'I'll have to be getting back, the guests are coming at four. How long are you staying, Mick? A week?'

'No, no; I'm off the morrow.'

'So soon? I thought you had a week.'

'Yes. Yes, I have, but . . . but a little goes a long way.' He nodded back towards the house. 'The cottage is still crammed and . . . and I want to do some visiting.'

They stared at each other for a moment before Mick added, 'You've never seen Carrie for years, have you?'

'No; no, I haven't.'

'Well, that's where I'm going. I often spend my weekends there; there's always a bed for me. My Uncle Stan and Aunt Alice are very good to me and more than good to Carrie, they've given her a start in life she would never have had here. She's on a secretarial course, you know.'

'Really?'

'Oh yes; she's a bright lass, is Carrie.'

Joe looked to the side. Funny, Mick had never mentioned Carrie in years. The subject had seemed to be taboo; and he himself had in a way pressed her down into his mind because thoughts of her conjured up a feeling tinged with regret and shame, centred round a scene in the bedroom and the rage of his mother. But here was Mick telling him something, he was talking about a young girl, not a little girl, a young girl who was going to be a secretary. She must be seventeen now; she was some months older than him.

'Do you ever go out for the day, Joe?'

'Oh yes; sometimes to Newcastle.'

'With your mother?'

'Yes, yes; or Harry.'

'Do you think your mother would let you go out with me for a day in Newcastle?'

It was on the point of Joe's tongue to say 'I doubt it', but what he said was, 'I don't see why not.'

88

'Good, good. That's agreed on then. What about tomorrow?'

'All right.'

'We'll have to walk to the station, unless we get a lift.'

'I don't mind that.'

'All right, it's fixed, tomorrow then.'

They turned away together and marched over the hills towards the estate.

'If you want to go into Newcastle, then I'll take you into Newcastle.'

'I want to go with Mick, Mother.'

'Spend the day with Mick, why?'

'Just . . . just because I . . . I like being with Mick.'

'Really! boy. You're hopeless . . . well, I forbid you.'

'I'm sorry, Mother, I'd rather you said yes, because in any case I'm going.'

'Now, now! Don't take that attitude with me, Joe. You're not too big yet to be locked in your room.'

Joe slanted his gaze towards her. 'I wouldn't try that, Mother. Remember the boys are at home and if I was to go and ask Martin he would immediately say yes.'

'How dare you! Go and ask Martin indeed!'

'Well, he's the head of the house.'

'He may be the head of this house but I am your mother and I'm in charge of you.'

'I'll be seventeen in a short while, Mother. I heard the master saying at school there could be a war, so next year I could be a man, couldn't I, and be in the Army? You couldn't stop them taking me.'

'What's come over you, boy?'

'Don't keep calling me boy, Mother.'

'I will keep calling you boy, because that's all you are and I repeat, I forbid you to go into Newcastle with Mick Smith. And I say again, don't you take that tone with me.'

As he stared at her he knew that he had come to a

89

crossroads, that if he gave in to her now he'd have to give
into her again and again and again. Although he had defied
her before, it had only been in words but now the thought
that he had the choice of putting those words into action and
so set a new pattern, and in doing so break one of the threads
that tied him to her, caused his whole body to tremble and
his voice to quiver as he said, 'Either you give me permission
freely to go with Mick tomorrow or I go down now and put
it to Martin.'

The trembling turned to slight fear as he saw her colour
rise. For a moment he was swept back into the past to those
days when her temper would flare into demoniac rage.

'Get out of my sight, boy. Get . . . out . . . of . . . my . . .
sight!'

He got out of her sight. He went out of the room, into the
corridor and into his room and there he stood with his back
to the door, his mouth wide, gasping at the air, still in fright,
yet knowing that in some way he had emerged as if out of a
deep canyon.

2

Joe sat on the wooden kitchen chair and watched Mrs Alice Carver flitting back and forth from the stove to the table, talking all the while. She had what was termed a comfortable figure, but her face was thin, her nose sharp and her voice seemed to take its pattern from her features, just as Mick had described her on the way here; although his Aunt Alice was sharp of nose and of tongue, she was broad in the shoulders and warm in heart, he had said.

Flinging a cloth over a side table, she now turned towards Mick and said, 'I'm not puttin' meself out for you, mind. If I'd known you were coming that would have been different; I mean, bringing company. You always have your meal in the kitchen and I'm not opening the dining-room at such short notice, but you can go and sit in the front room if you want to.'

'Who wants to? We're comfortable here.'

'Well, it's up to you.' She was now piling crockery on to the table. 'Your uncle, as you know, comes in at ten past twelve on the dot and Carrie a few minutes after, that is if she hasn't stopped to gaze in the shops. Well, she knows I put it on the table all at the same time; if it's cold, that's her look out. Would you like a drop of tea while you're waitin'?'

She had now turned abruptly and was addressing Joe, and he, taken by surprise, stammered, 'Yes . . . oh no. No, thank you; I can wait for my dinner.'

She now pushed out her chest, drew in her chin, looked at Mick while thumbing towards Joe and said, 'He expects his dinner! Did you hear that? He expects his dinner!'

Mick looked at Joe, whose face had turned scarlet, and nodded solemnly as he said, 'Aye, he does, Aunt Alice. It's a bloomin' cheek, isn't it?'

Then they were both laughing, and the little woman, coming up and slapping Joe between the shoulders with such force that he coughed, said, 'Don't look as if you are bein' confronted by a whale. I'm not gonna swallow you whole, not just now anyway.'

Joe managed to force a smile. Then looking back at Mick who was grinning at him, he bit on his lip and moved his head slightly as if to say, 'How am I to take her?'

Mick now turned to his aunt and asked, 'Did Carrie pass her test?'

'Of course she did! She could have done it on her head. And I'll tell you something else—' she paused, went to the oven, took out a tin holding roast potatoes, flicked them over expertly and put the tin back in the oven before she continued, 'She won't be long in that school, she's a way ahead; and you know what?' She put her hands on the table and leant towards Mick. 'He's going to buy her a new typewriter; that old thing she practises on makes a noise like a candyman's trumpet. But she doesn't know, so don't let on. And she's doing shorthand, Pitman's, she calls it. Funny that is, isn't it, to call shorthand Pitman's.'

Joe had gauged that the 'he' she referred to was the uncle and the reference to Pitman's shorthand brought his eyes to Mick and his face ready to go into a grin; but something in Mick's expression checked it and he listened to him saying, 'She's a bright lass, is Carrie.'

'Now you've said it, Mick, you've said it. Yes, our Carrie's a bright lass. And she's going places.'

Joe noticed that the little woman referred to Carrie as if she belonged to them: it was Our Carrie. In his mind's eye there was dawning a picture of this Carrie. He could see the smart business girl: she'd likely be wearing three-inch high heels and her hair would be permed; and not only would she look smart, she'd talk smart. For a moment he wished he hadn't come: he didn't want to see this new Carrie. On the way here this morning, the picture of the Carrie he had once known and played with . . . and loved, had been plain in his mind; and the nearer he had come to the house where she now lived, he imagined the Carrie he expected to see would be merely an older replica of the one who had run out of his life the day his mother had hit him and knocked him out. That memory too had been brought sharply into focus on this journey. It was as if his mind was digging down through the years and bringing up pictures of past events . . .

Stan Carver was a thick-set, medium-sized man, and strangely, Joe thought, he resembled his wife, at least in features: they had the same sharp-edged face. What was obvious, though, straightaway was that Mr Carver didn't talk much and his greeting of Mick was as to one of the family, indicated with a nod and a 'Hello, there!'

When Mick introduced him, Mr Carver shook his hand in the conventional way, saying, 'I'm pleased to see you, lad. You're welcome,' then went to the sink in the far corner of the kitchen to wash his hands, came back to the fireside to sit down in a chair to the right of the oven, and watched his wife putting out the meal.

It was as she put the last plate on the table that the door opened and Carrie Smith entered the kitchen.

Automatically Joe rose to his feet, although Mick remained seated. The girl who was now confronting Joe was someone strange and of whom he held no memory in any corner of

93

his mind. She wasn't smartly dressed as he had imagined: a slack grey coat reached halfway down her calves, her hat was in plain brown felt and from under it her hair hung loose. It was rather unusual, he thought, to see a girl with long hair hanging loose. Her hair was dark brown, as were her eyes; her face was round, her cheeks naturally red. She was wearing no make-up; she could have been a girl fresh from the country. That was until she spoke.

When her voice came to his ears it denied the ordinariness of her clothes and the simplicity suggested by her powderless face and loose lying hair, for her tone was crisp, each word clear. Unlike her uncle and aunt, who spoke with the Northern inflection, drawing one word into another, she pronounced the last syllable of each word. This, however, he didn't realise until later when he let himself think about the meeting and how, after the first keen glance, she looked past him as if he weren't there, to greet Mick with 'Hello. You didn't say you were coming. Why aren't you at work?'

'I'm on holiday. The boss knew I was worked to death, and not wanting to lose me said, "Mick, you take a few days' rest. If anybody's earned them, you have."'

'Oh yes?' She inclined her head towards her brother. 'I can quite understand that he would say that.' She was taking off her hat and coat as she spoke; then going over to her aunt, she bent down and kissed her on the cheek, and followed this with the same salutation for her uncle; and in response he patted her on the shoulder.

'Haven't you noticed we've got a visitor?' She had been looking at Mick, but turned slowly and looked at Joe, and smiling slightly said, 'Yes; yes, of course.'

'Well, don't you know who he is?'

When she looked back at Mick she allowed her gaze to rest on him for some seconds before she answered, 'Of course I know who it is. He hasn't changed much.'

94

Joe felt a heat seeping up through his body, finally coming to rest in his face, which he knew now had turned scarlet. It was more than five years since she had seen him and she was saying he hadn't changed. He imagined for a moment that he was still in short pants, until she turned to him and added, 'What I mean is, I would have still recognised you,' and as if to soften her first statement she added further, 'Of course, you've grown much taller. You would have, wouldn't you?'

As he stared at her he actually did feel as if he were in short pants, and he couldn't find words to answer her.

The situation was saved for him by Mrs Carver's crying, 'Well, there it is! It's on the table. Take your seats; there's nothing worse than a cold dinner.'

As he moved towards the table Joe noticed that, although they had been bidden to take their seats, neither Mrs Carver, nor Mick, nor Carrie did until Mr Carver was seated; then, each pulling a chair out from under the table, they sat down; and having done so, Mick pointed to a carved chair with a leather seat and said to him, 'Come, sit down. You're honoured; that's from the parlour; I hope your pants are clean.'

Joe sat down and, shyly taking up his knife and fork, he began to eat; but with some difficulty, for there was no conversation. And he was embarrassed further when he realised he was the last to finish. They waited for him, and when his plate was clean, Mrs Carver, leaning towards him, said, 'Spotted Dick or rice?'

He blinked and opened his mouth once before he managed, 'Spotted Dick, please.'

Spotted Dick. That was what Mary called currant pudding, and his mother referred to as boiled fruit suet.

He enjoyed his Spotted Dick; but this, too, was eaten in silence.

The meal finished, Stan Carver, placing his hands on each side of his plate, slowly raised himself up from the table and, standing still for a moment, said, 'Thank God for a good dinner.' And without another word he left the table, went out of the kitchen, presumably through the scullery, and into the backyard; and when the sound of the door shutting came to them, Mick turned with a laugh towards Joe, saying, 'I bet you're wondering where the first part of grace before meals went.'

Managing a smile, Joe said, 'Yes; perhaps I am.'

'Well, I might tell you that Uncle follows a pattern that was forced upon him. You see, he came from a family of ten lads and four lasses and food was the main object in their lives; and if you weren't careful and hung on to your plate one or the other swiped it.' He nodded. 'It's a fact. They did it laughingly, but they did it; so that cut out forever the grace that says, what we are about to receive, so he only gives thanks when he's got it down.'

As they all laughed, Joe glanced towards the little woman, and she, nodding back to him, said, ' 'Tis true.' Then, looking towards Carrie, she said, 'Mash the tea, girl. Time's going on; you'll have to be on your way again.' And with this she went into the scullery, Mick following her.

Left alone with Carrie, Joe sat watching her pour the boiling water into the earthenware teapot, and after bringing it to the table and setting it on a stand, she smiled at him and said softly, 'How are you?'

'Very well, thank you. And you?' His voice was as low as hers had been.

'Oh, I'm fine, fine.'

It was as if they had just met.

'I wasn't meaning to be rude when I said you hadn't changed.'

'Oh, I know, I know,' he said and smiled widely.

'It was just that I was a bit surprised at seeing you. When I've been back home you've always been at school.'

96

'Yes; yes, I would be. I suppose they arranged it like that.'
He bit on his lip; he hadn't meant to say that. What had
possessed him?

'Yes, I suppose they did. Anyway, I don't go very often.
Dad comes here but not Mam; she and Aunt Alice never got
along.'

'Are they sisters?'

'Oh no!' She shook her head; then jerked it backwards,
indicating the scullery, as she added in a much lower
tone, 'They're not really my aunt and uncle. We call them
that. Mam and Aunt Alice are cousins twice removed,
so to speak.'

'Oh . . . Are you happy here?'

'Oh yes. Well! what do you think, after that cottage!'

The statement was somehow a reflection on his uncle and
now on Martin as his successor . . . And yet he himself had
often thought the cottages should have been extended or
pulled down and rebuilt. There was still no indoor sanitation
or running water. 'You prefer living in the town?' he said.

'Every time' – she bobbed her head at him – 'especially
when you have a room to yourself and a decent job ahead.
What was there for anybody, back there?' She now poked her
face towards him, for her words had not been a statement
but a direct question, one with a touch of bitterness, and
when he didn't answer she went on, 'It was all right for
you. Not that I'm blaming you. Don't you think that. But
in your position you had decent surroundings. Decent! What
am I talking about? Magnificent surroundings would be a
better description. Well, not really magnificent,' she again
contradicted herself, 'but you know what I mean.'

'Yes, yes, I know what you mean, but you know something?' It was he who was now leaning towards her, and his
voice and face serious as he went on, 'A big house, a room
to yourself, and all the food you can eat isn't everything; you
can be as miserable as sin with it all. And anyway, I'm only

there for a very small part of the year; I spend most of my time at school, where there's twelve beds to a room . . . dorm . . . and one can never be alone, it's not allowed.'

She bowed her head as she apologised, 'I'm sorry. I do yarp on, and I know you're right.'

They started now as the sound of breaking china came to them, followed by Mrs Carver's voice on a note so high-pitched it was almost a scream, as she cried, 'Out of me way! Leave them! Leave them! You never come in this kitchen but you break something: when you help it spells disaster. Now go on, get out!'

Mick appeared in the doorway with his hands going through his hair, his head thrust forward and his mouth in an elongated O, to be greeted by Carrie saying, 'Eeh! our Mick, not again. What was it this time?'

'A dinner plate and cup.'

'My goodness! There'll be nothing left shortly.'

'I'll get her a new set.'

'That isn't the thing; she likes her old china. She'd had it for years until you started helping.' She now grinned at him as she pushed him, only to cry at him under her breath as he lifted the teapot, 'Leave it! We don't want that all over the floor.'

As Carrie was pouring out the tea, Mr Carver came back into the room, followed by his wife, and he said to Mick, 'Stay out of that scullery from now on. D'you hear me?'

'Aye, Uncle.'

Mr Carver gulped through his tea, then muttered, 'Well, I'm away. Are you ready, Carrie?'

'Yes, Uncle.'

As Joe watched her put on her coat and hat he experienced a keen sense of disappointment, for he was realising it had been in his mind to escort her to work. Whether Mick would have proposed this he did not know; he only knew that the desire had been there; but it seemed to be the pattern that she and her uncle left together at dinnertime.

98

She was standing in front of him and when, conventionally, she held out her hand towards him, saying, 'Good-bye, then,' he hesitated for a moment; then his arm jerked forward and he was holding her hand. He felt the warmth of it flowing up his arm like an injection; it was as if everything in her was being transmitted through their palms. But as quickly as his arm had gone out, it returned to his side, jerked back there as if by a spring; and he noticed that his action hadn't gone unnoticed by Mick.

He now watched Mick follow Carrie to the doorway that led into the scullery, and he found himself also stepping in that direction, until he could take in the whole of the scullery and the open backyard door through which Mr Carver was now passing, saying as he did so, 'Ta-rah, then.' It was a salutation to cover all those present. Then he saw Carrie turn and look at Mick and Mick take her by the shoulders and look down into her face.

He heard him speak some words, but he couldn't make out what they were; he then saw him bend and kiss her, not on the cheek but on the lips. Then Mrs Carver's voice from behind him cried, 'Out of me way! lad,' and he sprang aside to let her enter the scullery with a tray of dirty cups and saucers.

3

3rd September, 1939

'Mother! Mother! listen. Will you stop ranting and listen. Look! Now look! War's been declared and all you can think about, all you can talk about is what you're going to do if I don't stop seeing Carrie.'

'I don't care about war being declared or anything else.' Ellen Jebeau's back was bent, her head thrust out. At this moment she looked to Joe like a witch and her voice and words sounded as ominous as any that could have been uttered by an authentic witch, as she hissed at him, 'I am more concerned about what happens to you than what a lot of stupid men do in their aim to kill each other. Don't you yet understand, boy, what you mean to me? You are all I've got, all I've got left to build my life on; my life has been one long frustration, and to stand aside and see you throw yourself away on scum like . . . '

'Don't you dare call Carrie scum!'

'And don't you dare, boy, speak to me like that!' She had advanced a step further towards him until now they were standing almost breast to breast. 'I am your mother. I have worked for you in all ways practically from the moment you were born and I'd die rather than see you throw yourself away on the likes of her; for she *is scum*, and I repeat it, *scum*. She hails from scum. Just look at her mother and the rest of them.'

He was unable to speak but he glared back into her infuriated countenance, and when she said, 'And don't bring Mary and Mick up as examples of paragons, for Mary is really witless; she's a good servant and nothing more. As for Mick aiming to rise above himself, he'll never do it. And he's crafty; you can see it in his face. And I know he's behind your meetings with that girl. Doubtless he wants to see her established in this house.'

It was now he who stepped back from her, almost pushing her aside with his forearm as he said, 'Don't be ridiculous. Neither you nor I have any claim on this house, and you know it. When I marry I can't live here. As for you, Mother, when Martin marries it'll be Uncle's case all over again; you'll either have to step down and be housekeeper or go.'

His lips were still pursed on the last words when they suddenly sprang wide as he saw her almost stagger back from him, her hand to her throat, the colour draining from her face. This was the sort of reaction that usually followed a burst of temper bordering on rage.

As she groped towards a chair he made no move towards her but watched her sit down, then bow her head for a moment before slowly raising her eyes to his again when, in a voice that had lost none of its bitterness, she said 'Leave me; but I'm warning you, I'll see you dead first, before you take that girl.'

He was still visibly shaken when he entered his own room where, going to the window, he placed both hands on the sill and bowed his head. She was mad. She was mad, she was; she was mad.

'Joe!' His head came up sharply. 'You there, Joe?'

101

That was Martin. He went hastily towards the door; he didn't want Martin to come into the room because then he might break down and say things about his mother that were best left unsaid.

They met on the stairhead and Martin cried, 'You've heard the news then?'

'Yes, it's awful, isn't it?'

'Oh, I wouldn't say that, laddie.' Martin put his arm around Joe's shoulders and together they went down the stairs. 'Come, let's have a drink before we're blown to smithereens; they'll likely start at any time.'

'You think so?'

'Oh, sure of it. There'll be bombs popping all over the place. They're bound to make Tyneside an early target. They're already organising air-raid precautions, and children are to be evacuated. Soon everybody'll be busy doing something, even right out here. What are you going to have? Whisky? Sherry?'

'A sherry, please.'

He followed Martin to the drinks cabinet that stood in a corner of the hall.

'What's the matter with you?' Martin asked. 'Not frightened of the war, are you?'

'No . . . no.'

'Then what's up? Had words with Mama?'

There was a long pause before Joe answered, 'Yes, something like that.'

'Take it in your stride, laddie, take it in your stride. Anyway, in a few months' time you might be called up.'

'Do you think so?'

'Sure of it; you'll be eighteen at Christmas. Harry knew what he was doing, didn't he? He's a fully fledged pilot now. Lucky dog.' And as he handed Joe his drink he added, 'I'm going in tomorrow.'

'What do you mean? To join up?'

'Yes. I've seen the partners; they agree it's the right thing to do.'

'I'll miss you.'

Martin's voice was low, with a note of sadness in it now, as he said, 'We'll miss each other, but still, that's life. Here, drink to it.' They clinked their glasses; then Martin, walking towards the long window, said, 'It's a good job I didn't become engaged; you shouldn't get married at a time like this.'

Joe's eyes widened as he asked, 'You . . . you were thinking about getting married?'

'Yes. Yes.'

'Who to?' The question sounded naive to his ears.

'Marion, Marion Crosbie; you know, the Hallidays' niece; you've met her.'

'Oh, yes, Miss Crosbie. She's the dark-haired one.'

'Yes' – Martin now laughed – 'the raven-haired one. Some girl . . . Marion.'

Of a sudden Joe was thankful that a war had been declared: Martin would join up and, because of his principles, he wouldn't then marry Miss Crosbie. That would be one less thing for him to worry about with regards to his mother, for she would still be mistress of the house, at least until the war was over, which might go on for a year, perhaps two.

For most people in England the war hadn't yet begun. The general opinion was that it had fizzled out; like a spent squib, it hadn't even given one burst. It was a fortnight now since it had started with such a hullabaloo, but there had been no raids, and no bombs had been dropped; the sirens went and people made for the shelters, but more and more half-heartedly, as days passed and nothing exciting happened. The only thing that seemed to be stirring most people was their scorn of Chamberlain. Of course there was

103

the black-out, and that was enforced, and everybody had to carry gas masks. There were no street lights any more and cars couldn't use their headlights, and it was being said that more people were being killed this way than if a real war had come upon them.

Joe should have gone back to school the previous week but it was being used as an evacuation centre. The upper school were remaining but it would be at least another week before he'd have to return.

The war hadn't seemed to touch the house, that is until the morning a lady arrived in a car from Hexham. She asked Ellen how many children she was prepared to take. She got no further than the hall and Ellen's answer could have been heard in every corner of the house: 'None!'

'None?' said the lady.

'None,' repeated Ellen.

'You might be forced to,' said the lady quietly.

'Then you'll have to go over the heads of the military and Sir Martin, for he's thinking of using this house as a convalescent base for officers.'

'Oh,' said the lady, slightly mollified. 'Oh, I'm sorry.'

'Good morning.'

The lady went out and drove away and Joe, who had witnessed the meeting, went into the kitchen where Mary was saying to Helen, 'Eeh! the lies rolled off her like butter off a hot griddle.'

'There's no truth in it at all then, you don't think?' said Helen.

'Not a word,' said Mary. Then turning to Joe she asked, 'You, Master Joe, you've heard nothing about officers coming here, have you?'

'No, Mary,' he said.

'No' – Mary turned to her sister – 'no, it's as I said, the lies.' Then realising to whom she was referring she stopped and, embarrassed now, she muttered, 'Well, it was a fib in a good cause; we don't want bairns scampering around this place, do we?'

'No, I suppose not,' he answered.

'You suppose not? Aye, Master Joe, you'd suppose not if you saw some of them from the towns. Lousy they are, their hair nearly walks by itself. I tell you I know. You can't help getting a nit or a dickie at school, but some of those town bairns are lousy. Oh, we don't want any like that here. Your mother was quite right. Do you want a scone?'

'Yes, please.'

She split open a newly baked scone and thickened it with butter and as she handed it to him she added, 'There's rationing comin', that's what they say, curtailing the food; well, it won't affect us, havin' cows and sheep an' chickens. But those pigs are more bloomin' nuisance than the horses. What do you say, Master Joe?'

'Yes, yes, I suppose so.' He smiled at her, the while thinking, why was it he always sounded inane when talking to any of the Smiths, with the exception of Mick? He didn't even show up brightly with Carrie.

'You suppose so? Well, I should think so; you'd grumble if you didn't get your butter, wouldn't you?'

He smiled broadly and he turned from her, munching at the buttered scone, and as he walked out of the back door he heard the sound of a car coming on to the gravel in front of the house. By the time he reached the end of the yard Martin was already out of the car and was running up the steps to the house.

Joe paused for a moment. He knew that Martin had seen him and yet he had taken no notice of him. Was something wrong?

Swallowing the last of the scone he ran over the drive and into the house to see Martin disappearing into the study. He did not go towards the study door because his mother, coming down the stairs, called, 'Who was that . . . Martin?'

'Yes.' He nodded. 'He's gone into the study.'

She made for the study door and he wanted to say, 'I wouldn't if I were you; he's in a tear about something,' but he knew that even if he did speak it wouldn't deter her.

He was a little way behind her when she knocked on the study door. When there was no response she slowly turned the handle and pushed the door open. Looking to the side of her, he could see Martin standing with his arms folded and resting on the mantelshelf.

'May I come in?'

It was some seconds before Martin turned towards them and said, 'Yes, yes; come in.'

Joe followed his mother into the room, and they stood looking at Martin, who had his back to the empty grate now and was staring at them as if he wasn't seeing them. Then his words came in a mutter so unlike his usual jaunty tones as he announced, 'They won't have me.'

Ellen stepped forward now, saying, 'You mean there's something wrong?'

'My eyes.' He tapped his right eye with his forefinger. 'Colour blind or some such thing. Damn rubbish. Did you ever hear anything like it? Colour blind. And me who's been firing a gun from when I was practically able to walk. Colour blind.'

Joe listened to his mother saying flatly, 'Colour wouldn't affect your aim.'

'No, I know. I said that.' He flung around from them and walked to the end of the room.

'What did they say? Have they offered you anything at all?'

'Oh, yes, yes' – he nodded his head at her over his shoulder – 'a desk job somewhere. I've been at a desk for years; I want no more of it and I told them. I told Ratler, you know, Colonel Ratler from over at Bellingham. He suggested I stay and farm the land. Farm the land, be damned! Most of it

106

hasn't been turned over for years. And what do they expect to grow on these hills?'

'What was decided?' Ellen's question was quiet.

'Nothing, nothing; they're to let me know, and they'll likely do that on the day they say the war's ended.'

Of a sudden he sat down in a chair and Joe, looking at him, had a strange thought, for his mind was saying that if men could cry, Martin would be crying now. He was about to take a step towards him when his mother said, 'Troubles never come singly. I'd better tell you I've had a call from Harry. He's going into hospital. He says it's nothing, just a check-up.'

Martin was on his feet. 'What time was this?'

'Oh, about ten this morning. He left a number where you can get him. It's on the pad in the hall.'

As he passed her he stopped and said, 'He didn't give you any idea what was wrong?'

'No, nothing. He sounded quite cheery. Just a check-up, he said. Perhaps . . . perhaps he's going abroad; they do have medicals before they're sent overseas, so I understand.'

'Yes, yes, that's right, yes.' He was nodding at her, obviously relieved now, and turning to Joe, he thrust out his hand and rumpled his hair as he said, 'Such is fate. As I was saying to you the other day, laddie, because I was aiming to be a fighting man I wouldn't get married. But now there's nothing to stop me, is there, eh?' He jerked his chin to the side; then seeming to stretch himself inches upwards, he thrust out his chin and marched from the room.

Joe turned and looked at his mother. She had her eyes on the figure striding across the hall towards the telephone table, and the look on her face caused him to close his own eyes for a moment, for he knew how she had taken what Martin had said: although it had been voiced lightly it was meant to have serious intent, and in her own mind his marrying would mean once again that she would have notice to quit.

4

'Well, it's up to you, Aunt Ellen, whether you stay or go. But one thing I won't tolerate is your continued manner towards Marion. You have shown your dislike of her since she first entered the house.'

'She dislikes me.'

'Well, you've given her cause from the beginning, haven't you? And get it into your head, Aunt Ellen, we're engaged to be married. You know – ' He pulled in his chin as he looked at her before continuing, 'It's odd, but none of the other girls I've brought to the house over the years have seemed to arouse your animosity. And why? Because you thought I wasn't serious. But now that I am, you see Marion as a threat to your position. I know I'm speaking plain, but this is a time for plain speaking. Don't you think so?'

Ellen Jebeau brought her lips tightly together and drew them inwards between her teeth before she said, with deep bitterness, 'I don't know about it being a time for plain speaking, I can only say that time has shown your ingratitude for what I've done for you over the years.'

'Done for me!'

They had been seated each side of the blazing fire in the drawing-room, but now Martin had sprung to his feet, his voice raised as he repeated, '*Done for me!* Oh, come on, come on, Aunt Ellen, think. Father took you and the youngster in twelve . . . no, thirteen years ago; he made it possible for you not only to live comfortably but well, and to educate the laddie. I took on where he left off . . . what have you done for me? Now, now! let's put matters straight. Besides being allowed to play mistress of this house for years, you've been given a good allowance. And, if I remember rightly, Father was not only going to continue that allowance but had bought a house for you, hadn't he? Well, I can't promise that if you leave I'll be as generous as he was; I'll continue your allowance certainly, but as for a house, no; for as you are well aware, because you know the books as well as I do, it takes us all our time, even with my salary, to continue living here as we have done of yore. So don't speak to me of ingratitude. And just in case I may say things I'll be sorry for, I'd better not go on, except for one last word. My wedding is set for April; whether I'm called up or not, it's going through. It could have been different if I had been accepted for the Forces, but this way I mean to make Marion my wife and I hope . . . well . . . well' – he jerked his head upwards – 'I may as well say it, that if I have a son, or for second best, a daughter, to carry on here. It may seem that I've never taken my title seriously, but below the skin I have great respect for it, and for this house too and the men who have gone before me who made it. So having said that, I advise you, Aunt Ellen, to see to your own plans.' He moved a step or two from her. Then, turning and looking into her tight, white countenance, he added and quietly, 'On second thoughts, I think it would be better if you decided definitely to make arrangements to live elsewhere. In fact, as things stand I see it as the only course for you to take . . . But,' he added kindly, 'there is no immediate hurry until April.'

As he made for the door he heard the phone ringing in the hall and when he entered he saw Joe turn from the telephone table towards him, saying, 'It's for you, Martin. It's . . . it's from the hospital, I think.'

Martin strode quickly towards him, picked up the phone, said, 'Yes?' then listened; and as he did so his head began to move in small jerks as he looked from side to side.

When at last he placed the phone down he turned and gazed at Joe, saying in a bewildered tone, 'It's Harry; they . . . they want me to go at once.'

Joe moved towards him, asking now, 'Is he bad?'

'Apparently so.' Before he finished speaking he had sprung towards the stairs and up them, shouting now, 'It'll be a longish drive; ask Mary to put something up for me; soup or something.'

'Yes, yes.' Joe ran to the kitchen, and was still giving Mary the order when his mother appeared in the doorway, saying, 'What is it?'

He turned to her: 'A message from the hospital, Harry's ill. They've . . . they've asked Martin to go straightaway.'

He watched her walk away without speaking and enter the hall again; he had expected her to come to the table to supervise Mary packing up the food. Mary had already pushed the soup pan onto the heart of the fire, and she said to him now, 'Get me the thermos, will you, Master Joe, and the picnic basket out of the bottom cupboard.'

Within a few minutes the basket was more than half full of food, and Mary was pouring the soup into the thermos.

She was screwing the top on when Martin entered the kitchen. 'Is he so bad, Mr Martin?' she said.

'I don't really know, Mary, but it would appear so. Oh' – he looked into the basket – 'I'm not going for a week; I just wanted a sandwich or two. But thanks.'

Joe picked up the picnic basket and the thermos flask from the table, and together he and Martin went out and across the dark courtyard towards the garage.

110

Martin took his seat in the car and was about to start her up when Joe leant towards him and asked, 'Would you like me to come with you, Martin?'

Martin looked at him for a moment and smiled softly at him as he said, 'I would, laddie, but you'd better not; I think your mother needs you tonight. She's had a bit of a blow. I'm sorry I had to deliver it, but there it is.'

The message in the words sounded ominous to Joe's ears, and he straightened up and said, 'Tell Harry I'll be thinking of him and I hope he'll be home soon.'

'I'll do that.'

The car gave a roar, then slowly moved out of the garage; the dim side-lights showed a pale flicker on the back of the house, then swung around for an instant on to the gardens. The next second the light was gone and Martin with it, and Joe stood in the yard oblivious of the fact that he was without a coat and that the cold was seeping through his pullover, for his outer self was no colder than the feeling within him that had been evoked by Martin's last words concerning his mother. He drew in a deep icy breath, then straightened his shoulders, a habit he was forcing upon himself a lot of late, then made his way towards the kitchen, to be greeted by Mary with, 'He's gone then?'

'Yes, Mary, he's gone.'

That was all he said, and he surprised her somewhat by walking quickly up the kitchen and into the hall. He would generally stop and have a word or two or listen to her. He was a good listener; he was about the only one in the house that was these days. Everybody seemed to be in a rush. It was the war, she supposed. She got a bit lonely when she was on by herself at nights. Things were changing in the house – you could feel it – and there was trouble brewing. She had only to look at Mrs Jebeau's face to see it; in fact, she could smell trouble in that direction. She was a funny woman, was Mrs Jebeau, nervy; what they called neurotic,

111

she would think. 'Yes' – she nodded to herself – 'that was the word, neurotic, which accounted for her nerves and her funny temper too.'

Going through Joe's mind as he mounted the stairs were thoughts which were very similar, except that he expressed his in a slightly different way. His mother, he knew, was in for another of her bouts, and he would have to bear the brunt of it. He should be used to them by now because they had become a frequent occurrence during the past few months, particularly since Martin had been bringing Miss Crosbie to the house. He had to think of her as Miss Crosbie so he wouldn't again make the mistake that had aroused his mother's anger when he had spoken of her as Marion. As if he were a child of five she had reprimanded him, saying, 'Don't be so personal; she is Miss Crosbie. And don't address her by any other name.'

It was almost a running dive he made across the gallery and to his bedroom, but he did it on tip-toe. He had no doubt that his mother was in her bedroom and that if she heard him she would come into his room and it would start, he knew it would: the upbraiding of Martin, and he wouldn't be able to stand it without checking her.

It came to him that he could lock the door, there was a bolt on it, but this conjured up the vision of her battering on it, for she certainly wouldn't be deterred by the fact that she was raising the house; she would know that Mary was the only one in it at the moment.

In his room he pulled on a dressing-gown and sat down and waited. He waited fifteen minutes, which seemed like hours, and still she didn't come. And he knew she was next door because he had heard her moving about.

Half an hour later he took off the dressing-gown and decided to go downstairs. He was puzzled: he could not understand this new tactic. Why was she leaving him alone?

* * *

112

Martin returned the following evening. Harry had died of pneumonia after an operation on his kidneys.

Joe, looking dumbly at him as he stood in the hall, saw a man whose youth seemed to have fled from him. He was standing well apart from them as he gave Joe and his mother the details, and as the tears rolled down his cheeks Joe sensed a great loneliness in his cousin that seemed to link up with a similar feeling within himself, and he was drawn to Martin to put his arms about him, and when their faces touched both were wet.

5

'Where's your gas mask?'

'In its box.'

'You'll say that once too often.' Carrie slanted her eyes and nodded her head at Joe as she added, 'And you can get into trouble for not carrying it.'

'That'll be light to the trouble I'll be in soon.'

'What do you mean?'

'They say it could come any time – calling-up.'

'Oh, that.'

They stopped and faced each other. Then Carrie jumped aside as a passing bus threw up some slush from the gutter, and as she brushed her hands down over the bottom of her coat, she said, 'You'd think they did it on purpose,' and as he went to assist her she stayed his hands, saying, 'It'll only make it worse. Anyway, what does it matter? You were saying about being called up.' They were walking on again.

'Yes, I was saying . . . '

'You want to go?'

'Yes and no. It all depends where I land.' He stopped again and, taking her firmly now by the arm, pulled her into a shop doorway and, looking into her eyes, he said, 'If it wasn't for leaving you I'd be glad to go, and . . . and I thought you'd be proud of me going.'

'Oh, Joe' – she turned her head slowly to the side – 'don't start on that again; you . . . you know nothing can come of it.'

'Why not?'

'Look, don't be silly.' She pressed her lips tightly together for a moment. 'You're asking the road you know, it's been spelled out so many times: the rich man in his castle, the poor man at his gate. Only the poor man happens to be me.'

'That's daft, rubbish. Look, there's a war on, everybody's changing. Everything will be changed after it. And, anyway, what are you talking about, the rich man in his castle? When Martin marries next month she'll be out. Mother, I mean. She hasn't said anything, but she knows all right. Even if Martin wanted her to stay, Marion can't stand her. And I don't blame her, the way she's been received. At the same time, though, I can see Mother's side of it, at least on this one point, for she hasn't considered herself as being just a housekeeper all these years, she's felt mistress of the place, and she's going to miss it.'

'Will you?' The question was direct and he blinked for a moment before answering: 'Yes,' he said, 'honestly yes, I will. It's a lovely house, it's a lovely place. And I'll miss . . . well, I'll miss Martin. We've . . . we've always been close, but more so since Harry went. But in a way I'll be glad when he's married; he'll have someone really of his own then.'

'Will you really be glad when he marries?'

'Of course I shall. What makes you ask?'

'Oh, just that . . . well, he could have children.'

'Well, I expect he will have.'

'And you don't mind?'

'No, I don't mind. And I know what you're thinking.'

'Yes, of course you know what I'm thinking, because you are next in line for the title and all it entails. And what if

115

Martin doesn't have any children; or, say, if he were to die in the war and you survived, what then . . . Sir Joseph Bartholomew Jebeau?'

'Oh! *Carrie*.' Joe turned away from her, thrusting his hands deep into his overcoat pockets, and he sounded very like Martin himself as he growled out, 'Suppose, suppose, suppose. There's as much chance of that happening as . . . '

When he hesitated Carrie ended, 'As your mother greeting me with open arms. I know, I know. And yet I'm wrong, there's more chance of that happening than your mother ever looking upon me with favour. Why, if she knew we were meeting, she'd go mad. You know she would. Every time you want to see me you have to make an excuse, haven't you, tell a fib of some sort? There's times I don't see you for weeks on end.'

'That isn't my fault.' He turned on her now, but was almost pushed aside as someone came out of the shop. And so he took her arm and pulled her into the street again and, still holding her arm, he said, 'And what do you think I feel like when I don't see you and knowing you're away dancing with that John Bennett or that Sweetman fellow?'

'Well, what do you expect me to do? Sit in the house and wait for you coming? And look, don't drag me any further, Joe, please. See where we are! This is where I work, remember?'

They stopped just beyond the steps of the food office and, all the irritation seeming to flow from him, he looked at her meekly now as he said, 'I may not see you again for weeks. I don't know what's going to happen, so, Carrie, I must say it – I've implied it in a thousand different ways for months now – I . . . I love you, Carrie. Looking back, I can't remember a time when I didn't love you. Do . . . do you love me?'

Her head was bent and her words were hardly audible above the noise of the traffic as she said, 'What's the good in loving someone you . . . you can never have?'

'But we can, you can. I don't care what my mother thinks, or anybody else, I'd . . . I'd marry you tomorrow if you'd have me. Will you . . . will you, Carrie?'

Carrie lifted her head and looked at him, and what she saw was a young boy, the same young boy she had known when she lived in the cottage. She didn't see the dark nineteen-year-old youth, for he didn't look nineteen: there was hardly any stubble on his chin, his face was pale, his mouth tender, his clear grey eyes filled with the hurt of love. She saw the boy who wrote poetry, and she loved him, but as the boy, not as the youth or the budding man. She thought of her brothers. They had all appeared to be like men when they were sixteen, especially Mick. Mick had always been like a man to her. Oh Mick, Mick was something. Oh yes, their Mick was something. And he understood Joe. He had explained his character to her by saying, 'He lives half in the air; it's only his toes that touch the ground.' She remembered him laughing kindly as he said this, because he liked Joe, he liked Joe very much; but at the same time he felt guilty about him, because in a way he had made use of him as a sort of cover. Her mind swung away from her brother and she told herself that she couldn't see herself spending her life with someone whose toes were just touching the ground; her nature demanded stability. She knew she had been brought up these last few years with her Aunt Alice and Uncle Stan because of the instability at home. Of course that had been mostly created by the lack of money, but the instability she saw in Joe wasn't that kind of lack, it was something she couldn't put her finger on. But Mick's description of him sort of fitted. Yes; nevertheless, he was nice. She liked him, she liked him a lot. Perhaps she loved him. She didn't really know. Could you love two people . . . two men like that? There was no answer.

'Look, Joe, I've got to go.' She put out her hand as if warding him off. 'I'm late already.'

'You . . . you don't care for me? You don't even like me?'

'Don't be silly.' She took a step towards him. 'You know I like you. But . . . but I'm not ready yet for what you want.' She knew she was lying, and she went on lying. 'I . . . I don't want to be tied down to anyone, and . . . and things are so uncertain with the war and all that. But . . . but I do like you, I like you a lot, Joe. Get that into your head, I like you a lot.'

'But you don't love me?' His voice was flat.

'Oh, why must you harp on about that! Look, I've got to go. Bye-bye.' She backed two steps from him, then turned and ran towards the building.

He remained where he was. The weight in his heart seemed to have tethered him to the pavement, and he had to force himself to turn away, and some seconds after she had disappeared through the doorway. What would he do without her? He wouldn't be able to love anybody else but her, ever. When some part of his mind prompted the words that he had heard so often, boyish fancy, his inside actually jerked in protest. It was no boyish fancy, the feelings he had for her; they seemed to have been born in him. They had lain dormant for some years after she had left the cottage, but he knew now they had simply been growing in the warm darkness of his being where love bred . . .

He had to meet Martin at four o'clock and he had to kill time till then. He did so by wandering the streets, and when for the second time he passed the food office where she worked, he knew what he was going to do. He was going to face up to his mother when he got home and have it out. If he could convince her that nothing she could say or do would make him change his mind about Carrie, the way would be open for him to prove to Carrie he had enough love for the two of them.

But there was so little time left now, for he could get his papers any day . . . He had the urge to run.

*   *   *

118

He had been so quiet on the journey home that Martin said to him, 'What's up, laddie?' and when Joe had replied, 'Everything,' Martin had nodded his head, saying simply, 'Carrie?'

It had been almost a minute before Joe replied, 'Yes, Carrie.'

'Well, better finish it now, laddie, because no good will come of you marrying into that lot. Oh, I know, I know.' He had taken one hand from the wheel and held it up in protest. 'She's a nice girl, what I've seen of her, the best of the bunch, I should say, next to Mick and, of course, Dick. Old Dick's all right, but if you marry her you'll be marrying her family . . . Does she feel the same way as you?'

When Joe gave no immediate answer Martin had sighed as he said, 'There are a lot of women in the world, laddie, thousands and thousands of 'em. And the right one is among them, the right one for you, that is. Some day you'll come across her and you'll know it, as soon as you look at her, you'll know it. As I know it. Something goes bang inside your belly. And as often as you tell yourself she's not your type, that you don't like blondes, your taste tends towards the browns, even redheads but not blondes, no; and what's more, her face is round, but you don't like round faces; and you've always gone in for a bit of shape and she's flat as a pancake. You're not having any of that, you tell yourself, but you're hooked, laddie, you're hooked.' He had glanced laughingly at Joe, and Joe had known he was describing his future wife, but his words had brought no consolation to him . . .

It seemed to Joe that his mother was waiting behind the hall door for him, because no sooner had he entered the house than there she was, staring at him over the distance.

'I want you upstairs a moment,' she said. Her voice was quiet, controlled.

He turned his head and glanced to where Martin was

119

taking off his overcoat, and Martin raised his eyebrows, pursed his lips and nodded his head, the action saying, 'You're in for it again, laddie.'

By the time he reached the gallery his mother was at the far end of the broad corridor, but she wasn't going into her room or into his room, she was making for the attic stairs, and now it was his turn to raise his eyebrows. What on earth did she want him up there for?

But he knew why the moment he entered the old school-room, for after allowing him to pass her she closed the door and stood with her back to it, her pale face, now tinged to a deep red, thrust out towards him as she cried, 'Think you're smart, don't you? Lying, sneaking, crawling individual that you've become, and all to see that little slut. Well, it's finished. Do you hear? You attempt to go near her again and I'll make it my business to go across there . . .'

'Shut up!'

She shut up and her mouth fell into a gape, the sweat appeared in globules on her upper lip, the colour deepened in her face and she seemed to have to force breath into her lungs as she listened to him now saying, 'You'll not tell me any more what I've got to do and what I haven't got to do. I've made up my own mind what I'm going to do. I'm sick and tired of your domination. Do you hear? Do you hear me?' He had actually taken a step towards her. 'If I want to see Carrie, I'll see Carrie, in spite of you or anyone else. Do you hear me?'

She blinked rapidly now; then, her face becoming suffused with an anger that seemed to send out rays of heat towards him, she cried, 'Yes, I hear you. And now you hear me. I'm your mother and I forbid you to take that tone with me. But the first thing I've got to say to you here and now is you're no more capable of keeping a wife than of keeping a — ' she seemed to search for the word, then brought out, 'rabbit. You've been at school for years and what have you

120

achieved? Nothing. The only thing you can do is scribble; and what is the result of your scribblings? Mediocre stuff, stupid rhymes. What's going to happen to you without me behind you? Have you ever asked yourself that? And here you are, eighteen and you don't even know what you are going to do. Go to university . . . Huh! and waste more years.'

She now drew her chin into her chest and in a voice almost as deep as a man's she said, 'And you dare to tell me to shut up, me! who's given her life to you. From the moment you were born your future has been my one aim, and now to see your trailing after that little slut, you who are in line for a title . . . '

'What?'

The anger that the insults to his intelligence had aroused in him was put aside by the amazement that surrounded the question, and again he mouthed, 'What?' then added, 'In line! You really must be mad; I'm . . . I'm as much in line for the title as the rabbit you inferred a moment ago I'd be unable to support. Martin and Marion will have a family. She wants a family; I've heard her say so, and she'll have a family, and I hope it's a big one, ten, twelve . . . In line, indeed!'

While they glared at each other he recalled that Carrie had said something similar earlier in the day.

'Don't be stupid.' She was biting on her lip now as if regretting her words; then she added, 'It isn't every woman that can bear a child, and she doesn't look a child-bearer to me. And I have a feeling – ' She now drew in a long breath before resuming – 'And it's more than a feeling, it's a certainty that, although we're leaving here, being forced to leave here, we'll return, for this is our home. If . . . if everyone had their rights I should be legal mistress of this place now. Whether you've known it or not, I was your uncle's mistress for years, and he would have married me. Yes, yes, he would.' She nodded her head before adding, 'But a man can't marry his brother's wife. It was a dirty quirk of fate. I . . . I feel

121

I've been robbed, all along the line I feel I've been robbed. But it can't go on forever. No, it won't go on forever and, I repeat, we'll come back here one day. I know inside.' She thumped her chest.

When she stopped speaking his feeling of animosity towards her seeped from him, and the pity that he always felt for her again rose to the surface and for a moment he himself knew the extent of her frustration and the reason behind her furious tantrums when she had known his uncle was going to marry again.

He could see now that she was placed in an almost similar position, for with Martin marrying, she was once more being cast adrift. He thought for a moment that if she would only accept his feelings for Carrie he would go to her this minute and put his arms about her and comfort her, but he knew she would never accept Carrie. But then Carrie hadn't accepted him, had she? So what was stopping him from going to her and telling her that she had no need to worry? Whatever it was, it was like a wall between them and he was honest enough to admit to himself that most of the time he was building on it brick by brick in order to blot her out of his sight . . . forever.

He watched her now lean against the door, her body slumped, her eyes closed. Of a sudden she looked old. She was forty-six: her face was unlined, her hair still golden without grey in it, her body trim, very trim, yet he seemed to be looking at an old woman. Pity for her again seeped through until, opening her eyes, she said, and in a quiet appealing voice now, 'Promise me, Joe, you won't see that girl again.'

It was on the tip of his tongue to say, 'I'll do no such thing,' but he found himself compromising by saying, 'I'm going to join up.'

'You're going to what?'

'Join up.'

She moved her head slowly now and seemed to be making

an effort to speak, and then she muttered, 'You'll be getting your calling up papers eventually, in any case, so why . . . ? Please.' She now straightened up and extended her hand towards him, and again she said, 'Please' – then added his name – 'Joe. Don't . . . don't go until you must. Don't leave me . . . until I get over this. I mean the move. You . . . you don't know what it's costing me.'

He turned from her now, shaking his head, saying, 'I'm . . . I'm sorry but . . . but I must do it.'

He had his back to her and he stood waiting for another outburst, but when neither answer nor movement came to him he turned his head slowly and looked at her over his shoulder. She was standing straight, looking in his direction but seemingly through him, and the strange look on her face brought him around fully, and he was about to speak, not with the intention of giving her the true version of why he wanted to volunteer, for it wasn't in him to hurt her to that extent, but she turned from him and, quietly opening the door, went out.

Her exit caused him more concern than if she had made it in the blaze of anger similar to that with which she had first confronted him. He put a hand to his brow and now out of all she had said there came into his mind her words: 'You couldn't support a rabbit.' And they stabbed at him and caused his whole body to tremble as if in shame because, in a way, he knew she was right: his inadequacy to face his future was there for even himself to see; he had considered volunteering in order to avoid the responsibility of making the choice either of going to University to read for a degree in English Literature or of just plumping for a teacher's training college course.

Why was life like this?

6

There was a high wind blowing. The night had turned rough and the rattle from the windows had seemed to be emphasised by the silence during supper. They had almost finished eating when Martin spoke. As if following up a train of thought, he looked across at Joe, saying, 'I wonder if those thieving scoundrels will be on the prowl again tonight?' and Joe answered, 'I shouldn't think they'd have the nerve to make a third trip, not in the same week, anyway.'

'Those beggars have got the nerve and cunning to tackle anything. But there's one thing sure, next time they come on this land they'll be met by a reception committee. Oh, yes.'

'Who's on tonight?'

'Paxstone, and I've given him orders to shoot and be damned. If those devils can wring the necks of chickens and slit the throats of sheep, then they shouldn't object to some shot, should they?' He poked his head slightly towards Joe, and after a moment's hesitation Joe said, 'He would really shoot them?'

'Yes, yes, indeed; aim for the legs to bring them down. Oh –' He now thrust out his hand in a flapping movement, saying, 'Don't look like that, there's nobody going to be murdered.'

'What . . . what if those men have guns too?'

'Oh, I wouldn't think so. But then you never know; they're probably ready to poach anything. No, you never know.'

Ellen Jebeau rose from the table, and they made the gesture of rising too. She was addressing Martin as she said, 'If there's nothing further you want of me, I think I'll go to bed. Mary will be here till eight.'

'Of course, of course.' Martin had pulled himself up to his feet now and he held on to the back of the chair as he nodded at her, then watched her go towards the door. Before she reached it, however, it was opened and Mary entered the room.

Mary looked first at Ellen and then towards Martin as she said, 'It's . . . it's me dad, sir. He's been to say that Bernard has put his wrist out, and it being Danny's day off he went for Bill, but Bill's gone over to see his mother in Consett, so he says, what about it, sir?'

'Oh.' Martin chewed on his lip for a moment. 'Tell him not to worry, I'll go.'

As the door closed on both Ellen Jebeau and Mary, Martin turned to the table and as he sat down said, 'Damn nuisance. And we really need two men out there, but I can't ask more of them than they're doing; they're making up for one short as it is. And this snow lying doesn't help.'

'Let me come with you tonight, Martin.'

'*Oh no. Oh no.*' Martin turned to look at him, a twisted grin on his face. 'You want your mother after me?'

'She's not to know; she'll be fast asleep before then.'

'What if there's a scrap and I do have to fire at them and they return it; for after all, as I've said, we don't really know whether they carry guns; all we know is they haven't used them yet.'

'Well' – Joe laughed now – 'it'll give me a bit of practice before I'm introduced to the real thing, and that shouldn't be long now.'

'Oh.' Martin nodded at him now, his face serious. 'But that shouldn't be for a while, they're not calling the twenties up yet . . . You want to go?'

'Oh, yes, yes; in fact – ' He dropped his head now and, picking up his pudding spoon, he traced it round his empty plate before he said, 'I'm going to volunteer.'

'You are! Well! Why didn't you say so before? Oh, you thought I might be upset. That's you, Joe, that's you. No, I'm over that. Does your mother know?'

'Yes. Yes, I . . . I told her tonight.'

'Oh my! Oh my! I don't need to ask how she took it.'

'No.'

'You're going to find it tough, Joe; I mean, Army life. You decided on the Army? No?'

'No, the Air Force. I fancy flying, something to do with flying, anyway.'

'Oh, they'll take you for that, all right; they're fishing for them like mackerel.' There was a pause before he ended, 'Your mother's going to be lonely, you know that, don't you, Joe?'

'Yes, yes, I do.'

Tapping his cheese knife in rhythm on the edge of the table, Martin said, 'I don't know whether you've noticed, but there's never been much love lost between your mother and me. She liked Harry. Well, who didn't? who wouldn't? but she's never cottoned on to me, and so I don't know whether or not she's told you . . . oh, to put it plainly, I had to give her her marching orders.'

'Yes, yes, I thought you had to.'

'But she hasn't told you?'

'No; but . . . but I guessed something like that had happened from what you said a while back.'

'She's got a decent allowance and they're wanting women in all kinds of work now. She . . . she needn't be on her own. Well, not in that way. But, nevertheless, I know she'll miss

126

this house. Most of all she'll miss you. But there it is, that's life, and she should know, if anyone does, that there's no straight path in it. Well' – he sighed – 'what's the time?' He turned to look at the clock. 'Quarter past eight. I think I'll go and change my clothes and have a drink to fortify me, because it'll be damned cold out there tonight . . . Listen to that wind! It's getting stronger.'

He rose to his feet now, smiling and, putting an arm around Joe's shoulder, he said, 'What are you going to do with yourself?'

'Oh, I don't know.'

'Well, it's too early to go to bed and the rooms are like ice. The drawing-room's nice and warm; go in there.'

They went into the hall together; then Joe watched Martin take the stairs two at a time, and the maleness of him, his virility seemed to leave an aroma behind him. He remained standing looking up the stairs. He wished he could be like Martin, if only in some small way, because he had the feeling he lacked something.

'You couldn't support a rabbit.'

Was it because his mind tended towards thinking about things, musing over them instead of tackling them? Or was there a deficiency in his make-up, in the maleness of him? *No. No.* His whole body jerked in denial as he made for the drawing-room. He was male all right. Inside he knew he was very male: he wanted Carrie and he knew how he wanted her. There was nothing airy-fairy about the way he wanted Carrie; he wanted to touch Carrie, he wanted to see her . . . He turned on himself, saying, 'Oh God! Give over!'

There was no light in the drawing-room except that from the fire, which was burning brightly and leaving deep shadows in the corner of the room. He sat on the chintz-covered couch to the side of the fireplace and, leaning his head back, looked about him. From one dim object to another he let his eyes roam, and he saw them all clearly:

127

the Louis Quinze couch between the long windows, the French glass-fronted cabinet in the corner opposite, the sixteenth-century iron-bound chest standing in the alcove, its lid flat against the wall, held there by a pyramid of logs. It was a beautiful room. It was home, the only home he could remember. He was going to miss it. Strangely, he knew at this moment that he'd miss this house as much as his mother would. He also knew that never in his life would he be in a position to own one like it.

'You couldn't support a rabbit.'

7

〜

'If the moon comes up I doubt we'll see any visitors the night, sir, and it's trying its best over there.'

Martin looked up into the dark sky where now he could see a faint pattern of grey, scudding clouds, then whispered, 'I don't think it'll last long with this wind, and there's more snow in the air. By God! it's getting colder. And I must say again, Dick, it's very good of you to join me. To tell you the truth, I wasn't looking forward to it. It's a lonely business at any time. I was only saying to young Joe earlier, we really should have two on. Apart from the company it's safer, because one really doesn't know how many of the beggars one has to contend with.'

'You're right there, sir. I've said the same to meself, but the way we are fixed . . . well, we couldn't do much else.'

'You're right. You're right, Dick.' Martin now leant his gun gently against the thick bush of the hedge behind which they were crouched and, putting his hand into the deep pocket of his overcoat, he drew out a flask, unscrewed the silver top, poured out a measure and handed it to Dick Smith, saying, 'It'll stop the shivers.'

'Oh, thank you, sir. Thank you.' Dick did not immediately hand the small cap back to Martin but, taking a clean handkerchief out of the top pocket of his short, thick coat, he wiped the rim of it, then handed it back, saying again, 'Thank you, sir.'

Nice chap, Dick; best of the bunch. Strange he had to father two sluts of women. But then he had married one, hadn't he? Any good in that family came from his side. It was a nice gesture to wipe the cup. Yes, yes, indeed he was a good man, Dick.

'Ssh! what was that?'

They had both slowly turned their heads, which were now very close as they stared to where a grassy bank rose to a narrow stretch of woodland that bordered the house gardens. It wasn't likely that anyone would come that way, for the hen crees were situated in the field just beyond the hedge, and the sheep were there too, having been brought down from the hills after ten of their already small stock had been taken.

'Likely a branch snapping in the wind, sir.'

'Yes, yes; it couldn't be an animal, it was too loud.'

'Couldn't be Master Joe out, sir?'

'No; he was playing the piano when I left.'

'Nice young fellow, Master Joe.'

'Yes, Dick; the makings of a good one there, though I don't know how he'll come off in the Forces.'

'Oh, it's surprising how the Army toughens the lads, brings out the fibre in 'em. And as our Mick has often said, there's more to Master Joe than meets the eye.'

'True. True.' As Martin whispered his reply he raised his head slightly above the hedge and peered into the field, where now he could distinctly make out the hen crees and the dark blobs of the sheep.

As a thought struck him he dropped on to his hunkers again and whispered quickly, 'They could come in by the far gate and force their way into the back of the crees: they're only planked.'

'I've thought of that, sir; we put wire trips up there 'safternoon. If they fall over them it'll ring the bell; you know, the old cow-bell that hangs in the shed.' He paused. 'Well, we put it up 'safternoon, sir.'

'Good. Good, Dick. It's a splendid idea. So the only way they can get at the crees is through the west field and along the path here.'

'Only way, sir. Only way.'

'Well, if they come, we'll get them. And by the way, I don't know why we're sitting crouched down here because we could stand up by the spruce there: its shadow is darker than the sky, and we could be more ready for them. No matter how many there are we'll give them a chance to show themselves first, eh? But if they start to run, we'll fire; at the legs, of course. Understood?'

'Oh yes, understood, sir.'

They had raised themselves but still remained crouched, and were moving slowly by the hedge towards the tree, when once again Martin's attention was brought round to the strip of woodland, not by a noise this time, but by a strange feeling of impending danger. But it came too late for him to do anything about it, for when he straightened up and turned towards the bank the bullet hit him in the chest and his body seemed to disintegrate and fly in all directions, and he knew that death was on him and that it was something that divided you into a million parts and each fragment screamed as it flung itself into eternity.

But as he sank into Dick Smith's trembling arms, he made no sound. Even while Dick was lowering Martin to the ground, he had his head turned in the direction of the dark blur standing out against the night and it was only a matter of seconds before he raised himself and his gun towards it. But his finger never pulled the trigger for he, too, felt an explosion in his chest and, as if going into a slow dive, he dropped to the earth, the gun still gripped in his hand, and as

131

he died he heard a voice yelling, 'Christ! Christ Almighty!'

It was half past ten when Joe placed the iron fire-screen in front of the dying embers of the fire and left the drawing-room.

The hall light was still on but Martin would put that out later. The house was very quiet. He stopped for a moment and gazed about him. It was strange, but he imagined that at such times as this, when there was only himself and his mother in the house, the building had left its base and was afloat in the air. It was the remains of a childish fancy, created by a story he had read, but it returned to him most vividly at this moment. He again sensed the wrench he was going to feel at leaving this house and never return to it as home . . . Then, not of a sudden but slowly, there crept through his being the most odd feeling: his stomach began to tremble, as if his bowels had become loose in their casing. No part of his mind said, 'It's silly to feel like this about leaving the house,' because he knew that this feeling wasn't in any way connected with his leaving the house. Suddenly he became vitally aware that there was someone in the hall with him. He didn't swing round but, his thoughts seeming to direct him, he moved slowly, turning a full circle, and he gazed about him, his eyes stretched wide. Had the house actually left the ground, he knew that he couldn't have felt more strange than he did at this moment, or more afraid: there was someone here. Had the poachers been chased and found their way into the house? No, no; it wasn't someone that was here, it was some *thing*.

He was feeling pain now and a great, great sadness. He couldn't bear it. Of a sudden he was running, flying up the stairs. At the top he stopped, brought to a halt by the sight of his mother entering her room. He had the impression that she was fully dressed but told himself that it must be a trick of the light. He felt odd, queer, as if he'd had a bad dream. He walked slowly now towards the room, but as he passed his mother's door he felt forced to stop and knock, not because he wanted to see her particularly, but because there was a great need in him for human company. He wanted to speak to someone and hear their voice speaking to him.

There was no answer to his knock, so he knocked again; and then her voice came to him: 'Wait . . . wait a moment.' It seemed as if it were coming from a long distance and he waited for a moment, and the moment went into a full minute, and then slowly he opened the door.

She was in bed lying on her back, and as he crossed the room towards her he noticed a number of strange things. Her woollen hat was lying on a chair: she was a tidy woman, over-tidy; there was a place for everything and everything in its place, was her motto. And her outdoor boots were sticking out from under the bed. What drew his eyes down to them was the fact that it was a strange place for them to be. And they were wet.

He moved slowly up by the side of the bed, and now he said, 'Are . . . are you all right?' and he saw the bedclothes that she was holding under her chin rise and fall with the movement of her neck before she said, 'Yes. I . . . I was asleep.' At this his lower jaw fell slightly and his head came forward and he said, 'You were what?'

She did not repeat her last statement but she said, 'Go . . . go away, please. I . . . I want to rest.'

Joe stood staring at her. That strange feeling he had experienced in the hall: had it been repeated on the landing? Was he having hallucinations? No, no. He shook his head at himself. True, he'd had that weird feeling in the hall, but seeing her on the landing a moment ago had been no illusion.

His hand shot out now and made an effort to grab the bedclothes from her, but she clutched them tightly against her throat. They stared at each other for a moment in tense silence; then gripping the side of the bedclothes, he

133

swung them upwards and exposed to his amazed gaze her grey outdoor coat. It was crumpled and wet in parts.

Once more he was overcome with a strange feeling, but this he could recognise, for it was made up of unadulterated fear.

When she grabbed the clothes and put them around her, saying, 'I was cold; I . . . I often sleep in my coat,' he backed away from her, all the way towards the door; then on the landing, and for no reason that he could give to himself, he turned and ran not towards his bedroom but across the landing, over the gallery, down the stairs, through the hall to the front door. There he stood leaning against it, his arms outspread, one cheek pressed on to the black wood, with his breath coming in gasps, as if he had just surfaced from drowning. A minute later he had wrenched open the door and was standing on the terrace. The night seemed light, the moon was scudding between white clouds, showing up the white world beyond the drive that had been cleared of snow. He drew in deep, deep breaths of air; then, almost quietly now, he told himself he must find Martin. He must talk to Martin . . . Perhaps he was going mad.

Was he going mad? No, no; he wasn't going mad. It was no illusion: he had pulled the clothes off her, seen her lying in bed in her outer clothes, and those soiled. What was she hiding? Where had she been? He must find Martin – he would be down near the chicken run – he must speak to someone, touch someone's hand, hear someone's voice. He was running again, taking the short cut through the gardens and towards the woodlands, calling now, 'Martin! Martin! Martin!'

He found Martin, and Mr Smith. Martin was lying on his back, his knees upwards. The moon was shining full on his face – it seemed as if he were staring up at it. He was obviously quite dead. Mr Smith was lying on his side. Joe slipped on the snowy slope as he neared him, and when his hand touched the man's chin above the collar of his rough

134

jacket and felt the sticky wetness on his fingers, he sprang up as if he had been stung by a hornet.

'Oh God! Oh God! Oh God!' he was yelling aloud now as he stumbled back towards Martin and then stood looking down at him. He tried to move, but he couldn't until a voice shouted in his head, 'Get help. Get help,' and then he scrambled up the bank and raced like a wild thing, screaming now, 'Bernard! Mr Swann! Danny! Help! Help! Mary! Mary!'

He had gone through all the Smiths' names by the time he reached the yard, and it was there that Danny Waggett caught hold of him. 'They're shot!' Joe screamed. 'They're shot! Martin and Mr Smith, they're shot, they're shot. Down in the spinney. They're shot! They're shot!'

At two o'clock in the morning the doctor gave him a sedative and he went into a deep sleep, but when he awoke he did not speak to anyone, and the police found great difficulty in questioning him too.

8

If the war wasn't actually forgotten, it was put aside for a few days in the district around Screehaugh. Until the day of the funeral, men and the police searched the grounds and land around hoping to find the murder weapon. Neither Sir Martin Jebeau's gun nor that of his stableman, Richard Smith, had been fired, and both guns were found not a yard from each other. The churned-up snow around the spots where both men had died had not helped the investigations either.

The immediate suspects of the murder were a local man and his son; but both these men could not have had stronger alibis, for the father was in hospital after having an operation on his hip bone, while his son had three days previously been called into the Forces. The second suspect was a resident of Consett, but on the night in question his wife had given birth to their first child, and the doctor and the midwife both vouched for the fact that the man had never left the house after he came in from work at half-past five until he went to work the next morning, an hour after he had heard his son first cry.

The police thought they were on to something when, following an anonymous 'phone call, they went to a butcher's shop. The voice on the telephone had informed the police the butcher was in the habit of buying stolen sheep and fowl. The police spent two days trying to persuade the butcher to give them the name or names of his supplier. When, worn down at last, he mentioned a man who lived as far away as Prudhoe, the police picked up a young fellow known as Billy the Badger, which apparently had nothing to do with his poaching activities, but was given him because he always wore a white muffler, the ends tucked into his trouser tops, and on Sundays, when he wore his best, which was a black coat and trousers, his pointed face above this ensemble roughly depicted the night creature of the woods.

Billy the Badger had much more difficulty in proving his innocence, although he admitted to stealing chickens. Yes, he said, he had raided at Screehaugh, but only for chickens. He swore he had never touched their sheep, and he swore by many Northern oaths that he was in Newcastle up till eleven o'clock on the night of the murders.

It took some further persuasion to elicit exactly where he had spent the hours in Newcastle. 'Pubs,' he had said briefly at first. When he found this wasn't good enough for the police, the result of speaking the truth being the lesser of two evils, he gave the name of a woman he had visited.

What happened when he faced his wife and when the husband of the lady in question, who was in the Forces, heard of her escapade, didn't reach the papers. There was a war on and such emotional family matters were really of no account. The police went on searching. They would find the culprits. But they were hampered by the fact that the stealing of hill sheep at this time was becoming a common occurrence.

During the five days between that dreadful night and the day of the funeral, Joe and Ellen Jebeau never looked at each other, nor did a word pass between them. There were no set meals; the whole Smith family was deeply affected and Mary and Helen did only what was absolutely necessary. They cried a lot, and Jessie Smith, appearing in the kitchen more than she had done in recent months, not only cried but wailed, nearly always when Joe was within earshot, and the substance of her wailing was, 'Left without a breadwinner,' which nearly always elicited, 'Oh! Ma, be quiet,' from Mary.

It was an understood thing that Mr Joe, Sir, as he was now – and that was hard to take in – was still in shock, for he walked about like someone in a dream and would stand staring in front of him for minutes on end.

Mrs Jebeau, too, appeared shocked. As Mary reiterated to the police, she'd had a job to wake her up out of a dead sleep that night, and when she did come to she just couldn't take in what had happened: she didn't seem able to speak for ages and she'd had to help her into her clothes.

But in private, Mary remarked to Mick that it was funny how that one always seemed to fall on her feet. She had been ready for the road, then Mr Arthur died. And there she had been again, almost packed to make way for Mr Martin's wife, when once again fate had taken a hand, and now she was set nicely. And for good, it would seem, for she'd rule Mr Joe, title or no title.

And poor Miss Crosbie. It seemed that she had been knocked silly too. Mary described to Mick how the young girl had stood in the hall, her face cupped between her palms, and gazed about her, while the tears ran down her face and she kept muttering, 'Oh Martin! Martin!' Her mother and father had had to help her down the steps and into the car. The house seemed fated somehow. What did he think . . . ? Did he think Master Joe would go off his head?

One part of Joe was telling him he had already gone off his head, but another section kept repeating, 'It'll soon be over and then you can tell her. Once you've done that you'll be free.'

He still had the numbed feeling on him, and that in itself was frightening, for as yet he could feel no sorrow for either Martin or Mr Smith. He knew that at night, alone in his room, he should be crying, but no tears came; that in itself was strange, for he'd often cried about small things, such as seeing a fox with its leg in a trap, still alive, its eyes begging for release. He had been too afraid and shocked to go near it, and on that particular night he had cried because of his cowardice. Then he had cried one night following a market day in Hexham, for there he had seen two men fighting. It was in a narrow side street and there were only a few people watching. The younger man had hauled his older opponent from the ground and held him up against the wall with one hand while he pummelled his face with the other, and the blood covered his fist. When the sight elicited from one of the bystanders, 'I know he deserves it, but enough is enough, and after all, he's his father,' another had answered, 'Aye, you've said it: he's his father; but then, the lass was his wife.'

He puzzled over that, but he kept remembering the older man's face, and the sadness in it, and the awful fact that he hadn't retaliated in any way. It was something about the old man's attitude that had made him cry.

But here he was in a deep tragedy: the man he had loved – yes, really loved – had been murdered, and he could shed no tears for him . . .

He was dry-eyed at the funeral, and there was a great crowd there. They came to the house on horseback, by car, by bicycle, by farm-cart; but most of them followed the hearse on foot; close friends filled the four cabs.

He himself sat in the first cab opposite Martin's two partners, Mr Alex Beecham, the senior partner, and Mr James Holden, now the junior partner. Martin's position in the firm had been between the two.

The Smith mourners were all on foot and there were no women present. Dick Smith's hearse followed that in which Martin lay.

Joe had insisted on this arrangement despite Mr Beecham's opinion that it wasn't quite seemly.

The day was cold, with flurries of snow and people were muffled up to the eyes. But Joe himself didn't feel the cold; when you were numb already, the temperature made little impression on you. In the cemetery he became aware of Mick Smith walking by his side, but he did not acknowledge his presence in any way.

Later, when like a waking nightmare, the business was over and he was once again sitting in the cab, Mr Beecham leant towards him and said, 'If you will excuse us we will be returning straight to Newcastle,' and paused before adding, 'Sir Joseph,' which remark drew the young man's attention to him.

For the first time a sensation pierced the numbness and it caused Joe's body to jerk and send a message to his brain that created the desire to shout, 'Don't call me that, because I'm not a sir. I never was and never shall be; you've left the sir in the grave.'

'Are you all right?'

'Yes, yes.' The words were clipped. 'You said you'd be leaving for Newcastle?'

'We'd like to make it before dark. With no lighting, the roads can be rather treacherous, you understand, and the weather is seeming to worsen.'

'Yes.'

There was a long pause before Joe said, 'I want to see you about . . . about business.'

'Yes, yes, anytime.'

'Tomorrow?'

Mr Beecham's eyebrows moved up slightly, and he said, 'Yes, if you wish, tomorrow. Say, eleven o'clock?'

'Very well.' Joe's reply was curt and Mr Beecham looked at this young man who, when he had last seen him just a few months ago, had appeared to him to be a schoolboy, immature for his age: but sitting before him now was a young man with no sign of immaturity on his countenance, for he seemed to have aged overnight, as it were. The eyes held a strange expression, and he guessed that even though their gaze was directed towards you their owner's mind was on something entirely different. He had certainly taken the tragedy badly. Doctor Nesbitt had suggested that the shock had perhaps temporarily deranged him, and up till this moment he had agreed with him, but suddenly now the young fellow seemed to know what he was about. Strange how he had given that start when he had addressed him as Sir Joseph. As yet he wasn't used to the title; indeed, he was perhaps the first to have addressed him as such. Even so, it had taken some little effort on his part, for here was this relatively obscure relation who had fallen into an estate, which, although small, was of no mean value, and he had fallen into it by a series of dead men's shoes. And that was putting it plainly. As fate had a habit of doing, it had played what he termed a rather dirty trick for although Martin and his father before him had both found the running of the estate anything but easy as far as money was concerned, this young man would be better off than either of them, for Martin had only within the last year taken out two very large policies on his life, the second when he knew he was going to be married. He wondered if the young man was aware of this. Well, he would be tomorrow morning.

By right and custom, he himself and James here should be going back to the house for the reading of the will, but this very new Sir Joseph had made it evident yesterday that he wanted no reading done in the house and that he would let them know when he wanted the matter dealt with. Well,

141

he had now let them know, and tomorrow morning he'd be interested to see what his reactions were.

'So there it is.' Mr Beecham placed the last sheet of stiff paper on top of a number of others and raised his gaze again to Joe, who was sitting opposite to him, and continued, 'There is no obstacle to your inheritance, as I can see. The insurance company, in due course, will settle the policies. These were a very fortunate investment.' He coughed, then went on, 'They won't make you entirely independent, but they will ease any worry about the maintenance of the house and estate. And as time goes by, your staff will likely decrease, for the age limits of call-up will rise. You have two men there under forty, isn't that so?'

'Yes . . . Yes.' Joe straightened his back against the wooden chair, at the same time reaching out and placing one hand flat on the edge of the long polished table and, looking across at Mr Beecham and James Holden, who sat by his side, he said slowly but firmly, 'I have no intention of . . . of living in the house after today. I've volunteered for the Air Force. And should I survive the war, I won't live there even then. But I wish to leave the control of the estate in your hands as sort of legal guardians. You will pay whatever staff have to be kept on to keep the house and grounds in order and . . . '

'But . . . but—' Mr Beecham leant forward over the desk now, his hand on the blotter in line with that of Joe's, and he said two words: 'Your mother?'

Joe now withdrew his hand from the desk and, rising to his feet, he looked down on to the upturned faces of the two men and said, 'My mother may remain in the house as long as she wishes, but the running of it, the accounts and such, I wish to leave in your control. Mary Smith will act as housekeeper and she will submit all bills to you.' He now watched both men rise simultaneously to their feet, and it was James Holden who, turning to his partner, said almost

142

in a whisper, 'Her . . . her allowance?' On this Mr Beecham, nodding now, spoke in a small voice: 'We will continue her allowance?'

'No.'

'*No?*'

'I said no. She can live in the house under those conditions or go. It's up to her.'

There was silence between the three of them for a moment as they returned each other's stare; then Joe said, 'If you don't wish to act for me I can make other arrangements.'

Mr Beecham's voice was stiff now as he replied, 'We have always acted for the house and I shall be happy to continue doing so. But, nevertheless, I must say that I find your orders rather disconcerting.'

Again there was silence between them, but as Mr Beecham stared at this young man, he remembered Martin hinting that his aunt kept the young boy on a tight rein; and he also went further back and recalled Arthur's confidence and how he had once described his sister-in-law as a frantic leech. Perhaps the young man had something on his side after all. But his measures were definitely drastic, smacking somewhat of retaliation.

'Good-day and thank you. One thing more, when you write to me, would you be kind enough not to use the . . . the title. In fact, I wish to disclaim it.'

The two older men made no reply to this, and neither of them moved towards the door to open it; nor did they say 'Good-day . . .'

Joe walked out of the offices into the thick driving snow. The fact that he turned his collar up against the seeping cold indicated that his numbness had been penetrated, yet he was unaware of it.

He was well on his way to the station when he paused and looked up towards a building, and he saw in his mind's eye Carrie running up the steps, and he recalled her voice saying,

143

'Oh! why must you keep on about that.' The word 'that' to which she was referring was love.

How long ago was it? Days or years? Had he ever loved anybody? Yes, he had loved Martin and Harry and his Uncle Arthur. He seemed to love people more when they were dead. But no, he had indeed loved them when they were alive. But there was nobody left to love now, and that was a good thing. Never, never again in his life would he say he loved anybody, for love was a destroyer, love was a madness that turned people into fiends and devils. He was going back now to confront one, one who supposedly did what she did out of love, and strangely he was no longer afraid. When your whole being was overflowing with loathing and hate there was no room for fear.

He said to Mary, 'Where is she?' not, 'Where is my mother?'

'Up in her room, Mr Joe . . . '

Mary was finding it difficult to change her way of addressing this new master. She had never yet addressed him as Sir Joseph, because somehow he didn't look like a sir; he didn't, in her eyes, fit the title; he was too young. Yet she had to admit he had changed over the last few days. By! he had that, and in more ways than one. She didn't like to own up to the fact that she now stood a little in awe of him, and she had never felt like that with either Mr Martin or his father before him because, in their own ways, they had both been free and easy.

Leaving Mary staring after him, Joe ran up the stairs, crossed the gallery, and went straight to his mother's bedroom. He didn't knock, but paused for a moment before opening the door.

She was sitting by the window at a little table she used as a writing desk, and she jerked round as he entered the room, but she didn't rise. Neither did he move from where he was standing, just inside the door, for almost a minute;

and when he did, he came quickly to the side of the table and stood within an arm's length of her.

Again they looked at each other in silence, and then he said very slowly, 'I've been to see Beecham and Holden. I've made arrangements with them how the estate is to be run. You, Mother, may stay or go, but you'll have no control of any of the affairs, either outside or inside the house. You can eat free and sleep free, but that's as far as your privileges will extend, ever. Do you understand?'

He watched her mouth fall open, then he saw her upper lip twitch and her eyelids flutter; then she muttered, 'No! no! you can't do it.' Her words were scarcely audible.

'I've done it . . . Will you stay?' He bent towards her now. 'You'll have plenty of company: three dead men and a woman.'

They were staring into each other's eyes now, both mouths agape. 'You fixed the car, didn't you; Vanessa Southall's car? You didn't expect Uncle to be in it . . . And then Martin was going to marry, wasn't he?' His voice was no more than a faint whisper now but it was as if his words were spraying vitriol on her face, because she tossed her head from side to side as if throwing off the spray. 'You couldn't bear the thought, could you, of that girl, that nice young girl, being mistress here? You told yourself it was for me, all for me.'

'It was, it was.' Her lips mouthed the words but no real sound came from them.

'You thought he was on his own, didn't you? You didn't count on Dick being so conscientious that he wouldn't let Martin watch alone.'

He put out his hand towards her now but didn't touch her, saying, 'Don't faint; it won't help you any because I'll only revive you with a jug of cold water and make you listen to the finish.

'Where have you hidden the gun? Where have you put it, eh? I know every gun in that room. I used to help Martin

145

clean them. But the police never thought to ask if there was one missing, because the lady of the house was fast asleep in bed, wasn't she? And there was only the maidservant and me. They could even have suspected me had they not found the two sets of footprints in the soft snow right up to the very hedge where Martin was hiding. The poachers had already been and got away with their spoils; or when they heard the shots, they made off. We'll never know, will we? But you know something, Mother?' His face was hanging over hers now. 'I could commit murder at this very minute. I have a great urge to throttle you, but that would prove I'd inherited your madness and I want no trait of you to show in me, ever. Ever!' He shouted the last word; then his voice dropping again, he said, 'The very smell of you nauseates me; you stink of death.' Now he drew himself upwards and stepped back from her, and it seemed to give her space to breathe, for she drew air into her lungs and for the first time she spoke, almost whimpering now: 'I . . . I didn't do it. It's . . . it's you who are mad. And . . . and you can't leave me like this, with nothing . . . My allowance.'

'You have no allowance. I've told you the terms: you are bed and board, as the saying goes, nothing more. And let me tell you this: should you in any way try to get in touch with me, even go to the partners and ask for my whereabouts, I swear before God—' He now raised his hand in a dramatic fashion and paused before he added, 'See, I'm taking an oath. I swear before God that I'll expose you for what you are: a four times murderess.' He took another step backwards and stared at her for a long moment before saying, 'This is the last time I'll ever look on you willingly.'

'Joe! Joe!' Her voice was cracked, coming like a broken note from a rusty instrument; and again she appealed to him as she watched him move towards the bedroom door. 'Come . . . come back a minute. Oh Joe. Joe.'

He stopped with the door handle in his hand and quietly said, 'Yes, I'll come back some day when you are gone and I'll find where you've hidden the gun, for you wouldn't have dared take it outside this room, would you? And this—' he moved his arm slowly to the side as he was about to add, 'This is going to be your grave,' but he stopped, for two reasons; the words sounded melodramatic, like those that might be used in an amateur play, and this was no amateur play; the second reason was that he felt sick.

He was stumbling as he walked across the landing. There was no sound from behind now, and he leant against the bannisters for a moment, his upper body swaying over them, and his stomach began to heave. She was insane. His mother was insane, yet she looked so normal, frail and normal. But she really was insane, mad. And he was her son, he was the son of a mad woman. What was in her was in him. No! No! He was running down the stairs.

Without stopping in the hall to put on an outer coat, he wrenched open the front door, ran over the terrace and down the steps. It was as he dashed along the drive that Mick Smith saw him. Mick was walking slowly, a haversack and gas mask hanging from his shoulder. He was on his way back to Newcastle, but when he saw Joe racing across the field that bordered part of the drive, he paused a moment before deciding to follow him. He didn't run but hurried in the same direction, and he kept him in view until Joe disappeared into the belt of woodland. When he himself entered it he couldn't see him ahead or on either side, although in most places the bracken and undergrowth was flat.

It was as he was about to emerge from the far end of the wood that the figure on the ground brought him to a standstill. Putting down his gas mask and haversack at the side of a tree, he walked slowly forward; then dropping on to one knee, he placed his hand on Joe's shoulder, and the contact brought the younger man round with a start.

147

'What is it, lad?'

'Oh, Mick! Mick!' It was an agonised cry. And then he was lying face downwards again, his knuckles pressed into his mouth, trying to smother the fearful sounds that were erupting from his being.

When the tears sprang from his eyes and nose and his body shook as with an ague, Mick put his arms about him and, pulling him round, cradled him as he would a child, saying, 'There! There! Let it up, an' out. It's over. It's over. It's over. What's done's done; nobody can bring them back.'

How long he lay against Mick he didn't know; he only knew that between the sounds he had been emitting and the wash of tears that seemed to have drained him dry, a voice within him had kept repeating: 'She killed your father, Mick; she killed your father. My mother killed your father.'

'I'm sorry,' was what he said, however, apologising for his tears.

'Nothing to be sorry for; it's the best thing that could have happened. You'd likely have been sorry if you hadn't, 'cos you've been on the verge of snapping. I've seen that. I wanted to talk to you, but I couldn't get through to you somehow . . . Anyway, what are you going to do now? Have you thought?'

Joe had hitched himself into a sitting position against the bole of a tree, and as he wiped his face he answered, 'I'm . . . I'm leaving today; I've joined up.'

'Oh.' Mick shook his head. 'Oh, well. What you in?'

Joe looked at the blue overcoat Mick was wearing and said, 'Same as you, the RAF.'

'Flying?'

'Signals – wireless-mechanic.'

'It's a tough life, mind.'

'I'll survive.'

'Yes, of course you will.' Mick nodded his head reassuringly. Then glancing at his watch, he said, 'Come on, get up out of that; I've got to be away, my train goes at four o'clock.'

Joe got to his feet and he stood with his head bent as Mick retrieved his things; then slowly he joined him, and together they walked back through the wood, silent now, until they reached the drive. There, holding out his hand, Mick said, 'You'll be all right now. And after all, perhaps joining up was the best thing you could do; you'll be among people. And who knows, but we might bump into each other . . . eh? Good . . . goodbye, Joe.'

'Goodbye, Mick. And thanks. Not only for now, but for everything; all the help you've always been to me.'

Mick stared at him for a moment, then again he said, 'Goodbye.' And Joe answered 'Goodbye', and they parted.

As Joe walked away he felt that he had said goodbye to the last phase of his youth, and that his storm of weeping had swept him into manhood and away from all connection with the woman back in that room. Yet he felt like someone entering a foreign country without knowing anything about the language.

PART THREE

Maggie

1

She was standing in the wings, leaning against a post that supported a wooden framework, which in turn held up a number of backcloths. She was just five feet tall, and fat. The Marie Lloyd costume she was wearing: buttoned boots, feather boa, black-straw, flower-trimmed hat, gave her the appearance of a child dressed up as an adult. She had full view of the stage and of the three female impersonators, kicking up their legs in a dance, the rhythm of which had gone a little awry.

She turned her head slightly as a voice behind her said, 'If those idiots don't come off soon they'll get booed. Five hundred rookies to choose from and that's the best they can turn out. Thank God for ENSA. What do you say, Lemon?'

Maggie LeMan lifted her shoulders slightly and smiled as she said, 'They're enjoying it, anyway.'

'They're not out there to enjoy themselves; bloody fools.'

The man now bent his long length down towards her and said quietly, 'You tired, Lemon?'

As she turned her face towards him there was a twinkle in her round brown eyes and a touch of sarcasm in her tone as she answered, 'No, sergeant, no; I've only been up since half-past six. I think I've sat down twice since then, because

153

one has to eat . . . And what is it now?' She turned round and looked at the brass-dialled clock sitting starkly on a red brick wall to the side of them and added, 'Only half-past eight.'

For answer he pushed her in the shoulder, and when she almost tipped over the bird cage at her feet his other hand came out and, steadying her, he laughed down into her face as he said, 'Sarky little bitch, aren't you? If your figure could match the length of your tongue you'd be over in Hollywood. 'Oh—' The smile slipped from his face as he said, 'I meant well. What I mean to say is . . . Oh' – he jerked his big head to the side – 'I never open me mouth but I say something.'

She flapped her hand at him. 'Don't let that worry you, Sergeant. If I got on me high horse every time somebody hinted that I wasn't like Betty Grable, I would have ridden to hell long before this.'

The sergeant was silent for a moment; then unconsciously taking his tactlessness a step further, he said, 'I always say it's a bloody shame, you with a voice like you've got. You should be in front of one of the big bands. When you hear some of those squawkers and what they get.' He bent towards her again, saying now, 'Have you ever thought of applying to join a NAAFI concert party? They're sending them overseas I hear, like ENSA . . . Oh, but' – he pulled a face – 'God's truth, I wouldn't suggest you join ENSA, not after some of the stuff we've seen here.'

Maggie LeMan kept her eyes rivetted on the occupants of the stage for a moment, where they were bowing and making the best of the half-hearted appreciation now being shown by clapping punctuated with cat-calls; then, slowly leaning to the side, she picked up the bird cage as she said, 'What do I want with a concert party? I wouldn't leave Madley if they offered me my own travelling dressing-room. Why, who in his right senses would leave here, sergeant? It's home from home.'

154

He pushed her again and smothered a deep laugh as he said, 'I don't think they'd let you go anyway, Lemon. Oh, my God! look at those silly buggers, they're going back to take an encore. Why doesn't someone throw a hand grenade?'

As the three impersonators left the stage they, too, were laughing, and it was evident, as Maggie had observed, that they had enjoyed themselves. Their painted lips were wide, and they continued to push up their false busts as they went past.

The sergeant muttered a deep oath, and Maggie remarked, 'If you don't think well of yourself, nobody else will. . . Are you going to announce me, sergeant, or am I going straight on?'

'OK, Lemon. Those silly buggers have got me goat.'

The sergeant marched to the middle of the stage and when, using what he called his stage expertise, she heard him say, 'Now I give you three guesses who comes next,' there followed ribald suggestions from different parts of the hall.

As the hubbub subsided he cried, 'Miss Maggie LeMan, our own Lemon!'

She watched him walk sideways towards the other end of the stage, his arm outstretched in her direction. The piano struck up *My Old Man Said Follow The Van*. She stood poised for a moment, stretched her mouth wide, licked her lips, moved her shoulders from side to side, then let her body sway, waited for the chorus to finish and the verse to start and she went on.

As she assumed her drunken pose and shambled towards the centre of the stage, she was deafened for a moment by the clapping and the shouting; and different names came to her ears, all meant for her: 'Good old Lemon! Good old Suck-it-and-see. Maggie McGee!'

She waited. The pianist softened his key. It seemed that he had stopped playing. She looked over the packed hall, from the front seat where sat Group Captain Peasmarsh and his

Wing-Commanders, through the different grades, all merged into a dusty blue mass dotted with white blobs.

She kept up her swaying motion, her mouth in a silly grin, until there was silence; and then she began to sing. Her voice, clear and pure, soared up to the roof of the theatre, and when it picked up the words of the chorus of 'My old man said follow the van. . .', no one in that vast hall joined in, they just listened. And not a few thought it was a kind of desecration to use a voice like that in uttering such common words:

My old man said 'follow the van,
Don't dilly dally on the way.'
    Off went the van with my home packed in it,
I walked behind with my old cock linnet,
But I dillied and dallied, dallied and dillied,
    Lost the van and don't know where to roam.
You can't trust the specials like the old-time coppers,
When you can't find your way home.

When she had finished, the applause was deafening; as she made her exit there were cries of 'More! More!'

The sergeant and a young NAAFI girl were standing waiting for her. They ripped off her hat, her feather boa, her coat; then she was unbuttoning her shoes and stepping into slippers. As she smoothed down her straight black hair over her ears the girl pulled her skirt straight and tucked her blouse into the back, and she said to her, 'Thanks, Peggy.' Then turning her head, she glanced up at the sergeant, and with definite bitterness in her voice, said, 'I'll never do that again. I hate that song, and the rig-out.'

'I don't blame you.' The girl Peggy nodded at her. 'Not struck on it meself. It isn't for you; it's a common kind of thing, cheap. Go on. Go on. Listen to them.'

When she reappeared on the stage it was to look over a sea of smiling faces and to listen to the chant now of

'Macushla! Macushla!' The pianist struck and held a long opening chord, the hubbub died away. And now, her face straight, her lips seeming to quiver, she went into the song; and so beautiful was her rendering of it, so touching the cadences, so tender with longing the words, that she seemed transformed before their eyes: she was no longer Lemon, good for a joke or a bit of ribbing, for her voice cut through the façade of brashness, of insensitivity and coarseness that seems to become necessary to men in war.

'Macushla! Macushla! your sweet voice is calling,
Calling me softly again and again.
Macushla! Macushla! I hear its dear pleading,
My blue-eyed Macushla, I hear it in vain.

Macushla! Macushla! your white arms are reaching,
I feel them enfolding caressing me still.
Fling them out from the darkness, my lost love,
    Macushla,
Let them find me and bind me again if they will.

Macushla! Macushla! your red lips are saying
That death is a dream, and love is for aye.
Then awaken, Macushla, awake from your dreaming,
My blue-eyed Macushla, awaken to stay.'

As always when she sang this song her eyes were moist, and when she had finished the applause did not come immediately, but there was that magic moment of silence that sometimes links a performer and an audience. When the applause did come it was deafening, and she stood there unsmiling, though with her head bobbing up and down in acceptance of the appreciation.

As she left the stage there were again cries of 'More! Lemon. More!' and in the wings the sergeant said, 'Do

157

you feel like it, Maggie?' and she shook her head, saying, 'I couldn't, not tonight, Sergeant.'

'Good enough. Good enough. They've had more than their share. By!' – he patted her on the shoulder – 'that was something. It always is something. By!' He nodded at her now, and again said, 'By!' before turning and running on to the stage.

'Coming for a drink?'

'Thanks, Peggy, but I'm all in; I think I'll go to bed. Anyway, I've seen enough of that lot for one day.'

'Aw, come on. There's a new batch in, about fifty, they say, to fill up the last posting. I want to see if my dream man is among them.'

Maggie started to laugh, saying, 'If you couldn't find him among the five hundred there's less chance you'll find him among the fifty.'

'There's always hope in here.' Peggy Ryan dug her thumb in between her small breasts, then added, 'Betty and Rona have just gone over. Of course our Rona—' Peggy pulled a long face and assumed a refined tone as she went on, 'She'll be sweeping the counter with those eyelashes of hers in that demure virgin-like way, and the poor bods'll rush like lambs to the slaughter. And there she'll sort them out. But she'll want their pedigree before they get their hands on her knee. Did you ever know anyone like her? She's got ideas about herself, has our Rona, and her a mother's help, as she calls it, before the war hit her.'

'Well, she can afford to pick and choose, looking as she does.'

'But she's brainless.'

'She's got brains enough to know what she wants.'

'Well, come and see what she picks up tonight across the great divide . . . That makes me a bit peeved, you know: we can serve them, but not mingle with them on the other side. And by the way, we'll have to run for it; it's coming down whole water.'

Their running was impeded by the mass of men coming out of the main doors and scattering in all directions, and heads down, they made their way between them to the back of the Naafi and into the rest room, which was empty; and they were just in the process of taking off their wet top coats when the supervisor came in, saying, 'Oh, I'm in luck; I was about to send to the hut for help. Betty has scalded her foot and there's the last-minute rush on. Will you give a hand?'

They both glanced at each other before saying, 'Yes' together, and when the supervisor said, 'Oh, one will do,' Maggie on a tired laugh said, 'It's all or nothing.'

Within minutes they had gone into the kitchen, donned overalls and caps and joined the tall girl at the counter who was coping with an admiring queue.

After Peggy had been serving a while she muttered, 'Spotted a likely in the new wave, duchess?' and the blue-eyed blonde with the full-lipped mouth shook her head as she said, 'They all look married to me.'

'How can you tell?' Peggy Ryan asked between saying to an aircraftman, 'That's two teas, two wads and a Rizla. Tuppence ... fourpence ... tenpence altogether. Ta. Thanks.' And quite seriously, Miss Rona Stevens answered *sotto voce* in between her serving, 'Oh, it's in their eyes: kind of a troubled, searching look, like ... well, like something that's escaped from a cage.'

There was a concerted splutter from Maggie and Peggy in which Rona didn't join; instead, her expression quite humourless, she murmured, 'Well, you arsked,' and Peggy, mimicking her companion's refeened accent, said, 'Yes, I arsked and you h'answered, h'as you always do.'

Maggie was looking at the corporal standing at the other side of the counter as she said, 'Sorry, no sandwiches left; only wads, I'm afraid.'

'Good enough,' he answered. 'Oh, by the way, that was a good show you put on tonight, Lemon. You get better.'

Maggie smiled at him and nodded her thanks, until a jocular voice from the queue called, 'Squeezed some high notes out tonight, Lemon. Juicy. Juicy. Only Lemon left in the country.'

When another voice said flatly, 'Ha-ha-ha! That quip could get you recommended to the witless corps, brother,' the speaker put in, 'Oh, I was only pulling her leg. Lemon knows that. Don't you, Lemon?'

Maggie looked blankly at the face grinning at her from the queue, and as she pushed a cup of tea across the counter she said, 'You were saying?'

'I said I was only pulling your leg.'

'Corporal' – her voice was clear and could have been that of a schoolteacher reprimanding – 'I haven't much opinion of my legs, but I can assure you you are not the type of man I would allow within parade ground distance of them, let alone pull them.'

A roar went up from those near by and the corporal to whom Maggie had just handed the tea, muttered, 'Good for you. He never learns, does he?'

Maggie did not answer, but she thought: no, they never learn. If they were of a kindly nature they stayed that way, if they were narrow, tactless, or big-headed they stayed that way. People didn't change much. And most of them were blind, even the decent ones, for they never seemed to see below the skin. For a moment, even while she continued to dispense tea and wads, she fell into the void of loneliness that seemed forever gaping at her feet and from whose edge, time and again, she had to forcibly drag herself back if she wanted to survive.

It was ironical that the man she had just rebuked should be the only one who had shown interest in her as a woman during the fifteen months she had been on the station. She had lost count of the number of times she had slapped his hands from her body whenever he waylaid her outside. He

160

would start with her shoulders and move down to her hips, and no amount of disdain seemed to get through to him. It was unfortunate also that he wasn't much taller than herself. His body was thick-set, but his head was narrow and set close to his shoulders. Yet he wasn't a bad-looking man. Had his character been different she would have welcomed his attention. Yet if his character had been different he would have attracted an ordinary-looking girl. Almost constantly she longed to be like ordinary-looking girls and have a fellow, even if, like most attachments on the station, it was only a temporary affair. But she knew she would have to be a great deal more in need of male company to tolerate anyone like Corporal Billings.

'You're hard on him.'

She cast a withering glance at Peggy now, then whispered back, 'Poor soul. Then go and comfort him; he's all yours.'

As she was about to hand a cup to another airman, Peggy happened to jostle her arm and the tea sprayed on to the counter, splashing the man on the other side. And as he pulled his waist inwards she exclaimed, 'Oh, I'm sorry. I'll get you another.'

'It's all right.'

'No, give it here.' She pulled the half-empty cup towards her, and after quickly filling another she passed it to him, smiling at him, saying again, 'Sorry.' But he gave no answering smile. This caused her to look closely at him.

He was tall, near six-foot, and he had dark hair, black, and deep grey eyes. He was young, yet his face somehow gave off the impression of age. It wasn't that it was lined or rugged, it was the set of his jaw and the expression in his eyes. Her glance rested on him only for a matter of seconds, yet his face could not have registered more in her mind had she been staring at him for an hour.

He made no further remark but followed his companion towards a table, and she followed him now with her eyes.

161

'Clumsy clot! He must be one of the new batch; I haven't seen his dial before.'

'It wasn't his fault: it was yours, you nudged me.'

'Me!'

'Yes, you.'

'Well, if you say so, ma'am.' They both laughed quietly at this.

The rush over, Maggie drew in a long breath, and turning to the supervisor who was hovering in the background, she asked, 'All right if we go?'

'Yes. And thanks, Maggie; and you too, Peggy.'

Before leaving the counter Maggie glanced to where the tall one was sitting. He had spoken only three words but they had sounded different . . . nice. She was sensitive to voices.

When she went into the rest room she sat down for a minute while waiting for Peggy to come out of the lavatory. Resting her elbow on the table, she let her head fall on to her hand, and again she thought of voices. A voice was all she herself had, and she had inherited it from her mother. That was about all she had inherited. Her mother had had a beautiful voice both when she sang and when she talked. She could recall sitting listening to her. She always pronounced the ends of her words, particularly those ending in 'g'. Even when she was being reprimanded she had still loved to listen to her mother's voice. Voices were more expressive than eyes. Eyes could lie, but voices couldn't, not really . . . She could still hear her mother's voice saying, 'Don't sit looking at me like that, child; say something.'

'What shall I say, Mother?'

'Anything, anything that will give the impression that you can think. Do you understand me, child? You will have to think: the only thing that will get you by in life is your mind because you are not presentable in any other way. You understand that, don't you?'

'Yes, Mother.'

162

'So you must use your brains, because you're not stupid, you know, you're calculating, too calculating. I have found that out. That's why your father gets annoyed with you. You understand that?'

'Yes, Mother.'

'You are nine years old and you are going to be sent away to a good school, and you must take advantage of all they teach you. You understand?'

'Yes, Mother.'

'I have had to persuade your father to fall in with my wishes on this matter. It wasn't easy, and it is going to cost a great deal of money, and business is not at all bright at the moment. People are not wanting good furniture. The big houses are selling up; they are in as much dire distress financially as the working classes. There is little call for antique furniture. So you can understand what a sacrifice it is your father is making in sending you to this school. I have also indicated to the headmistress that you take singing lessons. You have a voice, though what use it will be to you I don't know. Oh . . . oh, go to your room, child . . . '

She never got to the expensive school. Her mother was killed in a train accident and her father, without looking at her, for he very rarely looked at her, told her that she would continue at the local school. This she did until she was fourteen. It was in that year her father married again. Perhaps he couldn't stand the thought of her being in the house all day, even though they rarely met; and never, never since her mother died had they eaten together.

The new stepmother did not take to her, and yet she could have for she, too, was plain and had little to recommend her except that she had a business head and she knew about antiques and was very good at sales.

Maggie had made herself useful to her stepmother by running the house, and yet continued to make herself scarce. In a way, the pattern of her life was much the same as during

163

the years following her mother's death: she ate alone and as soon as she heard her father's key in the door she went upstairs to her room.

She was seventeen when her life changed.

She met her aunt for the first time and was invited to spend a holiday with her. She knew that her father had two sisters, although he never kept in touch with them. They were common people. So much her mother had told her about them. She had recognised that her father, too, was common, but that he was a good imitator: from the time he had taken up with her mother, who was from the middle class, he had aimed to act accordingly.

But as common as his sisters were, the one who had died had become quite wealthy through a progressive small business. She left no will and was unmarried, so because her nearest relatives were her brother and sister, they shared her estate.

Her Aunt Elizabeth lived in a small house in the depths of the country near Hereford, and as she herself had never in her life been outside of Birmingham, the journey was like visiting a foreign country.

She was to stay a fortnight. At the end of the fortnight she wrote to her father, saying she wasn't coming back. She received no reply; nor had she heard a word during the five years that had passed since, and she didn't know to this day if he was alive or dead, and she didn't care.

She had never known what love and tenderness were until she met her Aunty Lizzie, and she knew that no one in the world would ever love her like that woman did; nor would she love anyone else. In any case she would never get the opportunity. It wasn't only because she was fat, and it wasn't only because she had no height, and it wasn't only because she was plain, it was because she was a combination of all three.

'What's the matter; you falling asleep, Maggie? You all right, you're sweatin'?'

She took a handkerchief and rubbed it across her brow and her eyes.

'You cryin?' Peggy's voice was a whisper. 'What's the matter?'

'Crying? No!' The tone was scornful. 'Me crying! Look, let's get out.'

They had just turned the corner of the NAAFI building on their way to the public road that ran through the camp when they bumped into two airmen. There followed the flashing of their torchlights and muttered excuses and a voice saying with exaggerated courtesy, 'Sorry, ladies. So sorry.'

The dimmed light from Maggie's torch swept over the face of the sombre airman. He hadn't spoken, just stepped aside. Then he and his companion walked away in one direction and she and Peggy took the opposite through the camp.

'What d'you think it's going to be like, Joe?'

'It's hard to tell; we're not trainees any more.'

'Aye. We are now fully fledged instructors. Doesn't seem real, does it? AC1, Leonard Forbister, Wireless Mechanic Acting Corporal Instructor. I never thought to see the day, and all because I said I fiddled with wireless. Air-Gunner, that's how I saw myself: pop, pop . . . pop, pop, pop. And then having medals pinned on me. I still get jelly in the belly, Joe, when I stand up and face those bods.'

'Well, you certainly have no need. You put over your stuff better than most.'

'Well, it's only because you gave me a leg up at the beginning, explaining the theory and such.'

'That was the blind leading the blind, Len. I don't know how I got through myself, because I was no good at school.'

'Oh, that's all me eye, Joe. You know something, Joe? What puzzles me, I hope you don't mind me saying this, but I . . . I would have thought you would have gone for a

165

commission. They had you before the board at Cranwell, didn't they? But you never said what for. Wouldn't you like to be up there, Joe?'

'No, Len, no desire.'

'I'm not probing, you know, Joe, but we've been together months now, nine of them, in fact, and I know no more about you now than on the day we met, except that you come from the wilds of Northumberland. On the other hand, you know all there is to be known about me: born Bigley Road, Grays, in Essex, twenty-six years old, wife Alice . . . who says if she had met you afore me I wouldn't have had a look-in — and she only saw you from a distance.' He now pushed Joe on the shoulder, and Joe said, 'You're a very lucky man having a wife and a mother who like each other, besides doting on you.'

'Aye, yes, I suppose you're right, Joe. And I miss them both, particularly Alice. She's a spanker, is Alice . . . Speaking of spankers, what do you think a woman feels like who's been born stumpy and fat and who looks as plain as a pikestaff, like that little one we bumped into back there. She was on the stage, remember? Must be pretty tough for them when they look at other lasses.'

'She had a beautiful voice.'

'Oh aye, granted, but that won't get her very far in life, not as she stands.'

'I don't know; you forgot what she looked like as you listened to her. And I think most of them there did, too: she seems popular with them.'

'Oh aye, I would say she was popular: anybody they can get a laugh out of is popular with thick-headed rookies . . . By the way, what do you think of the WO?'

'He seems decent enough, but we'll know more tomorrow.'

'Phew! it's a snifter.' Len pulled the collar of his great coat up over his ears, then added, 'I hope they've got that stove going. But then I don't suppose it'll matter much with twenty of us in there; our combined breaths'll be enough to give us a steam bath. That's when we get there. Number eight, isn't it?'

'Yes, the next block, I think.'

They had left the path and turned up by the side of the long Nissen hut when Len paused and, half turning to Joe, he said, 'You know, you still didn't answer my question earlier on information concerning one Joseph Jebeau. I don't even know if you have a mother or father, or whether they made you up in a test tube. And by the way, that's another thing. I read today about someone prophesying there'll be such a scarcity of blokes after this war that they'll be injecting the women. It's a fact. It's a fact.'

Joe walked on towards the door of the hut. As usual, Len had side-tracked himself, but what would his reaction have been if he had satisfied his curiosity and said, 'Yes, I have a mother: she is now living alone in a manor house in Northumberland,' and had gone on to tell him why. He wouldn't have believed it, of course; he'd likely have thought he was mad. And there were times now, even amidst the hubbub of men, when the numbness reared its head again and made him think that eventually it would take over and he'd descend into silence, cold unthinking silence. Strangely, the prospect didn't frighten him as much as daily living did.

167

2

'Look, Joe; for the last time, why don't you come home with me, if only to prove to Alice you're still on the station. She's getting suspicious now, and she's saying, "You don't mean Josephine, do you?" As you know, it's no palace, but it's home, and she'll make you welcome. And Mum will an' all. And she's a damn good cook.'

'I'm sure she is. And what I'm also sure of is she won't want to see me. Your leave's short enough. What's forty-eight hours and a good part of it taken up on the train! It's very good of you, Len; but don't worry yourself, I'm all right.'

'You're not all right. What's for you here? Cycling in the hills on your own or sitting in the NAAFI! Look Joe—' Len leaned towards him from where he was sitting on the side of his bed and, lowering his voice, he said, 'I don't want to probe, and I know I've said this before, but I . . . I feel bound to bring it up again. You must have somebody, a young fellow like you; you say you weren't brought up in a home. Well, you wouldn't be, would you, with your education? So isn't there anybody you want to go and see?'

Joe smiled tolerantly at the man who had made himself his friend. In the ordinary course of events he would have said Len Forbister wasn't the kind of man to associate with

him. It wasn't that he was a good few years older than him
or that, like Mick, he had been a working chap. He had
been very fond of Mick, and of his company. But Len wasn't
Mick: there was no deep depth in Len; he was an honest,
open fellow who was a father of two children and had a
good wife, by the sound of her. But when that was said, all
was said. Nothing about Len was compatible with anything
in himself. And yet he had grown fond of him, and he
had to admit to himself that when Len was away from
camp he missed him. It was then that the feeling of utter
boredom would assail him and he would be driven to join
the crowd for the buses and the queue for a seat in the
pictures in Hereford to pass the Saturday afternoon away.
On Sundays, unless the weather was really rough, he rode
out into the hills. On these journeys, however, he hadn't been
fortunate, as some of the fellows in the camp had been, in
finding a cottage or a house where they were invited in to
tea, which often meant, so he understood, eggs and chips or
even bacon, particularly if it was a farmhouse. And he had
no inclination to spend his off-duty time working in the jam
factory that ran cheek by jowl with the camp; he wasn't in
need of extra money.

He also knew that there was a cure for his loneliness.
He wasn't blind to the fact that he only had to say, 'What
are you doing tonight?' and he needn't be alone anymore.
There was that tall girl in the NAAFI. She had looks too.
But he doubted if he could have stood her voice for a
full evening; it grated on him when she chatted him up
over the counter. Now if she'd had the voice of the little
dumpy one they all took the mickey out of, Lemon, as
they called her, he just might have put the question to
her. Yet what would have been the result? What would
they say about a fellow who didn't make a pass at them,
for to make a pass you had to feel something? Well,
he felt nothing, not in that way, and he doubted if he

ever would again. He was dead inside. All except his head was dead.

It was impossible at times to imagine that he had been in this camp all of eighteen months. He had seen men come and go; squads of them went through their training and came out bright-eyed WOP-AIRs thirsting to get on to an aerodrome to finish their training and then into action. But here and there some found action on this very camp, and didn't live to tell the tale. They'd be taken up in a trainer plane by a pilot who had survived the Battle of Britain and, as Len put it, was zonked out with combat. In showing off to the raw recruits he might even throw the small plane into such daring bankings or dives that it couldn't be manoeuvred out of. If they were lucky his and his recruit's parachute might have time to open. But only yesterday one of his own batch hadn't been so lucky, and it was when the news broke in the camp that he knew he could still feel emotion. And Len had witnessed his reaction and this had prompted Len to do what he had said he wouldn't do again, and that was to try and persuade him to accompany him home.

Hitching himself over to sit beside Joe on the edge of his bed, Len now persisted, 'You must have some place, you know.' And after a pause, he went on, 'I sometimes think you've got something on your mind, Joe. If it would help any, I'm a good listener. I know I'm a good chatterer' – he grinned – 'but I can keep my own counsel, and yours an' all, if you want to talk.'

Joe turned and looked into the kindly face as he said, 'I really haven't any family, Len. The only relative I now have . . . well, I became estranged from her.'

With his head to one side Len stared at him for a moment, then asked, 'No friends or acquaintances, like?'

'Oh . . . oh yes. But they are scattered.'

'In the Forces?'

'Er . . . yes, mainly in the Navy.' That was a good place to put them: you didn't know when ships were docking these days.

'Well, haven't your friends any families or . . . ?' Len now swung his head to the side. 'I'm probing I know, but, man, I'm concerned for you.'

'Well, don't be, there's no need. If it'll make you happy, I'll take a couple of WAAFs out . . . officers.' He laughed now. Then assuming the voice of a certain discip. WO that neither of them liked, he clicked his heels together, gave an imitation of a salute and said, 'Corporal Joseph Bartholomew Jebeau caught making advances to a female of superior rank, sir.'

'What have you got to say for yourself, Jebeau?'

' 'Twas an irresistible impulse, sir; couldn't stop myself.'

'That's good! That's good!' Len was thumping him on the arm now with his fist. 'You could get on ITMA. Do Colonel Chinstrap . . . But, on second thoughts, I don't think you would do on ITMA. But I can see you on the Brains Trust.'

'Brains Trust!' Joe got to his feet and cast a disparaging glance down towards Len as he said, 'Whose place will you put me in, Joad's? or Huxley's?'

'Oh, they're not so clever; they read up the stuff, man.'

'Yes, and they've been reading up the stuff for years. Oh, Len.' He shook his head. 'Go on, get yourself packed up and away. And remember me to Alice.' He bent down towards Len now and pulled a face at him. 'Tell her that I do exist and that I'll see her one day.'

'She won't believe me.' Len now rose from the bed and began his packing, while Joe, picking up his cap, looked at him for a moment, then said, 'Well, be seeing you.'

'And you, mind how you go up them there hills.'

'I will.'

Joe walked down the length of the hut, between the beds, where here and there men were sprucing up ready to grab a few hours' freedom away from the camp. With the exception

171

of two others and himself, all the men in this section were married. It was odd when he came to think about it, but every now and again one or two of them would be posted, yet the five men who had accompanied him from Cranwell, and whose beds were at the far end of the hut, were still here. Jack Bisley, Sam Temple, Amos Bernstein, Angus McBride and, of course, Len. Even Warrant-Officer Gilbert, who had arrived just a week before them, was still here. Sometimes he longed for a posting just to see different surroundings. He wasn't so much concerned about the men or this particular job, because his work as a corporal instructor was to teach his squads the theory and practice of wireless communication, and especially the operation of the transmitters and receivers used in aircraft. No, it wasn't this that got on his nerves, but the monotony of his surroundings, the long, long road through the camp, the huts going off here and there, the airfield dotted with little planes, looking like toys, the new hall that was used for entertainments, pictures and the church services, standing out like a sore thumb.

He turned up a side path to go into the NAAFI. There were very few people in the building and no one at the counter. The little dumpy girl was one of two serving. He was glad to know that the tall languorous one wasn't about.

'A cup of tea, please.'

She poured out the tea, and as she pushed it across the counter to him he handed her the penny. Then she spoke, 'You must be enjoying this war,' she said.

'What?' He put his head forward as if he hadn't heard her clearly. He had heard her but he didn't understand what she meant. And she repeated, 'I said, you must be enjoying this war.'

'What makes you think that?'

'Well, you never seem to be dashing off here, there and everywhere like the rest. I've got the idea you've fallen in love with the camp.'

172

He smiled at her now as he said, 'Yes, you're right, I do love it.'

'Aha! Aha! I thought you did.' She took a cloth and wiped down the counter. 'And you always look so happy.'

He closed his mouth and ran his tongue round the inside of his lips. She was pulling his leg. She always gave as much as she got, more, he should say. She was always quick on the uptake but she had never got at him before.

'Brought up in Barnado's were you. Like the feeling of a large family?'

'Yes' – his face wore a serious expression – 'I was left on the doorstep in the proverbial washbasket.'

'The what?' She seemed to be straining her head and shoulders over the counter, and he repeated, slowly and emphatically, 'The proverbial washbasket; you know.'

'Oh.' She nodded. 'Oh, yes, the proverbial washbasket. Well, isn't that funny, the same thing happened to me. But it wasn't the proverbial basket, it was just an ordinary laundry one.'

Suddenly they laughed together, and he looked at her, really looked at her, for the first time, and he saw that she had a lovely set of teeth. All her good points seemed to be in her mouth, her voice, her singing and her quick wit, and he noticed, too, something different about her: she'd had her hair waved. Previously she had worn it flat, practically plastered down on her head, until it looked as if it was almost painted on her scalp, like that of a wooden doll. Her cap was set well back on her hair today too. For a moment he wondered about her, what she thought of all the ribbing and chipping that she received almost every day in this place. The fellows never seemed to rib the other NAAFI girls very much: they joked with them, but not in the same way as they did with Lemon. And the answer came: she was like a break in the monotony, like a resident jester. At one time jesters were picked for their hunchbacks, or some deformity. But

173

she wasn't deformed, only dumpy. It was a shame, really, that she should be used as a butt, yet she didn't seem to mind; in fact, he thought she enjoyed it. And anyway, what was there for a girl like her? In civvy street she would have found it hard to find a fellow to chat with and so she likely considered the war a godsend.

He showed his surprise on his face now as she leaned still further over the counter and whispered, 'The sleeping beauty's at a loose end: she's off from three.' She nodded towards the door behind her.

For a moment he was taken aback as he realised she was so sorry for him she was arranging a date.

He leaned towards her and in a whisper he said, 'I don't think I'll waken her.'

She held his gaze for a moment; then, her lips pressed tight, she made a small laughing sound before saying, 'Not your type?'

'Not really . . . too thin.'

It was a backhanded compliment, the best he could do, and he straightened up and nodded to her before taking his cup from the counter and making his way towards an empty table.

He did not take long in drinking his tea but by the time he had finished it, he saw that she was no longer at the counter, her place having been taken by another girl. He went out thinking that, behind all her brusque banter, she was a kindly little soul. She seemed a thoughtful person, someone of like nature to Mary Smith, but with much more up top. Oh yes, Lemon had quite a bit up top, he should imagine, and all concealed under the cap and bells.

He cycled out of 3-Wing on to the Hay-on-Wye road that ran through the camp. He passed the technical section and 2-Wing, both looking oddly deserted, except for a figure here and there moving between the nissen huts and the NAAFI or the discip. buildings.

By the time he reached Tyberton, which was only three miles from the camp, he was sweating, for the sun was shining fiercely out of a clear sky. It was near the end of August, and for the last few days it had been like high summer. He had reached Blakemere, which was only two miles further on, when he pondered if he should take another direction and make his way to the river, but the thought that even this far out there'd be a number of people on the banks today, mostly youngsters, he guessed, swimming or playing the usual dangerous game of swinging out over the river on a rope attached to a tree branch, deterred him. He wasn't very fond of the river Wye, for its rocky crevasses had claimed too many young lives even during the short time he had been there.

Thinking of young lives, his mind jumped back to yesterday, when he had heard about young Harrington. He had been a recruit in his class, a bright young lad.

He knew now that he himself would never have made a flyer. Regulations said that instructors must go up periodically, but he was always glad when they touched down. And he wasn't alone amongst the instructors who felt this way: Jack Bisley, Sam Temple, and Amos Bernstein, they all admitted that they hated it; but Angus McBride and Len looked forward to their trips as if they were half-day school holidays.

It had come to him over the last year or so that there was only one thing that made him different from other men, and that was the weight he was carrying on his mind. It deadened his days and brought him upright in the night, running with sweat and fear, his arms held out clutching the gun with which he had just shot his mother.

When he set out today it had been his intention to make for the hills bordering the Golden Valley, but when he got

175

through Blakemere the sweat was dripping from his chin and the sight of a stream tinkling its way not three yards from the road automatically brought his legs off the pedals. He hadn't noticed it before because of the hedge growing along the side of the bank, but here, and for some way ahead, it was open to the road.

He laid his bike on the grass verge and went down to the water's edge. Kneeling down, he bent over and sluiced his face with handfuls of the surprisingly cold water. He did not immediately dry his face but knelt over the stream, looking down to where the sun was glinting on the pebbles, turning them momentarily into stars. His mind became still. This was the kind of moment when words formed into meanings and, when you transferred them to paper, they turned into poetry. He hadn't put pen to paper since the day before Martin died, and he doubted if he would ever do so again. But this was the moment when it should happen.

As he continued to gaze down into the sunlit water a sound intruded into his mind. If he had been alert to everyday things he knew he would have heard it sooner. He lifted one knee from the ground and turned his head slowly and looked up the slight incline to the path, and in his sun-blinded vision he saw a shape. It was a small broad shape dressed in blue and the face was topped by a straw hat. He had the vague impression that the face was of an oriental and was beautiful in a strange way.

As he took his handkerchief out and wiped away the water that was still dripping from the front of his hair, a voice said, 'I wouldn't drink that if I were you; the cows wash in it just round the corner.'

He twisted himself to his feet and looked in amazement at the girl standing above him. He had recognized the voice and he had her in focus now. She was wearing a slack blue dress and a straw hat pushed to the back of her head.

176

'Oh! Hello, there.' He sounded embarrassed, as though he had been caught in some misdemeanour.

Having climbed the bank he looked down on her and smiled as he said, 'I didn't recognise you in civvies. Well, they make a difference . . . '

'Partly.'

He stared at her. What could one say to that? It was her habit of disparaging herself.

'I've never seen you along this way before,' she said.

'I've never been this way before. I was making for the hills, and hoping to come back through Peterchurch.'

'Well, you're on the right road, but I would say you had chosen the wrong day.'

'Yes, I've been thinking that myself.' He was smiling at her again. Then looking around, he said, 'Are you out walking?'

'Well, you could say that . . . compulsory walking, I'm looking for Simon, our dog. He's gone out on the razzle again.'

'Is he a labrador, a yellow one?'

'Yes, that's him. Have you seen him?'

'I passed one just as I was coming out of Blakemere.'

'Oh, that's where he's got to. Oh well, I needn't trouble: he'll be back. He's got a lady friend down there.'

'Do you live near here?' There was a surprised note in his voice.

'Yes, over there.' She pointed into the distance, and when he said, 'I never knew,' she answered on a small laugh, 'Well, why should you?'

Yes, why should he? It was a silly thing to say. He felt a heat rising to his face that wasn't caused by the sun. He was always awkward in women's company, girls' company. There had only ever been one with whom he had been at ease. He didn't think of her as often now, except perhaps on a long weekend when he was off-duty; the rest of the time he had things to occupy his mind.

177

'What?' he asked.

'I said, could you do with a cup of tea?'

He hesitated just a fraction of a second before saying, 'Well
. . . well, yes. Thank you.' And he immediately told himself
there was no compromise in accepting a cup of tea; RAF
men were invited into all kinds of homes in the district.

She was walking on ahead up the narrow path now, he
following behind pushing his bike, when he said, 'Your
people live here?'

'An aunt. She has a cottage.'

The word cottage conjured up in his mind the Smiths'
dwelling; but a few minutes later, when he saw what she
had called a cottage, he realised it was far removed from
the Smiths' dwelling as Screehaugh had been, in that it was
a substantially built house. Its side wall was covered with
the dead fronds of a massive wisteria; the front showed six
large windows, and the front door appeared to be at the end
of the house. The roughly cut lawn led right to the stone
doorstep and was bordered by a flower garden at one side
and a summer house at the other, beyond which was a yard
showing some outhouses.

The door of the house was open.

He paused in the doorway and watched her go into a dim
hall, calling, 'Hoo-hoo! Where are you?'

The voice that came back to him was unlike hers in tone
but matched it in substance, 'Where do you think I am?
Up the pole?'

She turned to him, smiling widely now, and beckoned him
into the hall. It was quite a large area for this type of house,
being all, he imagined, of sixteen feet square. He noticed,
too, that it was stone floored, and immediately he took in
the feeling of clinical cleanliness.

'I've brought a visitor.'

He didn't move from the middle of the hall, but watched
Maggie standing in a doorway to the right, and she turned

her face to him, laughing now as the voice from the other room came to him, saying, 'Male or female?'

'Male.'

'Thank God for that! Haven't seen a man for a week.'

Maggie now beckoned him towards her, and somewhat reluctantly he followed her along a short passage and into a long sun-lit kitchen, where a woman was standing at a wooden table mixing some ingredients in a bowl. On the sight of him she stopped immediately. Her mouth opened and shut; then looking at Maggie she said, 'You silly daft lump, I thought you were joking and it was Simon you had brought back.'

'Well, he'll bark for you if you ask him nicely, won't you?' She turned and looked up at Joe, and he, smiling now, said, 'I'm always willing to please.'

'This is my Aunt Elizabeth, otherwise Mrs Robson. And this, Aunt Lizzie, is Corporal Jebeau.'

It was the first time he had heard his name pronounced correctly since coming into the camp. He was generally called Jabbie or Joe-boy.

'I'm pleased to meet you, Corporal Jebeau.'

He was shaking hands now with the woman, who was the exact antithesis of her niece, being thin and bony; even her arms, showing bare where she had her sleeves rolled up almost to the armpits, looked fleshless.

'How do you do?'

'I do nicely, thank you. I bet you could do with a cup of tea? I've got a batch of scones in the oven; I must have known you were coming. You look hot; have you ridden all the way? Sit yourself down, or better still go into the sitting-room. That's it' – she waved them both away – 'get yourselves into the sitting-room, out of this.'

He found himself smiling widely as he went to obey her and for a moment he felt he had dropped into a home which was familiar to him. Then Maggie's fingers touching

179

his sleeve lightly stopped his departure as she said, 'Don't take any notice of her, sit yourself down there.' She pointed to a high-backed wooden chair, adding, 'If she makes you sitting-room company she cuts your rations.'

He hesitated for a moment as to what to do; then looking again at the woman at the table, who was now smiling at him, he sat down in the chair, and for the next ten minutes he listened to the banter between the two of them. There was no pause between exchanges; all the while their tongues wagged their hands worked, for the woman at the table went on making her cakes, while Maggie walked back and forth into and out of what he took to be a pantry at the far end of the kitchen, bringing out all that was necessary for a tea. She looked so different in the blue dress; still fat, but more like a schoolgirl might do, and she seemed as light on her feet as a dancer. There were things he consciously noticed about people which he brought to mind long after he had ceased to watch them, but now he noted for the first time that she had very small feet – they could have belonged to the oriental he had imagined her to be through the sun haze.

Also, strangely, he noted there was a similarity in the faces of the aunt and niece. Yet their features were as different as chalk from cheese. The woman at the table had, he should imagine, once been quite good-looking, even beautiful, whereas no one, not even with the kindest instincts, could attribute any beauty to Maggie's features. Yet looking from one to the other, he now realised where the similarity lay: it was in the eyes. But where the older woman's eyes lay in elongated hollows, the younger one's were round, lying almost flush with the unlined skin. Again he had the impression that she was a young girl, for there was a smoothness about her skin that one sees in the young before the face reaches the border of adulthood. Yet why, with such skin, such eyes, and that good mouthful of teeth, did she still appear so very plain? What constituted beauty? The bone formation, how each feature was set? He didn't know. All he did know at this moment was that it seemed a shame a girl such as Maggie here, with brains, because she was no fool, and a talent such as she had, should be encased in a body that held no appeal.

'Where are you from?' Maggie's Aunt Lizzie was asking.

'What?'

'It's the heat; you were nearly asleep, I think. Hurry up with that tea there, Maggie! I said, where are you from?'

'Northumberland.'

'Oh. I know Northumberland and all that district. My first husband was from those parts. I've been married three times. You wouldn't think so, would you? But anyway, how's one to tell that? And the strange thing about it is they were all orphans. Funny, that, isn't it? All orphans. Good job in the long run. He was from Hebburn, my first. Mouldy place, Hebburn. That's in Durham, though. But I went into Northumberland a number of times, to Hexham. Did you live anywhere near there?'

He swallowed deeply before he answered, 'Not far. Up . . . up in the hills.'

'Farmers?'

'Yes, sort of.'

'Sort of? Well, you are, or you aren't, laddie.'

'Well, in a very small way: chickens and pigs and things like that.'

'Oh, a smallholding, you mean?'

'Yes, yes, a smallholding.'

'Well, you've got it ready?' She was looking at Maggie now. 'Not before time. What about having it outside in the shade? I'm almost roasted, myself, in here.'

'Can I carry that?' He took the tray from Maggie, and she, picking up two plates from the table, said, 'Come on, I get sick of listening to her.'

181

They passed through the hall again; then he followed her across the lawn to where a rough wooden table was placed near the trunk of a large oak tree, to which was nailed an equally rough seat.

As Maggie took the things from the tray and set them on the table she said, 'I know what you're thinking: we're slightly barmy.'

'Not at all.'

'Oh, you needn't be polite; in fact, I would say to you' – she now paused with her hands on the table and stared up at him – 'please *don't* be polite. Imagine you're at home and you're not going back to that madhouse. That's what I do every time I'm home; because it *is* like a madhouse, isn't it, most of the time?' She was smiling quietly at him now; and equally quietly he answered, 'Yes, it is.'

She sat down and began to pour out the tea and, her voice still quiet, she went on, 'I don't suppose it's really so bad for you, instructing or teaching, whatever it is you do, but in the Naafi, amidst the clatter—' she now looked at him and her words were spaced as she went on, 'and the chaff and the ribbing; well, I sometimes think I have died and gone to hell, because that's what I think hell must be like; constant joking, especially when you hear the same thing repeated over and over again.'

As she handed him the cup of tea her tone changed: 'Not that I'm against joking, but everything in its place; when I'm here with Aunt Lizzie, we chaff each other, but . . . but not all the time.'

He was staring at her, amazed at the reaction her words were having on him; it was, in a way, as if she were suffering an agony similar to his own.

'Well, now, this is better.' The spell was broken by her aunt as she came across the lawn, devoid of her apron now, her long cotton dress flapping against her thin legs. 'There's a bit of a breeze coming up, I think. We could do with it. Likely have a storm tonight, shouldn't be surprised.' And as she sat down she added, 'Now tuck in; we're not short of a thing or two up here. Not that, mind' – she now wagged her finger in Joe's direction – 'she brings me anything.' The finger was now pointing at Maggie. 'She could, I know she could, but she won't. She's soft in the head. I know there's lads get eggs and butter and stuff from the farms, but everybody hasn't got farms, and I could take you to some cottages that are well supplied with butter, sugar and cheese and what have you, that's not from the farms.'

'Oh, shut up, Auntie.'

'I'm speaking the truth. The fiddling that goes on down there would set up an orchestra, and not one, but a couple of dozen.'

'Well, where did you fiddle the fat to make these scones, those tarts, and that sandwich cake?' Maggie was stabbing her finger at the different plates on the table, and her aunt wagged her head and pursed her lips before she said, flatly, 'I'm courting one of the airmen; he comes to Donald's farm.' She jerked her head backwards, and on this both Joe and Maggie burst out laughing.

'Think I'm past it?' She poked her head now towards Joe, and gallantly he now replied, 'I could never imagine you being past anything, Mrs Robson.'

'You're right, you know. I was a beauty in me day. Do you know that? Could take me pick, and I did. Oh' – she closed her eyes for a moment – 'I wish I had me life over again. Yet' – her voice became serious – 'I wouldn't want it to end anywhere else but here' – she now looked about her – 'with the hills behind me and the river at me feet, so to speak.'

During the silence that followed Joe experienced the most odd feeling, for he had the desire to reach out across the table and to take her hand: not Maggie's, but this woman's, the hand of this woman who would never see sixty again. Then he saw her face change and there was his mother staring at him,

183

and as if his hand had already been extended he felt himself jerking it back. So real was the sensation that his fingers slipped on the handle of the tea cup and when the tea spilt into the saucer he exclaimed, 'Oh! Oh, I'm sorry!' Then on an embarrassed laugh, he added, 'I'm not used to polite society.'

'Well, we're not polite society, lad, so tip it on to the grass and we'll pretend we're not looking. And we could do with some hot water. Will you get some, Maggie?'

Maggie hadn't reached the house door before Mrs Robson asked, 'You married?'

'No.'

'One of a family?'

'No. I . . . I'm the only one.'

'Your parents alive?'

Again he paused; then lifting the cup, he almost gulped at the tea before saying, 'No, they are both . . . dead.'

He became embarrassed when he found the woman's eyes tight on him. Then she was smiling, saying, 'Funny how I always run into orphans, isn't it? You known Maggie long?'

What did the question infer? He didn't know, and he almost stammered as he replied, 'We . . . Well, not really. Well, I see her in the Naafi quite a lot. My first acquaintance with her was when I heard her sing. She has a beautiful voice, really beautiful.'

'Yes, she has that. It should have taken her places, don't you think?'

Again he was forced to pause. 'Yes, I . . . I think it should.'

'She's a clever lass, you know; she doesn't only sing, but she plays the piano; composes a bit an' all.'

'Really?'

'Yes.' And without any lead-up she said, 'From what I gather some people take the mickey out of her down there because of her name, punning it like, and she being a bit fat. She didn't tell me, but I heard. By! if I . . . I ever heard anybody doing that I'd scalp them, I'd scalp the buggers.'

184

The word was said with such vehemence, yet at the same time sounded so funny, that he almost laughed. Fortunately he didn't, for what she said now was, 'There's no one likes a laugh more than I do, but there's a time and a place for everything. She was born small, she was born fat, and there's no denying that she's no beauty, but her face has got something. At times when I look at her it strikes me as it's got something; not beauty, but something that goes beyond it. And she's worth a thousand of your so-called beauties. By God! she is.' As her head wagged his embarrassment grew; then in a low tone she muttered, 'Here she comes. Now mind, don't say I ever mentioned this.

'Taken your time, haven't you? Heated it with candles, have you?'

'No, me flashlight.'

'I thought so. You're not eating.' She now pushed a plate of scones towards Joe, and he, taking one, said, 'I've already had two. They're lovely.'

'I never bake anything that isn't.' She now laughed as she added, 'And should you make a habit of coming here you'll soon learn I'm a very modest woman; hate self-praise.'

As he joined in with her laughter he felt a qualm of uneasiness as to what ideas she was getting into her head with regard to his visiting in the future. My! that would be something to cope with, if it got round the unit that he was going up to Lemon's place. Of all the girls he could have taken up with in the camp, she was about the most unlikely.

When the tea was over Maggie brought out two deck chairs from the summer house and after putting them up she pointed to one, saying, 'Make yourself comfortable, I'm going to help Aunt clear up. But before I go, let's get things straight, eh?' Her face was on a level with his; she stared at him for some seconds before she said quietly, 'You needn't be concerned that you might have started something; I've got no ideas that way. As my aunt would say, I happen to be a sensible lass.

185

And I won't suggest we ride back into camp together either, so sit yourself down there and relax, for underneath all your politeness, you're on edge.'

He knew his face was red to the roots of his hair and he stammered, 'O-oh now, now please.' He put out his hand towards her, but she waved it aside with a flick of her own, saying, 'Look, we both know what it's like down there, don't we? So let's leave it at that, shall we? And loosen your collar and tie; there's enough sweat on it to wash it.'

He had risen and now stood watching her go towards the side door. Such bluntness, such honesty, it was embarrassing; you weren't prepared for it, so you didn't know how to react. He wished . . . he wished he liked her. Oh well! He jerked his head at himself. He liked her, you couldn't help but like her, but he wished in this moment it was in him to more than like her. He wished he was big enough to forget that she was a fat young woman with nothing about her but her voice.

He sat down in the deck chair, loosened his collar and tie, then lay back and looked up into the dark coolness of the oak branches. For a moment he imagined he was in another world, a simple uncomplicated world: a world where there was no place down below in the valley where men were being prepared for war; that there was no place in Northumberland where a woman sat in a room all day with only her thoughts for company; that there was no one called Carrie Smith; that the world had dwindled and there was only this secluded garden and a secluded house, as had been said, with the hills to the back of it and the river at its feet and two women so unalike, yet alike: so understanding, so thoughtful of each other, and not only of each other, but of him. His head fell to the side; his cheek to the canvas of the deck chair, and his feet slowly slipped forward as he fell into a deep sleep.

He was aware of being awake long before he opened his eyes. At first he felt more relaxed than he had done for a long time.

In fact, he couldn't remember ever feeling like this. He lay in a sort of mental haze until a feeling of restriction just below his buttocks penetrated his still slumbering state. The pain increased and when he attempted to move his legs the right one went into an agonising cramp that caused his eyes and mouth to open simultaneously.

He pulled himself into a sitting position on the chair and began to rub his calf vigorously. Then, his head bent forward, he noticed that the shadows were long on the grass; in fact, there was but merely a streak of sunshine bordering the flower garden now. He reached out for his tie that was on the table. He didn't remember putting it there. He was on his feet now, turning up his collar, pulling the tie around his neck the while he looked towards the house.

He was about to move towards the back door when Mrs Robson appeared. As she made her way slowly towards him she said, 'You're awake then. If you had been dead drunk, you couldn't have slept deeper. Feel better?'

'I feel fine, but I'm very sorry. I . . . I never meant to fall asleep. It . . . it must have been the heat. What time is it? Oh!' He gave an embarrassed laugh, then looked at his wrist-watch, saying, 'No, it can't be ten past seven. Oh, I am sorry. Have I kept you in?'

'Kept me in? You mean, have you kept me from going out? Don't you . . . no, I rarely go down into the town at the week-ends. Too many of your lot in there: can't get moved. In fact, I don't go unless I'm forced. Maggie sees to most of my shopping. It's lucky she's stationed so close. Oh yes, that was a bit of luck. By the way, the bathroom's in the first door on the landing.'

'Oh, thank you.' He smiled at her, then went into the house.

Five minutes later, when he returned to the lawn, she was sitting with her back to the tree and, standing before her, he said, 'I don't know how to thank you for your kindness. It's

187

. . . well, to put it poetically, it's been like finding an oasis in a desert.'

'Well, lad, if that's how you think, you may come and drink any time you feel thirsty.'

His smile broadened as he said, 'Thank you, Mrs Robson; I might take you at your word.'

'Well, I'll expect you to. As I said, I'm never often out, and if you're a long way from home it's always good to have some place to drop in to. Not, mind you, that anybody else's house can come up to your own. That old song's right, you know: there's no place like home.'

His face was straight as, staring back at her, he said, seriously, almost stiffly, now, 'It all depends on the place you call home, don't you think?'

She did not immediately reply; her eyes narrowed and her eyelids blinked a number of times before she said, 'Yes, I suppose you're right . . . and no suppose about it, you *are* right. As you said, it all depends on the home you've left behind you, or were likely so damned glad to leave. And I'd like to bet there's quite a few of the blokes down there' – she jerked her head to the side – 'look upon this war as a godsend because it's given them a legitimate excuse to leave their shanties. A lot of the old sayings are damned silly when you apply them wholesalely, but we keep saying them because some clever bod wrote a song around them. We don't think . . . no, we don't think . . . Well now' – she rose to her feet – 'you're on your way. But don't forget you're welcome any time you like to come.'

He half turned from her looking towards the house, saying now, 'Is Maggie ready?'

'Ready and gone this good half hour since.'

'What!'

She had been walking away from him towards the path that led to the gate and she turned her head and said, 'Didn't want to disturb you; you looked so peaceful, asleep.'

188

He stood still as he recalled her plain speaking, and, his head hanging, he experienced a mixture of relief and a feeling that was most akin to shame. But there was no getting away from it; the overwhelming feeling was one of relief, because if they had ridden in together they would undoubtedly have been spotted.

'Goodbye, Mrs Robson.'

'Goodbye, lad.'

Her voice had a sad note to it and he knew that she was standing at the gate watching him as he rode away.

He again knew what it was to feel embarrassed when, on the Monday dinner time, he went into the NAAFI, and looking at her over the counter, he said, 'Hello there,' and she answered, 'Hello, yourself.' The perky waitress was back. 'Tea or coffee? Take your choice, there's not much difference.'

He stared at her for a moment before saying, 'Tea, please.'

As she turned away, Rona, who had just finished serving, came and stood in front of him. Her eyelashes fluttering, she said softly, 'Had a nice weekend?'

For a moment he thought there was a double meaning in her words, but he dismissed the thought when he recognised it was one of her usual openings to draw him into conversation. But he answered her pleasantly, saying, 'Very nice; exceptionally nice.'

'Lucky you.'

'Move it.' He watched Maggie bump the tall girl with her hip, then add, 'There's a gang of parched Arabs coming in from the desert; see to them.' For the first time in what seemed an age to him, he wanted not only to laugh but to guffaw, like he used to do when Harry or Martin came out with something funny. At the same time he realised that there was some form of seniority behind the counter, and that Maggie was in charge.

189

Just as he had been wont to do as a boy, so this morning after waking, he had lain and thought of the day ahead and what he had to do in it, and he was aware that life had taken on a tinge of colour. The feeling was still with him, and it wasn't unpleasant.

'Thanks, Maggie.' He took the tea from her, put a coin on the counter and smiled at her, then turned away.

Some minutes later, the rush having subsided, Rona, bending down to Maggie, said, 'Since when has that one called you Maggie? He hardly opens his mouth. I think he's got ideas about himself.'

'Oh.' Maggie took up the cloth and began to wipe a section of the counter. Her head on one side, she bit on her lip, looked up at the waiting face above her, then said in a not too certain tone, 'Eeh, let me think. It must be since we were first married.'

Betty Allsop, who had overheard the exchange, let out a hoot of laughter, while Maggie went on rubbing at the counter, but Rona's reply was, 'That'll be the day, even with a fellow like Billings.'

Still rubbing away at the counter, Maggie had to resist the desire to turn round and bring the wet cloth across the beautiful face to the side of her. Yet, at the same time she knew she had laid herself open for such a reply. She drew in a deep breath; then, the cloth still in her hand, she turned about and went into the kitchen. And there she wrung the cloth out in the sink. Then still holding it, she went to the toilet and, just as she was, she sat down on the edge of the seat and, bending forward, she went through the motion of wringing out the cloth once again. Presently, her teeth pressed tightly down on her lip, she turned her head and leant her brow against the stone wall.

3

As Mrs Robson said, people had taken to war like they did to life: they had accepted it and were living with it and with all the things it did to them; but why did them up top have to go and stop the flower trains coming from Cornwall? There was nothing like a flower to cheer you up on a dark day. It was to save transport, the government said. That was just a gimmick, like when they stopped the holiday trains. Yet, when there was any racing on, transport could be found for that, couldn't it? And who went to the racecourses? she wanted to know. Aha! And income tax eight and sixpence in the pound. And then the daft things they were up to: ordering booksellers to destroy their maps, and ordinary folk an' all, as if the Germans when they landed wouldn't know where they were going. Men, really! It was women they wanted up there to spread some common sense among them.

Next to Churchill there was only one man whom Mrs Robson apparently favoured, and that was Sir Arthur Harris, because wasn't he sending bombers over by the thousand to knock hell out of them over there? Giving them a taste of the Battle of Britain, hitting their churches and cathedrals, just as the Jerries had done here.

Dealing with wireless every day, Joe rarely listened when off duty to accounts of small successes put over in the announcer's authoritative tone and the defeats intoned as if reporting a death: which it was, though not a single death, such as when Tobruk had fallen in June and Mussolini went into Libya. Names like Rommel, Auchinleck, El Alamein sounded as common to the ear as Smith, Jones and Robinson; yet Joe had the feeling that he was being forced to stand on the sidelines and watch a game in which he had not the slightest interest. Yet he knew, at least in this he wasn't alone: the feeling, if it didn't pervade the camp, certainly pervaded his section.

This part of the country didn't seem to be in the war. The munitions factory in Hereford seemed to be the only concession to it. The people went about their daily work in an ordinary fashion: there were no air raids, no scurrying to shelters, no fire engines tearing through the countryside. Naturally, most of the staff in the camp considered themselves lucky to have been posted here and dreaded the idea of a move, which created the feeling of being on the sidelines.

For himself, he wouldn't have minded a posting; in fact, he would have welcomed it, because there was another complication entering his life: vague, but nevertheless there.

Since that day in August when he had first visited the house up the valley, he had, during the past ten weeks, made a dozen return visits. But only once had he ridden back with Maggie. And then it was dark and their entry into camp had gone unnoticed. But it wasn't the camp reactions he was troubled about at the moment, it was Mrs Robson's. He liked Mrs Robson, he had become very fond of her: she was down to earth, and she seemed to bring him out of himself, but she seemed to be harbouring serious ideas about Maggie and him. And that was ridiculous.

Maggie herself, he knew, understood the situation well enough: there was no one more sensible than Maggie; but

192

her auntie, who seemed to have taken the place of her mother and, like a mother, had her future interests at heart, was always bringing her qualities to the fore for him to admire.

He was well aware of Maggie's qualities. She was an extraordinary human being, and it was a damn shame that her personality and talents should have been encased in that little dumpy body of hers.

Last week, after a concert, he had listened to a small group of airmen, seated at a table next to his, discussing her. One had said, 'Her height doesn't matter. I tell you, if she was out in Hollywood they would send her to one of those beauty farms, where they starve them and batter them about and knock them into shape; then they would give her a plastic nose, or make the one she's got more pointed, put false eyelashes on her, give her hair an expert cut, and walla! she'd be a sensation. They would call her The Little Nightingale.'

There had been laughter and one of the men had said, 'But you're not far wrong.'

'No,' the former speaker had replied, 'I know I'm not, because you don't hear a voice like hers every day. And she's got it up top, an' all. There's nobody readier with her tongue than our Lemon.'

Another voice had said, 'Then why don't you have a go?' and the answer had been a bit of a scuffle and more laughter.

And now here, this very minute, her aunt was saying almost in as many words to him, Why don't *you* have a go?

'Marriage is a funny thing, Joe. I know what I'm talking about. I've had three goes at it, and I can tell you that looks are the last thing to be considered; it's what's underneath that matters in the long run. I married me first for looks, and my God, didn't I pay for it! If he hadn't had the business I would have left him within a month. Oh, I'm being honest.' She nodded her head at him from where she sat to the side of the fireplace in the sitting-room. 'Anyway, I thought I was

193

entitled to my share of what he had, for from the time I'd gone there five years before, I'd pulled the business up out of nothing. He hadn't as much in his head, that one, as an addled egg. His dad had died long before his time, and that's how he came into it . . . the business. And you know another thing, Joe? Marriage is a business, and after the bed business is over you've often got twenty-three hours in the day to live with your partner; especially, that is, if you're working together like I was with him. Me second one wasn't bad; he had a business head on him. It was when I married him that we bought this house here, just to escape to at the weekends, you know. But me third was the best of the bunch. He had a face on him like a battered pluck; he was gangly, you know' – she shook her arm – 'loose-limbed; but he was the kindest, most considerate man you could ever wish to meet. But life plays you dirty tricks. I'd spent most of it with the other two, one bad and the other indifferent, now I'd come across a good one and fate gave us four years together, that's all. But looking back I think of them as compensation for the rest of me life before, and what's to come . . . Maggie's a fine girl, Joe; she's one in a thousand.'

'I know that, Mrs Robson, but we understand each other.'

'Aye—' she rose from the chair, went to a basket at the side of the hearth and, taking up a log, she almost flung it on the fire, and as she dusted her hands she ended, 'that's what she tells me. Anyway, you'll say it's none of my business, but I can tell you, you'll go further and fare a lot worse. Aye, by God you will, Joe.'

What could he say? He sat, his head bent, his fingers clasped together, each one twitching; and then she was standing in front of him, apologetic, saying, 'I've gone past meself, Joe, I'm sorry, but I'm concerned for her. She's like a daughter, the daughter I never had, and I lie awake at nights thinking what's going to happen to her when I'm gone, because

194

men being what they are, they'll take her on because of the money. And she'll get all I have, which isn't to be sneezed at.'

He looked up at her now and said quietly, 'I ... I don't think you need worry about her being hoodwinked by anyone; she can see through most people.'

'Aye, Joe, I know that. There's nobody more sensible, but underneath all the sense there's the woman, and her needs, and the feeling that she's going to go down through the years alone. It's a comfort, you know' – she smiled now – 'to think that there's somebody opposite you for the first meal of the day, even if it's to have a row with.'

'Mrs Robson.'

'Yes, lad?' She now moved a few steps backwards and sat down again, straightening out one leg and rubbing it as she did so. And he paused a moment until he imagined that the pain of her rheumatics had eased, and then he said, slowly but firmly, 'I don't think I'll ever marry; in fact, I'm sure I won't.'

Her head jerked up, her eyes narrowed.

'Why?'

'There's a reason.'

'Physical?'

'Oh no!' The words came out on a shaky laugh. 'Oh no, nothing like that.'

'That's something to be thankful for, anyway. Well, what else is so serious that it'll stop you from marrying?'

'It's ... it's a family matter.'

'Some sort of disease?'

Had his mother some sort of disease? Yes, in a way she was mad. And so he answered, 'Yes, in a way.'

'Physical? Mental? Or what?'

She was clever in the way she whittled things down. He swallowed deeply, then said, 'Mental.'

'Oh.' They stared at each other in the lamplight, then she sighed and said, 'Well, it isn't always hereditary; it misses generations, so I understand.'

195

When he didn't answer she said, 'I'm sorry, lad.'

'So am I. So am I.'

'It explains a lot. Thank you for telling me. But I can't see in the long run that it would make any difference to what we've been talking about, seeing who Maggie is. But I can understand you more now, 'cos I never thought you were the kind of fellow to lead anybody up the garden, then jump the railings. Again, lad, thank you for confiding in me. Well, now that's out of the road I'll get you something to eat before you're on your way.'

'No, no' – he was on his feet – 'you'll get me no more to eat today; I've had two marvellous meals. You sit still there; I'll make us a drink, and then I'll be off.'

As he made for the door she said, 'You won't forget to take that bottle in for her, will you? That cough of hers worries me; she's had it for weeks. Should be showing some signs of ease now.'

In the kitchen, which had now become familiar to him, Joe set about making the two cups of cocoa. He had let out a number of slow deep breaths as if he had got out of a tight corner, but no sooner had he entered the room again than Lizzie said, 'Does Maggie know of this?' And when he shook his head saying, 'No,' she came back to him: 'Mind if I tell her?' There was no pause before his answer came, saying, 'No, no, not at all.'

When he handed her the cocoa she looked up at him and said, 'Only three weeks to Christmas. Will you be off on Christmas Day?'

'I won't know until the rota's up.'

'If you are, will you have dinner up here?'

'I would like nothing better.'

'Good! Good! Well' – she lifted her cup of cocoa towards him – 'here's to a happy Christmas.' And he, touching her cup with his, smiled as he said, 'To a happy Christmas.'

4

'I would see to that cough if I were you, Maggie: it's been troubling you on and off for weeks. Why don't you report sick?'

'What! And stand in a queue in the rain and get pneumonia?'

'Well, it's affecting your voice, and when Old Starch Drawers notices it's bad she'll get you a private session, if you ask her.'

'She'd get me on the carpet too, if I asked her.'

'Oh, she's not so bad.'

'Who said she was? She's like a mother superior compared to some of those WAAF brass.'

'You goin' up to your aunt's today?'

'Yes.'

'It's pouring.'

'I've noticed that.'

'She won't expect you a day like this.'

'She always expects me. Where are you going?'

'I've got a date.'

'That Temple fellow?'

'Yes, that Temple fellow.'

'What good's going to come of that?'

'Just a little relief from boredom for a few hours.'

197

'His wife could be bored too, not having him home this weekend.'

'Aw, Maggie' – Peggy Ryan shook her head with impatience – 'you don't understand.'

Maggie turned her body slowly around and stared at her, and after a moment she said, 'I don't feel things like other people because I haven't got what it takes: that's it, isn't it?'

'Oh, the way you put things, Maggie! I just mean . . . well, you don't seem to need anybody. We all . . . '

'What do you say?'

'Aw, I'm sorry, Maggie. Yes, I know, it's stupid; you're bound to need somebody. But . . . well, you seem able to cope. But me, I get all burned up inside, feel I'm going to explode. I need a bit of fun.'

'I agree with you. Oh, I agree with you.'

'Aw, don't be so sarcastic.' Peggy now pulled on her overcoat and, picking up her cape from the foot of the bed, said, 'Well, I'm off, and if you have any sense you'll stay put. See you.'

'See you.' . . .

You don't understand. No, that was true, she didn't understand why she should feel as she did inside. Why, in this fat, unshapely body of hers, there could be such beautiful feelings that took her into dreams at night, dreams which always began with her standing at the top of a shallow bank and looking down on a man bending over a stream. Then she was running down to him, but as she ran the bank became longer and longer, and not once did he turn his face towards her. The dream, she knew, was symbolic. Joe didn't dislike her, but he didn't like her enough to come into the open and claim her, even as a friend.

Anyway, what was she thinking about? What man would put even the caption of friend to an association with her, let alone Joe?

Here was a good-looking fellow who could have had his pick had he cared to make the gesture. He had got the name of being a loner, a reticent type, so the reaction in the camp to their association, were it brought into the open, could stop the war for two minutes, for it would be entirely obliterated by the laughter at little Lemon hooking a fellow. And such a fellow, he tall and slim, no waste flesh on him, and she an undersized bundle of flesh. 'Mutt and Jeff,' they would say. 'The long and the fat of it.' She could hear them. She wouldn't be able to serve him over the counter but some quip would come flying their way.

Oh, she could understand the predicament he was in, the predicament in a way she had forced on him, the predicament she had begun to live for: counting the hours until Saturday or Sunday, her heart racing painfully as she pushed her bike into the shed and made for the door, some trite remark ready should he have already arrived, and an equally trite remark if he hadn't. And when he hadn't put in an appearance, as sometimes happened for a fortnight or more, the quietness would descend on her. And this would cause her Aunt Lizzie to reminisce more and more about her first two husbands in an effort to make her laugh. And she *would* laugh, dragging it out of the painful quietness that was filled with questions regarding the futility of self-education, for she knew nothing could come of this association, no more than the affairs that went on down in the camp. Oh, much less in fact.

He was in the house when she arrived and he helped her off with her cape, then her coat, the while Lizzie reprimanded her, saying, 'You shouldn't have come with a cold like that on you.'

'What do you expect me to do? Sit on the edge of my bed or in the steaming pictures. And don't suggest I could have gone to the NAAFI.' She glanced up at Joe here and they exchanged a smile.

'Get yourself in the room, and less of your backchat. And get those shoes and stockings off.'

'What are you putting in that tea?'

'Never you mind. Get it down you and say thank you.'

'How do you manage to get whisky up here?'

'You'd be surprised.'

A few minutes later she was sitting before a roaring wood fire, her bare feet resting on the rim of the brass fender, while she sipped at the whisky-laced tea and glanced at Joe sitting opposite her. In his shirt-sleeves and without a tie he looked so much at home that it pained her, and when he said, 'She's right, you know, it was a mad thing to do to come out in this,' she could have said to him, 'Is that why you came, because you thought you wouldn't find me here?' But for answer she replied, 'You're not so sane yourself.'

'That's different.'

Yes, his purpose in coming was far different from hers: her purpose was twofold, to see him and to come home to her Aunt Lizzie, whereas his touched on neither of them; this house was merely a bolt-hole from the monotony and restrictions of the camp ... Yet no, that wasn't quite fair to him, for she knew he had become very fond of her Aunt Lizzie; in fact, he talked much more to her, she noticed, than to anyone else, herself included.

'What kind of a week has it been for you?' She was asking the question as if she hadn't seen him for days; but then, when she served him in the NAAFI their exchanges would be brief; in fact, she would have less to say to him that she had to the other fellows.

'Oh, a bit testy. We've got a lot of new pieces of equipment in, but we can't use the damn things.'

'Why?'

'Oh, well' – he moved his head – 'it's rather complicated. It's American stuff, radio amplifiers and transmitter receivers. They use frequency modulation instead of amplitude modulation.'

'Oh yes?' She nodded at him and they both laughed, and he said, 'Well, I can't explain it in any other way, except to say we don't yet really understand the blinking things. They are sending a fellow over from Cranwell, somebody with brains, I understand, to explain to us dim-wits how to turn a knob.'

'Free French, Australians, Canadians, Poles, you don't have to go abroad to meet the natives. Did you hear about the two Canadians who nearly caused a bust-up last night?'

'No. What was that?'

'Oh, they got on about that raid business back in August, when so many of the Canadians were killed or taken prisoner. They said they had been given no support, and they were on about Montgomery. Anyway there was a punch-up among some of them, and of course the SPs came on the scene, so there would be some fizzers flying about this morning.'

'I never heard anything about it. Was it in our section?'

'Half and half, I think. And some of the discip. wallahs were in it too.'

'Oh, my heart bleeds for them.'

'Yes, I bet it does, and I can understand why. They were on about just that at the counter one day this week, saying, when you lot are on guard, you have to go straight on to instructing the next day while guard was merely part of the discips.' duty. I suggested they should go on strike.'

Again they were laughing. It was easy to talk to her about the doings of the camp.

He stared at her. She was looking towards the fire. Was it his imagination, but her face was thinner? Perhaps it was the reflection of the flames; she looked different sitting there.

201

Again he had the impression of an overgrown child . . . well, of a schoolgirl.

'Joe.'

When the voice came from the kitchen Maggie turned to him, laughing now, saying, 'There's your mother calling,' and her eyes widened just the slightest at his change of expression. It had been momentary, like the flicker in a film, but nevertheless the word 'mother' had struck a disruptive chord in him. It was, she supposed, that mental business Aunt Lizzie had told her about. With a sense of deep sadness, she thought it wouldn't have mattered a jot to her if all his people were mad, and he too, as long as she could say he was hers.

A few minutes later he returned from the kitchen carrying a pair of slippers. He was smiling now, and as he handed them to her he said, 'I am to deliver the message word for word: you are up the pole, asking for trouble; nobody in their right mind goes round in their bare feet, not with a chest like you have.'

She gave a little huhing sound as she eased herself forward out of the deep chair to take the slippers from his hand. Then he could find no explanation to give himself why he should have dropped on to one knee and, lifting one bare foot after the other, put her slippers on.

Their faces were on a level now; her eyes were round, the colour dark and bright, and for a second he again had the impression, as he had had that day by the river, of looking into the face of an oriental, a beautiful oriental.

He was saved embarrassment by her again making the huhing sound as she said, 'Well, well! that's the first time I've had me slippers put on for me. I can remember back to when I was two, putting them on meself. I must have gone barefoot before that.' She laughed outright now, and he with her.

He had just seated himself in a chair once more when again his name was called: 'Joe!' and as he rose he looked at Maggie, but this time she made no reference to his mother. Instead, she said, 'She'll keep you at it; far better to stay in the kitchen.'

When he returned, he was carrying a heavily laden tray of tea things; Lizzie followed, carrying the tea-pot, and saying, 'Ah, this is nice. This is nice.' Then, 'Don't you sit back there as if you were finished: get that table set.' She pointed to a little table, 'What do you think the cloth is for?'

The tea was a jolly, bantering affair, brought about by Lizzie and her reminiscing on her past life: no mention of air raids, sunken convoys, Russia, Tobruk or missing planes.

The tea over, Joe went to gather the dishes together, but Lizzie said, 'Oh, just leave them; I think I'll have a ding-on.' She inclined her head towards the piano, then looking at Maggie, she added, 'I set the notes out for the verse. 'Twas tricky, that bit: it's in a different key to the chorus altogether. I think you should alter it.'

Joe looked from one to the other, slightly amazed now, and put in quickly, 'You write music? You compose?' while at the same time recalling that Lizzie had once mentioned this.

'She does that.' It was Lizzie nodding at him.

'I don't. I don't.' Maggie shook her head, and now thumbing towards her aunt, she added, 'She's an expert at it.'

'Don't look surprised, laddie' – Lizzie was pulling a face at him – 'I did eleven years hard labour from six to seventeen. But she's as good as me' – she jerked her head towards Maggie – 'and with only a couple of years learning.'

'Nonsense.' Maggie was looking at him. 'I can't write music. I put notes down, you know, but anyone can do that.'

'Yes, anyone can do that.' Lizzie was at the piano, and after rubbing her fingers over the keys she began to play a melody.

A moment or so later Joe, looking from Maggie, who was sitting by the fire, to Lizzie at the piano, said in a soft voice, 'It's a lovely tune; what are the words?'

Maggie didn't reply but Lizzie stopped playing, and reaching to the end of the piano, took up a sheet of manuscript, placed it on the rack and, in a voice that held only a slight tremor and was pleasantly husky, began to sing:

Do not go, do not go
My love, from me,
For no blanket can warm
My frozen heart.
Do not go, do not go
My love, from me,
For the years ahead are dark,
So dark without you,
So full of lonely fear;
What does life hold for me,
Without you, my dear?

Age has touched me
And I can charm you no more,
But remember, when you go to her,
She but thirty and you all of three score,
There'll come a day
Not far away
When, like me, you'll beg her to stay,
Saying:

As she now went into the chorus again Joe found his back stiffening against the chair. He looked at Maggie. She had her head turned fully towards the fire, her feet were tucked under her, and her arms folded across her breasts, a hand under each oxter. Her pose suggested someone in deep pain. She had written a song about an aged woman losing her man. What knowledge had she of such a situation? He had the urge to go to her, to put his arms about her and say, 'It's going to be all right; you'll come through.' But she wasn't an old woman who had lost her man, she was still a young girl, and she'd never had a man to lose.

'There, did you like that?' Lizzie had turned round on the swivelling piano stool and, looking towards her, he said quietly, 'I did, I did indeed. It's a beautiful song; it should be published.'

'That's what I say. That's what I'm always telling her.' She was coming across the room towards them when the sound of a knock on the back door caused her to stop. At the same time the sound brought Maggie twisting in her seat to sit upright.

Getting to his feet, Joe said, 'I'll see who it is.'

'You'll not bother yourself' – Lizzie flapped her hand at him – 'I know who it is. But why has he come to the back door? It's Donald from the farm. He usually drops me in something on a Saturday.' She winked at them. 'It's good, as the saying goes, to have friends in court.'

As she went out of the room Joe, on impulse, went over to Maggie and, pulling a low stool from the side of the fireplace, he sat down by her side and, leaning his elbow on the arm of her chair, he looked at her for a moment before he said, 'You're a clever girl, aren't you?'

'Oh, aye, clever as owt.'

She sounded almost like a Northerner as she derided herself, and he smiled for a moment, then said, 'I'm serious. We're friends, aren't we? and so I can say this to you: you've got a lot inside that head that very few people know about, and I think you should use it, make something of it, especially through that.' He pointed towards the piano.

Her voice was as serious as his now as she answered, 'As I said, I can't write music, although the tunes come easy to my mind; as for rhymes, I've always been able to knock them off.'

'Well, now' – he was smiling broadly at her – 'we have something firmly in common, because so have I. I've always been able to knock them off, too.'

'Really?' She was laughing at him now. 'What kind?'

'Well . . . so-called poetry.'

'Come through. Come through.' They both turned their heads sharply towards the door, and then almost simultaneously their mouths fell slightly agape. But their astonishment wasn't anything to that of the man standing looking at them.

Bill Regan was one of the corporal instructors in Joe's section. He was, if a vote had been taken, the only unpopular man there. The others got on well together, but Bill Regan was an argumentative individual, always finding something to grumble about. He didn't make friends, and was aware that he didn't.

Joe had turned slowly on the stool as the man came into the room, with Lizzie explaining, 'This young man's after a spanner; his bicycle chain let him down. If you have a bicycle you should always carry tools, that's what I say. But sit yourself down; I'm sure you could do with a cup of tea. You'll have it in a minute. Go on, sit down.' She pointed to the chair that Joe had previously been sitting in, then limped out of the room.

Neither Joe nor Maggie had moved, and it wasn't until after Bill Regan had slowly lowered himself into the seat, and had brought out two words that spoke volumes, that Joe got to his feet; and it was he who repeated the two words. 'Well! Well!' and, coming straight to the point, he added, 'And what are you going to make of it?'

'Make of it?' Regan pursed his lips, then wagged his head as he said, 'No business of mine, only I never knew you two were thick.'

'We are not thick, as you put it.' It was Maggie speaking now, her tone vehement. 'Joe here' – she nodded towards

206

him – 'well, he knew my Aunt long before he knew me, and so he comes up to see her. Is there any harm in that?'

'No; and don't get yourself aerated, Lemon.'

He now looked at Joe and, his face going into a grin, he said, 'Lucky you, knowing someone with a nice place like this,' while his eyes took in the absence of Joe's jacket and tie.

As if made aware of this Joe went quickly out of the room into the passage, and there put on his jacket and tie and his greatcoat, then returned to the doorway, saying in no small voice, 'You want a spanner?'

'Oh, yes, yes.' Regan got to his feet. But before he went down the room he turned to Maggie and said, 'Glad to see you're enjoying yourself, Lemon.'

As they passed through the kitchen Lizzie said, 'Aren't you going to have this cup of tea?' But before Regan could answer, Joe said, 'He's got to get back, Mrs Robson.'

'Oh, I see, I see. Well, it won't go to waste.'

Out in the shed, Joe took tools from his tool bag and handed them to Regan, and he directed his flashlight on the chain until the job was done. Neither of them had spoken since they had left the house, but now, as Regan prepared to push his bike towards the house, Joe said, 'Don't make anything out of this, Bill.'

'What could I make out of it? It's all above-board, isn't it?' There was a sneer in his voice. 'You and Lemon are just pals, aren't you? Nothing else.'

A swift rise of anger suffused Joe, so much so that he found himself wanting to hit out. He glared at Regan through the light of the torch and growled at him. 'What do you mean?'

'Well, she's not everybody's cup of tea, is she? And with one or two lookers in the camp, I would have thought . . . well, you know what I mean, I don't have to go into detail. But after all, it's your own business. Every man to his taste.'

'Now, you look here!'

'Oh, don't get on your high horse.' Regan was pushing his bike across the yard now. 'But I'll say this.' And now his voice was stiff. 'If you weren't ashamed to be seen with her why couldn't you have brought it into the open? I mean, you're never seen together in the camp, are you?'

Joe was stumped for words for a moment; then he muttered between his teeth, 'I have my reasons. And so has she.'

'Oh, well. If you understand each other, that's everything, isn't it?' He adjusted the dimmed light on his bike, mounted it and half turned as he rode slowly away, calling, 'I could've done with that cup of tea. But thank her, anyway.'

Joe stood in the dark yard, his eyes closed, his hand to his brow. He knew what would happen now and he'd be ribbed to death, they'd both be ribbed to death, and all kinds of assumptions would be put on their association. How would she take it? Oh – he moved slowly towards the back door – she would likely laugh it off; she'd had long practice of that kind of thing. But what would be his reaction? He didn't know.

'He's gone then?'

He nodded across the kitchen table at Lizzie, saying, 'Yes, yes; he's gone.'

'He was quick.'

'He wanted to get back.'

'Aye, yes. Well, here, take it inside; I'll be there in a minute.'

Having put the tray down on the table, he turned and looked at Maggie, and she, returning his gaze, said, 'Well, that's blown it, hasn't it? I'll have to run the gauntlet tomorrow. But that's nothing; I'm used to it. What about you?'

'Huh!' He forced himself to smile. 'Let them think what they like; we know where we stand, don't we?'

Her eyes were unblinking as she looked at him and it seemed minutes before she said, 'Yes, we know where we stand.'

208

Then in a low voice she added, 'May I give you a word of advice?'

The smile widened and he made no answer, and she said, 'Laugh at it, make a joke of it, make a joke of me . . . '

'I'll do no such thing!' The smile had gone from his face. 'We're friends, and I'll stand by that.'

After staring at him for a moment longer, she turned away and said softly, 'Thanks, Joe. Thanks.'

5

'Why have you kept it to yourself? Surely you could have told me. I thought we were friends.'

'Oh, Len' – Joe jerked his head to the side – 'our meeting happened by accident and the association just grew, and we both knew what the reaction to it would be down here.'

'Well, if you had come into the open right away, it wouldn't have been anything like it is now. They skinned her alive in the NAAFI.'

'Well, very little has been said in front of me.'

'That's true; you've lost a bit of esteem though. Oh, you can look like that, but what did you expect? What you don't seem to understand, Joe, is that Lemon's a sort of mascot in that NAAFI, and be what she is, I mean in looks, she's well liked, and not only because she can sing as she does. Then here's you, takes her off on the side, too ashamed to come out in the open. All right. All right. That's what they're saying. Anyway, if you had taken up with her in the ordinary way you might have had to stand a bit of chipping, but nothing like this. And then there's her boss: the fellows usually have to ask her for a pass.'

'Look here!' Joe pulled Len to a stop. 'Whose bloody business is it, anyway?'

On another occasion Len might have laughed, for it was the first time he had heard Joe swear, and his 'bloody' seemed to have a peculiar ring to it, sounding like 'bleedy'. But this wasn't an occasion for laughter. He liked this fellow, he had even felt protective towards him because, he had surmised, he was carrying a load of some kind on his mind, and so he would have been the first person to applaud him taking up with a girl, even if it had been Lemon. But he was disturbed by the reaction to Joe in their own section. Sam Temple and Amos Bernstein were, last night, still talking about it, and the sensation should have died down now, being a week old. But they kept bringing it up. It was an underhand business, they said. If he hadn't been ashamed to be seen with her, he shouldn't have taken up with her on the side, for it was bound to be discovered sooner or later. And they had endorsed what others had often said: a close, secretive sort of fellow, something odd about him. And that's what Len was thinking himself: there was something odd about Joe. He was a young, very presentable looking fellow, educated, too, yet apparently had not thought about putting in for a commission . . .

He said now in a mollified tone, 'I . . . I had to speak like this, Joe, because . . . well, I felt a bit hurt. And, of course, when big-mouth Regan went into details about you both being comfortably ensconced before the fire, you in your shirt-sleeves, et cetera, well, what could I think but that you hadn't just met up that afternoon? And I also thought that . . . well, when I used to invite you home you could have told me the reason why you didn't want to come.'

'Len. Len' – Joe's steps slowed as they neared the labs – 'it . . . it didn't start until the end of September. I was out bike-riding. I was hot. I knelt down by a stream to take a drink and there she was on top of the bank looking at me. She told me her aunt lived near and would I like a cup of tea? Now what could I say? That's how it started. I may have been up to the house a dozen times since but, believe me, half those times she hasn't been there: she's been on duty. The aunt's a dear old soul and she's somebody I can talk to. As for Maggie and me, well she, Maggie, understands the situation, and there's nothing between us. Believe that, Len. Not a thing, not a damn thing.'

'Well, you've put yourself in an awkward position then, haven't you? Anyway, you'd better get a move on and meet this bod from Cranwell, who the sergeant says has it all up top, being one of the back-room boys.'

A moment later they entered the first lab, in which a group of airmen were standing around waiting for instruction. They walked past the benches which held set after set of radio equipment and through a door into another lab which, this morning, was unusually crowded with about twenty instructors, together with lab sergeants, flight-sergeants, and a warrant-officer.

The warrant-officer was standing apart talking to a flight-sergeant as Joe and Len took their places at the end of the almost half circle of instructors. The flight-sergeant turned slowly about to face his audience and Joe's mouth, snapping into a gape, unconsciously uttered the name, 'Mick.'

His voice wasn't loud: in fact, he could hardly hear the name himself, and it only reached Mick as a whisper. But Mick turned in the direction from where it came, and then he said, 'Joe.' Immediately he turned to the accompanying officer standing just at the side and said, 'Sorry, sir. An . . . an old friend.'

The warrant-officer smiled and said, 'It's good to meet old friends. But shall we get on?'

'Yes, sir.'

Len, his head lowered, whispered, 'You know each other?' And Joe whispered back, 'Yes, very well.'

For the next half hour, Joe, with the rest of the company listened to Mick talking about the intricacies of frequency modulation and of its advantages over amplitude modulation and all the while he felt happy inside, happier than he had been for years. If he had ever desired to see anyone from the old life, it would have been Mick Smith. Mick, who seemed to know all the answers, level-headed, deep-thinking Mick.

It was almost half an hour after the Saturday morning session was over, during which Mick had been introduced into the sergeants' mess and shown his temporary quarters, that Joe and he really met up. They stood in the biting wind outside the hut, their hands clasped, and all Mick seemed to be able to say was, 'Well, I never! Well, I never!' And then he added, 'The last person on earth I expected to see. Yet I've been looking out for you, because, if you remember, when we last met you said you were coming into the Air Force. Nobody seemed to know where you had gone.' The bright light slipped from his face and he stared at Joe. 'You don't go home?' he said.

'No, Mick; I don't go home. Oh!' Joe rolled his head. 'Oh! I am glad to see you.'

'Reciprocated, lad. Reciprocated.' Mick had spoken in a broad Geordie accent, and now they both laughed.

'What are you doing this afternoon?'

'Nothing.' For the moment Joe had forgotten he had intended to go up to the cottage and that Maggie, also being off, would be expecting him. Or would she? This had been a test week: if he didn't put in an appearance today she would think that he had been scared off.

Mike broke in on his thoughts, saying, 'You'll never believe who's living in Hereford.'

'One of the family?'

'One of the family: our Janet.'

'Janet? No!'

'Yes, a roundabout story, Janet's. She met a sailor in Portsmouth. His mother lived in Hereford, so when she married him she came and lived with his mother. That was

213

two years ago. Well, the mother died last August gone and Janet's going back to Portsmouth again in the New Year to be near Reg when his boat comes in. I'm going down there this afternoon. What about coming with me? Oh come on. That's if you've got nothing very special on.' He now punched Joe in the arm.

'No, I haven't. No, nothing that I can't cancel.' Joe's voice was hearty. 'What time are you going?'

'Oh, any time you like; half an hour. There's a bus, they tell me, at two-thirty.'

'See you at the bus stop then. Oh, Mick' – Joe put out his arms and gripped Mick's shoulders – 'am I glad to see you!' They stood a moment looking at each other, slightly embarrassed, then Joe turned abruptly away and made for the NAAFI . . .

'Well, thanks for telling me, Joe.' Maggie smiled at him across the counter. 'Aunt will be sorry, but I'll play rummy with her as a sort of compensation.' She still continued to smile and he, smiling back, said, 'Tell her to get that Christmas dinner ready for me, because I'm going to starve for a couple of days beforehand.'

'I'll do that. This fellow you met: he's a very old friend?'

'Yes, yes.' He nodded at her. 'I was brought up with him; he was on the staff.' He bit his lip as if he had said too much.

'Is he here permanent?'

'No; he's been sent from Cranwell, temporarily, to knock something into our dim heads about some new sets we have.'

'Oh.' Her chin moved up and down. 'I'd like to meet him.'

He paused. 'Yes, yes; you will,' he said.

'Would he like to come to dinner on Christmas Day?'

'Oh, I don't think he'll manage that: he's got a sister in Hereford, so he's likely already made arrangements in that quarter.'

214

'Oh well, enjoy yourself.'

His voice was low as he said, 'Be seeing you.'

'Be seeing you.'

As she watched him making his way between the tables, the weight inside her chest sank lower with every step he took away from her. It seemed that fate in the form of an old friend had taken a hand, saved him, sort of, from openly riding with her out of the camp. Who was this friend that could make him look so happy? She had never seen him really look happy before: his eyes had shone, he had looked handsome, beautiful. But then, he had always looked beautiful to her.

'Where's he off to?' It was Peggy at her side counting out change and when she had passed it over the counter she came back and said, 'Scuttling?'

'No, he's not scuttling.' Maggie turned on her fiercely, her voice a threatening undertone now. 'He's met a friend from home. They're going into Hereford for the day.'

'Oh, all right, keep your hair on. I just thought with . . . '

'Well, don't think. Or if you do, keep it to yourself. And listen.' She now pulled Peggy to the side. 'I've had just about as much as I can stand for one week, so don't you add to it.'

'I'm sorry, Maggie; you know me. I'm for you, I just want things to go right for you. It hurt me to think you're flogging a dead horse.'

'I'm off now. Bye!' The fire had gone out of Maggie's voice.

'Bye.'

Flogging a dead horse. Peggy was right, and she might as well face it now as later: for all their so-called friendship, he was a dead horse, a very dead horse, and she'd always known it.

6

The house in Hereford was one of a terrace: it had a large
sitting-room, an equally large dining-room, a kitchen, a
scullery, and a long garden beyond. Upstairs there were
three bedrooms, a box-room and a bathroom. Janet Morgan,
as she was now, showed Joe round with pride, as she well
might, for the house was her husband's property now and,
as she had just told him, she was letting it for a mighty good
rent from the middle of January.

He had been in the house an hour and she had never
stopped talking. He had wanted to talk quietly to Mick.

It had been impossible in the bus, and it was even more
impossible now, because she was bent on raking up all
the events that had happened back in the house since she
could remember.

He knew if he had met her in the street he wouldn't have
recognised her. She had been very pretty, as he remembered
her, but now she looked coarsened, and blowsy. Yes, that was
the word, blowsy. Her fair hair was crimped into a big halo
round her face, her eyes were heavily made-up, and her mouth,
rosebud as it had been termed when young, was now a big
lipstick pout. He knew instinctively that he didn't like Janet,
and she was saying to him now, 'Do you like Hereford?'

Before he could answer her she went on, 'I hate it; dead-and-alive place, more dead than alive. They don't know there's a war on. They should have been in the North last year when I went through to see my mother. Or in Portsmouth. And they're so damned snooty. Her next door . . . well, you would think she owned the bloody town, and she only rents her house, mind: doesn't own it, like us. She never got on with Reg's mother and she doesn't get on with me either. Of course, mind—' she now stubbed out half a cigarette, patted her lips and added, 'It would have taken a saint to get on with Reg's mother; I don't know how I stuck it so long. I suppose it's because I knew she wasn't long for the top. I might as well be truthful. Still it paid off. Look, you're not eating.' She pushed a plate towards Joe. 'Don't worry, I'm not short of stuff; I get bits and pieces on the side. There's a little pub I go to not three streets away; I'll take you to it after. Talk about the black-market centre; Finnegan's Fair would be a better name for it.' She put her head back and laughed, and her breasts wobbled beneath her tight woollen jumper; then again she went on, 'What's the matter with you, our Mick? Lost your tongue?'

'No, no, Janet, but I can't get a chance to wag it.'

'Oh, you!' She laughed as she flapped her hand towards him. 'You used to always say I'd swallow meself in me gob one day, didn't you? Eeh! the times we had in that house. House did I say? Pigsty. Mind' – she turned her attention now to Joe – 'your people had something to answer for, by God! they had. Things will be different after the war: you won't get people to slave like our lot did for a pittance.'

'Shut up, Janet. Joe had nothing to do with that.'

'No? Well, perhaps he will have in the future when he goes back. They tell me your mother's in a bad way.'

Joe brought his eyes fully on her now, staring into her face, and she went on, 'Well, I mean since she had her stroke.'

217

'Stroke?' His lips formed the word but made no sound, and she said, 'You didn't know? Oh, but then you never go back. Do you? I don't know how our Mary puts up with it. I told her she's mad, I did. I told her to her face last time I was through there. The place is like a shambles. The military were going to take it over, you know, but then the solicitors stepped in. And then there was your mother; she couldn't be moved. She can talk and move her right hand, but that's about all. But some officers were billeted for a time.'

He felt sick. He was going to vomit. He pushed the chair back from the table, saying, 'Ex . . . Excuse me,' and made for the door and the lavatory upstairs.

She'd had a stroke, she could only talk and use one hand. Why didn't he feel compassion? Why couldn't he think to himself, it's payment for her sins and let it go at that? Why was he still battling against her inside? Why did he hate her so?

Because she had killed three men and a woman, a young lovely woman.

But to be paralysed. And he had condemned her to that house. He had, in fact, chained her up with the corpses.

It was just retribution.

But who was he to play God?

Nobody should play God. He should do something. But what?

As he bent over the sink and swished the cold water around his mouth, he was overcome by a strange feeling, a recognised strange feeling; a numbness that he had felt before, the numbness he sank into on the night he'd found Martin and Dick Smith, and from which he had willed himself not to return, because in it he did not feel anything: there was no pain in the numbness, just a slight awareness that you were still alive, in spite of your body being dead.

218

'You all right, Joe?' It was Mick's voice from outside the bathroom door, and after a moment he opened the door and said, 'Yes, yes.'

'You didn't know she . . . your mother had had a stroke?'

He shook his head, then muttered, 'No.'

'Why don't you ever go back?' Mick's question was a soft whisper, and he answered as quietly, 'I can't, Mick. There's . . . there's a reason.'

'Strong enough to keep you away from her, when very likely she's dying?'

'Yes' – he bowed his head – 'strong enough even for that.'

'Well—' Mick turned about and gripped hold of the bannister rail as he said, 'You know your own best. But when we're on, I'd better tell you the place is going to rack and ruin. Our Mary does her best. She keeps the house cobweb free. That's about all she can do, cooking and seeing after your mother. As for the outside, you can hardly get through it for grass. Danny does his best, but he can't make up for half a dozen men. And I'm going to say this: I've tried to persuade our Mary to leave and let the solicitors get on with it, put your mother in a home somewhere. But she won't. She said it would be on her conscience.'

'What you two gassing about up there? About our Carrie? I forgot to tell him.'

At the name Carrie, Mick, without looking at Joe, said, 'Carrie thinks she might be here for Christmas,' And on this he went down the stairs and Joe slowly followed him.

In the sitting-room again, Janet said, 'She's not sure; but if things go as she hopes she should get here on Christmas Eve.'

It was the first time Carrie's name had been mentioned, and now Joe looked at Mick, who had seated himself at the side of the fireplace and taken the poker in his hand. He now stirred the fire as he said, 'She's in the ATS. She's billeted in Grantham.'

'Really?' His voice sounded ordinary, yet her name had dispelled the feeling of numbness and he said again, 'Really?'

This made Janet mimic him. Putting on a high-faluting tone, she muttered, 'Yes, rerely, rerely.' Then reverting to her own voice she added, 'And here's another thing that'll surprise you, she's been recommended for a commission. Now what do you think of that? She was on the clerical staff and she did so good that we'll soon have a ma'am in our ranks. Eeh!' – She now looked at Mick saying – 'Can you believe it, Mick? Our Carrie.'

'Yes, yes, I can believe it.'

'Oh, of course you would. That was a damn silly question to ask, especially of you.' She pulled a face towards Joe now. 'The apple of his eye, always has been. But what'll it be like if he has to call her ma'am?' She had turned her attention again to Mick and he said quietly, 'Don't be silly, Janet. Don't be silly.'

'Don't be silly? Who's silly, eh? Who's the silly bugger in this family? 'Tisn't me: I'm married, done well for meself. What do you say, Joe?'

He stared at her for a moment, slightly perplexed about something, but he just couldn't, in his mind, have said what, yet it lay in Janet's attitude to Mick. But he said, 'You've got a very comfortable home, and you should be happy here after the war.'

'Don't you believe it. I've no intention of staying here after the war. He'll be selling it, because prices will go up then. Drive me mad staying in this dump . . . '

For the next two hours Joe listened to Janet's prattle, and when on six o'clock she said, 'Look, I'm just going to slip out; there's an off-licence round here. She's very kind to me. I'm gettin' the stuff in for Christmas just in case Reg should turn up. If he doesn't, it won't go to waste. I've got a well-stocked cupboard already, but a little more won't do any harm: never does any day in the week;

220

but at Christmas you need a drop of extra cheer. What do you say?'

Neither of them said anything, until they heard the front door close; then Mick, sinking back into the chair, said on a laugh, 'Poor Reg.'

'As you say, poor Reg,' said Joe, answering in the same vein.

'She never stops. She's always been the same. She's not a nice character really, our Janet: and she's me sister, but I've got to say it. She was the mischief-making one in the family; right from a bairn she knew how to stir it.'

'How is Carrie?' He had been wanting to ask this question since her name had been first mentioned.

'Oh, she's grand. Loves the job.'

'Do you see her often?'

Mick pursed his lips, moved his head, then said, 'It all depends on what you mean by often. Cranwell isn't all that way from Grantham; just on seventeen miles. When our leaves coincide we meet up and have a trip to the pictures, or some such.'

'She's not married?'

'Married? No. No.'

The answer was so emphatic that Joe said, 'Why do you say it like that? She was and still is, I suppose, a beautiful girl.'

'Oh, I don't know.' Mick now moved his head from side to side on the back of the chair and looked up towards the ceiling before saying, 'She doesn't seem inclined that way: somehow she's serious-minded, you know, very serious-minded.'

'Carrie, as I remember her, was . . . well, light-hearted, sort of gay.'

'You thought her gay?' Mick was looking at him now. 'Funny; I never saw her like that. She always seemed to me to have a serious turn. And it's developed these last few years. It must be all of, what, nearly three years since you saw her?'

221

The numbness completely gone, Joe remembered vividly the last time he had seen Carrie. It was on the day a gun exploded his life. He replied slowly, 'About that.'

'Well, a lot has happened since then, as you yourself only too well know. And you have changed, an' all. You know that, Joe? You were a young lad the last time I saw you.' He paused, giving them both the chance to recall the time one of them cried; then he went on, 'But now you've matured; you've grown, not only in height and breadth but in depth, I should say, and beyond your years, for you certainly don't look just twenty.'

'Twenty-one on Christmas Eve, please.'

'Oh yes' – Mick laughed now – 'twenty-one on Christmas Eve. Well, Joe, I would never take you for that. Put another five years on it. And I don't know whether I intend that as a compliment or not.' Again they both laughed.

After a moment's silence Joe asked, 'How long will she be staying?'

'Carrie?' Mick said the name as if it had suddenly been introduced into the conversation and was not the essence of it, and Joe said, 'Yes, Carrie.'

'Oh, she'll arrive likely on Christmas Eve, and leave on Boxing morning. That's if she's lucky, which she's hoping to be.'

'And you'll be here all over the holidays? I forgot to ask you.'

'To the first week in January, I think.'

'Good! Good! Does Carrie go home, I mean, back North much?'

'No, not very much. Look.' Mick hitched himself towards the edge of his chair, saying now, 'I wanted to have a natter with you on the side about this frequency business, and there won't be much chance when Janet comes back, nor can I see much more opportunity in the camp. You see, it's like this . . . '

The conversation regarding Carrie was adroitly cut short, and when Janet returned, happily laden with four bottles of beer and a bottle of Scotch, the latter which she insisted on opening, it was impossible to get a word in edgeways . . .

Two very large whiskies and three beers later . . . It entered Joe's mind that one disliked more people in life than was the reverse, and that the one he disliked most at this moment, above all others, was Janet Smith, as he still thought of her, for she was sitting now on the couch beside him, her arm around his shoulder, her breast flopping against his side with every movement she made, and emphasising her words here and there by hugging him to her. She had a body smell that was a mixture of sweat and cheap scent. Her close presence was translated in his mind by one word: whore. She was a whore. He had overheard Martin, years ago, saying that most of the Smith family were whores.

He wondered why Mick didn't tell her to behave, but Mick had had three glasses of whisky and four beers, and he had slumped into his chair, not drunk, just apparently in deep thought and seemingly oblivious of his sister's chatter.

It was in desperation that Joe, of a sudden, pulled himself away from the clutching hand, exclaiming, 'Look at the time, Mick. If we lose that last bus, we've had it.'

Stirring himself, Mick said, 'What time does it go?'

'Just on ten.'

'On ten? That's early, isn't it?'

'Not for our part of the country.'

There would be buses running for the next hour or more, and perhaps camp transport of one kind or another, but he knew he couldn't stand the sight, sound, or feel of this woman a minute longer.

She was still talking at them when they walked into the dark street. 'Christmas Eve, mind, Joe. Christmas Eve. Good-night, our Mick . . . An' good-night . . . Sir Joe.' Her loud laugh followed them.

Spend Christmas Eve in her company? Not if he knew it. But then there had been stirrings in him all evening, and excitement borne of an old desire: he must see Carrie again, for at this moment she was appearing to him as a life-saver. His drink-hazed mind was telling him that to love and be loved by Carrie would erase all the misery of his life.

When he got in the bus the future stretched brightly before him, so brightly that for the first time since he had been in the camp he joined in the singing:

Kiss me good-night, sergeant-major,
Tuck me in my little wooden bed.
We all love you, sergeant-major,
Nobody wishes you were dead.
Until you awake me in the morning,
And bring me up a nice hot cup of tea . . . Gor blimey;
Kiss me good-night, sergeant-major,
Sergeant-major be a mother to me.

But once out of the bus and about to say good-night to Mick, there passed through his fuddled mind the sound of Janet's voice saying, 'Good-night, Sir Joe,' in mock civility. And now, putting his hand on Mick's shoulder, he said, 'The "Sir" business, Mick, the "Sir" business: you won't let on in the camp? And tell her, Janet, will you? Will you? Not to keep it up.'

'Aw, don't worry, I won't let on. Nor her. I'll tell her. But can't see why not, though.'

'Don't want it.'

'Should be an officer. That's what you should be; you should be an officer.'

'Don't want to be no bloody officer.'

They both laughed now and clung together for a moment, before pushing each other away and going towards their separate sites, while still calling their good-nights.

7

He was in agony to know if he'd be off on Christmas Eve or on Christmas Day. It wouldn't be so bad, he told himself, if he was on duty on Christmas Day, for Maggie and Mrs Robson would understand. But to be tied up on Christmas Eve as well, and to miss seeing Carrie, brought a feeling of anxiety and rebellion into his being.

It turned out that he was booked for duty up till five o'clock on Christmas Eve, but he had a forty-eight hour pass to cover him from then on.

Maggie had a forty-eight too; she told him so over the NAAFI counter, and she added, 'Aunt Lizzie is baking like mad, although I don't know where she's got the stuff from; you wouldn't think there was a war on. Don't eat too much tonight and don't have any breakfast.' She paused before adding, 'It's nice for you to have met old friends.'

'Yes, Mick's here till the New Year. You'll likely run into him.'

'I'd like that.' She stared at him. 'I'm looking forward to tomorrow too.'

'Same here.' He nodded as he smiled at her, while at the same time wishing he'd had the courage to make his excuses, because then he could have spent the day with Carrie. Perhaps they could have gone out for a walk together and talked, picked up where they had left off. Oh, no, no, not where they had left off, where they were when they were young, really young. She had once said she loved him, before he'd had the nerve to say the same words to her. He would remind her of that. He smiled inwardly and the warmth of it spread to his face.

Seeing it, Maggie said, 'It's going to be a nice Christmas all round. I've made up my mind that from two o'clock this afternoon, when I'm off, I'm not going to listen to the news until Boxing Day, if then. Is it right?' She now leant slightly across the counter and in a low tone said, 'I hear you hit the bottle last night; sang your head off in the bus.'

The smile slid from his face and he answered stiffly, 'You can't wink here without it being broadcast, can you?'

'Well, as you happened to be the only two who had managed to get . . . under the influence, it was noticeable when you started them all off. Did you have a sore head this morning?'

'No.'

'Well, you're lucky; it must have been good stuff. I can't promise you the same tomorrow. As Aunt Lizzie says, beggars can't be choosers in that line, but she's got a drop in.'

He made himself smile now as he nodded and said, 'Good! Good!' then added, 'What time shall I come up?'

'Oh, any time. Please yourself. The sooner the better.'

'Right. Right.' He stepped back from the counter. ' 'Bye then.'

' 'Bye, Joe.' She had said the farewell more to herself and her eyes watched him making his way towards the door. He looked so smart, so straight, so slim, she ached inside, and she soothed herself by thinking, there's tomorrow, all day tomorrow. Then her practicality rounded on her: what difference would it make? She was only prolonging the agony. If he was posted, or the war ended tomorrow, that would be that, and she knew it. The sooner she stopped crying for the moon, the better.

'Don't worry, he'll be back, Lemon.'

She snapped her eyes away on to the speaker, who now said teasingly, 'And don't look at me like that, I haven't said nothing.' He leant towards her. 'The fact is, I'm one of them that's glad you hit it off, sort of, in a way, like, because he's not so sullen since he got in with you. Like a clam, he was, when he first came.'

'Well, that's never been your complaint, has it, Ritchie?'

'No, you're right there. But I'll tell you another one who hasn't got the complaint either: Billings.' He made a small movement of his head backwards. 'Billings was gone on you, you know; he still is. Came as a kind of shock when the news broke about you and Joe-boy. By' – he wagged his head now – 'you are lucky, aren't you, Lemon, to have two blokes after you and you not the size of three pennorth of copper?'

Maggie had a cup of tea in her hand ready to pass over to him, but she kept a hold on it as she looked at him and said quietly, 'If you say one more word, Ritchie, in that condescending, patronising tone, I'll let you have this all in one go in that big loose mouth of yours.'

'Ah, Lemon, Lemon, I was only . . . '

'I know what you were only trying to say. Well, you've said it. Now, there's your tea, and if you're wise you'll say no more.'

'By, you're a little spitfire when you like, Lemon.' Self-consciously now, he picked up his cup of tea and pushed the copper towards her, and as he turned away, two airmen being served further along the counter smiled at her, and both simultaneously took their thumbs from the handles of their cups and pointed towards her. She smiled faintly at them, jerked her chin upwards, then turned round and went into the back room, and there she said to Bett Allsop, 'Take over for me for a few minutes, Bett, will you?'

'You feeling bad?'

'No, no. Well, just a little dizzy . . . faint.'

'Dizzy? Faint? Ho! Ho!' Bett nudged her in the arm as she said on a smirking laugh, 'Eeh! don't say that; that's when the loaf starts to rise . . . But that'd be the day, eh?'

Maggie watched Bett adjust her overall, then straighten her cap. The smirk on her face as she went towards the door, the improbability of such an event seeming to have fixed it there.

Maggie went to the sink and stood gripping the cold edge of it, and as she looked down on to the mass of dirty crockery she had the strong urge to take up the pieces, one after another, and dash them against the wall.

Even knowing she was friendly with Joe, they could not give her the benefit of the doubt that there could be a possibility of him wanting to take her; or even Billings, for all his pestering, having the same desire. Her suitors were apparently a joke, a sexless joke.

Turning about, she looked in the mottled mirror that showed her reflection from the top of her cap to her knees, and she bowed her head against herself.

8

It was just on three o'clock when Mick came hurrying into the picket post where Joe was on duty and, taking him aside, he whispered, 'Carrie, I've . . . I've just been on the phone to her; she won't be able to get in until after ten tonight.'

Joe looked at him blankly but made no reply, and Mick, jerking his head, said, 'You can come in if you like, but . . . but somehow I don't think you enjoy our Janet's company.' He grinned sheepishly, then added, 'Can't you put that dinner off the morrow?'

'No.' Joe shook his head. 'No, I can't.'

'Will you come to tea, then?'

Joe looked away for a moment. It wouldn't be fair, not only to Maggie, but to her aunt, to have his dinner and then leave them when they were expecting him to spend the rest of the day with them.

It came as a surprise and a solution of sorts when Mick said, 'If it's a girl friend, bring her by all means.'

'She isn't my girl friend.' Joe's retort came in a hissing whisper and he cast his glance at the sergeant sitting at the table at the far end of the room, supposedly writing; then he added rather shamefacedly, 'But she's been kind, she and her aunt, and I feel under an obligation.'

'Well, do as I said and fulfil your obligation by bringing her. Janet says there'll be a good few there tomorrow night, so one more won't make any difference.'

Joe bit on his lip, thought for a moment, then said, 'Leave it for now. If I can manage it I will come. When's Carrie got to go back?'

'I told you; Boxing morning.'

'Even if she doesn't arrive till late tonight?'

'That's what she said. She asked after you on the phone, she . . . she's looking forward to seeing you.'

Joe stared at him, and for a moment Mick returned his glance; then his lids blinking, he said, 'I've got to go; I want to catch the bus. I hope to see you the morrow then? If I don't, a happy Christmas. And by the way, a happy birthday an' all. Twenty-one. Some place to celebrate, isn't it?' He glanced around the post. 'Anyway, we'll make up for it, tomorrow, let's hope. See you.'

Joe remained still for a moment; then, turning to the window of the hut, he watched Mick hurrying down the roadway, and there came into his mind a strange thought: although Mick had said, 'See you tomorrow, then?' he had received the impression from somewhere beyond the words that Mick wasn't over anxious for him to go. It was a silly idea. He knew how he felt about Carrie; she was bound to have told him. Could it be there was someone else in the offing, and Mick didn't want him to be hurt? Could be.

He turned from the window. The sergeant was still writing. He wasn't the talkative kind, rather sullen in fact, which suited him, because he himself wasn't the talkative kind either. But at this moment everything looked sullen; the weather, this damned hut, the whole camp, his life. Oh yes, his life . . . What was he going to do with himself tonight? Buses would be packed, as would Hereford . . .

There was Maggie and Mrs Robson.

* * *

At half past six he carefully placed the two boxes on the carrier on the back of the bike and set out for the hills. The sky was high and bright with stars, the air cutting, and for a moment he was taken back to the northern winters, when the lungs would object to the searing iciness of the air, and suddenly he was back in the Hall. He could see the firelight flickering over the Christmas decorations; he could see the young lad he once was, filled with excitement. It was his birthday and tomorrow was Christmas morning, and there would be all those presents. There was always the hope in him that Martin and Harry would like what he had got them. It didn't matter so much about his mother, or his Uncle Arthur, but it had been important that his cousins should exclaim loudly with surprise at his gifts.

He stopped on a turn in the hill just before the last run to the cottage and looked away into the night, where he knew the valley lay. In the far, far distance the thin line of a searchlight played across the sky, and as he watched it he thought that even tonight there could be raids and people would die. They were lucky in this quarter of the country. He supposed he was lucky, too; but no, he'd rather be where things were happening, so thick, so fast that there'd be no time to think.

As he mounted his bike again he wondered how they would receive him; he wasn't expected until tomorrow . . .

They received him with bright faces, a gabble of words and, in a way, open arms, for Lizzie, in an impulsive movement, pulled him to her, saying, 'Happy Christmas, lad. Oh! I am pleased to see you. What's happened? I thought you wouldn't be here until the morning?'

'What went wrong; you were for Hereford, weren't you?' Maggie was taking his coat.

'I . . . I changed my mind.'

'You did?'

'Well, I'm here, aren't I?'

231

Maggie looked at him through narrowed eyes, and for a moment the smile left her face; and then she said, 'In the life. In the life,' and turned and led the way into the sitting-room.

'Oh, this is nice. It is.' Joe stood looking around him. The mantelpiece and the pictures were trimmed with holly and in the corner of the room stood an artificial Christmas tree, decked with tinsel, coloured glass baubles, and a traditional fairy on the top. The fire was blazing in the grate and a lamp standing on a side table was sending out a soft glow. He turned and looked at Maggie and for a matter of seconds there was a stillness between them and in it they exchanged a warm glance. Then Lizzie came bustling into the room, saying, 'Well, sit yourself down and take that tunic off, and put your feet up . . . Oh! this is nice. Now this really *is* Christmas Eve, to have a man about the house once again. How much leave have you got?'

'Forty-eight hours.'

'Well, in that case, there's no need for you to go back tonight. You can camp out on there.' She pointed to the sofa.

'Oh, I couldn't do that.'

'Away with you! You'll do what you're told. You're nothing but a lad, after all, and I have a way of dealing with lads.'

'It's my birthday, I'm twenty-one.'

Now why on earth had he said that? There had been no need to tell them . . . Yes there had; he wanted someone to know it was his birthday, to be pleased it was his birthday; there was some part in him at this moment that was craving for comfort. He started as the thought occurred to him that they were both about to fall on his neck and kiss him; but it was Lizzie grasping his hand and shaking it up and down, saying, 'Happy birthday, lad. Happy birthday. Now isn't this something, having a birthday on Christmas Eve? And a twenty-first. My! My! This calls for a drink.'

232

He had pulled off his tie and was handing it to Maggie when their fingers touched for a moment; then she too had hold of his hand, shaking it, saying, 'Twenty-one. Well, you could have fooled me; twenty-six, I would have said, at least, if not more. Oh, don't look like that; I meant it as a compliment.'

'Twenty-six! What are you talking about, girl? He just looks a bit of a lad. A bit serious, mind' – Lizzie poked her head towards him – 'a bit too serious, I'd say, for your age. Twenty-one. Isn't that wonderful, twenty-one! Oh, we must drink on this. Go and bring the bottle in, Maggie; we'll never have a better occasion for opening it.'

The most strange sensation was almost overwhelming him, there was a tightness in his chest, causing a constriction in his throat, there was pricking in the back of his eyes. On a note of desperation, he said to himself; for God's sake, don't cry. Yet he knew that if he could just sit down, put his head in his hands and let this feeling wash out of him, he would know some sense of relief. They were so kind, they were so good. Once again he was back in his early boyhood days amid the warmth of all those in the house.

'Sit down, lad.' Lizzie took her seat beside him on the couch and, looking tenderly at him and her countenance straight and the tone of her voice serious, she said, 'Before she comes back I want to say this to you: thank you for coming; you've made her Christmas. I've never seen her look so glad for years.'

As she put her hand on his a strong feeling of guilt pierced his emotions, and he blamed himself for making use of them. That's all he was doing, making use of them, both of them, but mostly of Maggie, and the feeling persisted, checking his efforts to be cheerful.

But two brandies and three glasses of home-made wine later, the guilt-feeling evaporated and was replaced by a desire to sing; and this he did, standing to the side of the piano and in a voice that should never be raised in song, for he was tone deaf. Nevertheless, he joined it to Maggie's and Lizzie's and they went through a repertoire from *The Old Bull And Bush* to *Come All Ye Faithful* . . .

It had been a grand evening. They all said so. And when at last they had made up the bed on the couch for him and he had bidden them a last good-night, he sat for a time staring into the fire, aware that he had a silly contented smile on his face and a wish in his heart that it would remain.

He didn't recall undressing and lying down, nor what it was that woke him some long time later, but slowly opening his eyes he saw through the glow of the dying fire the figure of Maggie bending down near the Christmas tree.

In an effort to clear the muzziness from his head he blinked. For a moment he didn't know where he was, and as he peered at the humped figure in the blue dressing-gown, he imagined that it was a child he was seeing.

When she straightened up he immediately closed his eyes and, breathing evenly, he feigned sleep. He did not hear her come towards the couch but he was aware that she was standing over him, looking down on him, and he found it an effort not to open his eyes. Then his inside gave a violent jerk, although outwardly he made no movement, as her breath came on to his face and he felt her lips touch his with a touch that was feather light, and in this moment he had the impulse to put up his arms and take her into them, to comfort her and to let her comfort him. And he might have done so had not the thought struck him, like a wedge rammed home, that Carrie was sleeping just a matter of ten or so miles away, and that it just might be possible for him to see her tomorrow. Or was it today? He had no idea of the time.

He was not aware that Maggie had moved away from the couch, it was only when he heard the slight creaking of the door that he knew he was alone once more, and he turned on his side and groaned.

234

9

Christmas Day was bright and dry; he had spent most of the morning cutting and splitting logs and kindling. The Christmas dinner was excellent but the jollity seemed forced, and he added his quota to the others'.

By half-past two in the afternoon they had finished the washing up and were all sitting round the fire. And after Lizzie had nodded off to sleep, Maggie startled him by leaning towards him and whispering, 'Look, if you want to go in and see those friends of yours, it's all right with me . . . with us.'

'What makes you think . . . ?'

'Shut up! and get yourself away while it's light.'

He stared at her face close to his, his eyes focused on her mouth. It was a nice-shaped mouth. He heard himself whispering now, 'Will you come too?' and only just stifled a sigh of relief when she said emphatically, 'No! No! Anyway, I wouldn't know any of them. Look, I'll make a cup of tea and . . . '

'What about?' He nodded towards Lizzie, and Maggie whispered, 'Oh, she'll understand. In any case, she's so grateful that you've spent the time you have with us.'

As he watched her go softly from the room his head drooped against the mixture of emotions that were passing through him: excitement at the thought of seeing Carrie and not a little shame that he should bolt off after the kindness he had received.

His head jerked up and he stared at the slumped figure of Lizzie. Her eyes were still closed and her words were scarcely audible, yet distinct to his ears, as she said, 'Take her with you, Joe, please; she needs a bit of jollification.' There was a pause and then the words, softer now: 'You owe her that much.'

God! What a situation. His face was red; he felt that his whole body was blushing, as if he had been caught committing an indecent act. He stared down at her, and for a moment he saw her through the eyes with which he viewed his mother, both going to any lengths to protect their own, to give them what they thought was best for them. Yet the difference between this old woman and his mother was that her desire was completely selfless.

Awkwardly he rose, gave one long look at the still supposedly sleeping figure, then went from the room and into the kitchen, where Maggie was just about to pick up the tray from the table, and like a young boy who was repeating a polite lesson he said, 'I'll only go if you come with me.'

She took her hands from the tray and rested them on the edge of the table while she looked at him, and she said flatly, 'Now you don't want me there; they're old friends . . .'

'Don't be silly. They're not really old friends, I mean the ones who'll be there; with the exception of two, Mick and his sister.' He gave a short laugh now as he added, 'The sister who's . . . well, who's giving the party, I can't stand, and you'll know her when you meet her. Go on. Go on, get yourself ready.' There was a command in his voice now, but she remained staring at him for a while longer until he said, 'Well, if you won't come, I won't go.'

Slowly now, her gaze dropped from his face and, lifting up the tray once more, she said, 'I'll have to explain to Aunt.'

236

'Here, give it to me' – he almost grabbed the tray from her – 'I'll do the explaining. You go on up and get ready.' And like a jovial suitor, he added, 'Don't take too long over it either.'

When he re-entered the sitting room Lizzie was sitting up straight in the chair, her eyes open, but neither of them exchanged a word; even when he handed her the cup of tea she did not give her usual, 'Thanks, lad.' Not until some fifteen minutes later, when Maggie appeared in the room, did she speak, and then, nodding her head at her niece, she said, 'Now, that's more like it . . . I've always liked that one.'

Joe said nothing, but he gazed at the figure for a moment with the same surprise as he might have done to see the ugly duckling turned into a beauty.

Although Maggie was still no beauty he had never imagined that she could look so presentable. For the most part he had seen her in the NAAFI overall and cap, or a skirt and blouse. Dressed in the latter, she had appeared like a sack pulled in at the middle. But here she was, strangely looking less fat and even a little taller; perhaps it was the dress. This was of corded velvet, the colour of which he would describe as a soft rose shade and trimmed with grey. It reached below her calves; it had long sleeves, and the square neck showed the cream tint of her skin at the top of her breasts, unlike that of her face, which had lately appeared slightly weather-beaten. Even this now looked less so, because her face was made up, and her brown hair, taken straight back from her forehead and behind her ears, took the podginess from it. He smiled at her softly as he said, 'That's a lovely dress.'

She said nothing, but Lizzie put in, 'I'm glad to see you in it again.' And, turning and looking at Joe, she said 'She's lost over a stone and a half in the last two months.'

'Oh! Aunt Lizzie.' Maggie went to put on her coat, and when he helped her into it he noticed it was a match to the dress; grey outside like the trimmings on the dress but lined with the coloured material. It was the kind of quality

237

his mother used to wear, being the clothes that belonged to his Uncle Arthur's wife.

'If she keeps on dieting she could be down to ten stone in another six months.'

'Aunt Lizzie, will you shut up!'

'Why should I? I'm in me own house, it's Christmas Day, and if you don't like it, you can get out and quick. And mind' — she now wagged her finger from one to the other — 'don't you come back here roaring drunk or else I won't let you in.' Then applying herself to Joe, she said, 'You're not due back in camp tonight, are you?'

'No, I have a forty-eight.'

'Then I'll have a bed made up for you. Now get yourselves off and enjoy yourselves.'

'You're sure you'll be all right?' Maggie was standing in front of her now, and Lizzie, looking tenderly down on her, said, 'My dear, did you ever know me not to be all right? I'm the one that can see to herself, remember? And—' she turned her attention to Joe now and, her voice strident, she added, 'and see to anybody who gets in me way, so watch out, you.'

They went out laughing, and they laughed more when Maggie, realising she couldn't ride her bike in high heels, had to dash back upstairs for her service shoes . . .

It was just getting dark as they rode into Hereford. The town seemed empty, for most people would be indoors, and there was little sound until they reached the house. Before knocking on the door, Joe could hear Janet's strident tones and laughter coming from within.

It was Mick who opened the door and he stared at them for a moment, his face blank. Then his features springing into a wide grin, he held out his hand, saying, 'Happy Christmas, Joe. Happy Christmas. And . . . ?'

They were over the step now and in the small hallway, and Joe said, 'This is Miss LeMan . . . Maggie.'

'How do you do, Maggie? Happy Christmas.'

'And to you . . . '

'Mick. Me name's Mick. He forgot to introduce us. Here, let me have your things.' He turned his head now and called, 'Janet! Janet!' Then looking at Joe, he said, 'She can't hear anything but her own voice. Listen to her.' Then pulling a face, he said, 'She's well away already; you know our Janet.'

Yes, Joe knew their Janet, and he found himself hoping that Maggie wouldn't be disgusted by Janet and her talk, forgetting that Maggie was very capable of handling all types, having had a great deal of experience in this line.

'Oh. Hello! Hello, there! Joe, boy. Happy Christmas!' He was enveloped in Janet's arms and her spirit-fumed breath was on his face and when she kissed him, he had the desire to knock her flying. He hadn't fully realized until this moment the extent of his dislike for this particular member of the Smith family, and that it had its beginnings many years ago when he had visited the Smiths' kitchen.

And when she stood back and dropped a curtsey and said, 'Welcome, Sir,' Mick cried at her, 'Give over and mind your manners. Look; this is Maggie, Joe's friend.'

'Oh.' Janet stood for a while surveying Maggie before she held out her hand. 'Pleased to meet you,' she said. Then she stared at her again before turning to Joe and saying, 'There's somebody in the next room who wants to meet you an' all.'

For the second time that the day Joe felt the heat passing over his body, but this time it was accompanied by the racing of his heart.

'Go on!' Janet thrust out her arm and pushed him. Then turning to Maggie, she said, 'Come on upstairs and I'll show you where to put your things.'

So Joe came face to face with Carrie, alone, as it were. There were six other people in the room, but that didn't seem

239

to matter, as long as Maggie wasn't present. Somehow, that would have put a damper on his greeting, made it awkward. As it was he found no words to say. After the introductions to the rest of the company, there they were standing behind the couch looking at each other.

She was more beautiful than he remembered her, and thinner, much thinner; and different somehow, yet her voice sounded the same when she said, 'Hello, Joe.'

There was a long pause before he could answer, 'Hello, Carrie. How are you?'

'Very well. And you?'

'Fine. Fine.' Again there was silence between them, and it seemed to envelop the room now until Janet burst in again, crying, 'Well, you've got it over, the great reunion? By the way, Bill and Polly, this is Joe, Sir Joe. We were brought up together. Would you believe that? We were. We romped together. Didn't we, Joe?' He found himself suddenly hugged to Janet's side. Then with a wave of her hand Janet indicated Maggie, who was standing near Mick: 'And this is Joe's friend,' she said. She now bounced her head towards Carrie, crying, 'Just mingle, mingle.'

'Come and sit down. Can I get you something to drink?' Mick led Maggie towards a chair to the side of the window.

'No, thank you.'

'Not a little sherry?'

'Well yes, perhaps a sherry.'

'Good.'

For a moment Maggie was left alone, and she surveyed the company. Her eyes travelled quickly over them and came to rest on the girl who was sitting beside Joe. So this was it. You could see by the look on his face that this was it. This was her. She was beautiful. She had everything: hair, eyes, teeth, skin, figure, the lot. If she hadn't sensed there was someone in his life, she would have known it now as she had watched them standing looking at each other a few minutes ago.

240

'There you are.' Mick handed her the glass.

'Thank you.'

'I've been in the camp a while now, and we've never met.'

'Well' – she smiled at him – ' 'tisn't likely, is it? I serve the lower grades.' They laughed together.

'Do you like being at Madley?'

She gave a little huhing sound, 'Well, I suppose I should say, since I've got to be in the war, I'm lucky, because my home's quite near. And it's beautiful countryside.'

'Yes, it is that, and I like the country. I'm a country man myself.'

'Yes?'

'I suppose Joe's told you our family worked for his people?'

'No. No. He doesn't talk much about them; about his people.'

He bent his head towards her and his whispered voice was hardly audible in the chatter as he said, 'You don't know who he is, then? Really is?'

'No; should I? Is it a secret?'

'Yes. I suppose in a way it is. Well, he wants it kept a secret. But I thought, you being a pal of his, he . . . well, he might have told you.'

'Told me what?'

'That . . . that he is a baronet. I think that's it. Anyway, he's Sir Joseph Jebeau.'

She screwed her face up until her eyes became almost pin points and, turning her head slowly, she looked to where Joe had been sitting with the girl. But they were no longer there. She hadn't noticed their going from the room. Returning her narrowed gaze back to Mick, she said, in an awesome whisper, 'Joe! Joe a Sir?'

'Yes, but don't let on if he hasn't said anything. And for God's sake, don't spread it round the camp.' She made no

241

comment on this particular request, but said, 'If that's the case, he should be . . . well, he shouldn't be just a corporal.'

'That's how he wants things.'

'Is . . . is there another reason?'

'Yes, you could say so. You see, he never wanted the title, and he came into it through dead men's shoes. His father died abroad and when Joe was five, he and his mother came to live with his uncle, Sir Arthur Jebeau. Well, he was killed in a motor accident. But he had two sons, Martin and Harry. Harry was only in his twenties when he died and then, not long after, Martin was shot . . . and . . . and me father along with him, by poachers. So that's how Joe came into the title. It seemed almost to turn his brain. Well, not the title, but the loss of all those dear to him. And the odd thing about it was, both his uncle and his cousin had been on the point of marrying when their deaths came about.'

'So that accounts for it.' She had spoken more to herself, but Mick said, 'Accounts for what?'

She shook her head before saying, 'His reticence, his sadness. There's a sort of innate sadness in him.'

'Yes, there is, isn't there? But he's always been a sensitive lad, right from a nipper. And although he was from the house, we . . . we were like . . . well, I won't say brothers, but we were very pally.'

'And . . . and your sister?' They were looking into each other's eyes now, a straight look. 'Was there anything between them?'

'Well' – he tossed his head slightly – 'they were fond of each other when they were little, but she was sent away to live with my Aunt and Uncle when she was just a bairn.'

'And now?' She was asking about the road she knew, and anyone with eyes had the answer to that.

'No. Well, no' -- he stumbled – 'what I mean is . . . well . . . well, I wouldn't think so. Anyway, the war has changed her, I mean, her outlook and things. But hasn't it done that to all of us?' He grinned at her.

'Come on, you lot, come on and have some tea and then let the jollification begin.' Janet was standing at the room door and as the company rose to obey the command Mick, turning to Maggie, said, 'You won't have to take any notice of Janet, she's a bit high.'

And Janet proved to get higher and higher as the evening wore on. At times Joe felt he could strangle her for she seemed bent on only two things: organising games where kissing and hugging were the prime objectives, such as passing a balloon down a line of people without it being touched by hands. She had manoeuvred herself next to him in this game and the contact of her body made him feel sick. Her second objective seemed to be to keep him and Carrie separated . . .

It was nine o'clock and Maggie was sitting at the piano playing one popular song after another, the whole company surrounding her in chorus, and it was now that, having edged his way towards Carrie, where she was standing near the door, he took her hand and quietly pulled her out into the hall, then along the corridor and into the dining-room. Once inside, he closed the door, and still holding her hand he stared at her and said softly, 'Hello, Carrie.'

'Oh.' She closed her eyes while smiling broadly and she shook her head as she said, 'Joe. Joe. You haven't changed, not a bit.'

'You don't really believe that?'

'No.' Her expression was serious now. 'You have changed. You . . . you look much older. But you're not the only one; we both have changed. Everybody's changed, everything's changed. The war's seen to that. And what's more, I . . . I changed once Dad went; something happened to me after he died. Life looked different, I began to think differently; deeper, if I can put it that way.'

'May I ask you something?'

243

'Anything.'

'Do you remember what we talked about when we last met?'

There was a pause before she replied, 'Yes. Yes, I do, Joe.'

'Then you'll know how I feel, still feel about you. I . . . '

'Joe' – she caught both his hands in hers now – 'please. It can't, I mean nothing can come of it, because . . . '

When she stopped he asked flatly, 'Why? Have you found someone else?'

'*Oh, no. No.*' She smiled at him now while shaking her head. 'No, nothing like that.'

'Well then, why not? Why not me?'

'Oh Joe.' She now let go of his hands and turned towards the fire and, lifting her hand, she placed it on the edge of the mantelshelf and bent her head towards her arm as she said, 'If I were to explain, you wouldn't believe me, and . . . '

'Well, try to explain' – he was standing behind her now – 'if there's no one else and you don't actually dislike me.'

She swung round now and faced him. 'Dislike you? Oh Joe! How could anybody dislike you?' She stressed the word 'anybody'. 'If I could love anybody else, it would be you.'

'What do you mean, anybody else?'

Again she had hold of his hands and what she said now, was, 'Promise you'll try to understand what I'm going to tell you. Promise?'

'I promise . . . '

'What the hell are you two doing in here! Eh? Come on, there's a party in the other room. We are going to play sardines. What's up with you, our Carrie? You can't come the sergeant-major here.' Janet pushed Joe to one side and, gripping Carrie by the arm, she pulled her out of the room, leaving Joe standing, his fists gripped by his sides, an impotent rage filling him.

244

Oh, that woman! His head drooping on to his chest, he gritted his teeth: if she wasn't careful he'd say something to her that he might later regret. He could still hear her voice coming from the sitting-room. It was well above the chatter and laughter of the party; she was likely arranging the game and could at any moment come back and haul him into it. Oh no, no, he couldn't stand that.

Mick's bed was in a box-room at the end of the upstairs corridor. The men had been directed to leave their outdoor coats there. The next minute he found himself taking the stairs two at a time, and he had just reached the top of the stairs when the whole party seemed to erupt into the hall and a voice came at him shouting. ' 'Tisn't fair, he's got a start.'

When he reached the box-room he stood for a moment leaning with his back against the door before groping for the light switch. The furniture in the room consisted of a single bed, a corner wardrobe, and a small dressing-table. He couldn't see a chair, and so, pushing the clothes to one side, he dropped down on to the foot of the bed and, his arm over the wooden rail, his body sagged as he sat listening to the confusion on the landing and with his eyes directed towards the door, hoping desperately that no-one would take refuge in here, except it be Carrie, or even Maggie. Oh, he wouldn't mind Maggie.

When the door opened abruptly his body, as if pulled by wires, jerked up from the bed and he stared at Janet who, having entered the room, now stood with her back tight against the door. And when someone apparently attempted to follow her she pushed her hand behind her and slid in the bolt.

'Well! here we are, then.' She moved from the door and took two steps towards him, and as she stood looking at him he imagined that she had sobered up somewhat, for her voice was steady as she said, 'I've . . . I've been wanting to have a word with you, private like, Joe, but there's been no chance.

245

Sit down.' She stretched out her hand and went to push him on to the bed, but he jerked his body to the side. At this, the expression on her face altered and she said, 'Don't take on like that; all I want to say is, half a loaf's better than no bread, and there'll be no strings attached.' Her face slid into a slow smile, her head drooped to the side and she said, 'I know I go on a bit loud like, but it's just a cover-up. I'm lonely as hell, an' so are you. Lonely folk recognise each other. Do I . . . I make myself plain?'

'Yes, very. Get out of my way!'

The tone of his voice brought her lips tight and her brows together, and when he went to pass her her arm shot out and she said, 'Don't take that tone with me. You might have a title but you're no better than anybody else, 'cos your mother's the biggest scrounger going. She an' you lived off the master and Mr Martin all your lives. They were class, they were. But not you or your mother. And I was a fool to lower meself to you. As for you looking down your nose at me, what was your mother but a whore? Everybody knew about her an' the master.'

'Then there's two of you.'

'You cheeky bugger!' Her hand came out across his face, and as he staggered back from her she screamed, 'You! to call me a whore. It's your lady-love you should give that name to. But no, that's too clean for her. You're a stupid young bugger! You know that? You always were and you always will be. Talk about flogging a dead horse. Carrie, dear Carrie, the dirty, unnatural little scut that she's always been.'

'Shut your mouth!' Even as he growled the words at her his mind was adding, What do you mean? Unnatural scut? And then she told him. Her voice rising now almost to a scream, she pulled open the door as she yelled, 'Go and ask her! And ask him, our Mick! Face up to them. See what they have to say to it.'

She was standing on the landing now and a bedroom door had opened and a number of people had emerged. Somebody had switched on the landing light and the guests were standing blinking as they looked towards Janet, who was flailing her arms now as Joe passed her and she was still yelling, 'Go on! ask them. I'd like to see their faces. They've been at it since they were bairns. She slept with him until she was nine and then me Dad moved her off out of the way. But that didn't stop it, did it?'

He was aware that he was standing beside Maggie and that she had caught hold of his arm.

'He called me a whore. Whores are clean compared with the likes of her. Aye, and you an' all, our Mick. Tell him. Go on, tell him the truth.'

'Good God! Good God!' Joe heard the whispered comments from both sides of him and they seemed to whirl around his head, and the voice of his thoughts joined them, saying, 'Good God! Good God!' Then as through a blur he saw Mick approach Janet and, taking her by the shoulders, drag her backwards into a room. He felt Maggie turn him about and lead him towards the stairs. And there, at the head, he came face to face with Carrie. There was no vestige of colour in her skin. She looked like a corpse, one who had died in shock. Her lips opened and twice they came together but they emitted no sound.

At the bottom of the stairs he pushed Maggie from him. He felt he was going to be sick. There was an outdoor lavatory, and he made his way to it.

But he wasn't sick. He came out of the lavatory and stood beside the door looking upwards. The sky was carpeted with stars and he heard a voice seeming to come down from the heavens saying, 'Promise you'll try to understand what I'm going to tell you. Promise?'

She . . . she had expected him to understand that . . . that she and Mick were . . . *No! No!* His mind, in a scream, was

247

refuting the very thought of it, when, down the path, he saw a dark figure coming towards him. It was that of the man who had once said to him, 'You mustn't say you love a man.' And he remembered he had made it sound as though it was slightly indecent. Yet, what had he done . . . had been doing, even then?

'Joe. Joe, listen to me.'

There he was standing in front of him, the boy who had taught him to fish, who had walked and run the hills with him, whose sayings had seemed to his young ears so mature, so wise.

'Joe, it isn't what you think.'

What did he think? Had he ever thought clearly in his life? All his thinking had been two feet above his head. That's what Harry used to say about him. 'I can see your thoughts wafting two foot above your head, laddie.'

He had always thought the best of everybody; nobody was really bad, until he had to face the fact that his mother had murdered four people. But again, murder was clean compared with this . . . this thing that this man had done to his sister, the girl who he himself had loved and who had once said she loved him; this thing was not clean, it was vile.

'Joe, you've got it all wrong. It's true I love Carrie and she me, but . . . '

'*Take your hands off me!*'

As he spoke Joe stepped back and tried to bring Mick's face into focus through the darkness. But it was blotted out by a series of pictures flashing in front of it! One showed him Carrie saying, 'Dad's going to send me to Aunt Alice's to live'; then another, a sharp-edged picture this time, in the kitchen at her Aunt Alice's. He was looking through into the scullery and Mick was kissing Carrie good-bye, not on the cheek but on the mouth.

He saw the reason now, too, why Mick had left the farm to go and live in the town; he was nearer to her there. And

248

Carrie. Hadn't she once said to him, 'There's nobody like our Mick. I love our Mick'?

'I've got to make you understand, Joe, there was never anything like that . . . I swear.'

That's what she had said, 'I've got to make you understand, Joe.' There shot through him now, like the explosion from a bomb, a wild rage and, like a bomb, its one aim was to destroy. So quick was his attack that when his hands gripped Mick's throat the two of them overbalanced and fell over the low stone kerb bordering the vegetable garden. As they rolled over Mick tore the thumbs away from his windpipe and, gasping, he endeavoured to stop the flailing of Joe's arms. Even when they stumbled to their feet and Joe's fists caught him in the mouth, he still did not retaliate. But he yelled at him, 'Joe! Joe, man, stop it! Listen. For God's sake . . . '

When they were dragged apart by other men from the party, Joe, the frenzy still on him, turned on them and when his fists caught one of the men on the side of the head, he received in return a blow that sent him staggering backwards. When again he came forward, another punch in the stomach this time brought him on to his back, and when his head hit the kerb he lay stunned, while the hubbub faded back into the house.

After being assisted to his feet, he stood swaying like a drunken man and dimly, as if from the end of a tunnel, he heard Maggie's voice saying, 'Will you stay with him till I get our things?' And a man saying, 'Yes, yes; but I can't see him able to ride.'

'No, you're right.'

As Maggie ran into the house, she could hear Janet's voice, tear-filled now, coming from the front room, babbling on in some form of explanation, and as she mounted the stairs she caught a glimpse of two men attending to the sergeant, as she thought of Mick.

It was at the top of the stairs that she ran into Carrie. Carrie had two clean towels in her hand, and they stared at each other for a second. It seemed as if Carrie was going to speak, but changing her mind, she turned and ran down the stairs, and Maggie ran first into the main bedroom, picked up her coat, hat and shoes, dragged them on, then went out on to the landing again and opened the doors until she found where the mens' things were; and having taken up Joe's overcoat and cap, she scrambled downstairs again.

At the foot of the stairs she met two of the women apparently about to make their departure, and one of them, nodding towards her, said, 'Disgraceful affair. Disgraceful. Tut! tut!' And the other said, 'I should never have come. George warned me about her . . . And such a carry on in the family. Really! Who would believe it?'

Yes, who would believe it? Maggie went out of the side door and down the garden. The man was still supporting Joe as he leant against the lavatory wall, and again he said to her, 'He's in no shape, miss, to go on a bike; he'll never make it.'

'I . . . I'm all right.'

'Here! get into your coat.'

Joe pulled himself from the support of the wall and she helped him into his coat and buttoned it up and placed the cap on his head. As she did so she felt a stickiness on her fingers. He was bleeding. Turning to the man, she said, 'Do you live in the town?' and when he answered, 'Yes,' she asked, 'Do you know anyone who's got a garage or a van who would run us out Madley way?'

'Oh, that's a tall order tonight. There's Foster's, round by the station. He supplies the camp, I know, so he gets a good ration. You . . . you could try him, but it'll cost you something. Do you know where the station is?'

'Yes, yes, I know where the station is. And I know Foster's. Thank you very much.'

'Nice how-d'you-do on a Christmas night.'

'Yes,' she repeated flatly, 'a nice how-d'you-do on a Christmas night . . . Would you open the back gate for me, please?'

Turning now to Joe, she said, 'Do you think you can walk?'

' . . . I'm all right.'

A minute or so later, she pushed the two bikes out into the lane, and when Joe lurched to the side she said quickly, 'Hang on to the handle-bar.' Then turning her head towards the man, she said, 'Thanks. Thanks for your help.'

'Wish I could do more.'

Slowly they went up the lane and into the street, and when they came to the end of it and turned into the main road she stopped and said, 'Do you think you'll be able to make it?'

'I'm all right.'

These seemed to be the only words he had left . . .

Mr Foster was having a party and he peered at her from the front door of his house, saying, 'You must be mad, miss, to expect me to go out tonight all that way. Anyway, I'm not a taxi service.'

'I . . . I know you're not.' Her voice was soft with a note of pleading in it as she went on, 'But . . . but my friend has . . . has had an accident and we can't make it home on our bikes. I'll make it worth your while; I'll give you double or even treble what you charge.'

He took a step towards her now, pulling the door closed behind him, saying, 'The damn black-out.' Then added, 'Well now, if you're willing to part with six quid I could make an effort. Where do you say you want to go?'

'Bramble Cottage. It's about five miles out of Madley. You could be there and back in an hour.'

He peered towards Joe who was leaning over the bike now, and he said, 'He's not just drunk, is he?'

'No, no, he's not drunk at all.'

251

'What kind of an accident has he had?'

'Er . . . well, he . . . he went to someone's aid and got mixed up in the mêlée, and he fell on his head.'

'Huh! anybody who interferes in a row deserves to fall on their head. Mind your own business, that's what I say. There's enough accidents without looking for them. Well, hang on, I'll be with you in a minute or so.' He went into the house again, and she turned to Joe and, using his words now, she said, 'It'll be all right; we'll soon have you home.'

Between them, she and the man helped Joe down from the high seat in the front of the van past a startled Lizzie and laid him on the couch in the sitting-room. Then after asking her Aunt for the six pounds, she paid the man, thanked him and closed the door on him.

Having quickly taken off her coat and hat, she now hurried into the sitting-room where Lizzie, kneeling by the couch, greeted her with, 'In the name of God! what's happened?'

'I'll tell you later. We've got to get his things off and see to his head. It's still bleeding, and I don't know where else he's hurt.'

'But what happened?'

'Aunt Lizzie, for the Lord's sake, don't ask me anything now, just let me get him undressed; he's in a bad way.'

Joe made no protest as they stripped him of his clothes. He wasn't quite aware of what was happening: there was a muzziness in his head, like a thick fog that was full of pain, in which snatches of conversation and words floated in and out.

'Will I get him a drop of whisky?'

'No, I don't think that's a good idea; he might have concussion or something. And look at that cut! A good two inches long. We'll have to cut the hair around it.'

'Look at his ribs. Good God! they're discolouring already. What'll they be like in the morning? And look at his shins,

252

all grazed as if he had been kicked. What kind of a fight was it, anyway? How many were there?'

'Shh! Be quiet for a minute.'

'What was it about, girl?'

'I can't tell you yet.'

'Nice thing to happen on a Christmas Day.'

For the second time that evening Maggie repeated, 'Yes, nice thing to happen on a Christmas Day.'

A spasm of pain shooting through the mist cleared his head for a moment as the hands turned him on to his side, and again, when they went to move him, he cried out and came to his senses, groaning now, 'Don't. Don't. My arm.'

'All right, Joe, all right.' Maggie's voice was soothing. 'Can you turn on your back again?'

When he tried to do this he realized he could only use one arm, and when slowly he dug his elbow into the couch it came to him he was almost naked.

'Push the cushions under his shoulder, Aunt Lizzie.'

When he fell back on the support of the cushions he lay panting for a moment. Gazing up at the two faces hovering over him, he muttered, 'I'm sorry.'

'Sorry? What are you talking about?' Lizzie's voice was brusque.

'Trouble, putting you to trouble.'

'Don't . . . don't talk such tommy rot. Just lie still there and I'll get a bottle for your feet.'

Lizzie gone from the room, he looked at Maggie and, his tone contrite, he said again, 'I'm sorry.'

'Don't talk, just lie quiet.'

'My head's splitting. What's happened to it?'

'You've got a gash in it. I've put some plaster on but it will have to be seen to.'

'What's . . . what's happened to my arm?'

'I . . . I don't know. Where does it pain?'

'The shoulder. I can't move it.'

She put her fingers gently on his bare flesh before saying softly, 'You've likely put it out. But if that was the case I don't think you could have borne us to touch it before. And Mr Foster helped you in on that side. Anyway, we'll get the doctor to look at you tomorrow.'

'No, no.' He shook his head. 'I . . . I have to get down to camp.'

'All right. All right,' she said soothingly. 'We'll see.'

Lizzie came in with the water bottle and a hot drink and three aspirins, and after they had settled him and he had closed his eyes and seemed to be resting, if not asleep, Lizzie beckoned Maggie into the kitchen, and there, closing the door quietly, she said, 'Now, will you please tell me how he came by that lot?'

Before answering, Maggie sat down on a chair and she drooped her head forward and let out a long sigh of weariness.

'He had a fight with his so-called friend,' she said; 'a man called Mick Smith. Apparently the reason he was anxious to go to that party was to see this fellow's sister, Carrie.' She raised her eyes and looked at Lizzie as she said slowly, 'He's in love with her and, from what I can gather, always has been. They were brought up together, this Smith family and him. There's another sister called Janet. She's a bitch of the first water, a common slut, everything that's cheap. Joe must have got on the wrong side of her when she was likely making a pass at him . . . Anyway, she spilled the beans about—' She stopped speaking and bit on her lip and lowered her head again, and Lizzie said, 'Well, about what?'

'She said that the brother and sister, this girl Carrie and Joe's friend, had . . . well, been at it for years, ever since they were young.'

'At it?' Lizzie's lips seemed to have sprung away from her teeth. 'You mean . . . ?'

'Yes, that's what I mean. And the shock was too much for Joe. He went outside and this Mick Smith followed him. There was a commotion and when I got into the garden they were rolling on the ground and the other men were trying to separate them. But it didn't seem to be the brother that knocked the stuffing out of Joe; it was one of the other fellows. He went punch drunk, I mean Joe did, and when he hit this man, naturally the fellow went for him.'

'Well, well!' Lizzie lowered herself onto a stool by the side of the table. 'Poor Joe,' she said. 'But these things happen; it isn't unheard-of.'

Maggie glanced at her aunt, for her attitude seemed now to be different from what it had been a moment ago when she had first given her the news, and the reason for it was in her next words: 'Well,' she said, 'that should clear his mind of anything transpiring in that direction. I always knew there was something worrying him, and this has been it.'

'Not quite, Aunt Lizzie.'

'What did you say?'

'I said, not quite. The other bit of news I've got for you is even more startling. Our Corporal Joe Jebeau isn't just Corporal Joe Jebeau, he happens to be Sir Joseph Jebeau.'

There followed a long pause before Lizzie said, '*What?*'

'You heard what I said: Sir Joseph Jebeau.'

Lizzie now scrutinised Maggie through a narrowed gaze and when she was about to speak Maggie put in, 'And don't say, you're joking or, who are you kidding? or, have you been drinking? He's a Sir and this Smith family were workers on his estate, or that of his cousin before he died. He was shot, apparently, just after the war began, at the same time as this Smith family's father, who was the groom or game-keeper or such. It's all very vague. There was another heir to the title but he died when he was young, I understand; and their father before them was killed in an accident.'

255

'Dear God!' The words were soft like the amen at the end of a prayer. Then Lizzie turned and looked towards the door leading into the sitting-room and when she again faced Maggie she said, 'He's got nobody, then?'

'Oh yes. I asked Mr Smith, during the evening, about his mother, who apparently had brought him to this estate in Northumberland when her husband died. He didn't seem to want to talk about it, but what I did get from him was that she is alive, and still living there; and Mr Smith's sister, the eldest one, looks after her.'

'His mother alive and he never goes near her . . . never goes near the place? There's something fishy there.'

'Yes, I should say there is. But it isn't any of our business.'

'I don't know so much.'

'Aunt Lizzie—' Maggie looked straight into the faded blue eyes and she said quietly, 'stop hoping, stop planning, because whereas before the gulf might have been jumped by friendship or compassion, not even love could get him across it now. You follow me, Aunt Lizzie?'

Lizzie drew her chin into her neck before she said, 'I hear you, girl, but I don't follow you.'

10

Len Forbister leant over the counter towards Maggie and, his voice low, he said, 'He's settled, and not afore time. My God! you could die in this bloody place afore they'd let a doctor come to you.'

'What's wrong with him?' Maggie's face looked blank as she asked the question.

'Well, as far as I can gather he's got concussion, his shoulder's out, and a couple of ribs are broken. How he ever managed to get down from your place on his bike I'll never know. And I didn't know there was anything seriously wrong with him till this morning, when I couldn't waken him. I got a shock, I can tell you.

'When I brought the WO and we got him round the only thing he would say was he fell off his bike. Some bloody fall, that, if you ask me. And another funny thing: when I went to tell that Sergeant Smith what had happened to Joe – I understand he was a lifelong pal of his – the fellow just stared at me, and out of one eye because the other one's bunged up. And his lip was split into the bargain. When Jack Bisley quipped him about it the fellow looked at him as if he could kill him. But he answered me quite civilly, said he was sorry, but that was all. Then he turned round and got on with the job.

'Look, Lemon' – Len bent still further towards her – 'you know more about this than meets the eye. Bernstein tells me he rode out of the camp with him on Christmas Eve and he was making for your place. But what I understood before I went on leave was that he was going with Sergeant Smith for a kind of family reunion. He didn't say exactly that; you know Joe, a clam is wide open compared with him. But that's the sort of impression I got, because this Sergeant Smith and him seemed to have known each other for years.'

Maggie was saved from having to answer immediately by the demands to be served of other men further along the counter, and as there was only Peggy on duty with her she went about her business for the next five minutes. But when at last she returned to where Len was still standing with a cup of tea in his hand, she looked across at him and said briefly, 'It's as he says, he fell off his bike.'

'Oh, Lemon.'

'Oh, corporal.' She mimicked him.

Then laughing, Len said, 'All right, have it your own way. You know something?' He poked his head towards her and in a low voice muttered, 'I wouldn't mind having you beside me in a tight corner.'

He turned and left the counter, and she called softly after him, 'Corporal.' And when he turned back to her she said, 'Let me know how he is. And see if I may pop in, will you?'

'Will do.' He nodded at her, then said again, 'Will do.'

For the first three days Joe slept a lot. His mind was hazy and every time he attempted to think clearly his headache increased. Some part of him was glad to be lying at rest away from the bustle of the camp, away from the labs. Oh yes, away from the labs, for as the MO had done, so would they have said, 'How did you come by this lot?'

And he would have answered, 'I fell off my bike.'

258

The words sounded inane even to himself and they seemed to be the only ones he had spoken for days. He didn't want to talk because talking was the outcome of thinking and, oh God! he didn't want to think.

But after the third day the more he tried to suppress his thinking the more it rose to the surface of his mind, and again, as if looking at a film, incidents from the past followed one another in front of his closed lids. The actors in the film were always the same two people, and at night-time they assumed life-size proportions and faced him from the bottom of the bed, even talking at him, as last night when Carrie had said, 'I tried to tell you, I tried to make you understand,' and Mick said, 'You had plenty of warnings of how things stood but, being you, you would never face up to reality; you still believed in Santa Claus.'

That last was Mick's voice from the past. It surged up from the Christmas Eve of his fifteenth birthday when Mick had ruffled his hair and said, 'You're a funny one. You know, I think you still believe in Santa Claus.'

What had elicited that remark he didn't know; he only knew now that he was sick. The sickness didn't only appertain to his bruised body, it was in his heart, but more so in his mind, because he had the strong desire to retreat into the silence that he had been introduced to when he inherited the title.

He lay for two weeks in the sick bay. Maggie visited whenever she could, and no-one in the bay or in the NAAFI chipped her about her attention to him. But towards the end of the second week, the nursing orderly stopped her as she was leaving the ward. 'I notice he speaks to you, miss,' he said, 'but we can hardly get a word out of him. It's a nod or a shake of the head most times. He seems to have difficulty in answering the MO. Has he always been like this?'

259

She could have replied, 'He's a quiet sort of fellow, reticent,' but what she said was, 'I think it's the effect of the accident.'

'Yes, perhaps. Anyway, he's for out next week and sick leave, after, likely . . . '

The following afternoon, after having struggled up to the cottage in a blizzard, Maggie had hardly got through the door before she said to Lizzie, 'He's due for sick leave; will you have him here?'

'Why do you ask such a damn silly question? Of course I'll have him here. Where else would he go, by the sound of things? Anyway, how is he? And get those things off, you're wringing.'

'Better, I should say, at least in one way. But he hardly opens his mouth. It's yes or no, or I'm all right, but he's never volunteered a word on his own since he went in there.'

A short time later as they both sat before the fire drinking bowls of broth, Lizzie suddenly asked, 'What do you expect to get out of this, girl?'

When Maggie didn't immediately answer, Lizzie went on, 'You said the other night the gulf was so wide that it couldn't be breached, and in your own mind you've made yourself sure of this. So I ask you again, what do you expect to get out of it?'

'The pleasure of his company.'

'Oh my God!' Lizzie spluttered on a spoonful of broth; then wiping her mouth, she said almost angrily, 'That isn't like you. When we've done some plain speaking, as we have on many occasions, you've always given the impression there'll be no half loaves for you. If you couldn't have the real thing, then there'd be no substitute; you'd faced up to the fact that men, being what they are, rarely look below the skin.' She paused and sighed, then ended, 'It's strange; I've never seen you like this before.'

'I've never been in love before.'

260

Lizzie slowly put her bowl down on the side table and looked at the young woman sitting opposite her. She was fat, but not as fat as she had been; the way she wore her hair did nothing to enhance her, nor did her uniform; but the quiet sadness that was expressed on her countenance seemed at this moment to make her beautiful. Lizzie leaned forward and put her hand gently on her knee, saying, 'I'm sorry, lass.'

'I know you are, Aunt Lizzie' – Maggie covered the blue-veined one with her own hand – 'but there's no need to worry about me; I've . . . I've known from the beginning it can come to nothing. I'm not one for deluding myself, you know that. There hasn't been much chance, has there?' She laughed and although the sound was without bitterness it caused Lizzie to close her eyes. And Maggie went on, 'I know a form of happiness when I'm with him; just to be near him is enough. I can't explain it to myself, the feelings he arouses in me; I only know I'd be quite content to go on as we are for the rest of my life. But that has as much chance of happening as of Hitler following Hess and telling us he's sorry for all the trouble he's caused . . . He's an attractive fellow, Aunt Lizzie, and he's not going to escape; he'll get over this last affair, or his first one – I don't know which it was – but somebody else'll come on the horizon and they'll have advantages that I haven't got.' She moved her head slowly. 'And that'll be that. Anyway, I think if the war were to end tomorrow he'd just walk off. You see, Aunt Lizzie, I've faced up to these things; I'm past the time when I thought miracles could happen and ugly ducklings could turn into swans.'

'You're not ugly.' Lizzie's voice was rough, and Maggie smiled at her faintly as she said, 'Well, that's some consolation. But you know, I would rather be ugly, Aunt Lizzie, than just plain. There's a WAAF down in the camp, she's got a face almost like a gargoyle, yet she makes it with the fellows because she happens to be about five feet seven, with a figure like nobody's business. You can get away with murder if you're slim.' Her smile widened.

'Well, it's up to you, isn't it? You should diet more.'

Maggie got to her feet, saying, 'I'll tell you something, Aunt Lizzie. If I eat less than I've been doing these past few months I'm going to lose the use of my legs.'

'That's daft; there's limits.'

'Well, you can't have it all ways; either you have me delicate and slim, or healthy and fat. The reverse is generally the case, but I'm an obstinate cuss.'

'You can say that again. Anyway, to get back to the point; you can tell him his bed's ready for him. I'll put him in your room.'

'Thanks, Aunt Lizzie. But there's one thing more I would ask of you and that is, don't talk about me to him . . . because it won't do any good.'

They looked at each other and Lizzie sighed, but she said nothing.

11

'Look, lad, why don't you talk any more?'

'I don't seem to have anything to say, Mrs Robson.'

'Call me Lizzie; it's easier, and you don't need to have anything important to say in order to talk, to have a bit of a chat. Is there something on your mind?'

'Yes.'

'You don't want to tell me about it?'

'I can't.'

'Well, fair enough. But that still leaves the weather and what's on the wireless, and the war.' She made a sound like a giggle now as she ended, 'All W's.'

Joe smiled faintly and as he looked at her there stirred in him a desire, a faint desire to do as she asked and to talk, talk about what was on his mind and what was under his mind, deep in the dark recesses where his mother lay staring at him; and about . . . the other thing. And if he could talk to anyone, he knew it was to this woman. He couldn't have talked to Maggie about it; no, not to Maggie. And now he was carrying another burden, forever. While doing his square-bashing and ramming a bayonet into a bag of straw, he had experienced no murderous desire, but now he knew what it was to feel the overpowering urge to kill, for that urge had been in the forefront of his mind when his hands had gone round Mick Smith's throat.

Lying in the little bedroom upstairs, the camp seeming to be a thousand miles away and war taking place on another planet, he wished fervently that he was anywhere else but in this quiet backwater. London, Coventry, any other place in the country where the bombs were playing havoc, or on some front facing an enemy, someone he could shoot at and who could shoot at him. That in the end was more important, that someone could shoot at him, because death seemed to be the only means of escape from his thinking. Except the quiet. If he could go right into the quiet he would find peace, because in there, there was no need to talk and no need to listen.

Once or twice during the past week he had almost escaped into it, but when you were living with someone like Lizzie, you couldn't entirely ignore them, because it appeared to be the height of bad manners, if not of ingratitude. He didn't have the same feeling concerning Maggie, because in a way he wanted to escape from Maggie, too; she knew too much about him now, for she had met Carrie and witnessed his humiliation.

There was another thing beginning to trouble him, and it was so alien to what his attitude had been over the past two years. Now, he failed to understand why the desire was strong in him to go home, back to the house. When he thought about the house he didn't see his mother in it; he only saw himself walking up the drive and in through the front door and Mary, Mary Smith greeting him. It was a troublesome thought for he knew it was the last thing he would ever do.

He had been back in the labs two days when the thin wire that kept his mind from sinking into the silence snapped.

His sense of relief had been almost overwhelming when he found out that Mick was no longer on the station and had returned to Cranwell. He had got over the first day of teaching pretty well, and the second day went smoothly too. In the evening there was to be another camp concert. It was being put on by a local group from the town. Len had tried to persuade him to come along, but he declined, saying he was going to read up some new stuff for tomorrow's lessons.

He was sitting on the side of his bed, a notebook on his knee, endeavouring to concentrate, but his mind kept jumping from one thing to the other. One of the lab sergeants had said to him earlier in the day, 'I don't know why you don't take up Morse; you can do it in your spare time and you would get promotion that way, out of this lot.' He didn't want promotion but he would like to get away from this lot. Yes, yes, he would, away to some place quiet.

There were half a dozen of his room-mates sitting round the stove. Their chatter and occasional bursts of laughter irritated him and the room became suffocatingly hot, fuggy. He'd be better sitting in the corporals' room off the NAAFI. He rarely made use of the room because it was usually packed, but he reasoned that tonight most of them would likely be at the concert.

He gathered up some loose sheets of paper from the bed, put them in his notebook, then put on his uniform jacket and greatcoat and went out. He had to pass the men at the stove, and although they turned and looked at him, no one spoke; they had given up trying to make conversation with him. All except Len.

Outside, the air was sharp and caught at his throat. He looked up into the sky. It was patterned with stars. He thought a silly thought: I could walk to you; if I kept on I could walk to you, and once among you I would write star-spangled poetry. When his shoulders gave a sudden jerk he almost stumbled.

There were only three men in the corporal's room and they were all busy writing. He wasn't aware of how long he himself had sat there writing, but when two of the men went

265

to leave the room and one remarked to the other, 'Saturday tomorrow, and I would be on duty, wouldn't I! He picks on me, he does,' Joe suddenly remembered that he too was on duty tomorrow, Naafi duty from dinner time till ten o'clock tomorrow night. He'd have to tell Maggie, because she would be expecting him up. At the moment she was helping out behind the scenes; she usually did at concerts.

He looked at his watch. It should be over now; he'd likely catch her if he hurried. There would be little chance tomorrow for, by the time he had finished in the labs and got cleaned up, she'd be gone.

When he came out of the NAAFI room he saw that the concert was already over, for the road ahead leading towards the main camp was thick with the departing audience.

He made his way round to the side door and, pushing it open, went through a passage and entered the area behind the stage. There were a few people still about packing clothes into boxes but they were already dressed for the road, some still wearing their make-up. There was an air of slight bustle, voices saying, 'Get a move on! Look slippy!' and, 'How do you think it went?'

He looked over their heads for a sight of Maggie. Away to the side of him, walking across the stage, he saw the sergeant who was usually in charge of these entertainments talking to an SP. To the right of him the back stage was clear. There was no sign of Maggie.

He walked the length of the back stage towards where a passage turned off, and as he neared it he heard her voice and it brought him to a stop for a matter of seconds, for she was saying, 'Take your hands off me! I said, take your hands off me! If I have to tell you again I'll scratch your eyes out. Do you hear?'

When he rounded the corner he saw her standing in the arms of Corporal Billings, who had her pressed close. But hearing Joe, he turned and looked towards him. His face was red, his mouth open, his lips wet. His grip on Maggie slackened, and as she thrust him from her and stood gasping, Joe looked from one to the other. But he didn't see either Billings or her; the faces before him were those of Mick Smith and Carrie.

As he sprang on Billings he heard Maggie scream: 'Don't! Don't, Joe. Joe, don't!'

He was pummelling the thick body, aiming for the red face, when, joined together, they fell to the ground and rolled over. Their bodies coming in contact with a piece of scenery brought it down on them.

There seemed to be commotion all about him, and when he was hoisted to his feet as if by a crane, he still continued to struggle.

'*Steady on! Steady on! Enough!*'

Of a sudden he became still as if in obedience to the voice. He felt his body sagging, he saw it sinking, going down and down; he felt the numbing quietness creeping over him, creating the desire to fall asleep where he stood, and when they turned him about and led him out into the open and across the square through the maze of huts to the guardroom, he went like a child between them.

He was aware he was being put on a charge; it also got through to him that he would be brought before the commanding officer on Monday morning. In the meantime he would report at set hours to the guardroom. Understood?

Yes, he understood; he understood everything that was being said to him but he could find no way to answer. And this annoyed the sergeant and the SP. But Warrant Officer Gilbert, who was present and had his own ideas of what was happening, or had happened to Corporal Jebeau, silenced them by saying briefly, 'Leave it . . . '

Later, sitting on the bed opposite, Len talked and talked at him: 'What possessed you, man? What came over you? She could have handled Billings, as she always has; it's a joke,

Billings being gone on her. And he's not a bad sort. Funny, but he's always been daft about her. Lays himself open. He cries when she sings, he does. You've messed him up, you know that? Lad, I can't understand you. You go round as solemn as a monk, then act like a madman. All I can say is, it's a good job you hadn't a gun in your hand.'

When Joe's body jerked in the bed and he turned his head to the side, Len said, 'All right, all right. Anyway, I've arranged it for tomorrow. I'm standing in for you, as your time will be taken up in reporting. You could be for the glasshouse, you know that? This is the second fight you've had within a few weeks. What's come over you, man?'

He would like to tell Len what had come over him in order to ease the pressure in his head, but every time he wanted to give an answer or to talk, a weird pain enveloped his whole body. When he remained quiet and said nothing he was at peace, or nearly so. But it was becoming more evident to him that he wouldn't really be at peace until he escaped from this place, because here he'd be forced to talk, answer questions, give reasons, and he was past giving reasons because all the reasons he gave were lies. And were he to give the real reasons, the truth, they would not call it a lie but the result of a twisted imagination that had gone into madness.

He slept heavily, and the following morning he went through the usual routine, but he did not go to the cookhouse for breakfast: in fact, he did not leave the hut until it was time to make his first report of the day to the guardroom.

12

It was half past four on Saturday afternoon when Maggie arrived at the cottage. Lizzie was waiting for her and before she had time to speak Lizzie said, 'Where have you been? I was worried. You said you'd be here at two and we were going to . . .'

'Aunt Lizzie.'

Lizzie became quiet and stared into the troubled face before her, and now she said quietly, 'What is it? What's happened? Is it him?'

'Yes, yes, it's him. He . . . he's absconded.'

'*He's what?*'

'He's gone AWOL.'

'But it's Saturday afternoon . . . well, I mean, he's off duty. What do you mean, gone absent?'

Maggie closed her eyes for a moment and bowed her head; then thumbing towards the stove, she said, 'Is that tea hot?' After Lizzie had poured her out a cup of tea she gulped on it before answering. 'He went for Billings last night as if he could kill him. You know, the fellow I told you about. He was making a pass at me, and Joe came on the scene. But I could have managed; I always do with that bloke; there was no need for him to belt him as he did. He . . . he's sick, Aunt Lizzie.'

They were looking at each other now. Then again Maggie gulped on her tea before she went on, 'He was put on a charge. He was to report every so often today. I saw him first thing; he was on his way to the guardroom. It was just after nine. I . . . I stood in front of him and said, "Oh Joe, I'm sorry." He . . . he tried to speak, kept opening and shutting his mouth, and then he said, "All right," and he touched my sleeve, like that.' She demonstrated by tapping Lizzie's hand. 'Then after a minute, when he tried to speak again, he said what I thought was, "Go home." I imagined he was referring to me coming up here this afternoon and I said, "Yes, Joe. All right, Joe. And I'll tell Aunt Lizzie." And at that, he smiled at me. It was a quiet reassuring smile. You know, he looked like he does when he's rested, relaxed. It was later when I saw Len Forbister; he's a pal of Joe's. He said Joe hadn't turned up for his second report. I hung on, and then at three o'clock I saw Len again. Joe still hadn't turned up, and he'd been reported absent without leave. Bill Regan and Amos Bernstein, two of the other corporals on the tech section, had been round the camp looking for him. But that was fruitless. His bike had gone. He must have walked out straight after the first report.'

'Dear God! the silly lad. Where on earth would he get to? Why didn't he come here?'

'I feel I know where he's got to, Aunt Lizzie.'

'You do?'

'He's gone to that place where apparently he never wanted to be; he's gone back to it. I know now he wasn't saying to me, "Go home" but "I'm going home".'

Lizzie got to her feet now, her head nodding as she said, 'Well, he won't be long there; they'll soon pick him up.'

'Likely that's the last place they'll dream he'll make for; most fellows don't go home unless they've got a wife there or some substitute. Anyway, I'm going to find out, Aunt Lizzie.'

270

'You're what!' Lizzie screwed up her eyes as she peered down at Maggie.

'I'm going to this place, this home of his, and I'll bring him back, because he's not a deserter, he's a sick man. And I feel ... I feel it strongly, Aunt Lizzie—' she nodded her head towards the old woman and she repeated, 'strongly, that whatever's troubling him deep inside started there; not only with that girl Carrie; you don't abandon your mother and all that goes with it for a girl like that.'

'But how in the name of God! do you propose to get that far, when you don't have a pass?'

Maggie was now on her feet bustling towards the hall and she called over her shoulder, 'My leave's long overdue. Miss Robertson was very accommodating; she gave me my pass and a travel warrant.'

'Did you tell her why you wanted them?'

'Don't be silly; I told her I was feeling very off-colour and if I didn't have a break I would likely have to report sick; I'm supposed to be visiting friends.' Maggie was running up the stairs now and Lizzie called up to her, 'I'm not with you in this; it's like a wild goose chase. If he's not there, what are you going to do?'

She didn't hear Maggie's mumbled answer but she turned about, went back into the kitchen and began to prepare sandwiches, and when Maggie next appeared in the kitchen there was a parcel of food ready for her and, standing beside it, a flask of tea.

'Can you get these in your case?' Lizzie's voice sounded ordinary, and Maggie, opening the case, answered quietly, 'Yes, twice as much; I've only got night-things.'

'And where do you expect to use them?' There was a tart enquiry now in Lizzie's voice and Maggie answered, 'Standing up in the train, I suppose.'

'That's another thing. Do you know where you're going? or how you're going to get there?'

'Yes, yes. I'm getting the seven-twenty from Hereford, change at Birmingham, and I should arrive in Durham some time after three in the morning. That's if we haven't got to crawl through any air-raids.'

'Yes, that's another thing' – Lizzie's face was screwed up tight – 'air-raids. You're walking straight into them. That end of the country gets blasted pretty often.'

'Well, it'll be an experience, won't it?'

'Don't be so bloody saucy; I'm serious.'

'So am I, Aunt Lizzie' – Maggie's words were slow and soft – 'never more serious. But if I can help in any way an air-raid's not going to put me off.' Then noticing Lizzie's moist, blinking eyelids, she altered her tone, saying briskly, 'It's about time I saw some action anyway. And just think, if I go through an air-raid, how I can brag when I get back to the camp, because I'll swear half of that ground staff have never seen an incendiary, even.'

'Well, listen to me; I haven't either, I mean, seen one dropped.'

Lizzie was standing very straight now, her hands folded one on top of the other at her waist, as she said, 'How am I going to know what's happened to you?'

Maggie hesitated for a moment, then said, 'I'll . . . I'll phone Donald down at the farm, and he'll give you a message. All right?'

After a moment Lizzie nodded and said, 'Yes, all right.' Then she went to Maggie and put her arms about her and hugged her close for a moment before she said, 'Take care, girl. And believe me, I understand why you feel you must do this, but I'll be worried every minute that you're away.'

At the door Lizzie said, 'Where'll you leave your bike?'

'Oh, at Mr Foster's; I'll need it when I come back.'

She turned and touched Lizzie's cheek as she said, 'Take care. Look after yourself.'

'Don't worry about me, it's you who'll have to take care . . . Go careful. Bye-bye, dear.'

'Bye-bye, Aunt Lizzie.' She paused a moment, then added in a mutter, 'I love you.'

Mounting the bike, she rode swiftly down the path, and as she did so she had the feeling she was leaving home for the first time and going into the unknown. And she was filled with a strange foreboding which had nothing to do with the journey or air-raids or even what would happen to Joe if she didn't get him back to the camp, but something indefinable that she couldn't put her finger on.

At seven o'clock the following morning, stiff and weary, she climbed up into the front seat of a milk lorry standing outside the station at Consett.

The milkman had come into the station with some packages to be sent by rail and as she had just got off the train and there wasn't a porter in sight she said to him, 'Can you tell me how I'll get to a place called Screehaugh?' He had stopped and looked at her curiously for a moment, then scratched his head as he said, 'Don't know no such place as Screehaugh, not as a place, miss. I know of a house by that name.' And to this she had answered, 'Yes, that's where I want to get to, a house called Screehaugh. From what I can gather it's just outside the town.'

'Oh no, miss' – he laughed as he shook his head – 'it's well beyond Edmundbyers and that's all of six miles away. And I should say Screehaugh is another good three. As for a bus, you'll maybe have to wait another hour or more, and then that just goes to Edmundbyers, not anywhere near Screehaugh.' He paused and looked down on the small figure, and his voice held a note of sympathy as he said, 'Come far, miss?'

'Yes, quite a way; I've been travelling all night.'

'Oh, well now' – he turned towards the entrance, saying

273

– 'me truck's outside; I'm cutting past Edmundbyers and if you'd like to hop in with me, you're welcome. And I can put you on the road to your destination like.'

For this she had thanked him warmly; but now, cold and tired, she was sitting perched on this high seat and being bone-rattled over very uneven ground.

Her companion, she discovered, was a talker, an inquisitive talker: Where did she hail from? Hereford. Oh, that was quite some way, wasn't it? Did she know anybody at Screehaugh?

A friend. Oh well, that would be Mary Smith then, wouldn't it?

The jolting of the truck had saved her answering and to save further questioning she became the talker: it was very wild country, wasn't it? It would be very nice in the spring and summer, but it must be dreadful when the snow fell. Had they had much snow . . . had they been isolated? Did they get many air-raids? Was he a farmer? On and on, until they came to a small village and he, shouting now, called, 'This is Edmundbyers. It's only a bit afore I turn off, but I can go out of me way an' ride you another mile or so along the road, an' show you the turning to Screehaugh. Half an hour should see you there. All right?'

'Thank you. Thank you very much.'

When, a short time later, he stopped the lorry, he leant across her and pushed open the door, saying as he did so, 'Good luck, miss.'

'Thank you,' she said; 'and thank you very much for your help. I'm very grateful.'

'It's nothing. That's what we are here for, to help one another, especially around these parts. And in these times. We've had a quiet time lately, thank God.'

She smiled at him, then stepped back on to the grass verge, and he called to her, 'Just do as I say. That turning over there, down the hill, keep on and then you'll come to a big belt of

274

trees. That's the beginning of their land. Might have to push your way up the drive.' He nodded at her. 'Gone to the dogs a bit . . . a place soon goes if neglected, or worse if the military get in. Well, so long.'

'So long,' she said. Then as he started up the engine she moved in the direction he had indicated and left the narrow main road for a narrower side one.

The early morning had been dull and grey but of a sudden it was as if a blind had been rolled up and there were hills stretching away, fold on top of fold, shining in the sunshine. They still looked grey and brown but the drabness had gone. The light became so clear that she could see into the far, far distance. Coming to a rise in the road, she stopped and looked about her, but wherever her eyes roamed they saw no habitation, not even the ruins of one. But there below her was the dark belt of trees that the milkman had mentioned.

When she actually came up to the trees it was as if she were about to enter a tunnel. She was walking through a plantation of fir. The road was narrow; it would take a car but that would be all.

It was almost ten minutes later when she emerged into broad daylight again. A few yards further along the road and there were the gates, iron gates, closed but not locked, and she paused a moment before them, staring through them up the driveway. As she took in the overgrown tangle of hedge and shrub she was again assailed by the strange feeling of fear.

She now asked herself what would she say to this Mary Smith. Joe might not yet have turned up. As she had reasoned out during the long night ride, he wouldn't have attempted to use a train, knowing that he might be stopped at any station and asked for his pass. His only chance of getting here was by lifts. And was it likely that having left the camp only just after nine yesterday morning he would have reached this far? Granted he was about ten hours ahead of her but it would have been difficult for him to find through transport from Hereford to Newcastle, so it wasn't likely she would find him here yet. Again she asked herself what she was to say to this Mary Smith.

She pushed open the gate and walked up the drive. It was long and winding. On coming round one curve she saw the house. At first sight it just looked like a big grey pile of stone; then as she blinked against the strong sunlight she could see that it seemed to be in three parts: a middle which had a trace of a chimney running right up its front, and two wings. The buildings were all of the same height and with the one roof, yet they looked separate. There were steps leading from a gravel drive to the front door, and from where she stood she could see the entrance to a yard on one side of the house and which was bordered by stables or outhouses.

Slowly she crossed the drive and mounted the steps. And now she was standing opposite the dark weather-stained front door. There were two bells: the one to the side was the old-fashioned, long iron pole type with a rusty ring on the end of it; the other was a modern button attached to the door itself. It was this she tried first. She pressed it three times, and each time there was no response; in fact she did not hear a bell ring, and so she tentatively pulled on the handle to the side of her. When again nothing happened she moved back over the narrow terrace and looked along each side of the house. Slowly now she turned and went down the steps again, and from the drive she once more looked at the façade of the house. The windows looked empty, blind. She was trembling a little as she entered the yard, thinking that if there was only this Mary Smith here, she would be in the kitchen.

And she was.

Mary was at the table setting the breakfast tray for the missis when the knock came on the back door. When she opened it, her mouth fell into a slight gape as she looked down on the small and plump young person looking at her. She was about to say, 'What do you want?' when Maggie spoke.

'Miss Mary Smith?' she asked; and Mary recognised something in the voice which told her that no matter what this one looked like, she wasn't common, not like those three mothers they sent with their bairns last year. She answered quietly, 'Yes, I'm Mary Smith.'

'May I come in?'

Mary hesitated a moment, then said, 'Well, yes,' and stood aside to allow Maggie to pass.

Maggie stood for a moment looking round the big kitchen. Unlike the outside of the house, at least this part of the inside looked as if it was well cared for.

Turning quickly to Mary, she asked in an undertone, 'Has . . . has he come?'

'Who?'

'Er . . . Joe, I mean Mr Jebeau.'

'Mr Jebeau?' Mary screwed up her face. 'You mean Sir Joseph. He's in the RAF Well, last time we heard, he was.'

Maggie nodded at Mary, saying, 'He . . . he's still in the RAF, but . . . but I'm afraid he's not well and yesterday he—' She gulped and paused. How could she put it Absconded? Deserted? What she said was, 'He left without leave; he . . . he wasn't quite himself.'

Mary stared at Maggie for a moment; then nodded her head as she said, 'I'm not surprised at that; he wasn't himself when he left here. And he's never shown his face since, not to see his mother or anything. Everything's done through the solicitors, everything's changed.' Poking her head forward now, she added, 'Have they sent you after him?'

'No, no.' Maggie shook her head, then said, 'Would you mind if I sat down? I've been travelling all night.'

'Oh aye, yes.' Mary now pulled the chair quickly forward, then said, 'I've just made a cup of tea; you'd like one, I suppose?'

'If you please?'

'And something to eat? You can have a meal, bacon an' that; we're not short, we've got hens and pigs. The cows have gone because there's only Bill Swann left to look after things and he's getting on. But you were sayin' about Master Joe: has he been up to something?'

'He . . . he got into a bit of a fight, and he should have reported and he didn't. But . . . but I'm afraid he hasn't been well for some time and something must have just . . . well' – she clicked her fingers – 'snapped.'

'Oh.' Mary now went to the fireplace and, lifting up a big brown teapot from the hob, she brought it to the table, saying, 'That doesn't surprise me either. He was odd afore he left. After the do he went to pieces, like her' – she thumbed upstairs – 'his mother.' Then her head nodding in small jerks, she said, 'She's in a bad way. Her mind is still clear but she can hardly move; rarely gets out of bed now. The doctor comes every week and he says he wouldn't be surprised if she goes out like a flash one of these days. There' – she pushed a cup of tea towards Maggie – 'let me take her breakfast up and I'll get you something as soon as I come back. I would take your coat off too.'

Maggie stood up and took her coat and hat off, and as Mary left the room with the tray Maggie looked about her. It was a fine kitchen. The stove was old-fashioned, being an open grate with the ovens to the side, which seemed to suit the place. The floor was made of great slabs of stone. There was a mat in front of the fireplace, but the rest of the floor was bare. Along one wall was a great wooden rack holding what looked like a full dinner, breakfast and tea service. By! her Aunt Lizzie would love to see such china. And to think this place was all Joe's, and he had left it, not wanting to own it; except that now he was sick, sick in the head.

She sat down and joined her hands on the table. What if he didn't come here? Yet that's what he had said, that's what

278

he had meant. 'I'm going home.' There was time enough. She would have to wait, and she would have to tell this Mary that she must wait. But she knew if he didn't come soon it would be too late, for they were bound to have put the SPs on to him. Who knew but they had already phoned Newcastle, because that city would likely be the headquarters for around here. And although she imagined a deserter, especially a single man, wouldn't make straight for home, she knew that the SPs would eventually leave no avenue unexplored.

She felt for a moment she was in a foreign land. The terrain outside was wild and strange; this house was strange. And the woman upstairs, his mother, what was she like? Would she ask to see her? Or would the woman herself want to see her?

The question was answered by Mary re-entering the room and saying, 'That's that for the next half hour, then I'll have to see to her. I didn't tell her that you were here; I mean that anybody connected with Master Joe had come. She's never mentioned his name since the day he left. Went off like a shot of a gun, he did, after telling me I had to take me orders from them in Newcastle, the solicitors. Not a bit like himself. He was always pleasant, was Master Joe, kindly like, but from the accident——' She stopped talking and went to the oven and took out a plate on which there were two slices of bacon and, bringing it to the table, she said, 'There's enough for two here; would you like an egg with it?'

'No, thank you. If you don't mind, I . . . I won't have anything to eat; I had sandwiches on the train. My . . . my aunt put me up more than I needed; but I wouldn't mind another cup of tea. And please continue with your breakfast.'

Mary poured out two cups of tea, then sat down opposite Maggie and began to eat the bacon. She got through one slice before she spoke again, picking up the words referring to the accident as if there had been nothing between: 'He

279

was altered from that time, Master Joe. It shook us all. Do you know about it?'

Maggie hesitated before replying, 'I heard something.'

'Master Martin and me dad were shot at the same time. They were out waiting for the poachers and they were shot.'

'Did they ever find their assail . . . the culprit?'

'No, never. But the general opinion is it was one of them from the black market in Newcastle. They're always after the hill cattle and sheep. If there hadn't been the war on, Mrs Swann says, the police would have gone about it more thoroughly and nabbed somebody by now. Well—' She swallowed on a mouthful of the bacon; then lifting up the corner of her apron, she wiped her mouth on it before going on, 'It certainly broke up the house. If a bomb had dropped on it, it couldn't have caused more trouble, or left it like it is now. I sometimes think it's a pity a bomb didn't drop on it and wipe us all out, 'cos it broke our family up. Me mother couldn't stand any more of it and she went to live with our Charlie and his wife in Middlesbrough. Our Helen went and joined up; she's in the ATS. As for our Florrie, I don't know where she is, but my mother's got the bairn.' She nodded towards Maggie now. 'She had a bairn, you know, before she was married . . . well, she never got married. And then our Janet . . . well, she's . . . she lives in Hereford. I just heard that from our Mick afore Christmas. She never writes; I've had nothing to do with her for years, but our Mick said she had fallen on her feet all right. Well, she would do, our Janet, she's like that. Mick's me brother. Then I have a younger sister called Carrie. She's in the forces an' all. But you see, we're split up and it was through me dad being killed. And then look what it did to the missis.' She again wiped her mouth before adding, 'But I'm not surprised at Master Joe going funny. As I said, he was funny the day he left, must have got on his mind. Well, it would, wouldn't it? It was like

280

him jumping into dead men's shoes, his uncle dying in the car crash. Yes' – she nodded now – 'he died in a car crash a few years back. Then his other cousin Harry, he took bad and died suddenly the first year of the war. And then Master Martin, and just afore he was going to get married an' all. That was the funny thing, that he, like his father, should die just afore he was going to get married. His father, you see, was going to marry for the second time.'

Like a twisted film reel, the picture was unfolding before Maggie's eyes. Yet somehow it wasn't complete. From what she herself knew about Joe, she couldn't fathom the reason why he would turn against his mother and this place simply because he had come into a title even, as Mary said, through stepping into dead men's shoes. There must be something else.

'Will he get court-martialled? I mean, Master Joe?'

'Well, not if he turns up soon and I can take him back to the camp.'

'Are you a WAAF?'

'No, I work in the NAAFI.'

'And' – Mary's head was on one side now, a puzzled expression on her face as she asked tentatively, 'and you're a friend of his?'

'Yes.' Her reply was flat sounding. 'He used to come and have a meal with my aunt when he was off duty; he didn't seem to have any place to go.'

'Well, it's a wonder he didn't know about our Janet living in Hereford. But it's likely a big place. Is it, this Hereford?'

'Yes. And the camp too is fairly big. It's about seven miles outside the town.'

'I've never been that way; in fact, I've never really been anywhere further than Newcastle.' Mary leant her elbow on the table now and rested her chin in her hand and, as if she were recalling the past to herself, she said, 'I seem to have spent me whole life in this place. Well, I have, haven't I?

281

This kitchen has been me home since I was ten. You see we all worked on the estate. The master was very good to us, although our cottage wasn't very much to speak of. We were crowded, like, and me mam was always going on. But me dad was always grateful to the master. I was very fond of me dad, an' I suppose that's why I stay on here. Anyway, I couldn't leave her in the way she was. Master Joe saw to it that I was left a decent wage, an' there's always plenty to eat, an' if I wasn't doing this I'd likely be doing war work. But they've never called me up. Well, you see, I don't suppose they would, me being over thirty-five, but I must admit there's times when I wish I had been called up and I had been made to go; you know what I mean, because it gets lonely here.'

Maggie felt a swift wave of pity for the woman as she watched her lower lip tremble, and she said softly, 'I think you're best off here; it's not too much fun being in the forces.' And after a pause she said, 'It's a wonder they haven't commandeered the house for evacuees or the military.'

'Oh, they did.' Mary was nodding at her vigorously now. 'Three women and their bairns they sent here, and they were awful, the lot of them; I had a job to keep them in their place. They were set up in the cottages but they wouldn't stay there; said they weren't fit for pigs. And—' She closed her eyes for a moment and nodded her head as she added, 'And they were right there, really. And then when they got in here, eeh my! Anyway, they didn't stay long, for as one of them put it, it wasn't just dead'n alive, it was dead'n buried. And they up one day and went back somewhere to the billeting office.'

She sighed now and gave a bit of a laugh as she looked at Maggie and went on, 'By, you get some eye-openers in this life; you would imagine officers to be superior types wouldn't you? Well, some of them billeted here, an' two of them must have been brought up in the slums of Newcastle, or Liverpool, or London, or somewhere low, because their habits . . . well, you wouldn't believe it. One used to smoke and throw all his match sticks behind the head of the bed. An' as for hygiene, well, you wouldn't credit it, too blooming lazy to go to the closet. And you should have heard what their batman said about them. They were better class than the officers; at least, the two I'm meaning. They were here four months and it was like four years. They found it a bit dull an' all, too far out, no communication, they said. But we haven't been troubled by anybody for the last year . . . How long do you think you'll stay?'

Maggie was surprised at the question. She had been on the point of asking if she could stay to see if Joe came home, but now she answered gratefully, 'I have a week's leave, but . . . but as soon as Joe turns up, that's if he does turn up, I'll try to get him back to camp immediately.'

'Well—' Mary rose to her feet saying, 'you can stay as long as you like for my part. I can put you in what used to be Mr Harry's room. That's away from the main corridor, so she won't hear you, because it might upset her if she heard there was somebody strange in the house, or any unfamiliar voice. I had to disconnect the door-bells. She used to get upset when she heard them, thinking somebody strange was coming. And she got terribly agitated when the others were here. She could walk a bit then but she wouldn't come out of the room . . . Would you like to see round?'

'Yes, I would like that very much.' . . .

So Maggie saw around the house in which Joe had lived since he was five years old, and as she went from room to room she was forced to wonder yet again what it was that could have driven him away from this lovely place. Although the windows needed cleaning and most of the furniture lacked polish, she saw that the place was kept in good order and dust free.

A short while later, when Mary left her in what had been Harry's room, she went and stood at the window and looked over the wide tangle of gardens, over a disused tennis court and to a stretch of woodland beyond. The sun was still shining and in her mind's eye she could see what the place had looked like when it had been kept in order.

She had been standing at the window for a matter of minutes, when suddenly she muttered aloud, 'Come on, Joe; come back, and let's get away. Come on. Come on.' It was as if he were in the garden and she were talking to him. Then of a sudden she was again overwhelmed by the odd fear; she became stiff with it. Whereas before it had been something distant, which she couldn't explain, now it was here, right here. It had, in a way, materialised and swung her round to face it. Her eyes wide, they moved from the single bed to the chest of drawers, on to a large, impressive, mahogany wardrobe and a matching dressing-table, then to an easy chair and a small table with a standard lamp on it. She had never been given to fanciful imaginings, she hadn't even as a child been addicted to nightmares from reading fairy tales, such as Grimms'; there hadn't been any time for such nonsense in her young life. Her reading had been books of instruction to prepare her for the battle of life that was forced upon plain, undersized individuals like herself. But this feeling wasn't any figment of fancy of the imagination, it was a real fear. And there was, she felt sure, a presence here, a malevolent presence, and for a moment she felt sure she must put her hand out to press something away. She stopped herself and clenched her hands tightly in front of her. She must get out of this room and down into the kitchen to Mary, the ordinary, sensible, level-headed woman.

Almost at a run now, she left the room, and when she reached the gallery she heard a voice calling, 'Mary! Mary!' It was a high thin wail of a voice and when she neared the top of the stairs she saw Mary hurrying up them, and as she passed her she said, 'She rang, but what's she calling as well for? She rarely does that.'

284

Maggie watched Mary scurry along a broad corridor and disappear into a doorway. Then drawing in a deep breath, she continued slowly down the stairs, and stood for a moment in the hall looking about her, before making her way to the kitchen.

Ten minutes later Mary entered the kitchen, saying, 'Well, what do you make of that? She knew there was somebody strange in the house. She couldn't have heard us going up there. But I had to say something, so I said it was me aunt from Howdon.' She nodded now, adding by way of explanation, 'She's the one that brought our Carrie up, my youngest sister, you know, that I told you was in the forces . . . Eeh! I don't know how she knew. Do you?'

Maggie could have answered, 'Yes', but instead she just shook her head, at the same time sitting down, for she was feeling slightly sick.

13

Maggie had had a restless night. For hours, so it seemed, she had lain staring into the darkness. Although she no longer felt there was an actual presence in the room, nevertheless she was experiencing a normal fear, not so much for herself now, but for Joe. And she knew that whatever had happened, other than the tragedies of his cousins, to turn his mind, had taken place in this house.

Being somewhat of the nature of her Aunt Lizzie she had up to now pooh-poohed anything in the form of ghostly phenomena or spiritualism. It was tommy-rot. But now she was faced with the fact that she wasn't as level-headed as she imagined, that there must be a sensitivity in her and that it had, in some way, prepared her for the experience she'd had in this room. She'd known this fear before entering here; in fact, since leaving the cottage. It had entered her as a mist which, by the end of her journey, had turned into a dense fog, and she was now deeply afraid of it.

She had lain thinking about the house in the hills, those gentle hills, so different from those surrounding this place; and, too, of that marvellous woman who lived there and without whose companionship she dreaded to think what her life might have been like up till now.

She didn't know at what time she fell asleep but she was startled awake with a hand on her shoulder and a remembered voice saying, 'I've brought you a cup of tea. I thought I had better look in as it's on nine o'clock.'

She sat up with a start, saying, 'Oh! I'm sorry.'

'It's all right.' Mary nodded at her, smiling. 'You didn't sleep well?'

'No,' Maggie replied. 'No, I didn't.'

'Well, it's natural; nobody does in a strange bed.'

While Maggie sipped at the tea Mary opened the curtains, saying, 'It's a nice morning; sharpish.'

'There's no sign of him, I suppose?' It was a stupid thing to say and she shook her head at herself as she turned and put the cup on the side table, and Mary answered as if the situation was normal, saying, 'No, he hasn't turned up.' Then pointing to the wash-hand stand, she added, 'There's cold water in there for a wash, but if you like to come down to the kitchen I could give you a drop of hot. This room's cold. All the bedrooms are cold. They've never had fires in them, not in my time. But we used to keep fires going downstairs, that was when there was plenty of wood chopped and you could get coal practically for the asking . . . What's that!' She turned quickly to look out of the window, then whispered, 'Eeh! it looks like one of those military cars with the hood over.'

Before Mary had turned from the window Maggie was out of bed and saying now, 'It'll likely be the special police. You'd better go down.'

'Special police?' Mary was across the room at the open door. 'My goodness me!'

Maggie had already stripped off her nightdress and was tumbling into her clothes, and it was but a matter of minutes later when she entered the kitchen. The two SPs were standing near the table and they turned and looked at her as Mary, pointing towards her, said, 'This is Sir Joseph Jebeau's friend. She can tell you he's not here; she . . . she came to find him.'

Both men looked from Mary to Maggie and back to Mary again, and one of them said, 'What do you mean ... Sir Joseph? We're looking for Corporal Joseph Jebeau.'

Stretching her neck out of the collar of her striped blouse, Mary said, 'Yes, he might be that to you but, nevertheless, he's Sir Joseph Jebeau.'

The two policemen looked at each other for a moment, then turned towards Maggie, and they had no need to repeat the question, it was in their eyes, and she answered it, saying quietly, 'She's right, he is Sir Joseph Jebeau.'

'But he is ... ' One of them looked at a paper in his hand, then said, 'But why?'

'That's his own business.'

The taller of the two men now brought his head forward, his chin moving up and down against his collar as he said, 'That might be, miss, but his whereabouts is ours. He's wanted; you know that?'

She paused a moment before saying, 'Yes, I know that.'

'Then may I ask you a question?'

She didn't answer, but waited, and he said, 'Do you know of his whereabouts? Is he here?' And to this she answered, 'To both those questions I can say no, and ... and I may add that you are not looking for an ordinary deserter; Corporal Jebeau is a sick man.'

'Oh, well, that's for the doctor to decide, miss, not you or me.'

'Yes, it will be.'

'Would you like a cup of tea?' They turned and looked at Mary now.

'It would be very acceptable, miss, but we'd like to look around first so, if you don't mind, would you give us a lead?'

'Yes, I'll do that, all except the missis's room.' She had moved round the table now, and when they looked at her enquiringly, she said, 'His mother's room.'

288

'We'll have to look everywhere, miss.' The smaller of the two men pursed his lips before saying, 'His mother's room's likely the place he'd make for.'

'She's not well, she's in a bad state.'

'I'm sorry, miss, but we've got a job to do.'

Before leading the way out of the kitchen, Mary glanced towards Maggie.

Maggie went towards the fire and held her cold hands out to the blaze. But only for a second, then she was at the window looking into the yard. If he had got this far, was it likely he would have come into the house? He could be in the outbuildings. And she was on the point of scrambling out of the kitchen when a thought checked her: if those men were searching the rooms, they could quite easily see her from a window, and that would bring them down at a rush; SPs were naturally of a suspicious mind . . .

It was a full half hour before the men returned to the kitchen with Mary and they passed straight through it and went outside. It was another half-hour before they had finished their searching of the outbuildings and the gardens right down, as Maggie informed her, to the greenhouses, almost scaring Bill Swann to death, coming on him like they did.

They had a last word with her in the kitchen and it was the tall one who looked at her straight in the eye as he said, 'It's your duty, you know, miss, to inform the authorities if he should turn up.'

'I know my duty,' she answered, 'you don't have to tell me.' The tone of her voice was that which she used when behind the counter and the man stared at her for a moment and must have thought it better not to make any retort. Then they both left.

As the sound of the car faded away from the yard Mary sank down into a chair, saying, 'Eeh! the things that happen here. I thought she was going to die. I had to give her some explanation. "It's all right, ma'am," I said. "These men are

289

Special Police. They are after an escaped soldier." I had to say something. She didn't move a muscle but she looked petrified. Her eyes followed them all round the room, and when they opened the wardrobe she gasped as if she was about to die. Eeh! why had he to do it . . . Master Joe? And they said they'd be back . . . How would they have got on to it so soon?'

'They would have telephoned from Hereford.'

'Oh aye; but it's a Sunday morning.'

'Every day of the week's the same when you're in camp.'

'Yes, I suppose so. Oh, this war; talk about turning things topsy-turvy. If anybody had told me that one day I'd be left here alone with just her upstairs and watching the place going to rack and ruin, I would have said they were barmy. But now I sometimes think I'm goin' barmy meself.' She nodded as she rose from the chair and went towards the stove, and as she put the kettle on the fire she said, 'Nobody should be left to live alone; everybody needs somebody, even if it's only a dog. We had two, and they died.'

She now took the poker and raked the bottom bars of the fire, then threw the poker back on to the fender and, straightening her back, looked towards Maggie and nodding her head vigorously as she said, 'That's another thing; I'm still cooking on an open fire. They were getting the electric brought over from the Doltons' place just before the war because they'd had it in for some time, being nearer the main road. But that fell through. Of course we had the generator, and that acted fine when there were men here to look after it. But old Bill can't see to it; he's got enough on his hands. And anyway, for the two of us it's not worth bothering about. And I don't mind the lamplight; I was brought up with it.' She sat down opposite Maggie now and, her voice dropping to a sad dispirited tone, she went on, 'But that's it, isn't it? being brought up with things like they were. Why, with our crowd you couldn't breathe in our cottage. But it

290

was company.' She spread out her hands, and then nodding as if to herself, she ended, 'You can put up with anything if you've got company.'

Maggie wetted her lips and swallowed deeply but could express no words, yet her mind was endorsing everything that Mary said: you can put up with anything as long as you have company . . . special company.

She was tired, she was depressed: she had walked the length and breadth of the estate, she had met and talked with Bill Swann, a taciturn-natured man who had said he wasn't a bit surprised that young Mr Joe had scarpered, because he wasn't cut out for it; too dreamy, wandered the hills with his eyes shut half the time. Then, of course, the missis was to blame; she had tried to tie him to her apron strings. As quiet as he was, he had a will of his own and she didn't get off with everything. By what Mary said, he had stood up to her. High jinks there used to be in the house between them, but of course his type, sensitive, almost womanly, you could say, couldn't take knocks like other folks. Everybody had been affected by the killings but it had seemed to turn young Mr Joe's head. One thing he couldn't understand and that was why he had never come to see the missis. As hard as she had been on him, she didn't deserve the life she was leading in that house there. Never saw a soul. Not that people hadn't come, at first, that is; Mr Dolton and the family were never off the doorstep. It was their cousin Miss Crosbie that Master Martin was about to marry just afore he died. But then the missis wouldn't see anybody; and then she had that stroke and that put the finish to her. 'And,' he had ended, 'I wouldn't have Mary's job for all the tea in China, not that she hasn't been well paid for it, and likely feathering her nest on the side, and I don't blame her for that, because who's going to see to her if the missis dies and the young master doesn't come back, and the place'll likely be sold? Oh, I don't blame her.' . . .

Maggie didn't care for Mr Swann. He was very like many others she had met who fitted nicely under her Aunt Lizzie's heading of 'bitter pills' . . .

The light was closing in when she entered the kitchen again, to be greeted by Mary with, 'You've never been off your legs; you'll wear them down to the stumps tramping the place,' only then to look her up and down as if she were recognizing something tactless in her comment . . .

During the day Mary had been thinking a lot about the visitor. It was beyond her how a fellow like Mr Joe, because he was a good-looking, strapping young fellow, could have taken up with anyone like this one. Seemingly, she had a nice nature and she spoke well, very like the master and the others had done, and much better than the missis upstairs, because she had a thin peevish voice. But the voice didn't make up for how this one looked: her being fat wouldn't have been so noticeable if she'd had height with it, but she didn't look to be five feet. You couldn't say she was as broad as she was long, but she was much too fat for her height. Added to which she was plain looking. Nice eyes, yes, and a lovely set of teeth, and when she smiled it changed her face, although she didn't smile much.

At first she had thought there was a foreign look about her, but from bits she had spoken about herself, she had been born in Manchester and her parents were English.

'I've made a stew,' she said. 'I hope you like it; you picked over your lunch.'

'I'm sorry. I . . . I didn't feel hungry, although it was a most tasty meal. You're a very good cook.'

'I don't know so much about that, but I suppose I've had enough training.' Mary smiled now and, aiming to make the visitor feel at home, she said, 'You can set the table for me if you like. The cloth's in the first drawer of the rack there.'

'Yes. Yes,' Maggie said, and it was as she turned towards the Delph rack that the distant sound of a scream halted her, and she jerked her head round and looked at Mary, who now had her eyes raised to the ceiling.

When the scream came again, louder this time, Mary exclaimed, 'Oh my God!' and ran from the room, and instinctively Maggie followed her.

As they reached the gallery, the screams came at them in a crescendo, and when Maggie, on Mary's heels, reached the bedroom she saw that the door was already open and there, in a bed opposite them lay what looked like the skeleton of a woman, one hand in her hair and her mouth agape, and, standing to the right of the bed towards the foot, was Joe.

Instinctively both Maggie and Mary made for the one each aimed to protect: Mary rushed to the bed and put her arms around the screaming woman, shouting, 'There now! There now! It's only Master Joe. It's only Master Joe.'

Of a sudden the screaming stopped, the mouth opened wider for a moment, then sagged closed; the eyes too closed, and the body went limp in Mary's arms. And she, looking to where Maggie had hold of Joe, said, 'She's passed out. Oh, Master Joe, you've frightened the wits out of her. Why . . . why did you do it?'

Joe said nothing; he had said nothing for a long time. He knew he couldn't say anything; all the words were locked in a dungeon deep down in him, although he knew he was home. And he knew why he had come home: he had to look at her once more; he thought that if he looked at her, just stood looking at her, she would turn into a woman, a mother, an ordinary mother, and love him just because she was a mother. And because she loved him she would let him go. But she had screamed, screamed and screamed, and he knew she wasn't a mother but a murderess. Domineering, vitriolic, dangerous, mad. He was looking at an old woman, an old, old woman, her head on one side, her mouth wide open, her eyes filled with terror.

He had wanted to say something to her; not to say, 'It's all

293

right; I know how you feel,' because he would never know how she felt. It eluded him for a moment what he wanted to say. And then he knew: he wanted to say, 'Look what you've brought me to. I'm as dead as Martin and the rest.' And he would say to her, 'If you had let me have Carrie I wouldn't be like this.' But then Carrie hadn't wanted him, had she? But he must see her. He would go over to the cottage; if she saw him she might change her mind.

His mother had stopped screaming; her eyes were closed now and she was moaning. He made to go towards the head of the bed but felt himself being turned about.

Oh, it was Maggie. Maggie was nice, Maggie was a comfort, like Lizzie. They were both nice. He wanted to say to her, 'Why have you come here?' She should be behind the counter serving tea and giving as much as was sent. She was quick-witted, was Maggie. He also wanted to say to her, 'Leave go of me. Where are you taking me?'

Her voice came to him as from a distance, saying, 'That's it. That's it. You'll be all right.'

He knew he was walking downstairs but his feet felt heavy; he had to lift each foot carefully as if he were sucking it out of mud. It was a long way to the kitchen and he was glad to sit down. The kitchen seemed small; it was taken up by Maggie's face. Why did she keep saying, 'You're all right. You're all right'? He knew he was all right. He was free. Nothing could touch him now for he didn't feel anything: pain, remorse, bitterness; there was nothing there. He felt comfortable. If only he could get rid of Maggie's face, he would go to sleep. Yes, that's what he wanted to do; sleep, sleep, forever.

As Maggie watched him drop his head on to his folded arms on the kitchen table she bit tightly on her lip in order to suppress her tears. She knew she would never get him back to the camp on her own; she also knew there were certain things to be done and that she would have to do them.

294

When Mary came rushing into the room she said to her, 'Will you call the doctor?'

'Eeh yes; yes' — Mary tossed her head from side to side — 'for both of them, I should say. My God! Did you ever?' She looked towards where Joe was slumped over the table and she said in a whisper, 'He's gone barmy, right barmy, and the shock'll likely finish her. Eeh, yes.' And she pressed her hand tightly against her cheek and closed her eyes for a moment, before saying, 'The doctor. Yes, the doctor. We'll have to get Bill to go to the Doltons' to phone for him.' And she ran from the kitchen intent on finding Bill, while Maggie pulled a chair close to Joe's side and sat down beside him and, putting her arm gently about his shoulders, she said, 'Oh, Joe. Joe.'

14

The doctor had aroused Joe from the table but had been unable to get any sense out of him, even to get him to speak at all. And he hadn't bothered to lower his voice when he said to Maggie, 'This doesn't surprise me: it began the night of the murders; it finished them both.' His chin jerked upwards. 'The military will have to be informed, of course. But it's late, and as they've already been here once today they won't relish coming back at this time of night. Anyway, it wouldn't do him any good to be hauled off as he is now. I should suggest you get him to bed and I'll come over in the morning and we'll take it from there.' Then shaking his head he added, 'By! woman, you've got your hands full.' And turning to Maggie he said, 'You'll be staying to see what transpires, I suppose?'

Maggie looked at him for a moment before answering simply, 'Yes.'

What did he think she'd be doing? Why did he think she was there? She felt excluded, somehow, from this strange set-up: Joe, Mary and this doctor, they appeared like one, they knew all about each other; she was certainly the stranger within the gates.

She now watched him leave, accompanied by Mary; and outside, in the yard, they stood talking, the doctor's head the while moving in little bobs.

When Mary re-entered the kitchen she said, 'He's very bad. Doctor says he's very bad; they'll likely send him to a . . . well, sort of special hospital.'

At this Maggie felt inclined to shout, 'Shut up! will you? Shut up!' Instead, she said, 'We'd better get him upstairs.'

'I'll have to make a bed up; there's no sheets on the others.'

'Oh, put him in my room; the bed'll be aired.'

'What about you?'

'Oh, I'm not likely to sleep tonight anyway. I . . . I think I'll sit up with him.'

'I can make another bed up.'

'No, no, don't bother. Come on, let's get him up.'

Coaxingly she said now, 'Come on, Joe. Come on.' And surprisingly, he got to his feet without protest, but when, one each side of him, they went to mount the stairs he became stiff, until Maggie said softly, 'It's all right. It's all right. Nothing's going to happen to you, dear. I'll be with you. I'll stay with you,' when he relaxed as a child might and, practically unaided, he went up the stairs. In the bedroom he went straight towards the bed and made to lie down, but it was Mary now who said, 'Oh, not in your clothes, Mr Joe. Come on, let's make you comfortable, eh?' Then nodding towards Maggie, she indicated that they should undress him. And the pity of it to Maggie was that he stood docilely and let them take off his clothes, down to his underpants.

When he was in bed, and as if he was still the little boy that she remembered, Mary said, 'There now. There now, that's better, isn't it? Now go to sleep. Go to sleep now.' And Joe, just as the obedient child would have done, closed his eyes, turned on his side and went to sleep. And Maggie went hastily from the room because her throat was tight, and the pain in her heart unbearable.

It must have been at about one o'clock in the morning when he began to talk, and the unusual sound of his voice startled Maggie out of a doze. She was sitting in an easy chair, her feet on a stool and a blanket around her, and she brought herself forward and peered through the night light to see him sitting upright in the bed, his hand out as if pointing to someone.

When she reached the bedside he took no notice of her but went on talking rapidly, 'No, Harry, no, I'm not going to carry them. Look at their feathers, they are beautiful. How could you! No, no, I won't eat them. Where's Martin? Martin. Martin. I'm seven years old. Yes, I long for Christmas, and my birthday.'

Maggie stood silently by the bed, watching him: his head drooped and his voice sounded almost tearful as he muttered, 'She hit Carrie. Poor Carrie. Ah, poor Carrie.'

'Lie down, Joe,' Maggie said, putting her hands on his shoulders, but he turned his body sharply around towards her and stared at her for a moment before he said, 'Oh, Carrie, you've come back. Look, I've written a poem about you, and a picture. I've drawn a picture of you. Oh, Carrie.' When he leant forward and his arms enfolded her, she fell across the edge of the bed. But her feet remained on the floor, until suddenly he dropped back onto the pillows, taking her with him, and her body became so twisted she could have cried out with pain. Yet, this feeling was superseded by the knowledge that he had his arms about her and was holding her close. It didn't matter that in this moment he was taking her for someone else: she was aware of only that she was feeling him close to her.

When she dragged her legs up on the top of the rumpled bedclothes, she kicked those aside until her body was close to his. He was still talking to this Carrie, telling her he was

298

so glad she had come back and that he loved her and would always love her.

The pain of his words were lost to her in the pleasure of his nearness. Everything else was forgotten for the moment: he was no longer a sick man, his body was warm . . . hot and pressing against hers; his voice was cut off as his lips moved over her face; her arms tightened about him while her mind soared on his name, crying, Joe, Joe. Oh my love. Oh, Joe, Joe . . .

Then it was done. She had made it happen. It would be all she would ever have of him or from life, but it was something.

It was something. It was all.

They were both sleeping peacefully, their foreheads almost touching, as Mary, a lighted candle in her hand, stood looking down on them. Her mouth, after being slightly agape, closed tightly and she moved her head slowly from side to side, before turning about and going out of the room as quietly as she had come in.

When Mary next saw Maggie, she was sitting in the chair, the blanket around her again. She was awake and when Mary silently handed her the cup of tea she said, 'Oh, thanks; I can do with that.'

'Sleep well?' The question was brief, and Maggie, peering up at Mary, nodded and said, 'Between times.'

Mary now looked towards the bed but she didn't ask how Joe had spent the night; what she said was, 'Are you going to phone the military?' And Maggie answered, 'Yes, I'll have to; I could never get him back on my own.'

Mary now turned and walked towards the door, but after opening it she looked back at Maggie, saying, 'I've been up most of the night meself; she's needed attention. A rare state she's in; I haven't slept much.' And she stared at Maggie for

299

a moment longer before going out and closing the door.

Maggie looked towards the bed and the sleeping figure, and she cast her eyes back to the door as she thought, Ah well. Ah well, what does it matter?

Joe seemed amenable when Maggie woke him with a cup of tea. He drank it greedily, but still didn't speak; yet he looked at her as if he remembered her and when she said to him, 'Can you get into your things on your own?' he made to get out of the bed immediately.

She was waiting on the landing when she saw him leave and go towards the bathroom. He was still walking in that strange way, lifting his feet well up off the ground.

He was some long time in the bathroom and she was beginning to get worried, when he reappeared. He did not make for the bedroom again but walked straight towards her; and when, like a child, he stood before her, she silently took his hand and led him down the stairs and to the kitchen.

When some minutes later Mary put a plate of bacon and eggs in front of him he pushed it aside, but at the same time he pushed his cup towards her. After drinking three cups of tea he sat back in the chair and stared, unblinking, in front of him.

Mary's voice was low as if in the presence of illness or death as she said, 'I can't see the doctor getting here before ten. What about the others?'

And to this Maggie replied, 'If, as you say, it's all that way to Newcastle and they were to leave straight off they should get here about . . . well, say half-past ten . . .'

The doctor arrived at a quarter-past ten and the SPs five minutes later. They weren't the same two who had come the previous day. They arrived in an open jeep and they both looked forbidding. The obvious elder of the two, on coming into the kitchen, looked down on Joe, saying, 'Well, well, what have we here?' And it was the doctor who answered,

300

'You have a very sick man here. Sir Joseph has suffered a breakdown.'

Now both men stared at the doctor, their faces slightly screwed and it was again the elder one who said, 'What did you say?'

'I said, Sir Joseph has suffered a breakdown. I am Doctor Morgan; I know this gentleman very well.'

The SPs exchanged glances and it was the younger of the two men who spoke for the first time, saying, 'But he's a corporal.'

'Yes, yes, he's a corporal. Apparently he had no wish to be otherwise; nevertheless, he is still Sir Joseph Jebeau.'

'Well, Sir, Lord, Duke, or commoner' – it was the elder of the two speaking again – 'he's still a corporal, and a deserter, so it's our business to get him back. Come on!' But as he took a step towards Joe, who hadn't moved, the doctor put in, 'I'm giving you a letter to pass on to your superior officer. I'll be sending my own detailed report to the authorities later. In the meantime' – his voice dropped' – 'I'd advise no rough tactics with him; he's a very sick man.'

The SPs stared at the doctor for a moment longer; then, one on each side of Joe, they each took an arm and a shoulder, the elder man saying sharply, 'Come on, corporal; let's have you.'

Joe made no move to rise; he was deep in the silence, and he liked it there, he felt rested. There were voices ringing all round him, but they were high up in the air, not touching him; except one, and now it was saying, 'Come on, Joe, come on, get to your feet.' That was Maggie. He thought he had lost Maggie, thought she had gone away. Maggie was nice, and Lizzie was nice. He would go and lie down on the couch and they would let him sleep.

Maggie had pushed aside the young man and was herself clasping Joe's arm, and she asked the SPs, 'Are you going straight into Newcastle?'

301

'Yes.'

'Well' – she looked from one to the other – 'I have to get back to Hereford. Could . . . could you give me a lift? And what's more, you know, he'd come quietly with me.'

There was a moment's pause before the older man said, 'No harm in that as I can see. Well, get him in.'

'I'll get my things.'

'I'll get them.' Mary was already hurrying up the room, and during the time she was away hardly a word was exchanged between the occupants of the kitchen, except when Joe made a move to sit down again and Maggie said, 'It's all right, Joe, we're going out.'

A few minutes later, her coat and hat on, her case in one hand, the other holding Joe's arm, she led him out into the yard and manoeuvred him into the jeep. And as she took a seat she looked at the doctor standing in the doorway, then to Mary at the side of the jeep, and to her she said, 'Thank you. Thank you for your kindness.'

Mary gave her no direct answer but, wiping her tears from each cheek with the back of a finger, she muttered, 'God help him! God help him!' And Maggie, sitting close beside the almost inanimate figure, repeated the words to herself, 'Yes, God help him! Indeed, God help him!' and entreated, 'Bring him through. Oh, bring him through.'

PART FOUR

The Residue

1

Lizzie switched off the wireless; she was sick of listening to the news. Here they were in June, 1943 and the end of the war seemed as far away as it had in 1941. She had thought, last October, when Montgomery had gone after Rommel and swept the board, that that would have been the end of it, but there were so many fronts now it seemed that when they did well in one they lost out on another.

But it was a lovely day, real June-like; she would take her tea outside while she was waiting for Maggie. She shouldn't be long now; the bus got in just after six.

She was worried about Maggie. What was the matter with her? She had definitely changed. And it wasn't only that she was concerned for Joe, because at times she seemed sort of happy. But it was an odd kind of happiness, because at other times when she had put on weight she had become depressed, and she had certainly put on weight these past few weeks. But then it wasn't surprising, because she was eating more than ever. There was no talk of diets now. It must be her worry for Joe was affecting her in this way.

She sat in the summer-house and sipped at her tea, her eyes all the while directed over the garden towards the gate, and she thought, as she often did these days, that it was hard to believe that at this minute men, women and children were being blown to bits, or that half the people in the big cities were sleeping underground. She was glad she had nobody to lose in the war. The Swifts had lost their youngest son; his ship had been torpedoed. That was last month. And only three weeks before, their two nephews had gone too. One had been a rear-gunner, the other a pilot in the RAF. And she had heard only yesterday that young Mrs Stoddard down in the town had lost her husband. He was one of Montgomery's lot. And she was left with three children. But she was lucky in a way for, having the newsagents' shop, she still had her livelihood, not like some.

Yes, she was glad she had nobody to lose in the war. Except Maggie of course and, in a way, Joe. But then Joe was lost to everybody, himself most of all. Poor Joe. Maggie had wanted her to go along with her to the hospital to see him, but she couldn't. Although, as far as she understood, it was a very nice place and they were well looked after, she didn't think she could bear to see men crying like babies, some of them having gone back into childhood, while others were so fear-ridden that they cowered from a kindly voice. And there were a number like Joe, Maggie had said, who just sat staring into space, obedient in everything but speech.

Oh, there she was. She rose to her feet and stepped down from the summer-house as Maggie dismounted from her bike, and she greeted her casually with, 'You look hot.'

'So would you be if you'd had to push that bike up the hills.'

As she pulled off her hat Maggie looked towards the summer-house and said, 'Is that tea still hot?'

'Yes, it hasn't been made but a few minutes. Here, give me your coat and go and sit down.'

Maggie had drunk a cup of tea and eaten a scone before Lizzie said, 'Well, how did you find him?'

'Oh, much the same. I had a talk with one of the orderlies. He said it could be a long job. It was like shell-shock but different. He'd had a shock of some sort, and he could be brought out of it, perhaps with another one.'

'Well, he's not likely to get a shock there, is he?'

'No.' Maggie picked up another scone and ate it, and as she put her hand out for a third one she said quietly, 'Do you think *you* could survive a shock, Aunt Lizzie?'

'Well' – Lizzie turned her head slowly and looked at Maggie – 'it all depends what it is; as you know, I don't like shocks. But tell me and let me get it over.'

Maggie bit into her scone, chewed on it for a moment, then said, 'I'm pregnant; I'm going to have a baby.'

Lizzie said nothing. Her back was straight, her head still turned towards Maggie; her mouth fell open; her eyes widened and moved over the small frame and settled on where the fruit of the shock lay.

'Well, say something.' There was an appeal in Maggie's eyes now as she looked at Lizzie, but still Lizzie didn't speak, and Maggie said, 'I'm happy, Aunt Lizzie. Try to understand. I'm happy as I never thought to be happy in my life. It's the only thing I'm likely to have of him. Whether he stays in that hospital forever or comes out, it'll be all the same between him and me, but I . . . I've got something of him and that'll satisfy me.'

'Oh, girl.'

'Don't say it like that, Aunt Lizzie, please. Can't you understand what's happened to me? I've been given something that I never thought, never imagined, would come my way: the chance to be a mother. Can't you understand?'

'Yes.' Lizzie's voice came throaty now. 'Yes, I can understand, but . . . but it's something I never imagined . . . well, with you, not for a minute, and it has come as a shock. Yes, yes, it has, girl.'

'You're ashamed for me.'

307

'Not a bit of it.' Lizzie sounded like her old self now. 'Ashamed for you, or ashamed of you, no; I'm glad for you; only it's the last thing on God's earth I imagined you would ever tell me. When's it due? How far are you gone?'

'One thing at a time.' Maggie sat back and wiped her mouth on her handkerchief. Then, her head slightly bent forward, she said, 'To answer your last question first, I'm almost five months at the beginning of next month. As to how and why, that's going to be difficult to tell.'

'It's Joe's?' put in Lizzie now, her head poked forward.

'Of course it's Joe's. I said so.' Maggie's voice was hard. 'Could it be anybody else's?'

'But when? He's been bad ... well, long before he left and ... '

'I said it was going to be difficult to tell, Aunt Lizzie. Let me put it this way. What's inside me doesn't belong here; it really belongs to the girl, Carrie; he took me for her. It was the night he arrived at the house; I was sitting up with him. He had a sort of nightmare, kept talking to her, and when I tried to quieten him he thought I was her. Deep inside he was back in the past with her, and ... well' – she sighed now – 'the rest was easy. Nothing to brag about. Mind, if that's it, I think it's overrated; more pain than pleasure. I don't know why they connect it with love. Yet that's the moment that gave life. Odd.' She turned her head towards Lizzie now, a sad smile on her face, then went on, 'But it was my one and only chance to have anything of him, and I took it. And I'd do it again and again should the opportunity arise; but it won't. So there you are, Aunt Lizzie, I'm like many another in this war; I've copped it, as they say.'

Lizzie's hand came out now and clutched at Maggie's and, bending forward, she kissed her on the cheek, an unusual show of affection, and her voice had a break in it as she said, 'Well, it's something to look forward to, lass, and other than yourself there'll be nobody more pleased to see it than I

308

will. Have you . . . I mean, do they know anything about it down there?'

'No.' Maggie gave a short laugh now. 'That's one good thing about being fat. There have been remarks from Peggy and Bett that I'm putting it on a bit, but it would be the last thing on earth they would dream would happen to me. And you know something?'

'No?'

'You know who'll get the blame, or the credit, for this?' She tapped her stomach.

'Who?'

'Billings.'

'That fellow?'

'Yes, that fellow. And being him I'd like to bet my bottom dollar he doesn't deny it.'

They both laughed now until Lizzie said, 'You'll be dismissed the Service.'

'Oh, that'll be a heartbreak; I can't wait. You know, I did think that after the war I'd start a union for waitresses. When you're behind a counter, Aunt Lizzie, people don't see you as a human being. They don't. You're a different species, especially dishing out tea and wads. The men aren't so bad, but you remember that time I was on the outside unit for a month or so? It's a wonder I didn't upheave an urn over some of those WAAFs, and ATS, too, who weren't above pushing their noses up. Some of them looked upon us as if we were a lower type of domestic servant. The worst ones were those who had come up from nothing and the pips went to their head. Yet, others were like Joe, you know, titled, not bothering about it.'

'It's the same the world over, lass, there's some and some in every class, but, as I'm in the habit of saying, like milk, we all come out of a cow and the cream among us rises to the top.'

'Oh! Aunt Lizzie.' Maggie pushed her, and then put her hand over her eyes and started to laugh. But when the note of laughter changed and Lizzie saw the tears running from beneath Maggie's fingers she quickly drew her into her arms, saying, 'There, girl, there. Don't worry, everything will turn out right, you'll see.'

After a moment, Maggie, gulping in her throat, said, 'Not for him, Aunt Lizzie, not for him. It's pitiable: he sits there like a child who's been told to sit still; and he's got thinner: he's like two laths. I'm glad of one thing though; the orderlies seem to like him. I suppose it's because he's biddable; some of them aren't. Oh—' she now moved her head from side to side and dried her eyes, saying, 'I'm glad you don't go to see him; it would upset you. I want to cry all the time I'm there. And yet, you can't help laughing at things that happen. There's one fellow who never stops singing. He makes up songs; parodies on this and that. When you're sitting in the garden he'll come and stand in front of you, quite naturally, and he'll give you a chorus or two, then go on to somebody else. And sometimes what he comes out with . . . well, it isn't fit for polite ears. Yet I had to laugh today. There's one of the lads keeps painting. It's nearly always the same kind of picture, a big black square with a hand in one corner, a bust in the other, and a leg in another. They are very weird. I understand his whole family were blown up in one go. Caruso, as they call the singer, always sings the same song when looking at this poor fellow's pictures. The words go to a hymn tune, but he doesn't only give him a couple of choruses, he goes on and on. One of the choruses goes like this.' And between chuckles Maggie began to sing:

> 'Oh glory, glory behold him,
> A student of the arts,
> Of busts and bums
> And other parts, silly bugger.'

As Lizzie let out a roar of laughter Maggie leant towards her with her hand on her shoulder, saying, 'Oh, Aunt Lizzie, it's the funniest thing to hear him, yet at the same time when you're laughing, you want to cry. He's a tall fellow and handsome. They said when he first came in two years ago they had to strap him down; he fought everyone and had the strength of a bull, picked up chairs, tables and threw them about; one minute he'd be quiet the next minute he'd be away. Then all of a sudden his pattern changed to this singing lark. I suppose it's the drugs they give them.'

Now Lizzie, wiping her face, said, 'Oh, that was funny, girl. I can just see it. But that's in my mind's eye; I don't think I could stand it in the flesh.'

'I didn't think so either after my first couple of visits, yet I knew I'd sit in hell to be near Joe.' She swallowed the lump in her throat, and the tears again sprang from her eyes.

'No more, girl, no more.' Lizzie now patted Maggie's shoulder briskly, 'Crying's not going to do what you're carrying any good, whether it be a he or a she. What do you want?'

'Doesn't matter.' Then smiling through her tears, Maggie looked at Lizzie and said, 'Do you think if I stuffed myself, really stuffed myself, I would have twins?'

Again they were laughing, but softly now, their heads together. Then Lizzie said, 'By the way, there's a letter for you. It's got the Newcastle stamp on it; it'll likely be from that Mary.'

'Oh.' Maggie rose to her feet. 'It's funny, I was only there for a couple of days, yet she seems like an old friend. You know something?' She pointed to her stomach. 'She knows about this.'

'How on earth . . . what do you mean?'

'She must have come into the room that night: I could tell by the look on her face and the way she spoke to me the next

311

day; so it's come as no surprise to her. I wonder what she's got to say?'

In the house, Maggie sat down and opened the letter, and she read it to the end before she raised her eyes and looked at Lizzie, saying, 'His mother's dead. She's to be buried on Monday. She's leaving it to me as to whether Joe should be told or not.'

2

It was three weeks later when she considered it to be the right time to tell Joe about his mother's death. It was a blustery day, and there was rain in the wind, so she sat indoors at the end of a glass-covered arcade. Most of the visitors were in the main rest room and so this end of the arcade was comparatively quiet.

The blue flannel suit that Joe was wearing seemed to hang on him like a bag. There was a collar to his shirt, but no tie, which was significant. His face wore a placid expression. Although he didn't talk she always maintained a conversation, feeling that he could listen and in part understand. But today she didn't know whether she was hoping he would understand or not, because whatever had turned his mind she felt it was connected with his mother. She took his hand now, saying, 'Aunt Lizzie sends you her love, Joe, and she's baked you some of the scones you like. She's always baking. I don't know how she gets her hands on so much fat. Joe . . . Joe, can you hear me? Joe, I feel you can hear me and . . . and I've got some news for you.' She now gripped his hand more tightly before going on: 'Your mother, Joe; your mother died a few weeks back.'

She waited for some response, and when she could detect none whatever she said, 'Mary wrote me. She's been writing regularly since we were there, remember? She said your mother went peacefully in her sleep . . . '

She was almost overbalanced by his arm jerking upwards, then flinging to the side as if in an effort to knock her over.

Rising quickly from the chair, she put her hand on his shoulder, saying, 'You understand! You heard me, Joe. Say something. Please say something. She's dead, Joe, your mother's dead.'

Then Joe said something, not in words but as part of an ear-splitting, high-pitched crackling laugh that brought the visitors at the other end of the arcade round to stare in some apprehension and an orderly to come hurrying from an inner room. He looked first down the arcade, then towards them and when he came up to where Maggie was standing holding Joe by the arm, her face screwed up against the eerie noise coming from his wide-open mouth, he pushed her gently aside and, almost lifting Joe to his feet, he said firmly, 'There now! There now, chappie! There now! Come on. Come on, let's go and have a walk, eh?'

Maggie watched the man lead Joe away, Joe still emitting that hysterical laugh. But once they had disappeared she dropped into a chair and endeavoured to still the trembling of her body.

A woman, leaving a group of people further along the arcade-balcony, came up to her now, saying, 'I shouldn't worry; it might be a good thing; it could be a breakthrough. He's never spoken, has he?'

All Maggie could do was make a slight movement, and the woman said, 'Well, it's something like what happened to my son.' She made a backward motion with her head, indicating another young man in blue. 'His turning point came when he started to cry. He was in water for days: they had to take their turns clinging to the life-raft; all but two died. You could say he was lucky, but it turned his mind for a time. I wouldn't worry because next time you come you'll likely see a great change in him.'

'Thank you.'

The woman left her alone and she sat waiting for she knew not what. Would they bring him back? She had just come and they were allowed two hours.

They didn't bring him back, but the orderly himself returned, saying, 'He's quietened down; he'll sleep for some time. Would you like to come along and have a word with the matron?'

A few minutes later, while sitting in an easy chair in the matron's office sipping a cup of tea, the matron came to the point of why she had asked to see her. 'Could you tell me, Miss LeMan, what you were talking about before the corporal started to laugh?'

'Yes,' Maggie said flatly, 'I told him that his mother had died a few weeks ago.'

'Oh . . . do you know what kind of relationship existed between them?'

'Not very good, I should say; she seemed to be the cause of his distress, more than the fact of losing his cousin, although he never confided in me.'

'Well, this may be a good sign. At least he is making a noise; that's something he hasn't done since he came here. I hope we have better news for you on your next visit.'

Maggie's pregnancy was close on seven months when she broke the news about her condition in the camp. The reaction of her superior was one of utter disbelief: 'No! Maggie. No! Not you,' she said.

'Why not me?' Maggie asked harshly.

'Oh, I didn't mean it that way. But somehow you seem to be a cut above such things. And then there was Corporal Jebeau. You were friendly with him and he was such a nice young man. Is it that Billings? Is that why he was posted?'

'No, it's not Billings, miss. It doesn't matter who it was; I'm pregnant and I'm feeling very much off colour. I can't stand the long hours at the counter any more, so what are you going to do about it?'

'That doesn't rest with me; you'll have to see Miss Robertson.'

Maggie saw Miss Robertson, who also thought her condition to be equally 'incredible'; but their reaction was nothing to that of the girls. Peggy took it as a breach of friendship. After a series of rapid questions, to each of which she was given a short, negative answer followed by a long silence, she said, 'I think you might have told me; I was supposed to be your pal.'

Bett Allsop's reaction was, 'Well, if it's happened to you, why couldn't it happen to me?'

Only the reaction of Rona Stevens aroused Maggie's anger, for after greeting the news with complete silence she turned away, muttering to Bett Allsop, 'Somebody must have been hard up.'

As Maggie's grip on her arm pulled her round, her face blanched: 'As hard up as he might be,' Maggie spat at her, 'he chose me rather than you, because a blind man could detect there's nothing under that skin of yours but meanness of spirit. And let me tell you this, Miss Stevens, if you ever hope to come across your gentleman, you'll have to learn to speak English.' And in emphasising this she thrust Rona aside and went into the back room; and when Peggy followed her she turned to her and said, 'She's always got my goat, but, nevertheless, I shouldn't have said that.'

'Oh yes, you should, and more; she's always been at you behind your back.' Then Peggy, turning away towards the sink, said, 'It was Jebeau after all?'

'You surprised, too?'

'No; no, not really, but you've always given out that it was just friendly, like, platonic, so to speak.'

'Well, it was and it wasn't.'

'Oh, that kind of answer clears things up, oh, it does. Anyway, when are you leaving?'

'As soon as they let me.'

Peggy now turned from the sink and, leaning her back against it, she said, 'I'll miss you, Lemon, we all will; except the duchess, of course. You know something, and you won't understand this, but she was jealous of you.'

'*What!*'

'You were popular, you see. You're fat. You can't get away from it now, can you? even without the added burden' – she poked her finger towards Maggie's stomach – 'and you're no beauty. I'm not being nasty; it's just a fact and you know it. But you have a good voice, both in singing and talking, and you were liked beyond the counter. You could always hold your own and the lads liked that. Yes, she was jealous of you.'

Maggie now moved her head from side to side as she said, 'That'll take a lot of believing, Peggy.'

'Well, you can believe it because it's a fact, and you couldn't have hit her harder than that bit about her English, because even when you're chipping, you talk as if you were educated . . . well, knowledgeable, like. And people can be jealous of that, you know; I mean education, when they haven't had it.'

'I left school when I was fourteen, Peggy.'

'Yes, but it all depended on what school, and what your people were like. Our Rona comes from the low end of Birmingham, so I suppose you can understand her wanting to change her voice.'

Maggie turned away, saying now, 'We all come from the low end of some place or other. I feel worse about it now than ever.'

317

'Well, I shouldn't let it worry you; you've got more to worry about than that, I should think. How is he, anyway, the corporal?'

Had she spoken the truth her answer would have been, 'Worse, if anything,' but instead, she said, 'About the same.'

'Doesn't he know about that?' Peggy nodded towards her, and Maggie said, 'No.'

'Well, it'll come as a surprise to him, won't it?'

'Yes, it will. It will.'

Maggie's discharge came almost two weeks later, for which she was grateful, for the news had spread through the wing, and although the quips were fewer, the questions in the eyes were many; in a way, Lemon had let them down; like a clown leaving the circus for the straight stage . . .

The day after her release she went to visit Joe, but she was unable to see him; although she did see the matron again; and this time, one of the doctors, too, was present. Couldn't she, he asked her, throw any real light on the relationship between Corporal Jebeau and his mother?

At this, she replied that she had already told the matron all she knew and that had been gleaned from the servant, Mary Smith, who remembered Joe's mother as a rather dominant woman who had tried to hold her son down, and one who was also given to fits of anger.

The doctor nodded, but then he brought Maggie upright and wide-eyed when he said, 'He's under the illusion that his mother murdered four people to enable him to assume the title. You do know he is titled, don't you?'

'Yes.'

'You have said that you saw his mother once; can you tell me what she was like?'

'I had a brief glimpse only; she seemed rather weird to me. It was when Joe, Corporal Jebeau, left the camp without leave and turned up at the house unexpectedly. I . . . I had gone on before him, hoping to bring him back; I didn't know he was in the house until I heard her scream. Mary Smith, the maid, and I rushed upstairs. That was the only time I saw her. Joe was just standing staring at her.'

'And she was screaming?'

'Yes. She looked scared, terrified.'

'It's a delusion that his mother killed four people, but there is something troubling him in his mind and when you told him his mother had died, in a way, it opened a door and his subconscious has twisted the facts of whatever was behind that door into delusion. Anyway, that is how we are seeing it at the moment. But there is one bright spot; he is talking, and this is more hopeful than his silence.' . . .

Back with Lizzie, she said to her, 'He thinks his mother killed four people. They must have been his eldest cousin and Mary Smith's father, and his uncle and his fiancée. But that's crazy, isn't it? Impossible. No woman like that could kill four people. What do you think's behind it?'

'God alone knows, girl, but there's something there, and only He can tell us what it is; and by the looks of things that'll be some time, some long time, I'd say.'

3

Maggie's baby was born on a Sunday morning in the middle of November. There was no need to hold it up by the feet to make it cry for it was lusty almost from the first moment it breathed air. It was a boy, and on top of his crumpled face was a tuft of black hair.

When the doctor put him into her hands Lizzie cried, 'That's it! That's it! Let it rip; it's the loveliest sound in the world.'

'Couldn't agree with you more, but stop blathering, Lizzie, and get him washed. And now, Nurse.' He turned to another woman at his side, saying, 'There you are then; I'll leave you to do the dirty work,' and then bending over Maggie, he smiled down into her tired face, saying, 'It's been a long haul but it's been worth it, eh?'

'Yes. Oh, yes, doctor, yes indeed.'

'Now what you've got to do is to go to sleep.'

'I'd . . . I'd like to hold him first.'

She looked to where Lizzie was still standing to the side of the bed, the child in her arms, and Lizzie, almost edging the doctor away, gave Maggie her son. Then, her voice breaking, but in her inimitable way, she said, 'First-class job that, girl.'

'He's beautiful.'

'Yes, I'll say he is. But come on, give him back, else they'll throw me out.' . . .

During the next few days Maggie had a number of visitors from the camp. She had expected Peggy and perhaps Bett Allsop, but not Rona Stevens, nor her boss, nor Len Forbister, and they had each brought her something that must have made quite a hole in their sweet rations, besides items that had black market written in invisible letters on them. And when a large bunch of flowers came with a card attached, simply saying, 'From the Lab Wallahs,' this reduced her to tears, for in a way she saw it as an acknowledgment that a certain member of their section was the father of her son.

It was strange, she thought, as she sat looking at the child in the cot by her side, that everybody seemed to know who the father was except the father himself. Poor Joe. It was a month now since she had seen him and, whereas earlier their meetings had been one-sided, she doing all the talking, their positions had later become reversed and he had jabbered about anything and everything, one subject running into another.

He always seemed pleased to see her, but even when her stomach was bulging, he seemed to be unaware of her condition. She had spoken about this change to the matron, but she had not seemed concerned, simply stating that this was a pattern and it would work itself out.

Christmas came and Lizzie put up the tree, and for the first time it had a real meaning for them both and they sat before the fire in the warm comfortable room, the baby contentedly nestled in the corner of the couch, the side-table showing more Christmas fare than they could hope to get through, for again many in the camp had shown her that she was not forgotten, even to the extent of bestowing on her two priceless oranges.

What was more, they had a duck for Christmas Day, a Christmas pudding, and plenty to wash it down with. Yet, sitting there, they seemed to emanate sadness for, as in many another family on this night, there was no man to share the festivities, and Lizzie brought this to the fore by saying, 'Well, girl, we've got to look at it this way: he could be in Africa, he could be on the high seas, he could be a prisoner in Germany, or he could be dead. Looking at it like that, we've got a lot to be thankful for.'

Yes, she supposed so; yet in a way he might as well be dead; in fact, inside himself she knew he felt he was.

They were both glad when the holidays were over and they had returned to the normal routine. Automatically they listened to the one o'clock news and the six o'clock news. At these times the war came into the house; yet once they had switched off they could have been on another planet. Their time was taken up with the child, the household chores and an added one outside when, weather permitting, they endeavoured to prepare part of the garden as a vegetable plot.

The break in the routine came on the days Maggie travelled to the hospital to visit Joe. But it wasn't until June of that year that she saw any real improvement in him; this was when he first spoke to her. To her amazement, he said, 'You didn't come last week.' When she could answer, she said, 'I'm sorry, but I had a cold.' She knew she couldn't say, 'The baby wasn't well and I was afraid to leave him.'

What was more heartening, too, was that since the news that the second front had been launched everything and everybody seemed to have bucked up, with one exception; and Maggie kept this exception hidden in her mind, as a small niggling fear told her that there was a change in Lizzie. Her manner and voice might still be the same, but the briskness had gone from her body: she would sit for long periods in a chair either inside the house or outside in the summer-house, her head drooped on her chest, dozing as she called it. The first person Maggie voiced her fears to was Joe. It was late

September and he had, during her past three visits, appeared utterly normal, not chattering all the time now and, although when he talked it was mainly to answer questions, they were sensible answers. And on this day he proved his return to normality by making an observation. They had been sitting together in the grounds for almost half an hour when he said, 'You've lost a lot of weight, Maggie.'

She smiled at him and, in a return to her old perky manner, she said, 'I thought you'd never notice.'

And to this he answered, 'Well, I did, before, but didn't like to remark on it . . . Are you all right?'

'Oh yes, I'm all right, Joe.'

'Aunt Lizzie? You've . . . you haven't mentioned Aunt Lizzie today.'

She looked away from him and then, her voice merely a mutter, she said, 'I'm . . . I'm worried about Aunt Lizzie, Joe.'

'Is . . . is she ill?'

'No, nothing you can put your finger on, but she seems to be sleeping most of the time, and, like me, she's lost weight, only she looks like a bag of bones now. And . . . and it isn't through the rationing' – she smiled faintly – 'we get more than enough . . . more than our share.'

'Have you had the doctor?'

'Some time ago, but he couldn't find anything wrong with her.'

It was at this point that she turned to him eagerly and said, 'Joe, why don't you come back now? She . . . she would love to see you; she's always talking about you.'

The effect of her words was to drop a screen between them, and for him to edge a little way back from her along the bench: his expression altered; the light went out of his eyes; and his voice a mumble now, he said, 'No, no,' as if in protest; 'I'm all right here. I . . . I don't want to leave. I'm . . . I'm settled . . . safe.'

For a moment she felt angry and her feelings were expressed in her voice as she exclaimed, 'Do you intend to stay here all your life, then?'

'Oh, Maggie.' He shook his head from side to side.

'Never mind "Oh Maggie". You're better now; you could be discharged, I'm sure you could, and you wouldn't have to go back, I mean, into the camp, or anything like that. And if you have to recuperate any more you'd do it better at home. Joe' – she put her hand on his knees – 'face up to it, you can't stay here forever.'

'Why not?' The words came as a whisper, but their reaction on her was to cause her to repeat almost on a shout, '*Why not?*'

At this she put her hand over her mouth and looked about her at other groups scattered over the grounds; then leaning towards him and her voice almost a hiss now, she said, 'Because it's cowardly; you're all right now. I know you are, except that you don't want to face up to life outside, but get it into your head that you can't go on being nursed all your life.'

'I'm not being nursed.' His voice sounded as angry as hers now.

'Yes, you are.'

'You know nothing about it. What do you know about how I feel? As for being nursed, you want to go through it. *Nursed, indeed.*'

He got to his feet now, almost glaring at her, and she, rising slowly from the seat, her head bowed, said, 'I'm sorry, I'm sorry if I've upset you, Joe. I'll . . . I'll go now.'

She was turning away when he put his hand out and touched her arm, and pleadingly he said, 'Oh Maggie, try . . . try to understand. I'm still at sea, all at sea. It's like this, Maggie; they tell me I've one more obstacle to face: once I can . . . well, face up to it, talk about it, I'll be OK.'

She was looking at him now and her eyes were moist as she asked, 'How long is it going to take, Joe?'

'I don't know, Maggie. Doctor Straker' – he gave her a twisted smile now as he went on – 'he's the chief head-prober, he says not to worry, I'll . . . I'll have done it one of these days and without realising it. I mean, I'll have got over the hump, so to speak.' He looked down now towards the ground as he muttered, 'I'd . . . I'd like to be with you and Lizzie again in the cottage. I . . . I often think about those times I spent there. Sometimes at night I fancy I'm back with you both.'

Maggie stared at him, her gaze still soft even as she repeated to herself: with you both. It would never be, with you, Maggie.

She turned from him, and he walked with her towards the lodge, and there they shook hands. She went out of the gates, and he returned up the drive to what had become for him a tomb, because for all his show of defiance he knew Maggie was right. He didn't want to leave here, ever.

4

But he did leave some three weeks later. Two visiting days had gone by and Maggie hadn't put in an appearance; nor had there been any word from her until this morning, and then her letter said she was very sorry she had been unable to visit him because Aunt Lizzie was very ill; and she went on to say that she thought her end was fast approaching.

He stood with the letter in his hand, his heart beginning to race, and his mind telling him that if there was one person he liked in this world it was Lizzie; Lizzie had been a mother to him, a real mother . . .

It was his morning for seeing the psychiatrist and when he sat before Doctor Straker and the jovial-looking man said, 'Well, how are we today?' he answered calmly, 'Very well.'

'Oh, that's a good start.'

'Doctor.'

'Yes?'

'You said some three weeks ago that I'd only one hurdle to jump and that was the gate. Well' – Joe paused – 'I'd . . . I'd like to take it, the jump; I'd like to leave.'

'Oh, yes? Well, I'm glad to hear that. Can you tell me what's made you decide?'

'A friend, a dear friend is very ill, she's . . . she's not expected to live and . . . and I'd like to see her.'

'Then you just want to leave?'

Joe's head drooped now and he thought a while before saying, 'Yes, perhaps; I . . . I don't know how I'll feel once I'm outside.'

'Oh, I should think you'll be all right.' The doctor now looked down at the folder holding the case history of Corporal Jebeau, Sir Joseph Jebeau, apparently, this strange young man who, he had decided, was so afraid of war and killing that he had transferred the whole onus on to his mother, with whom it seemed he hadn't got on very well. It wasn't an unusual case; nothing appertaining to the mind surprised him any more. Even without a war the grey matter was often taxed too much and would spew up from it hidden thoughts and desires. But when it was also carrying the load of war it often sank under the weight, as it had done in this young fellow's case.

'This business about your mother; it's all cleared up now, eh?'

Joe realised that if he were to answer truthfully, it would have meant that no leave would have been granted, and so he simply said, 'Yes,' instead of, 'No, because her deeds are still with me, and will remain with me, even though I'm looking at them in a different light now. The only other thing I want to do in connection with her is to find the gun, for only then will I know for sure that it is not all a figment of my imagination.'

But the doctor was smiling broadly at him now and saying, 'Well, I'll set the wheels in motion. But remember, if you feel any kind of strain, just come back.'

'I will, and thank you.'

As Joe walked through the waiting-room he glanced at his fellow inmates with a deepening sadness, as one might have done when about to leave a happy family. There

327

was Ted and Gerald and Hookey and 'Caruso'; only he had stopped singing of late and had become very quiet, even sad. His singing had got on everybody's nerves but his sadness affected them more deeply.

He had the silly desire to go back among them and reassure them that he would return. Yet would they mind? Some of them were like children: their flights of happiness were ephemeral, their regrets without substance, and they were unaware of the overall sense of loss that pervaded them. These were the light cases; in the big block at the other end of the grounds were lives that were filled with protest and fear and the great void into which only the fortunate among them slipped.

The car deposited him at the station, and there the driver, used to such leave-takings, remarked, 'Good luck, fellow. You sure you'll be all right on your own?'

'Yes. Yes, thank you.'

'You should have had somebody come and meet you, they generally do. Sure you'll make it?'

'I'll make it.' Joe's voice and a nod of his head conveyed a firmness that he was far from feeling: every nerve in his body seemed to be tingling; already he was finding the outside world strange; it was as if he had been away a lifetime; and he had, many lifetimes.

A few minutes later, standing on the platform, he was wondering why people weren't looking at him: the strangeness of him; he must look odd, like a walking skeleton; all the flesh seemed to have dropped from his bones.

The train arrived and he took his seat. Opposite him were a couple who kept holding hands. Neither of them was in uniform, yet there was a tenseness about them, as if they were on the verge of parting.

It wasn't until he had alighted from the train that he thought he should have written and told Maggie he was coming. When he had given the address of his destination to Admin. he had told them he would write and tell his friend of his coming, but he hadn't. Why hadn't he? He knew why, because at the last minute he was afraid he wouldn't be able to jump the hurdle of the gate and then they would have been disappointed.

Hereford looked the same as if he had been here yester-day except that, it being mid-afternoon, the invasion from the camp of the cinemas and bars hadn't started yet.

On enquiry he found he had three-quarters of an hour to wait for the country bus that would pass through Madley to Hay, and so he sat on the green for a while, and then, making an effort, he went into a café and had a cup of tea . . .

As the bus approached Madley he experienced no feeling of either apprehension or excitement, but two miles or so beyond the camp, when he alighted, a feeling of excitement did rise in him, and it increased as he approached the cottage, touching on joy as he realised that he had made it. It was like a successful escape, for he had no desire to return to the confines of the womb; indeed, he felt like running the last few yards to the gate and up the path; the only thing preventing him being the thought of what his sudden appearance might do to Lizzie, her not being well.

He passed the front door and went round the corner of the house. The back door was open. Maggie was in the kitchen. She had her back to him and was bending over what looked like a baby in a high-chair. He stared fascinated as he watched her scoop something out of a bowl and put it in the baby's mouth; he heard a gurgle and a splutter and then her voice saying, 'You've had enough? All right, you needn't spit it at me.'

Fascinated, he now watched her bend quickly and kiss the baby on the top of its head; then she turned round, the bowl in her hand, and almost dropped it as she gasped, 'Oh! Oh! Joe,' and looked from side to side as if searching for some place to put the bowl. Then almost throwing it back onto the table, she moved towards him, her hands outstretched, and when she drew him over the threshold they stared at each other, both unable to speak.

When at last she did speak, she gabbled, 'Well, of all the things to happen. Why didn't you let me know you were coming? Good gracious! Sit down. Sit down. I . . . I don't know where I am.' She put her hand to her brow. 'When did you leave? Have you had anything to eat?'

He put his hand out and caught hold of her wrist, saying quietly, 'I'm sorry I gave you a start, and I know I should have told you, but there was so much to do, so many people to see, so many forms to sign.'

'Oh, Joe.' She pulled a chair up close to him now and, leaning forward, she gathered both his hands in hers, saying, 'Oh, I am happy to see you out. Oh I am, you've no idea.'

'I'm happy to be out, Maggie . . . How is she?'

'Not too good, I'm afraid. I'll have to prepare her before you go up.'

He didn't answer, but turned his head and looked at the child who was looking at him now and he asked, 'Evacuee?'

'No, no.' She was looking down towards their joined hands.

'No? Are you minding it for someone?'

'No, Joe.' He looked at her steadily; he could feel her hands being withdrawn from his; he watched her rise to her feet and go and stand behind the baby's high-chair; and from there she looked at him straight in the face as she said, 'He's mine.'

330

His face screwed up in disbelief and he made small movements with his head; then as the colour flooded over his face he whispered, 'Yours?'

'Yes. Does it surprise you?'

As he, too, rose to his feet he said, 'Yes . . . well, it does in a way, Maggie.'

'Oh.' There was that old astringent note in her voice. 'You think like the rest: I'm not made in the image and likeness, so therefore I'm not capable of bearing a child.'

'Oh no, no, Maggie, nothing like that, only . . . well, I just . . . er' – again his head was moving – 'Doesn't seem like you, somehow. Are you? I mean, have you . . . well, have you got married?' His words ended on a high enquiring note and she answered flatly, 'No, I haven't got married. And I'm one of those bad girls; not so bad now, because there's a war on and it's happening all the time. No, I'm not married; he's what you would call illegitimate, commonly known as a bastard.'

They stared at each other, her face as red as his now, and when he muttered, 'I'm sorry,' she said, 'So am I, Joe.'

'Oh, Maggie.'

'You're shocked, aren't you?'

'No, no, I'm not shocked, I'm only . . . well . . .' He could find no words to explain his feelings and yes, truth to tell, he was shocked. He searched round in his mind to name a father. The only man he could think of was Billings. He had forgotten that he had ever hit Billings. He could only remember that Billings had been fond of her and had made himself the butt of her sarcasm. But that often happened where affections were concerned; she had likely been trying to hide what she felt. And yet he had thought . . . What had he thought? That she was in love with him? Yes. Yes, he had. Well then, he had been mistaken, hadn't he? Of a sudden he experienced a feeling

331

of loss, and added to this he felt hurt, his mind telling him that she should have told him, that it wasn't fair. Yet, when he came to think of it, she had never brought Billings up here.

Perhaps Billings was married. On the thought, he turned and put the question to her, 'Is he married?'

She stared at him open-mouthed for a moment, and then she added slowly, 'No, he isn't married.'

'Then . . . then I think he should marry you.'

'I don't think he would agree with you.'

'I . . . I don't see why not; he . . . seemed very fond of you.'

'What? Who? Who seemed very fond of me?'

'Well—' He lowered his head, his eyelids blinked rapidly, then he jerked his chin up to the side and, looking at her, said, 'Well, er, Billings.'

When she made no answer he raised his head. She was still standing near the child and what she said both puzzled and amazed him, for her words held deep bitterness: 'You know something, Joe? At this moment I could hate you, really and truly hate you.' And on this she turned about and went out of the kitchen.

She stopped at the top of the stairs, her fingers gripping her throat. She drew in a deep breath in order to compose herself, for she mustn't let Lizzie see how she was feeling.

When she went into the bedroom she made a gallant effort to bring into her voice the same note of happy surprise it had held when she first saw Joe at the back door.

Lizzie was propped up against the pillows. Her eyes were closed; she was dozing again.

'Aunt Lizzie.'

'Oh. Oh, yes, lass? I must have dropped off.'

'I have a surprise for you.'

332

'You have? They've doubled the rations?' A weak smile spread over the wrinkled skin. The spirit of laughter was not yet dead in her.

'No, something better than that; somebody's come to see you.'

'Ah lass, I'm past doctors. I know it and you know it; now let's face . . . '

'Aunt Lizzie, it isn't the doctor; it's someone you'd like to see.'

'Oh yes?'

'It's Joe.'

'Joe?' Lizzie's face took on a brightness and she made an effort to pull herself up, saying, 'Joe, here?'

'Yes, Aunt Lizzie. But listen. Will you do something for me?'

'Anything, lass, anything in the world, you know that.'

'Well now, listen to me, please. I don't want him to know that Charles is his.'

'You don't want him . . . ?'

'Aunt Lizzie, he . . . he was shocked when he saw the child, and I don't know if he's really better or not. I don't know if he's just out for a time; I know nothing yet; and I've no idea what his reactions would be if he knew Charles was his. It might even knock him back to where he was before. You never know with Joe.'

'But, girl, he should know he's the . . . '

'*Aunt Lizzie.*' She took hold of the wrinkled hands. 'I implore you; please do this for me, will you?'

They looked deep into each other's eyes for a moment; then Lizzie said, 'It'll be as you wish, girl; but I think you're depriving him of something.'

Maggie straightened her back, saying sadly now, 'Perhaps you're right, Aunt Lizzie. But he has no memory of what happened, and if he could recall any part of it he wouldn't see me as the woman who lay beside him; in

333

fact, I think now it would do more harm than good if he ever knew.'

'Oh Maggie, my dear.' Lizzie was stroking Maggie's hand now. 'You shouldn't have to put up with all this. You've had enough on your plate all your life; you deserve some love and comfort.'

'I've had love and comfort in you, all I ever wanted, and now I've got it in the child. I'm satisfied . . . I'm lucky. Now, now, now, now, don't cry or you'll have me at it. I'll . . . I'll send him up. But take things quietly. You will, won't you?'

Take things quietly. Lizzie smiled to herself. She'd soon be taking things quietly for a long, long time. She was surprised she hadn't started on her journey before now, but she was glad she was to see Joe again before she went, because she liked the boy; in fact, she could say she loved him. If she'd had a son she would have wished for one like him . . .

She hardly recognised him when he came into the room. She looked up at him as he held her hands and she said, 'Why lad, you're nothing but skin and bone. What have they been doing to you?'

And Joe answering in the same vein said, 'Keeping me on bare rations. I told them what you would say when you saw me.'

'It's good to see you, Joe.'

'And you, Lizzie.'

'Sit down, lad.'

He pulled a chair up to the bedside and again took hold of her hands, and when she said, 'How are you now?' he answered, 'Fine. Fine.'

'All the tangles straightened out?'

'Most of them.'

'Well, you know, if you had confided in me when I told you to, you wouldn't have had any more trouble.'

'You're likely right, Lizzie. Yes, you're likely right.' He smiled at her. Then leaning his face close towards hers, he said, 'Do you know something, Lizzie? If I had confided in you the exact truth, you would have had me put away even before they did.'

'As bad as that, lad?'

'As bad as that.'

'Well, they sorted it out for you, anyway.'

'No, they didn't, Lizzie.' He gave a shaky laugh now. 'When I was telling them the truth they thought it was my worst time; they put it down to delusions, traced it back to my childhood, even said I was afraid of being in the war; yet, you know, most of my time, all I've wanted to do was to get to the front line with a gun and shoot somebody.'

'Oh—' Lizzie turned her head away, the old quirk in her voice now as she said, 'Don't you tell me that; you want to get in the front line and shoot somebody. Never believe it.'

'It's true, Lizzie.'

She brought her face to his fully again, saying, 'It is, lad?'

'Yes.'

'Well, the source must have been pretty bad.'

'It was.'

'Do you want to talk about it?'

'Yes; yes, I do, but perhaps later on, that's if you're strong enough.'

'I'm strong enough for anything. I lie here doing nothing, waited on hand and foot. By, if anybody deserves medals in this war, it's that little one downstairs... What d'you think of the baby, Joe?'

He paused and looked away before saying, 'He seems a very bright little fellow. But ... but I was surprised to see him there, Lizzie.'

335

'Yes, I suppose you were. But, you know, Maggie's a very human human being. Perhaps you've never noticed that?'

'Oh yes; yes, I have, Lizzie. But . . . but you see I never knew there was . . . anyone else.' As the thought came into his mind he bent over her and wetted his lips before he spoke the next words softly, saying, 'She . . . she wasn't, well, I mean, she wasn't ra . . . ?'

'Raped? No, no, Joe; nothing like that. As far as I can understand she did it off her own bat, very much off her own bat.'

'Oh. Do . . . do you know who it was? I mean the father?'

'Yes, Joe; yes I do.'

'Corporal Billings?'

'*Corporal Billings?* Him! Oh no, Joe. What in the name of God made you think of Billings? I haven't met the bloke, but by what she says she hated his guts. No, it wasn't Billings.'

'But you do know who the father was?'

'Yes, Joe; yes, I do know.'

'Is . . . well, is he a decent fellow?'

'One of the best, Joe. One of the best.'

He rose from the chair now and, a stiffness in his voice, he said, 'Then why doesn't he marry her?'

'Perhaps . . . perhaps he can't, Joe. There's a war on, as you know, and lots of things . . . '

'Is he dead?' The words were a whisper.

Lizzie was about to say, 'No, no; very much alive, Joe,' but she changed her mind and what she said was after a moment's hesitation: 'There's a doubt, and because of it, Joe, I want to ask you something. I would like you to promise me something.'

As Maggie had extracted a promise from her a few minutes ago, she now waited for her answer, the answer from

336

Joe, and it came as hers had done. 'Anything, anything, Lizzie,' he said.

'Will you look after them both for a time until she finds her feet? When I'm gone they are going to need someone. She hasn't anyone in the wide world: her father's as dead to her as if he was in his grave; she has no one to turn to; life's going to be pretty lonely for her, pretty rough. Although she won't be in need, money-wise, and she'll have a roof over her head, that's small compensation when you're devoid of human company. And she'll have the child to bring up. She'll need someone, Joe. And somehow or other I was under the impression that you liked her a bit.'

'Oh, yes, Lizzie, I like her. I like Maggie very much, in fact since . . . since my cousins went, and . . . and I was very fond of them, no one has filled the gap but your two selves.'

'So, you'll do what I ask, Joe? Will you?'

What could he say but, 'Yes, yes Lizzie. Don't worry! I'll do what you ask.'

'Thanks Joe.' Then on a gentle laugh she said, 'She called the child Charles after my third husband, because Charlie was a good man. Charles Joseph LeMan; nice sound, hasn't it?'

'She's named him Joseph?'

'Yes. We thought about it, talked it over and asked ourselves, was there anyone we'd like him to be called after, and we thought of you.'

'What about the father's name?'

'Oh.' Lizzie, looking down towards the eiderdown, started picking at an imaginary thread as she said, 'You had better ask her that yourself; but I'd leave it for a time, she's touchy about these things. Now get yourself down and have something to eat, and tell her I could do with a nice strong cup of tea . . . laced.'

337

'Oh, Lizzie.' He put his fingers on her brow and stroked the white hair to the side now; and leaning over her, he placed his lips on her cheek, then stood up and went slowly from the room.

It was three nights later and Maggie was sitting close to Lizzie's bedside. She knew that her heart was nearing the end of its long day's work and at the thought her own heart was full to bursting, and she had a desire to give vent to it in a long lamenting cry like the fabled banshee's. Yet Lizzie seemed calm, utterly at peace and still able to talk quietly, and she was talking now, softly between gasps for breath: 'I'm going to tell you something and I want you to believe it as I believe it. He told me the cause of all his trouble; his mother. Last night, he talked and talked.'

'Well . . . well, we guessed that, didn't we? But rest now, Aunt Lizzie, rest now.'

'No, no; I'm all right, girl, I'm all right. But I must tell you this: his mother is a murderess; she murdered three men and a woman all to gain a house and a title for him.'

As Lizzie felt Maggie's fingers tighten on hers she said, 'It's the truth, girl; that fellow's as sane as me or you, and he told me the whole story from the beginning.' And gradually Lizzie related to Maggie all that Joe had told her: about the affair of his mother and his uncle; of the manner in which the uncle and his fiancée were killed; of the violent deaths of his elder cousin and the groom. And she finished: 'He told me how he found out. But now he seems a bit . . . well, a bit obsessed with where the gun is . . . I mean, where she hid it, somewhere in her room. And . . . and I believe him, Maggie, every word.'

'Oh, Aunt Lizzie, no wonder . . . no wonder he went off his head.'

'No wonder . . . And you believe him?'

'Yes; yes, I saw his mother. Remember? She was terrified at the sight of him. Oh, how awful.'

'Take care of him, Maggie, he needs looking after; I think in a way he'll always need looking after. He'll need a mother as much as he will a wife. And . . . and don't worry, girl, it'll all come right, you'll see; it'll all come right.'

Never in this world, Aunt Lizzie, never in this world. Her mind said the words loudly but her lips remained unmoving.

5

They buried Lizzie a fortnight later, and three weeks after this, Joe was finally discharged from the Air Force. Sitting in the kitchen facing Maggie, he said, 'I'd like to stay, but . . . but there's your reputation to think of.'

'Oh my God!' Maggie closed her eyes, and he came back at her swiftly, saying, 'Don't say it like that; there was Lizzie before, the three of us made . . . '

'Well, there's three of us now.' She pointed to the child strapped in his high-chair. 'And who cares anyway? If you are worried about those down at the camp . . . '

'I'm not worried about those down at the camp.' He had risen to his feet and, his voice harsh and strong now, belying his pale, thin features which were emphasised by the blackness of his hair, he said, 'To hell with the camp and all in it!'

'I second that, so what have you got to worry about? There's only the Cuthberts at the farm; and as for them in Blakemere, why, they don't know we're alive up here. Even if they did, would it matter so much to you?'

'It doesn't matter to me at all what people say. And don't twist my words. It's you I'm thinking about; you don't want any more—' He stopped; he had been about to say scandal. But it did not constitute a scandal today to have an illegitimate child. Or did it? What did he really know about it? He was aware that the war had turned the morality issue topsy-turvy: what had been mainly the rich man's prerogative and the licence of the soldier at war was now every man's . . . and woman's choice, if they wished to indulge themselves. He recalled Florrie Smith being sent away from the cottage. The fact that she was going to have a child had been a scandal, yet the scandal was created merely by the term 'unfortunate'. And this set his mind recalling scenes, faint now as wisps of cloud, of entwined couples in the hay-field in the summer, of grunts and orders of 'Get yourself away!' from the stable loft in the winter, and of how fortunate many had been: Helen and Janet Smith . . . Janet Smith. He hadn't thought of her in a long time. Thinking of her brought a curl to his lip; he couldn't at the moment think why he disliked her; so much of the past had sunk deep into his mind. All he knew now was he didn't want people to think badly of Maggie, and if he stayed here that's what would happen. But he wanted to stay here; this had become home to him. And there was a way he would stay here, a legal way.

But his whole body jerked with rejection at the idea.

Noticing his agitation, Maggie said softly, 'Don't worry, Joe, please. I would like you to stay but if you don't want to stay, well, that's up to you.'

'I want to stay, Maggie.'

'You could go home and pick up the threads,' she said. Yet even as she spoke her mind screamed at her: 'Don't push him.' But when, instantly, he replied, 'I couldn't, Maggie, not yet, anyway,' she drew in a deep breath, and, getting to her feet, said briskly, 'Well, let's say it's settled.' And she rose from the table, adding, 'I'll be glad of another pair of hands; that plot in the field is getting me down. I don't know how the grass ever grew on it; it seems like solid rock. And then there's him.' She pointed to the child. 'The little beggar's one

341

person's work, and more . . . And stop grinning at me. Yes, I'm talking about you.' She was leaning towards the child, and for answer he banged his spoon on the table.

'Talk about cheek,' she said, turning to Joe; 'he knows every word I say and he doesn't take a blind bit of notice.' And now she turned back to the child again and, saying, 'Oohoooh!' cupped his small chin in her hands as if intent on squeezing it; then lifting him out of the chair, she said, 'Come on, I'll wash that mucky face of yours.'

As Joe watched her carrying the child into the back kitchen he thought, she loves him, and again he wondered who the father might be. And he also wondered why he didn't like the child. In a way he saw it as an intruder and this made him feel out of place. When there had been only Lizzie and Maggie and himself he had never felt like that; in fact, he had imagined that he, in some way, was Maggie's main concern. How far could one delude oneself?

His gaze fixed on the kitchen door, he told himself he'd better face up to the fact that she was letting him stay because she needed his help and in a way felt sorry for him, but that her main concern now was that child, and always would be.

6

'At six twenty-five this evening, five German pleni-
potentiaries in the presence of Field Marshal Montgomery
put their signatures to the surrender of the German Armies
in the North.'

'It's over! Oh, Joe, it's over.' They were standing in front
of the wireless, and they joined hands; then for a moment
they fell against each other, laughing; at least, Maggie was,
almost hysterically.

'Oh, let's drink to it. I'm going to get drunk tonight.
I am, I am.'

'Don't be silly.'

'Who's being silly? Didn't you hear? It's over.'

'Not quite; there's still the Japanese to be sorted out.'

'Oh, we'll soon finish those off . . . Where's that bottle? I
said I was going to get drunk, but I doubt if there's enough
left in it to make me tiddly. By' – she turned round now
and looked at Joe again – 'if Aunt Lizzie had been here,
she would have had that cupboard stocked. It's a pity I
didn't keep up her contacts. But still, there's enough for a
couple each.'

She bent over now, arms outstretched towards her son,
who had toddled into the room and, lifting him up, she

held him above her head. He gurgled; then when she brought him to her breast, his arms about her neck, he looked over her shoulder and said, 'Joe . . . Joe.' And Joe, coming towards him, tickled his chin, which caused the child to wriggle in her arms. And she said, 'Go on then. Go on,' and she pushed him now towards Joe.

Joe's feelings towards the child had altered somewhat over the past months, because from the day he had settled in permanently the baby had insisted on holding his attention, even at times crying when he left the room. At first Joe had found this embarrassing: the very fact that he had never held a child in his arms before made him awkward, and his attitude towards this particular child, which had made itself evident in the first weeks he was in the house, had one day brought the forthright enquiry from Maggie, 'Don't you like him?'

Of course he liked him, he had lied; it was just that he wasn't used to babies.

And he had thought this explanation satisfied Maggie, but Maggie knew why he apparently didn't like the child, and a tiny section of her mind gathered hope from it, even though, as her honesty told her, it was a weak hope.

It would appear in the months following that the pattern of her life was set, and the residents of the two villages down below seemed to have accepted them without having to condone a scandal, having decided that the young man suffered from shell-shock and had been sent to Madley camp for a rest. But it hadn't worked and he had gone off his head for a while; now . . . well, he was still a sick young fellow.

So did the kindly distort the truth in order to provide a moral excuse for the association of the couple living in what had been Mrs Robson's cottage.

344

But one morning, like an overcasting cloud penetrating a sunny sky, the postman brought two letters: one addressed to Maggie and one to Joe. Maggie read hers and looked at Joe. He was still reading his. Maggie said simply, 'Mary says she's going to be married,' and Joe, raising his head here, said, 'Yes, they are telling me that, too, and they are coming here.'

'Who?'

'My solicitors. They quote that if Mohammed won't go to the mountain, then . . . '

'Oh!' She got to her feet. 'When are they coming?'

He looked at the letter again, then said, 'This was written last Thursday, so it'll be tomorrow, Wednesday. And there's only Holden coming, as far as I can gather. He's the younger partner.'

'How young?'

'Oh, in his fifties.'

'Young?' She laughed; then beginning to bustle, she said, 'I'll have to get something ready; cook something we can have cold. If it's fine we can have lunch outside and . . . '

'Look, he'll likely have lunch down in Hereford. And anyway, let him take what's going. I'm not going to bother my head, and you're not going to bother yours.'

'Oh, am I not? The man's not coming all that way without having a meal.'

'Well, he can have my week's meat if he brings his ration card.'

She laughed at him now; then turning from him, she opened the double doors of the wall cupboard and, standing back, surveyed the contents. And as she did so he surveyed her, thinking, What will Holden make of this set-up; me, the child, and this fat young woman? But no, she wasn't really fat any more; she was plump. She had lost almost three stone in weight and had altered in other ways since those days when he had first seen her

345

across the NAAFI counter: she no longer wore her hair pulled straight back from her forehead, she'd had it cut and waved; her face was still round, her cheeks full, but her skin was clear with a slight bloom on it, brought about, he supposed, by the constant fresh air up here. She could now be a younger sister to that fat dumpy creature he had first seen dressed up as Nellie Wallace.

But how would Holden see her? Likely a young girl in her puppy fat. At least so, until she spoke, when the very tone of her voice would alter his first impression, because apart from her voice sounding unusually pleasant, there was nothing girlish about its substance: when she talked it was as a mature woman, a woman with a sharp wit which, he knew from experience, could adjust itself to any grade.

And what would he say to Holden tomorrow? I'm not coming back? But he would have to go back sometime. Yes, he would have to go back. Anyway, why was Holden making the trip? They had done everything through letters so far, and there was always Mary there.

But that was the point, Mary was about to leave. Likely that was what was bringing him.

James Holden sat on the lawn in the sunshine and as he sipped his third cup of tea he told himself, and not for the first time since his arrival three hours ago, that he was puzzled: if the child wasn't Joe's, and he said it wasn't, and if he had no intention of marrying this young woman, and of course he could see the reason quite plainly why he shouldn't; not that she wasn't a very nice person, very entertaining, with a certain charm, but she was so small and tubby and very plain. Yet one forgot about her plainness when she began to talk. She was really very amusing; he hadn't laughed so much for a long time. Her reminiscences on her NAAFI days would make a book. And she had a most unusual voice; 'cultured'

346

was the word he would use for her voice, it was so pleasing to listen to.

Her child was a fine little fellow too. Now if young Jebeau had been the father of it he could have understood his desire to stay here with them both, but almost right away he had made it evident that he had no connection with her in this way. He had stated that they were living as friends, definitely just as friends. It was a queer set-up, to say the least, but now he must get him to do something definite; that's if he could, because here was a different man from the one he had last seen in his office in Newcastle. Then, he had been a young man determined to go his own way, but here was a man, outwardly still young-looking yet inwardly seemingly as settled as someone who had experienced all the rigours of a hazardous lifetime and had now come home to rest. And the picture he now presented exemplified this, for there he sat in a basket chair, his long legs stretched out before him, and to the side sat the young woman, and on the grass was the child playing with a wooden truck. It was a scene of domestic contentment which he had to explode, and so he said, 'Miss Smith has given her notice in; she'll be gone within a month. Sam has been gone this long time; well, almost five months. His back gave out. And I must tell you that in the spring the Army sent an overflow there. They were in the house for nine weeks and if they had been in nine years they couldn't have done more damage. The old chimney in the hall caught fire; it's a wonder the place wasn't burned down. Of course, there'll be some form of recompense, but it will never be enough to make things as they were. And the place is in a bad shape, Sir Joseph.'

How odd to be called Sir Joseph. Joe smiled quietly to himself. He would never feel a sir. He didn't want to be a sir. Oh no, he didn't want to be a sir. He said now, 'Is there any way of getting rid of the title?'

347

'What?'

'You heard what I said: is there any way of getting rid of the title? Can one sort of disown it, write it off?'

'Not that I'm aware of.'

'It's worth looking into.'

'If you say so.' Dear, dear, he was a very queer fellow. Both Arthur and Martin would be turning in their graves if they were hearing this now. Somewhat stiffly, he said, 'Title or no title, the place needs someone in authority; it's in a dreadful state and it's such a shame. It was a lovely house and the grounds were delightful, I remember.'

'Yes, yes, I know. Well, I've been thinking about what's to be done with it and I think I'll sell it.'

'Sell it?'

'Yes; there'd be no obstacle to that, would there?'

'No, no; it isn't entailed.'

'Well, we'll leave it at that then, shall we?'

'But in the meantime, when Mary goes there'll be no one to take charge, unless I appoint a husband and wife as caretakers. It isn't fair to ask anyone to live there alone.'

'Yes, do that. Do that for the time being.'

James Holden stared at this odd young man. Why had he made the journey? There was a saying: Is your journey really necessary? And Alec had thought it was. 'Go and see him,' he had said. 'State everything in black and white: tell him the state of the place; tell him if it is left empty it could be ransacked.' Well, it had been ransacked already, hadn't it? The soldiers had seen to that.

In a short while he took his leave.

He had arrived by taxi and as he was asking the driver to return at a certain time to pick him up, Joe had interrupted, telling him it would be all right, he would run him down to the station. A few months earlier Maggie had bought

348

an old car from someone in the village. It had belonged to a young man who had been killed, and although she knew she would only be able to run it at very odd times because of petrol rationing, the possession of it had given her pleasure.

And so Maggie had shaken hands with James Holden and told him that she had been very pleased to meet him. On his part he had assured her the pleasure was reciprocated. And she had watched the car being driven away and down the winding road.

Picking up the child from the grass, she went into the house and, sitting down, she hugged him to her breast and rocked him to ease the pain that seemed to be gripping her heart like an iron band.

'May I ask if you intend to marry?' She had overheard the solicitor talking as she had been about to come out into the garden with the tea tray, and she had stepped back and waited for the answer.

'No, no; she's a friend, that's all, and . . . and the child's not mine. No, I have no intention of marrying.' Joe's tone had been definite.

Well, she knew, didn't she? She had known all along. Yes, but she hadn't heard it in so many words before. Well now, she had, hadn't she? And that should settle it once and for all.

It wasn't fair.

No, of course it wasn't fair, but was life ever fair? To some, yes; some people had all the breaks.

Well, she'd had a break, hadn't she? She was holding him now. She had told herself, when the child came, that she wanted nothing more from life. But life was such that it made you lie. Her Aunt Lizzie had once said that life gave you salve for the sores it created for you, then when you weren't looking it picked off the scabs again.

It was a crude analogy but a fitting one in her case, at any rate.

And why did life give you the power to hate where you loved? for at this moment she hated Joe. Again she hated Joe.

7

'Captain William Parsons of the United States Navy, who observed the attack from the Super Fortress which dropped the bomb, said, "When the bomb fell away, we began putting as much distance between us and the ball of fire as quickly as possible. There was a terrible flash of light, brilliant as the sun. That was the first indication I had that the bomb worked."

"Each man gasped at what had been Hiroshima going up in a mountain of smoke . . . " '

Three days after the news had broken Maggie was still saying, 'Why had they to do it like that? To wipe out the whole place; it's terrible, like a massacre.'

'The war was a massacre.'

'Yes, but not like that, to be burnt up all at once.'

'You never saw London at the height of the Blitz?'

'No, I never did.'

'Well, parts of that were burnt up all at once. And anyway, the Japs would have held out, and men would have gone on being killed by the hundred or the thousand.'

Changing the subject Maggie said, 'I'm going to take Charles down to Mrs Cuthbert. Donald said yesterday his mother would like to see him; he wasn't a year old when she last saw him; she's been in bed so long. I felt I should have called on her but I didn't like to. Anyway, now he's asked me, I'll go along this afternoon.'

'Do you want me to carry him part of the way?'

'No, no.' She shook her head. 'I'll take the pushchair.'

'It's windy; you'll have your job cut out.'

'I can tackle the elements.'

When she smiled at him he smiled back, saying now gently, 'You're capable of tackling anything you put your mind to, Maggie.'

'Oh, is it complimentary day? Anyway, what are you going to do?'

'I was thinking about getting on with that article.'

'Good, good. And I think it's an excellent title, "You've got a nerve"; it'll help people.'

'You think so?'

'Sure of it.'

'Ah well, each to our own task. Sure you don't want me to come along?'

'Anything to get out of work. Go on, get in there, and get sat down and at it.'

On a free laugh he did as she bade him; and ten minutes later, as he saw her pass the window, he knocked on it and waved to her, and she waved back, and the child did too.

He had only written half a dozen lines when he sat back in the chair and looked out of the window to where the summer-house stood on a small green patch of grass, surrounded now on two sides by a vegetable garden. And an air of utter contentment seeped through him.

Since James Holden's visit there had, as it were, crept up on him the knowledge that, for the first time in his life, he was experiencing happiness; perhaps not complete happiness but a measure of it, and for the first time in his life he had a glimpse of where he was going. The route he intended to take offered no great excitement, no adventure,

352

but at the same time, no discord, no striving. As he saw it now, he had been held back from making the start on the journey by a prejudice, but he had overcome that now.

Before he set out on any new journey, however, he must return to the house, just this once; he must finish things there, satisfy himself that he was right. There were times, even now, that he doubted it; just a small doubt, but he knew that if the doubt became a certainty and the certainty should prove that he was wrong, then indeed he had been mad.

As he brought himself suddenly upright in the chair, and forward over the small table, he saw a car enter the drive. And he said to himself, 'Surely not Holden again, and Beecham with him.' But no, it wasn't a taxi, it was an old car, one that could give even Maggie's a number of years.

By the time the car had drawn up he had opened the door; and when he saw the driver step on to the gravel, his mouth fell into a gape; there came a restriction in his heart for a moment; his eyes narrowed as if in disbelief; and then he had walked from the door and was standing in front of the visitor.

'Hello, Joe. I . . . I didn't think I would find the place. Doubtless you're surprised to see me.'

'Yes, Carrie. But . . . but come in.'

She followed him through the door into the small hall, and then into the sitting-room where, seemingly now unable to speak, he directed her to sit down with a motion of his head.

'What a nice house.'

'Yes. It isn't mine, it . . . it's Miss LeMan's. I . . . I'm only staying here.'

He stood looking down at her. What did she want? Why had she come? And at this time when everything was straightening out for him. But for whatever reason she was here, it wasn't, he sensed, having the effect upon him he would have imagined only a few months ago. She was still beautiful, but nonetheless different; there was a placidness about her. No, that wasn't the right word . . .

'You're wondering why I'm here?'

'Since you ask, Carrie, yes, yes I am.'

'Are you better? Quite better?'

'Yes, I'm better.'

'I was sorry to hear you had been ill.'

'Thank you.'

'I felt I had to come and see you before I . . . well, go away.'

'You're leaving the country?'

'No' – she smiled at him – 'not the country.' Her head now dropped and she gave a small laugh. 'I've never found it so hard to explain before. I remember, Joe, I tried to tell you the beginnings of it some time ago, but . . . but you seemed to misunderstand. First of all, I'll . . . Please sit down, Joe; I can talk to you better when you're not looking at me like a schoolmaster.'

'I'm sorry.'

'Well, it happened after father died. I suppose it was his going and the war, the devastation of the air-raids, *the* air-raid, one particular one, that did it, I think. I happened to be working alongside a nun. She went on, hour after hour; she seemed almost superhuman. She was so upset at the condition of one child that she swore at the Germans, then spoke to Our Lord and asked him to overlook it. I laughed until I cried, not knowing that I'd been crying all the time. Anyway, I think it was there that it really started, and to cut a long story short I became a Catholic. It . . . it was that I wanted to tell you about on that particular Christmas night, Joe, and also that I had my mind set on joining the Church, whole-heartedly joining it.'

His eyes narrowed again, and now he said quietly, 'What do you mean, whole-heartedly?'

354

At this she gave a clear laugh which sounded like an echo from their long ago childhood, when she said, 'Hang on to your shoe-laces, Joe, in case you leave the ground, but I'm going to become a nun.'

He felt his face screwing up as if in protest as he repeated, '*A nun?*'

'Yes, yes; dreadful, isn't it?'

'But . . . but I don't understand. Why you? I mean.'

'Yes, why me, of all people? That's what everyone says. The whole family think I've gone doolally-tap; all except Mick, that is.' Her face was straight now and her voice was low but her words were firm as she said, 'Everything our Janet said that night was lies, Joe; there's never been anything like that between Mick and me. Oh, yes' – she nodded her head quickly now – 'we love each other; yes, we found that out early on; perhaps a little stronger than brother and sister should love, but that's as far as it ever went. You see, he had cared for me since I was a baby. He always thought that . . . well, I was different from the rest. In a way, I know now that he was protecting me from my mother, as Dad was when he sent me away to Aunt Alice's. I love Mick now as I loved him then; I'll always love him, Joe, and he me. But don't let me give you the impression that I'm going into the Church to evade this. Speaking frankly, love between a brother and sister is not unknown and if we'd had a mind, things could have developed and no one been any the wiser.' She gave an embarrassed laugh now and drooped her head as she said, 'I don't sound like a prospective nun, do I, Joe?' And he, his face slightly flushed now, smiled back at her and said, 'I have to agree with you, Carrie, you don't.'

'Well, there's one thing I've learned about nuns latterly, and that is, they are very, very human – oh my! You wouldn't believe – so don't look upon me as a potential saint, Joe. Anyway I . . . I felt I had to come and explain

355

things to you before I go in, and that'll be the day after tomorrow. You . . . you don't mind me being here?'

'Oh no, no Carrie.' His tone was steady. 'I'm glad you came. It's funny, but I wanted something cleared up in my mind and . . . well, your arrival has done it for me.'

She stared at him for a moment, waiting for him to go on, and when he didn't she said, 'I'm glad of that. And Mick will be happy too. I wanted him to come up with me, but he wouldn't.'

'Where is he?' He looked towards the window. 'He's not out there?'

'Oh no; he's down at Hereford. He . . . he thought it would be awkward after what happened between you, and it was better that I should explain. But I know he would be delighted to see you, Joe. You see, in a way he's taken the same line.'

'Not becoming a priest?' Joe's voice was high and Carrie laughed outright now, saying, 'Oh no; he won't even turn; I mean, become a Catholic, no, but he has joined The Third Order of the Society of Saint Francis . . . You've never heard of them?'

'No.' He shook his head.

'Well, he'll be a kind of layman priest. No, no, that isn't the word, priest; but they take vows of poverty and such.'

'He's going into a monastery, a Church of England monastery?'

'Oh no, no. As soon as he's discharged from the RAF, which could be any day now, he's opening up a wireless shop. He will live an ordinary life, but he must promise to . . . well, to attend Communion regularly and set a special time aside for prayer and self-denial, and go into retreat during the year. One of the main objects is to help others.'

Joe got to his feet now, his head shaking as he said, 'I . . . I can't really take it in yet. Looking back, there was

356

always something deep in Mick, and at this moment I can understand him more than I can understand you.'

She smiled up at him. 'I've no doubt about that, Joe. Sometimes I can't understand myself. That's one of the things I hope to achieve in the end. Look, would you come down into the town and have a word with him? He's never really got over that business at Janet's. He says one of the things he's continually fighting is his hate of her. Will you come, Joe? By the way' – she looked round – 'where is Miss . . . ?'

'Maggie? Oh, she's gone to visit a neighbour. She's taken the child with her.'

'She . . . she has a baby?'

Now it was her mouth that dropped into a slight gape, and he was quick to close it by saying, 'Yes, but it's got nothing to do with me.' And, strangely, again he only just stopped himself from adding, 'More's the pity.'

Dear, dear. He turned his head away from her. Here he was with Carrie, the girl he had loved since he was a boy, and in this moment he was wishing he was the father of Maggie's child. Well, it just went to show, didn't it? what he had been thinking a few minutes before that car stopped opposite the window.

He smiled broadly at Carrie now, saying, 'Yes, I'll come down with you. I too will be happier after I've cleared the air with Mick. What a day! But would you like a cup of tea first?'

'No, no; I've just finished lunch.' She was standing up now looking about her, and again she said, 'This is a nice house.'

'Go and have a look round while I'm getting my coat.'

Up in the bedroom he bent down and looked in the small mirror: his face was smiling, his eyes were bright, he looked alive.

357

When he came downstairs again Carrie was walking into the kitchen, and he joined her as she said, 'I would like to have seen her.'

He did not follow this up, but said, 'I'd better leave a note,' then added quickly, 'No, no; I'll tell her everything when I come back. Oh, Carrie' – he took her by the shoulders – 'I'm happy for you, and I'm happy for myself. You've done something today.'

On this he leant towards her and kissed her on the brow; then taking her by the arm they went out.

It was almost two hours later when he returned to the cottage. His meeting with Mick hadn't gone as smoothly as that with Carrie; both he and Mick had seemed embarrassed, not, Joe thought, in recalling the last time they had met but rather at the turn of events that were taking the brother and sister into the religious world. Whereas he had been able to speak freely when with Carrie up in the cottage, Mick's presence formed a barrier to speech, not least in himself, and as he had listened to the bantering tones of the conversation between these two people who had been so dear to him at one time, and who, by Carrie's confession, were still very dear to each other, there had arisen in him a feeling of inadequacy and the not pleasant knowledge that these two people, brought up without any advanced education, had gone far beyond him in their thinking.

But here he was back. He had caught the bus to the village and had run the last couple of miles and he was panting as he entered the kitchen calling, 'Maggie! Maggie!' A feeling of happiness had earlier returned but now it had heightened itself on to the border of elation. Oh, he had been blind. And that girl, what she had put up with, and how she had cared for him. Right from the beginning she had cared for him. But why had she had the

358

child? Damn that! He liked the child; he loved it; yes, he did, he had come to love it, and who was he to blame her for having it? And he had blamed her. He had a nerve when he came to think about it. He should really alter the substance of that article he was writing.

'Maggie! Maggie!' He was in the sitting-room now. She hadn't come back. Well, he would go over and meet her.

He was trotting now down the lane along by the Cuthbert's fence; through the gate and into the field, closing the gate behind him, over a fence and through another field; and there was the farmhouse and the duckpond, the quacking of the ducks and the honking of the geese coming to him on the wind. He was out of breath as he came to a stop against the railings overlooking the home paddock. He wouldn't go any nearer but he would wait for her here.

He had been standing against the railings for about ten minutes when he saw Donald Cuthbert come out of the farmyard and make his way towards the pond. He watched him stoop and pick up a duck, which, unlike the rest, didn't scamper away. He saw him stroke its leg before putting it on to the ground again, and when he straightened up he was looking across the paddock, and, instinctively, Joe lifted his hand in salute.

Donald Cuthbert walked slowly towards him, and when he was within speaking distance, Joe called, 'I'm waiting for Maggie.'

The farmer came to the fence and peered into Joe's face, and he repeated, 'You're waiting for Maggie? What's up?'

'What do you mean, what's up?'

'Well, I don't get this. She's gone. You had a row?'

Joe's face crinkled. His lips apart, he went to speak; but then he closed his mouth and, his hand going to his throat, he gulped for a moment before saying, 'What do you mean, she's gone? She can't be gone. I only went down into Hereford, and we haven't had a row. No.'

'Well, something upset her; I've never seen her like she was. She was all right when she first came, but you see, it's me mother's birthday and she thought she would like you to come over and have a cup of tea along with the rest of us, so Maggie left the child and went back for you.'

'Oh, my God!'

'What did you say?'

'Nothing. Do you know where she's gone?'

'Not a clue. She was gone some time, and then she arrived with the car piled up, takes the child, saying she was very sorry. At least that's what she said to me mother. She said, "I'm very sorry, Mrs Cuthbert, but I've got to go and see about some business. I'd forgotten about it." Me mother was puzzled; there was such a change in her. And then when I came outside with her I saw the car. Piled up to its roof it was, as if she had thrown the stuff in.'

'Did she say where she might be going?' Joe asked; but then shook his head, saying, 'No, no; silly question.'

'Haven't you got any idea what's upset her, then?'

Joe looked at the older man now and said frankly, 'Yes; an old friend came unexpectedly. She, I mean Maggie, must have come back when we were talking. She's likely misconstrued things.'

'That happens; women are made that way. Oh yes, that happens. Well, I wish I could be of some help to you. We are very fond of Maggie, you know. When she first came here to live with her aunt she was like a roly-poly pudding. But she was nice, always nice and cheery. She had a cheery tongue.'

'Yes,' Joe went to turn away repeating, 'Yes, she had a cheery tongue.' Then looking back at the farmer, he said, 'Thanks. And I'm sorry about your mother's birthday party.'

360

'Oh, that's all right; it was just a little tea. But she's puzzled about Maggie. I'll have to tell her what happened. Anyway, what are you going to do now?'

Joe took in a deep breath as he said, 'I don't know, except look for her. Yes' – he nodded his head vigorously now – 'I'll look for her. I'll find her.'

'Yes, I'm sure you will. She can't have gone all that far and she has a child, and all that clobber. She's got to stop somewhere soon. And anyway, there's the petrol; she'd never get very far on the ration, would she?'

'No, no; you're right. Well, thank you. Thank you, Donald.'

'I wish I could help.'

Joe made no answer to this, only inclined his head and turned away.

He did not run now; there was no need. When once again he entered the cottage he wondered why he hadn't noticed that the kitchen floor was clear of toys and that the mugs weren't on the rack. Slowly now he went into the sitting-room and, standing in the middle of the room, he stood gazing about him. This house had come to be home to him; what was he going to do now? Where would he start to look? Dear God – he swung around, his hand to his head – to think that she should come back during the short time that Carrie was in the house. And what had she heard?

What had he said? And where had she been while she was listening? It wasn't likely that she had heard the conversation from this room if she had been in the kitchen, but if she had been in the scullery or even outside the scullery door, which opened out on to the cobbled enclosure where the coalhouse and wood store was, she could have heard from there anything that had been said in the kitchen. But then, what had he said in the kitchen? The only thing he could really recall was that he had kissed Carrie on the forehead. But she couldn't have seen that. Had his kiss been audible?

361

He sat down at the little desk before the window; and there on the pad in front of him was an envelope with his name on it: Joe. He tore at it and pulled out a strip of paper with a perforated top. It had been torn from her shopping pad and on it he learned what she had heard, for it stated simply, 'You have no need to come home and tell me; I have listened to you for the last time. I don't want to see you again, so, please, don't come back. I won't return home until I know you are gone for good. So do me this one last favour; get on with your life and let me get on with mine.'

As there had been no heading, so there was no signature. *Oh Maggie. Maggie.*

He read the letter again and again, and one thing came through from it; she couldn't be that far away if she would know when he left the house for good. Why did things happen to him? Why couldn't he be like other men whose lives ran smoothly? But did their lives run smoothly? Did he know anybody whose life had run smoothly? Just taking his own family: his father, his mother, Uncle Arthur, Martin, Harry. Yes, Harry's life had run smoothly, happily, until the Gods became jealous. Only the good die young. There was something in that. Oh, at this moment he wished he was dead . . . No, he didn't! He was on his feet. Enough of that; he was going to find her. Whether it took a long time or a short time he was going to find her. But where to make a start? Down in Hereford.

He walked round Hereford for three days. He had always imagined it to be a small town, but each day it seemed to grow bigger. Every time he saw a push-chair he made eagerly towards it. But Charles was never in it.

Next, he tried the villages, riding from one to the other on his bike, making discreet enquiries. But no one seemed to have heard of a Miss LeMan who had a two-year-old

362

child. In fact, the enquiry raised eyebrows, especially from the occupants of small hamlets, and as one pious lady said, 'Is she one of the victims of the war's mishaps?'

They were all victims of the war's mishaps.

He had been in the house ten days when two letters arrived. One was from Alec Beecham, the other for Maggie. And he recognized the handwriting as being Mary's.

Alec Beecham's letter said that the new will was ready for signing and would need to be witnessed. Would he care to make the journey back north or would he prefer that James came to him and settled the matter there.

'I won't come back until you've gone.' Well, he could be gone, couldn't he? He could go north and settle the will business and go to the house for the last time and settle the business there, too. And knowing he had left the house she would, as she said, return. Yes, as he had surmised, wherever she had settled she had him seemingly in view, or had detailed someone to report to her. Well, he would stay away a week and then he would return. She couldn't stop him, no matter what she said. And anyway, now he came to reason it out, she must know that he wasn't with Carrie if he was still in the cottage, so why was she making it difficult? Was she really wanting to be rid of him? No – he shook his head at the thought – she had seemed so happy; at least, up till a short while ago. He could put his finger on the time; it was from the day James Holden had visited him. A slight stiffness in her manner had appeared. What had caused it? Had he also said something then to hurt her? No, no. He shook his head. But yes; now he remembered something that James had asked him about getting married. And what had he replied? That he had no intention of ever getting married. Had she heard that too? And about the new will he intended to make?

363

He was tactless; he was senseless; had he ever grown up? Had he ever stopped to think about anyone else but himself and the burden that his mother had laid on him? As a boy he had cried because he couldn't have Carrie. And then, faced with the fact that he had a mad mother for a parent, he had tried to escape from the responsibility, and had eventually succeeded. And when he found that his young love had a deeper feeling for her own brother than she had for him, and at the same time that he had been betrayed by his one and only friend, he had decided that it was too much and had given up. And who had stood by him during all this, and before this when he had become lost in the mass of men down in that camp? A small fat girl. And such had been his ingratitude, even from the beginning, that he had tried to hide their association. And then it was she who had forced her way into the silence and pulled him back into the world again. And it was she to whom he had returned as if by right, only to be upset, even shocked by the knowledge that she had, in the meantime, given birth to a child. Lizzie apart, it was Maggie, the little fat girl to whom he had clung as a life raft over the past years. And now she had got tired of his clinging; as she saw it he had left the raft for a lifeboat.

What must she think of him? God! what must she think of him now?

8

'I think you are making a mistake.'

'That's as maybe, but I've made up my mind to sell.'

'It's in a dreadful state; it should really be put into order before it's put on the market.'

'I'm not doing anything about that. Let it go as it is; take what you can get for it.'

'Why not leave it for a while, think it over?'

'You said it's in a dreadful state; it will only get worse.'

Alec Beecham heaved an impatient sigh. 'It could be a lovely place,' he persisted.

'It was, once; it never could be again; too much happened there.'

'Too much happened everywhere.'

'Yes, you're right. Anyway, I'm going over today to see Mary and say goodbye to her. She's been very good.'

'Good isn't the word for it, stuck out there all alone in that place; it's a wonder she's been able to stand it. I feel that she should be recompensed. Would you like us to see to it for you?'

'No; I'll do that myself.'

'Very well.'

Alec Beecham rose from his chair and extended his hand to his client. Difficult one, if he knew anything: his attitude had been stubborn with regards to his mother. That was a very, very sad affair; couldn't get to the bottom of it. But his attitude now was just as rigid with regard to the house. He was an odd man. And this business of wanting to get rid of his title, it wasn't understandable.

Joe could almost guess what the solicitor was thinking and when he smiled at him and said, 'I'm a nuisance, aren't I? Always have been,' Alec Beecham denied it strongly, saying, 'Nonsense, nonsense; you've been through difficult times. Anyway, do what I ask, will you, and think it over about the selling? I've always had a soft spot for Screehaugh. I used to envy Arthur such a house and I always enjoyed my stays there and the shooting.'

Without further comment, Joe took his leave, and as he went out into the street he repeated to himself, 'And the shooting.'

He was unable to persuade a cabby driver to take him all the way to Screehaugh; and so he went by train to Consett, from where he was able to hire a taxi.

He had expected to find the grounds overgrown, but the tangled mass they presented saddened him long before he reached the house. He had no memory of his last visit here, for his mind was comparing the condition of the place now with that on the day he had walked out, the day he had lain in Mick's arms and cried.

The appearance of the house was even worse than that of the grounds: windows were broken; the dark stain on the brick-work, outlining the chimney, had widened.

He walked through the grass-strewn yard to the back door, and when he found it locked he stood back from it and stared upwards, wondering if Mary had already gone. Alec Beecham had given no indication of it.

The wind was whistling down the yard, bending the tall dry grass that had grown up between the stones, and a half-door of a horse box swung drunkenly on one hinge. He shivered: the day was raw, but there was an added iciness in the atmosphere surrounding the place.

He looked in at the kitchen window, shading his face on either side with both hands. The room looked tidy; and after some further positioning of his hand he could see that there were some embers of the fire still glowing in the grate. Mary must have only recently gone out.

He pushed his open pocket-knife between the upper and lower half of the window, released the catch and pushed the bottom half upwards, then climbed in over the sink and into the room.

The kitchen was tidy, although the Delph rack was clear of all but a few ordinary dishes; there were no copper pans hanging on the wall, and the brass candlesticks and horseshoes had gone from the mantelpiece.

He walked from the kitchen and into the hall, but remained standing just within the doorway. The noontime sun slanted through the windows and showed up the floor that had once been so highly polished you could almost see your reflection in it, but now presented a large square of scuffed boards. There was no furniture whatsoever in the hall.

Standing opposite the fireplace, he could see where the fire had been. The whole wall was black with smoke, the big oak beam that formed a mantelshelf was charred. As James Holden had said, it was indeed a wonder the place hadn't burned down. What a pity it hadn't.

The drawing-room presented the same bareness, as did the dining-room. It wasn't until he came to the long billiard-room and the study that he saw where the furniture was stored. The billiard table was piled high with carpets, and surrounded by couches, chairs, tables, bureaux, drawers, chests and every article of furniture stacked one on top of the other almost to the ceiling.

The same pattern was repeated in the library.

Slowly now, he walked to the bare staircase, and when he reached the gallery, he became still as he looked along the corridor towards the room that he knew he must enter once again.

When he thrust open his mother's bedroom door, he half expected to see her sitting in the bed facing him. And yet, he had no memory of seeing her sitting upright in bed; the only memory was of himself stripping the bedclothes from her and revealing her in her outdoor clothes. The bed was bare except for a mattress and, but for the wardrobe, the room was bare of furniture.

Slowly he walked across the floor, looking at the boards, his eyes searching for a loose one that could indicate a hiding place. He even pulled the brass bedstead away from the wall and examined the exposed floor; but each board showed not the faintest sign of having been moved.

The bedstead spring and the mattress on it he found was intact on both sides.

Next he looked in the wardrobe. It was an old Dutch wardrobe, just one large empty space inside. The top was flat with just a slight rise of ornamentation at the front. He reached up and groped across the top with his hand, but felt nothing; he hadn't really expected to find anything there.

It had to be somewhere. What other furniture had been in the room? The wash-hand stand with the marble top, a dressing-table with two short drawers and one long one, which he could see now as if it were standing before him, and a writing table.

He walked to the window. It was an odd-shaped window. There were two of them on this side of the house, one at each end of the wall. They called them the triangle windows, this one set above the central bow of the library.

368

The bedroom window itself was no more than three feet wide and both bottom panes opened outwards. For some reason which he couldn't explain to himself his eyes became riveted on the cup of the drainpipe that ran down the side of the wall towards the ground floor. Rising from it was an angled pipe connected to one leading down from the main roof guttering.

Slowly he opened the window, a gust of wind catching it and almost wrenching it out of his hand. Pushing the window open to its fullest extent he now leant well out until his head was above the cup of the drainpipe. Looking into it told him nothing, only that it was rusty and blocked with leaves.

Hanging on to the window sill now with one hand, he eased himself further out until he could thrust his arm down the cup. This resulted in his having to pull out handful after handful of black, rotting, mulched leaves, but nothing else. He withdrew himself back into the room, pulled off his overcoat and his suit coat, rolled up his sleeve well above the elbow and once again leant out of the window; and now thrusting his forearm down into the cup's outlet, he found what he was looking for. His fingers recognised the shape of the wooden handle. He gripped it and pulled, but it remained fast. Again he tried while the wind tore at him and the window flapped against his shoulder.

He was breathing heavily and, far from feeling cold, he was now sweating as he pulled himself back into the room. He'd have to get at it somehow or never sell the house, because whoever bought it would, if they cared for the place at all, clear the drain-pipes, the blocking of which any householder knew was one of the main causes of decay in the brickwork. And what would happen when the gun was found? The war being over, newspapers had to be fed, and they would grab at this. You could even see the headlines: Poachers hunted and blamed for killings.

369

But perhaps the new occupants would have the spout taken down and thrown away. Yes, but once it was loosened, the gun would probably be loosened too.

Once again he had his arm in the drainpipe, but tug as he might he couldn't move the gun.

Minutes later, his top coat on once more, he heard himself laughing; then he checked it; but he could not check the words that came out of his mouth as he looked towards the bare bed. 'You were determined that I should have it, weren't you? This seems to be your final card.' And then he almost left the ground in one leap as he swung round to hear his name being spoken. 'Eeh! Mr Joe, you did give me a gliff. I saw you from the road hanging out of the window. I . . . I thought you were one of those fellows after the lead. And then I recognised you.'

'Oh Mary—' He put his hand to his brow for a moment, and she came towards him, saying softly, 'Have I given you a turn?'

'Yes; yes, Mary, you've given me a turn.'

She now walked past him and stood by the window and, looking downwards, she said, 'Were you looking for something?'

He stared at her. 'I . . . I think the drain's blocked, Mary. It . . . it was full of leaves. I cleared it.'

'It's been blocked for a long time, Mr Joe.' They stared at each other and he found his head moving in disbelief, while his mind told him that *Mary knew.*

His voice was a mere whisper now as he said, 'You know, Mary?'

'Yes, Mr Joe, I know.'

'And . . . and you did nothing about it? You continued to look after her?'

'Well, you see, I didn't believe it, not at first. She used to have sort of nightmares and she would wake up yelling about the spout. "Get rid of that spout," she would shout.

370

Then just before she died her mind was clear and . . . and she told me. With her own lips she told me. And she kept saying she did it for you. But after, when I came to think about it, I know why she did it; it was only a bit for you; most of it was for herself, 'cos she had been mistress of this place for years and she couldn't bear the thought of leaving it. You know, Mr Joe' – Mary now looked towards the bed – 'I nearly committed murder meself that night. The only thing that stopped me, I think, was that I knew she was near her end. She did a dreadful thing, but by God, Mr Joe, she paid for it. Eeh! she did that. When I saw her lying there dead, all I felt against her kind of vanished: she had never been a very happy person and she had gone through hell in her last years . . . When did you find out, Master Joe?'

He drew in a shuddering breath before he said, 'The night she killed them. I saw her as she came back, and I surprised her in bed with her clothes on.'

'She was a clever woman in her way, your mother. If it hadn't been for that, you spotting her, she might have carried on normal, like, and no one any the wiser. But about this spout. I've thought about it a lot. I tried to get the gun out last year. Well, I mean, what I did was, I put my arm down to see if there was anything there to satisfy meself that it hadn't all been a sort of me own imagination playing havoc with me, because sometimes when I've been left here on me own, I wouldn't have been surprised if I'd gone off me head meself.'

'I can understand that, Mary. I just don't know how you've stood it.'

'Well, it was either here, or going to live with me mother or going into munitions, and I didn't fancy either of those two. This was the lesser of all the evils; I was me own boss so to speak. Anyway, about the spout, Mr Joe, I understand . . . well, there's a rumour, I got it from the solicitor, that you might be thinking of selling, and

I think something should be done about it.' She nodded towards the window. 'It's all past and done with now; let sleeping dogs lie, I think; I'm not one for stirring up trouble, never have been. I often thought if I had help I could have unscrewed the whole pipe; it isn't all that long; but I couldn't do it on my own, and to ask anybody, they would want to know the reason, wouldn't they?'

'Yes, Mary, they would want to know the reason.' He paused. 'Do you think we could do it together?'

'I don't see why not, Mr Joe; but . . . but first of all let's go down and have a cup of tea.'

Ten minutes later they were sitting opposite each other at the kitchen table, and once again Mary caused him almost to leave the ground when she said, 'How is Maggie and the bairn? I bet he gets more like you every day.'

'Like *me*? What do you mean, Mary, like *me*?'

'Well, why shouldn't he be?' Mary narrowed her eyes at him now. 'Have I said something wrong? I hold nothing against you for not marrying her. I . . . I mean, you know your own business best, but when she had the bairn by you . . . well.'

'*Mary*—' He was on his feet now and, his hands flat on the table, leaning across towards her in such a manner that she scraped her chair back away from him as he cried, 'What on earth are you talking about?'

Pulling herself to her feet, she went round the back of the chair and held on to it as she stared at him, thinking for a moment that he too, like his mother, had gone mad. 'Well, it's your bairn, Master Joe, and I thought . . . '

'Mary' – he had closed his eyes now and drooped his head – 'what are you saying? It's not my bairn.'

'Master Joe—' The tone of her voice brought his head up and as he stared at her she said slowly, 'Well, I reckoned from the time you were together to the time it was born, it was yours.'

Slowly he sat down on the chair and, staring up at her, he said, 'Mary, sit down and tell me what makes you think the child is mine.'

Mary sat down, but cautiously, and she pressed her hand against the side of the table as if for support as she said, 'Well, when you deserted from the Air Force, she came here looking for you. She was here before you got here. We found you upstairs in your mother's room; she was screaming. You were very strange, didn't speak or anything, and we got you to bed and the doctor to you, and she sat up with you. Well' – she looked down now – 'your mother had a bad night, dreadful, and I had to get up and see to her, and I thought I would look in and see how you were. And there you were, both of you, in bed together.' She lowered her head now as she said, 'She was tight in your arms and you were both fast asleep.'

'Oh, dear God!' He let his head drop back on to his shoulders and his mouth fell into one large gape and he seemed to stretch it wider and wider before finally bringing his head forward again. 'Of all the bloody fools in this wide world, you're looking at one, Mary,' he said.

'Well, I wouldn't say that, Mr Joe.' There was a faint smile on her face now.

'I would, Mary, I would. I accused her, at least I did in my mind, of going off the rails. And to think . . . Oh, my God!' He got to his feet, 'No wonder she walked out on me.'

'She walked out on you?'

'Yes.' He nodded at her. 'Carrie came to see me, and Maggie must have got the wrong impression . . . '

'But our Carrie's going into the Church.'

'Yes, I know, but Maggie didn't know that and she'd had enough.'

'Eeh! what a mix-up. But then our Carrie was always one for mixing things up, in a different way, I know, from our Janet and the rest. But for her to go and be a nun. Eeh! Mr

Joe. Well, it floored me mother; she won't speak to her. It was bad enough when she became a Catholic. But now a nun! Somebody's got at her. That's what me mother says. And our Mick is almost as bad; he's gone for a sort of holy Joe. Oh—' She put her hand over her mouth. 'Oh, Mr Joe; it's just a saying.'

He had to smile. Dear Mary. In a way she was like Maggie, a leveller, bringing things down to earth, and she had certainly brought him down to earth. Charles was his? He couldn't believe it. Oh! Maggie. Maggie. He must get back. And he repeated the words aloud; 'I must get back, Mary,' he said; 'and so let's get on with that spout, eh?'

'Yes, Master Joe, let's get on with it.' . . .

It took them almost two hours to undo the rusty bolts; and when they had the pipe on the ground and had forced the gun from its resting place, neither of them made any comment as they stood looking down at it. It was covered with the black slime of the decomposed leaves. As Mary went to pick it up, Joe stopped her and, taking a handkerchief from his pocket, he put it round the barrel, saying, 'Get a spade, Mary.'

Down in the wood he dug a narrow trench almost three feet deep, and there he laid the gun at the bottom of it, and again they stood looking down at it without speaking.

Joe had asked the taxi driver to return in three hours, and so he should soon be here. They were sitting in the kitchen waiting.

'I'm glad you're going to be married, Mary,' Joe said, 'and it goes without saying that I wish you every happiness; you deserve it.'

'I'll be happy, Mr Joe, never fear; he's a good man. I've waited a long time' – she laughed now – 'but I know I've chosen right. He's been married afore; his wife died in the Blitz in Liverpool. And he limps a bit, because a foot was hurt in one of the raids. We're thinking about setting up

374

a tobacconist's shop, Confectionery and Tobacconist.' She nodded at him. 'He's got an appointment with the bank manager next Monday, because he's got his eye on a nice little business; it's a corner shop in Gateshead. And quite a nice neighbourhood an' all.'

'May I ask how much they're asking for it, Mary?'

'Eeh! quite a lot, Mr Joe. But he'll get it. He's got a hundred and fifty saved up, and I've got a bit, 'cos I've never used me wages and it's in the same bank. We want about another two hundred. Oh, he'll get it.'

'There won't be any need, Mary, for him to get it.'

He went to the table whereon lay a small case that he had brought with him and, opening it, he took out a leather folder, and from this he extracted a cheque book, and on a cheque he wrote: Miss Mary Smith. Five hundred pounds.

When he handed it to her she stared at it for a moment and put her hand tightly across her mouth, while the tears sprang from her eyes and she muttered, 'Oh, Mr Joe, you needn't give me this because of ... well ... ' He now caught hold of her hand, and he said, 'I'm giving it to you, Mary, in thanks for your loyalty to this house since you were a little girl, and not for anything else. You're a good woman, Mary, a brave and kind woman, and I'll always be in your debt. And you must tell me when you're going to be married, because I mean to be there and meet this lucky fellow.'

'Oh, Mr Joe.' She was sobbing audibly now. 'I ... I never thought to see the day that I'd be so lucky. In all ways I'm lucky. In a way, I've always been lucky. No matter what this house has done to you, Mr Joe, I've always felt lucky because I was connected with it; I've never gone hungry, never wanted for anything because of it, and now me future's settled. Oh, Mr Joe.'

He had his arm around her shoulders now, and it was with a touch of sadness that he thought of how little it took to make some people happy. She thought she had always been lucky. She'd worked herself to a standstill in this house for years; she had looked after a mad woman; and even when she knew that woman had killed her own father, she continued to look after her and had kept her secret all this time. There weren't many such Marys in the world, but thank God there were still a few.

She was still crying when he bade farewell to her, and the driver closed the taxi door on him.

And now for Hereford and Maggie. He caught the night train from Newcastle to Birmingham. With luck, by lunch time he could be at the cottage.

What if she wasn't there? She had got to be there. She must be there.

9

It was raining heavily. He was drenched between leaving the bus and the time he reached the gate of the cottage, and when, pausing for a moment, he wiped the rain from his face and through narrowed eyes looked upwards to where a thin spiral of smoke was being spread out as soon as it left the chimney pot, he closed his eyes tightly, bit on his lip, then went up the path and round to the back door.

As if he had just returned on that particular afternoon after saying goodbye to Carrie and Mick, there was Maggie seeing to the child's wants: she was actually placing a bowl of hot cereal on the table when he opened the door. As she turned her head and looked at him a little of the contents of the bowl spilled over; then turning her gaze back to the table she reached out and, taking up a napkin, she dabbed at the spilt milk. And he couldn't believe his ears when, her back to him, she went towards the stove, saying, 'You've taken your time.'

His throat was tight, his chest was tight, his whole body seemed tight, fit to bursting with the things he had to say, and what does she greet him with? 'You've taken your time.' A gurgle of laughter spiralled up through the centre of him, but he didn't give vent to it. What he did was to play her at her own game, and, going to the table from where the child had already turned and was shouting, 'Joe! Joe!' he lifted him up and stared into his face; and then he said something that surprised her for the moment: 'Not Joe, Joe; it's Dada. Say Dada.'

'Joe, Joe.'

He stared at the child for a moment longer and saw in his face the reflection of himself; then on a wave of emotion he pulled him tightly into his breast and, holding the child's face against his own, he looked at Maggie where she was surveying him now from the other side of the table, and he said, 'That's one thing I'll never forgive you for, do you hear? Keeping it from me.'

'Huh!' She tossed her head as she again turned from him, saying, 'If you want the truth, you had very little to do with it. In fact—' She paused now; and then, her face twisted with a peculiar pain, she muttered through trembling lips, 'You didn't even know it was me; you thought it was her, or else it would never have happened.'

Slowly he put the boy down into the chair again, where he proceeded quite unconcerned to get on with his breakfast, and he moved round the table to stand in front of her to take her hands and pull them tightly into his breast, and his voice had a deep tremble in it as he said, 'We've . . I mean, I've got a lot of talking to do, Maggie. Come. Come on.' And with this he led her out of the kitchen, through the little hall, and into the sitting-room.

The fire was smoking slightly, and as he went to draw her down on to the couch she reached out, saying, 'I must push that wood on.'

'Damn the wood!' He jerked her round, and with a 'plop' she found herself sitting on his knee.

His arms were about her, their faces were inches from each other and when he began, saying brokenly, 'How . . . how can I start to tell you? What a fool I've been, blind, selfish,'

378

she agreed with him, saying, 'Yes, you've been all that.'

'Oh, Maggie' – he bowed his head – 'I feel so ashamed. How I've used you. But at the same time—' His chin came up now and his voice changed as he went on, 'You . . . you should have told me about the child. No matter what the circumstances, you should have told me. I wouldn't have known even now if it hadn't been for Mary.'

'Yes, Mary' – her voice sounded level – 'we've got a lot to thank Mary for. I wouldn't have known that your friend was going to be a nun if I hadn't called in and got her letter. In fact, I wouldn't be here at all if it wasn't for that because . . . because, Jo . . . e—' Her mouth widened on his name, her body began to shake and now in a mumble of words she said, 'I . . I couldn't stand any more. I thought I could, just . . . just to live here with you, but I knew I couldn't, at least I thought I couldn't. I kept telling myself I couldn't; I had to face up to the fact that you didn't love me, you didn't even care.'

He now took her face between his hands and shook her head from side to side, saying, 'I do, I do. I have for a long time, yet didn't really recognise it. I only knew I wanted to be with you. My trouble was, I took you for granted; you were there, you would always be there, just as much as if we were married. But I must tell you, and it's the truth, that I found out how I felt before Carrie came. It was after I told James Holden that I had no intention of marrying, the very words seemed to open my eyes and my mind to what it would be if you decided to marry, say, the father of the child. It was always looming in the back of my mind; the father of the child. I wouldn't own up to the fact that I was jealous of this man. And you kept quiet because you didn't want to hold me to any responsibility. I can see that now, Maggie; look at me, open your eyes and look at me.'

It was some seconds before she did as he bade her, and then the locked-up tears rolled down her cheeks and she listened to him saying, 'Maggie, I've never been so happy; I couldn't imagine ever being as happy as I am at this moment, when I tell you that I love you in such a way that my life won't be long enough for me to prove it to you. I feel, in a way, that I've just been born, and I have, Maggie, because you've given me new life. Oh, Maggie, Maggie.'

Still holding her face, he put his lips on hers, and such was his touch that she felt she was unable to bear it. He had said she had made him feel that he had just been born and, strangely, in a way, his words were prophetic for she knew deep within her that because of his past he needed a mother as much as a wife. Her Aunt Lizzie had been right.

'Oh, Aunt Lizzie. Aunt Lizzie.'

Their arms were about each other, holding tight, when he said, 'What did you say?'

And she muttered, 'Aunt Lizzie.'

And he repeated, 'Oh, yes. Aunt Lizzie. Aunt Lizzie.'

THE END